DUNGEONS & DRAGONS
NEVERWINTER TALES

THE LEGEND OF
DRIZZT

Credits

Written by	**R.A. Salvatore** **Geno Salvatore**
Art by	**Agustin Padilla**
Special Thanks to	**Jose Avilles**
Colors by	**Leonard O'Grady**
Letters by	**Chris Mowry** **Neil Uyetake**
Series Edits by	**Denton J. Tipton** **John Barber**
Collection Edits by	**Justin Eisinger** **Alonzo Simon**
Collection Design by	**Neil Uyetake**
Collection Cover by	**Gonzalo Flores**

Special thanks to Hasbro's Michael Kelly and Ed Lane, and Wizards of the Coast's Jon Schindehette, James Wyatt, Chris Perkins, Liz Schuh, Nathan Stewart, Laura Tommervik, Shelly Mazzanoble, Hilary Ross, and Chris Lindsay.

IDW founded by Ted Adams, Alex Garner, Kris Oprisko, and Robbie Robbins

ISBN: 978-1-61377-635-3

16 15 14 13 1 2 3 4

IDW

Licensed By: Hasbro, Official Wizards of the Coast Licensed Product

Ted Adams, CEO & Publisher
Greg Goldstein, President & COO
Robbie Robbins, EVP/Sr. Graphic Artist
Chris Ryall, Chief Creative Officer/Editor-in-Chief
Matthew Ruzicka, CPA, Chief Financial Officer
Alan Payne, VP of Sales
Dirk Wood, VP of Marketing
Lorelei Bunjes, VP of Digital Services

Become our fan on Facebook **facebook.com/idwpublishing**
Follow us on Twitter **@idwpublishing**
Check us out on YouTube **youtube.com/idwpublishing**
www.IDWPUBLISHING.com

DUNGEONS & DRAGONS
NEVERWINTER TALES

THE LEGEND OF DRIZZT

I am **Drizzt Do'Urden**, once of Mithral Hall, once loved in marriage, once friend to a king and to other companions no less wonderful. Those are the rivers of my memory, flowing from distant shores, for now I reclaim my journey... and my heart.

With the last of his trusted companions having fallen, Drizzt is alone—and free—for the first time in almost a hundred years. Guilt mingles with relief, leaving Drizzt uniquely vulnerable to the persuasions of his newest companion—Dahlia, a darkly alluring elf and the only other member of their party to survive the cataclysm at Mount Hotenow. But traveling with Dahlia is challenging in more ways than one...

(The events depicted in this book occur during the **Neverwinter Saga** *novels.)*

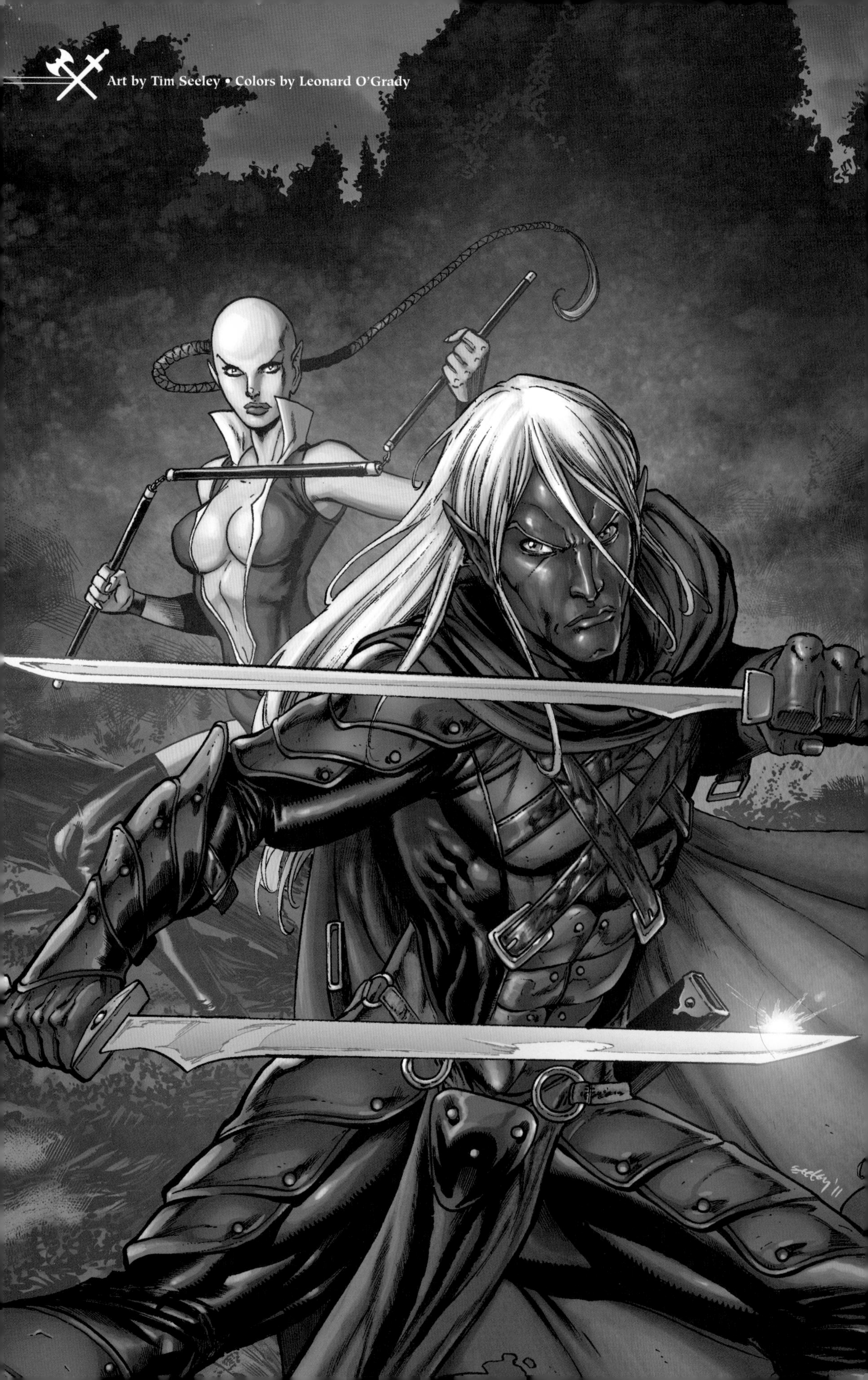
seeley '11

Art by Tim Seeley • Colors by Leonard O'Grady

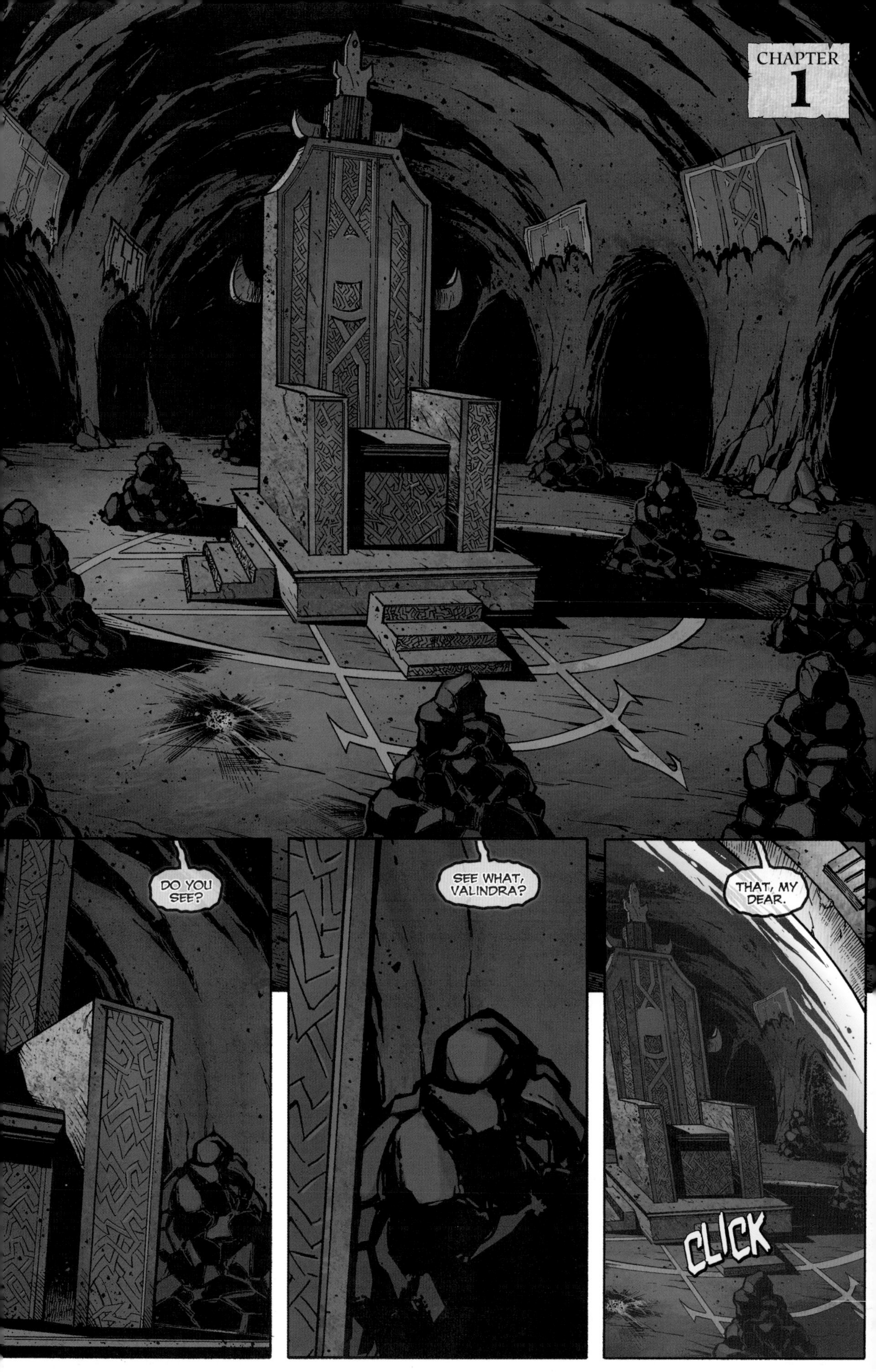
CHAPTER
1
DO YOU SEE?
SEE WHAT, VALINDRA?
THAT, MY DEAR.
CLICK

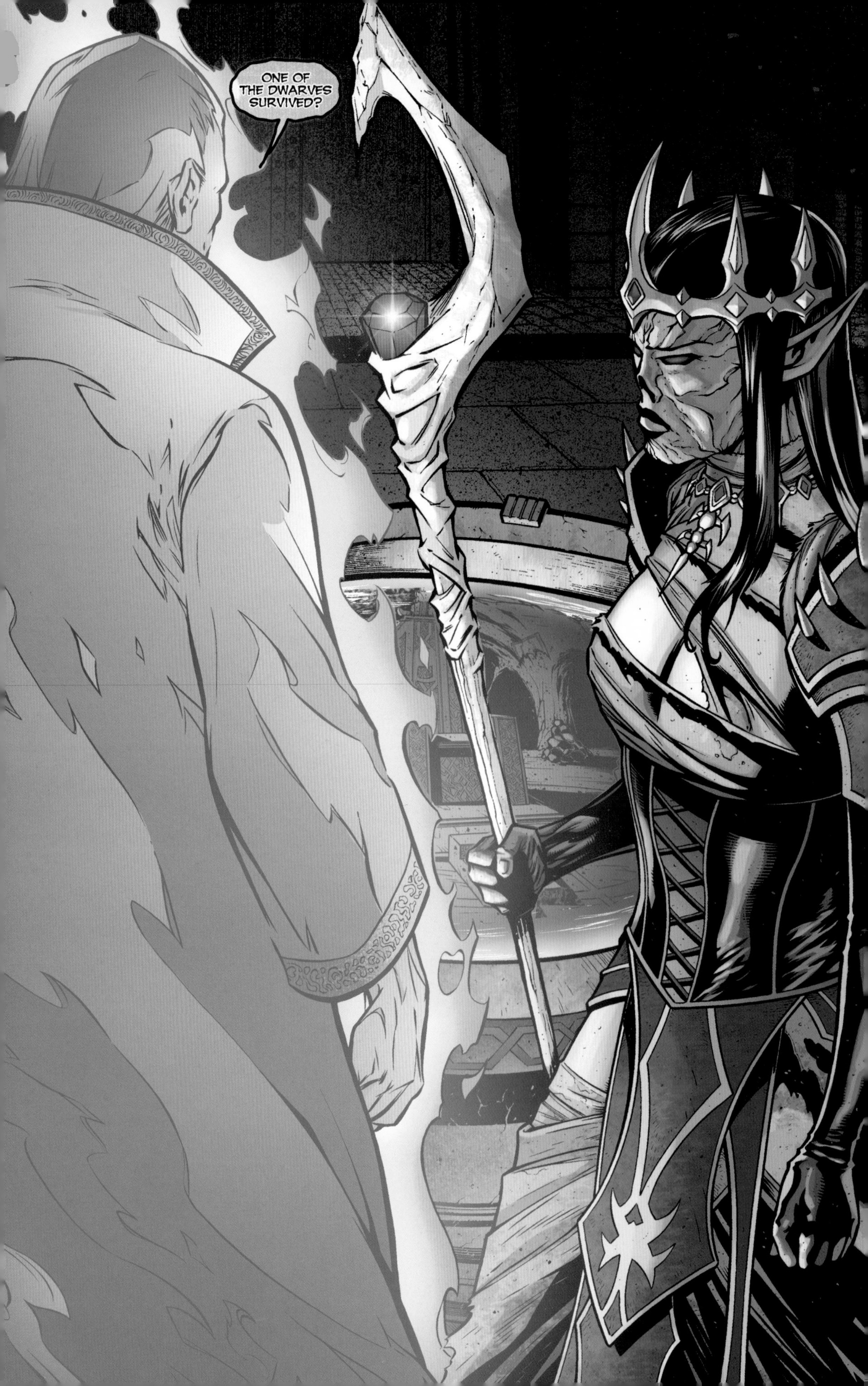
ONE OF THE DWARVES SURVIVED?

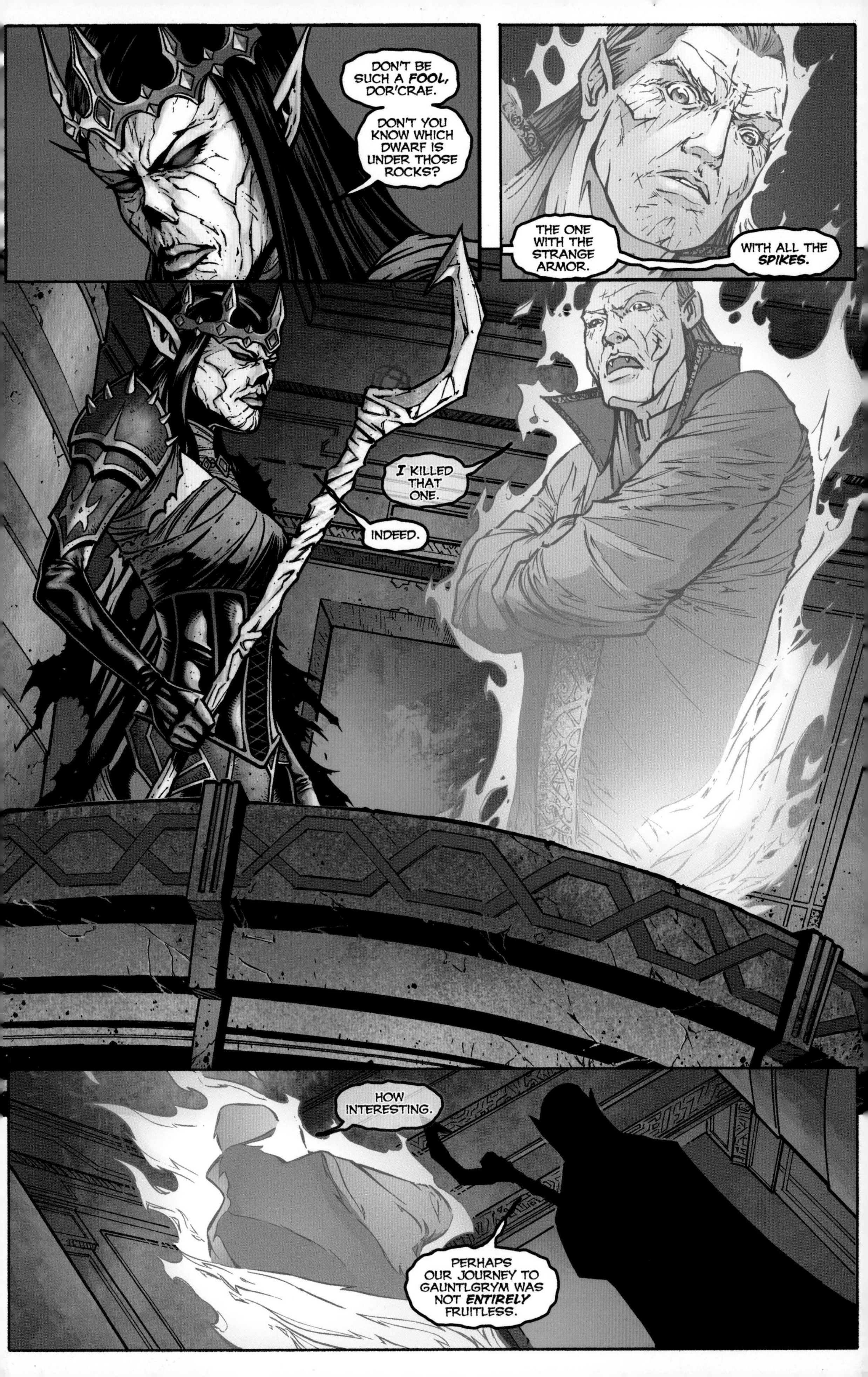

DON'T BE SUCH A FOOL, DOR'CRAE.
DON'T YOU KNOW WHICH DWARF IS UNDER THOSE ROCKS?
THE ONE WITH THE STRANGE ARMOR.
WITH ALL THE SPIKES.
I KILLED THAT ONE.
INDEED.
HOW INTERESTING.
PERHAPS OUR JOURNEY TO GAUNTLGRYM WAS NOT ENTIRELY FRUITLESS.

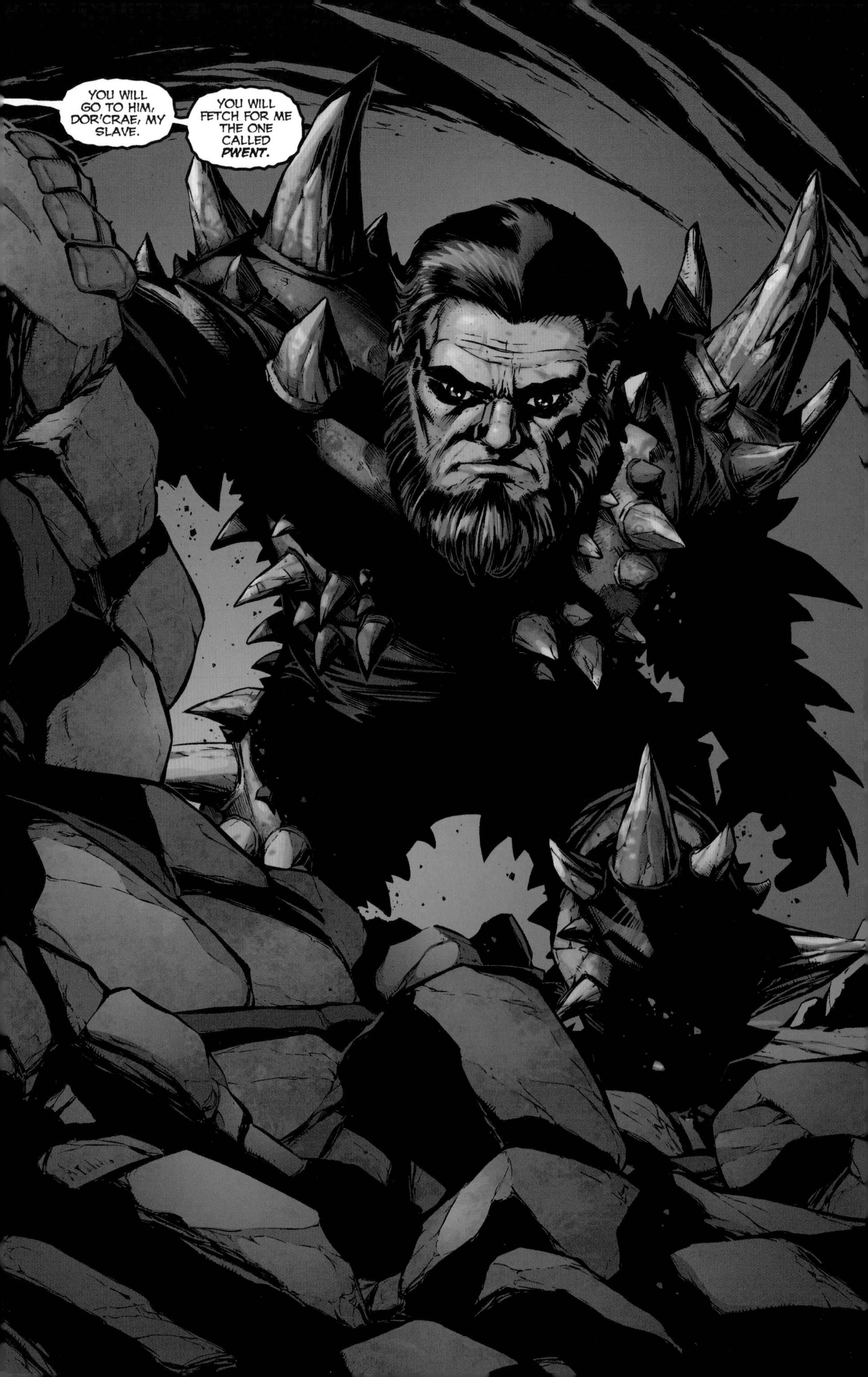
YOU WILL GO TO HIM, DOR'CRAE, MY SLAVE.
YOU WILL FETCH FOR ME THE ONE CALLED *PWENT*.

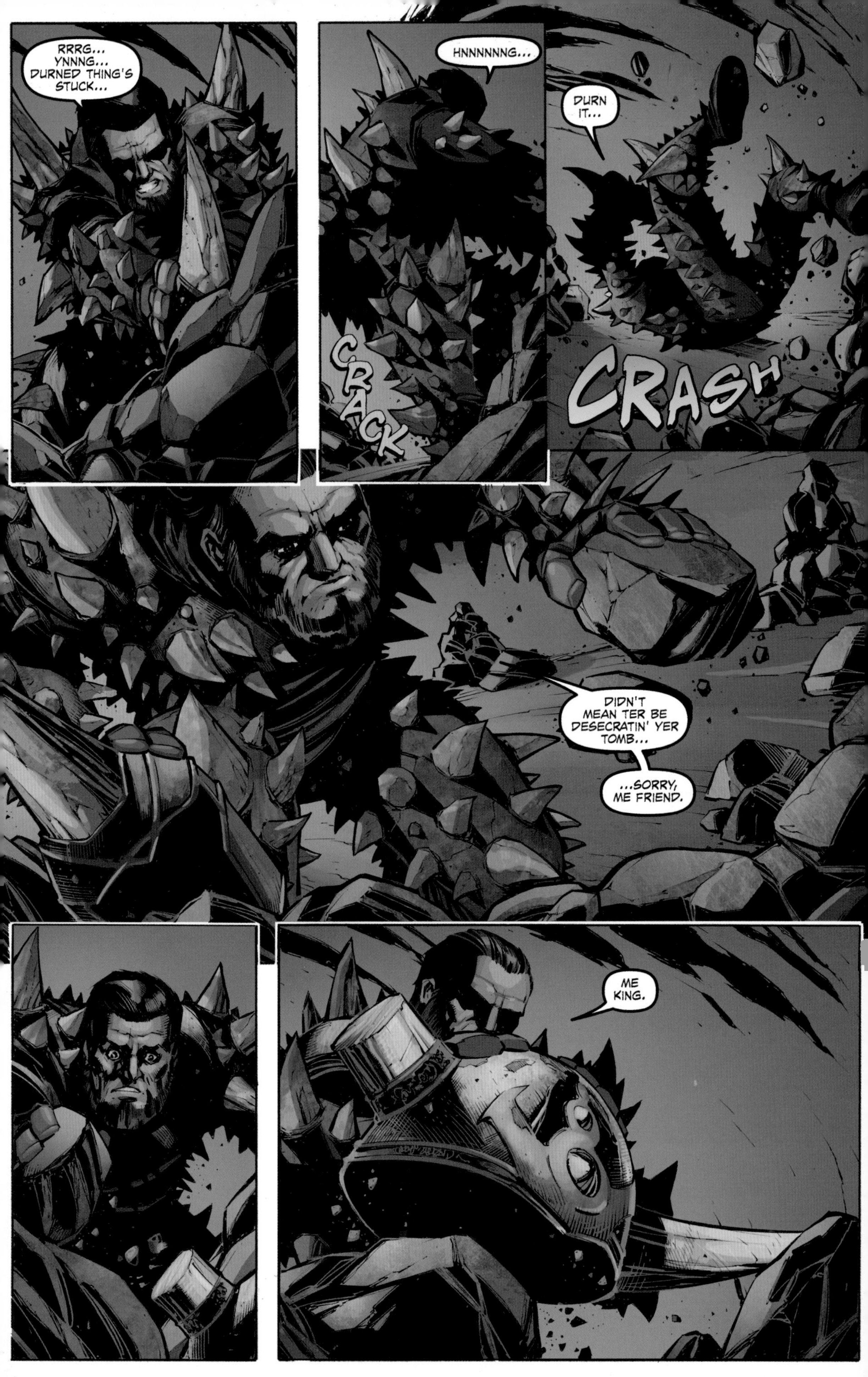
RRRG... YNNNG... DURNED THING'S STUCK...
HNNNNNNG...
CRACK
DURN IT...
CRASH
DIDN'T MEAN TER BE DESECRATIN' YER TOMB...
...SORRY, ME FRIEND.
ME KING.

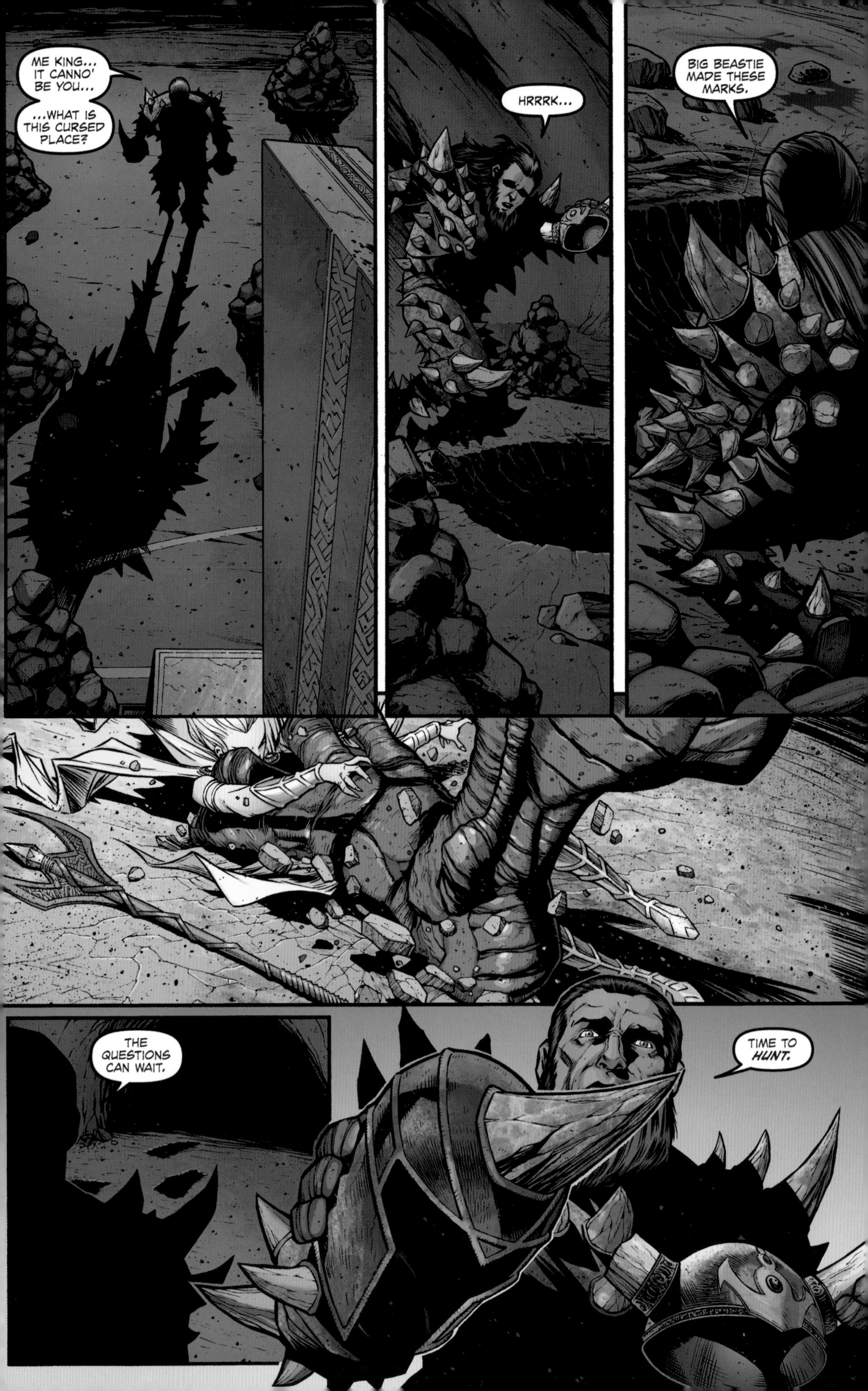
ME KING... IT CANNO' BE YOU...
...WHAT IS THIS CURSED PLACE?
HRRRK...
BIG BEASTIE MADE THESE MARKS.
THE QUESTIONS CAN WAIT.
TIME TO *HUNT.*

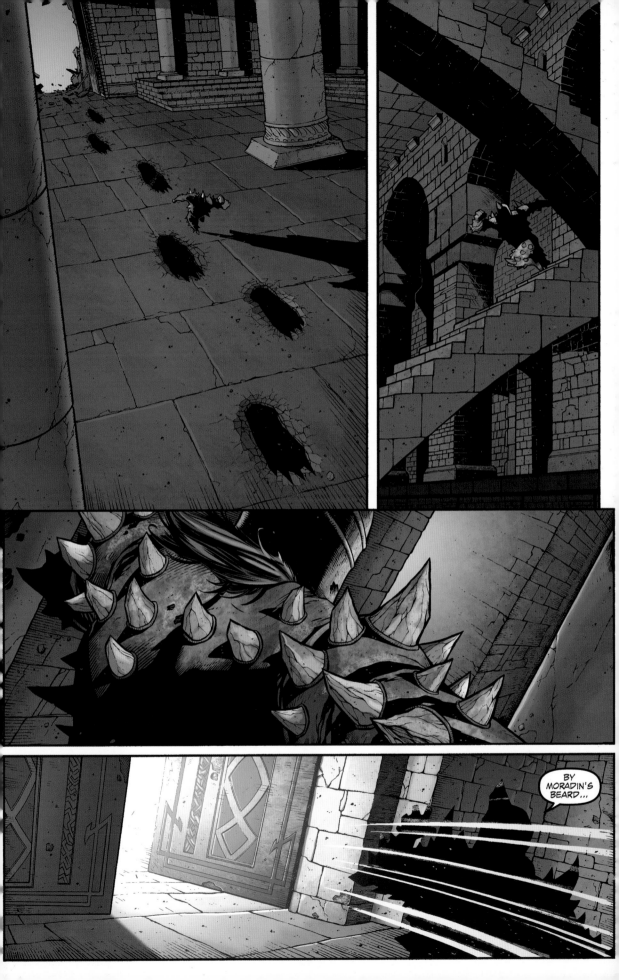

BY MORADIN'S BEARD...

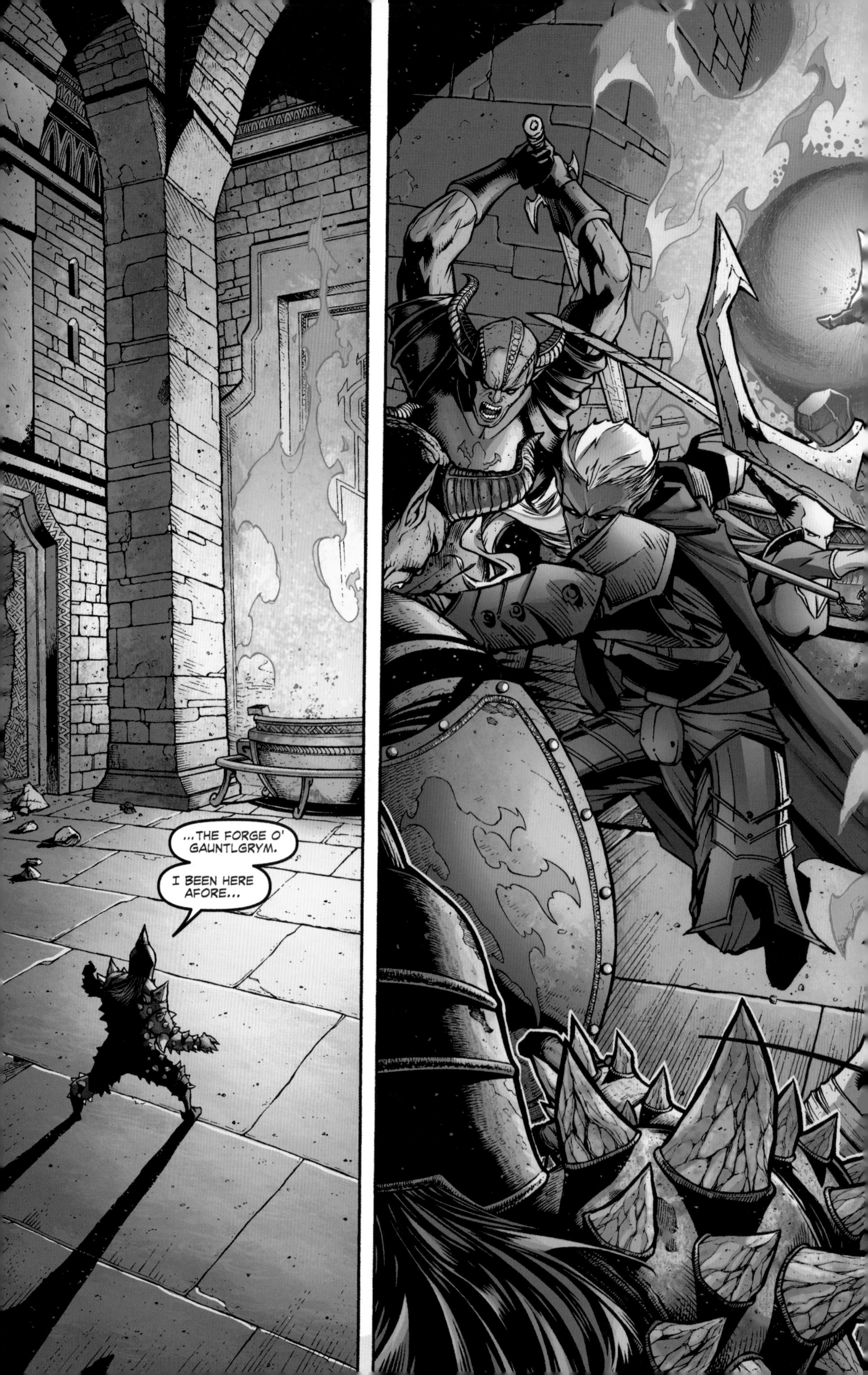
...THE FORGE O' GAUNTLGRYM.
I BEEN HERE AFORE...

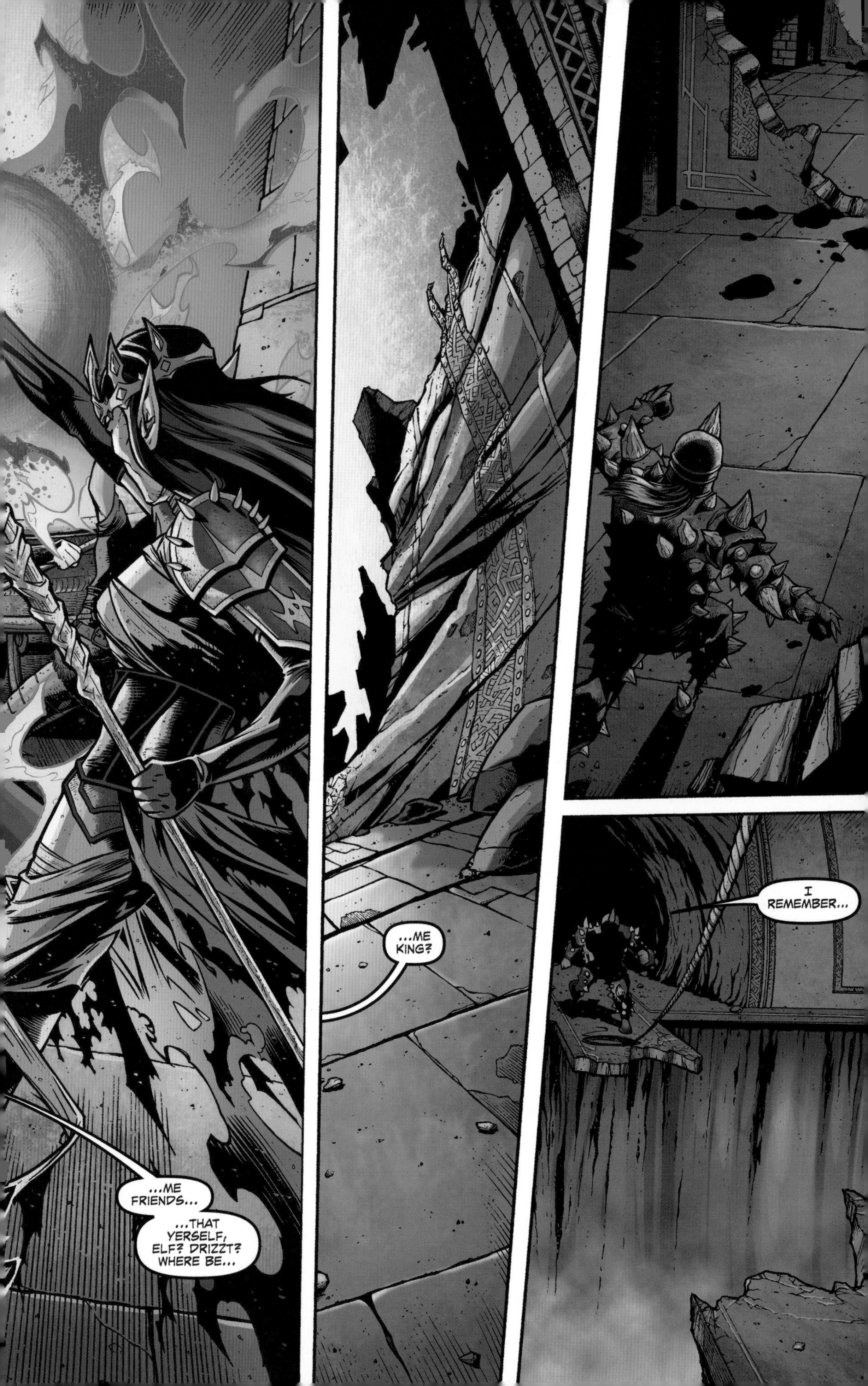
...ME FRIENDS...
...THAT YERSELF, ELF? DRIZZT? WHERE BE...
...ME KING?
I REMEMBER...

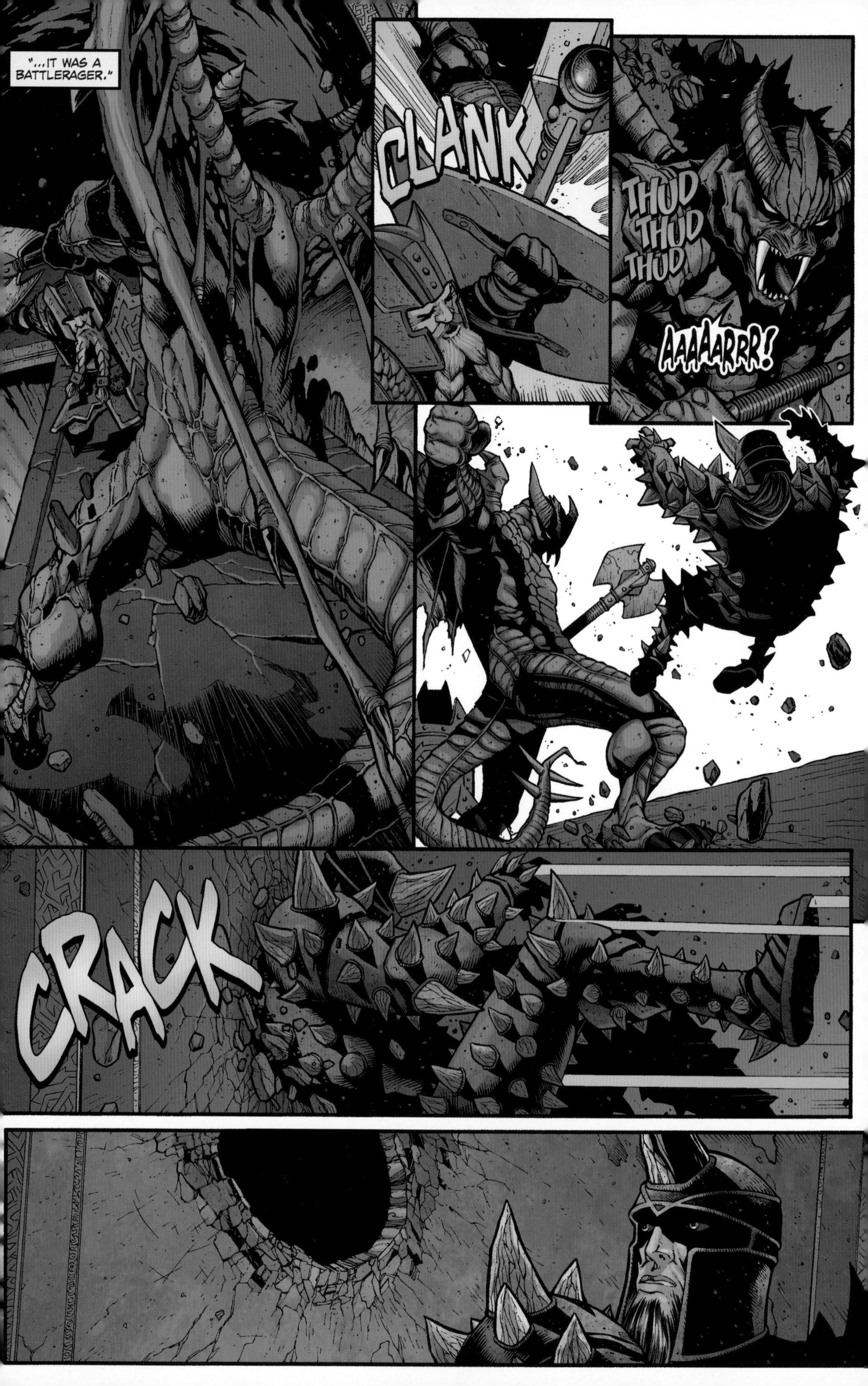
"...IT WAS A BATTLERAGER."
CLANK
THUD THUD THUD
AAAAARRR!
CRACK

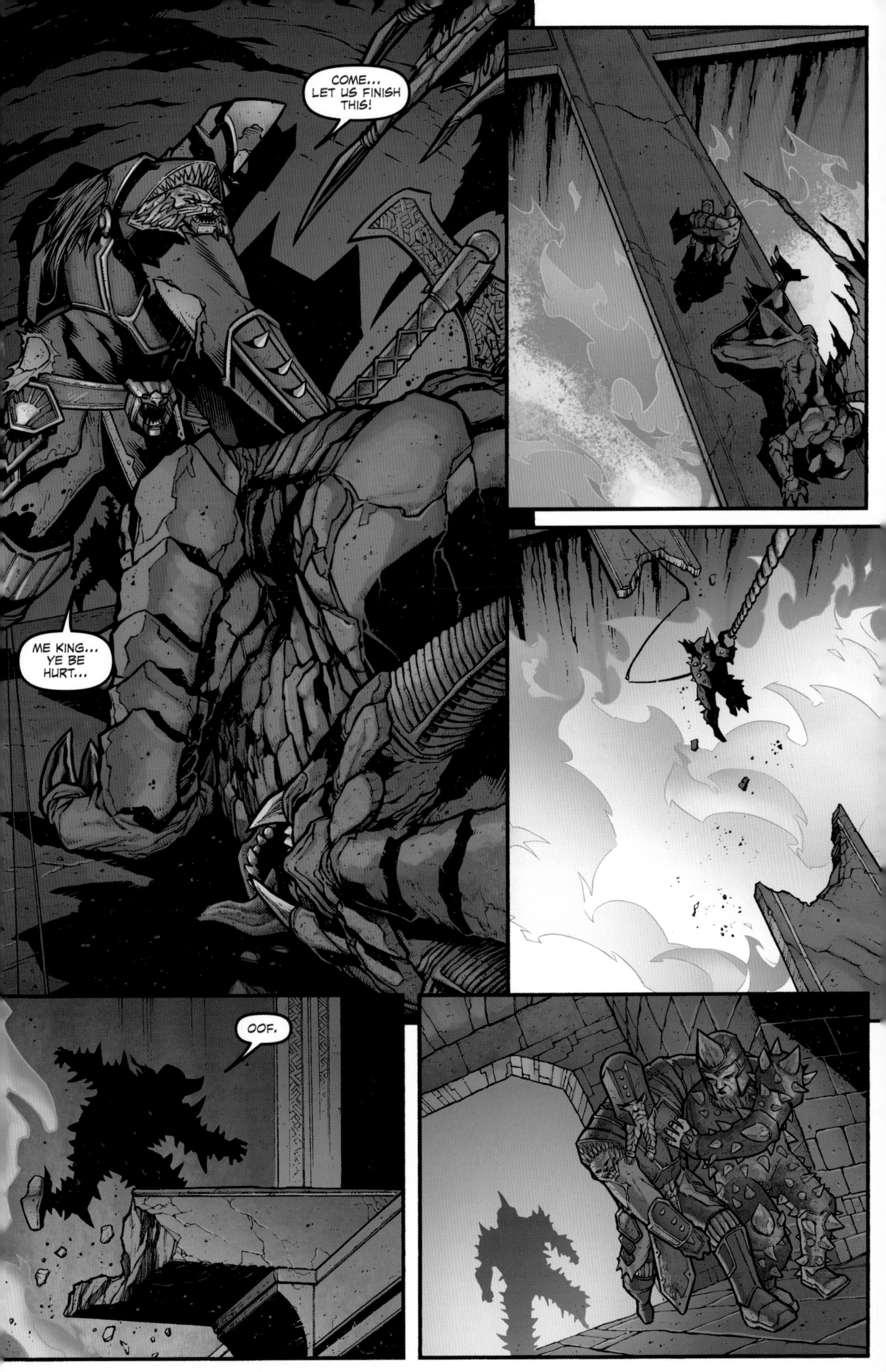
COME... LET US FINISH THIS!
ME KING... YE BE HURT...
OOF.

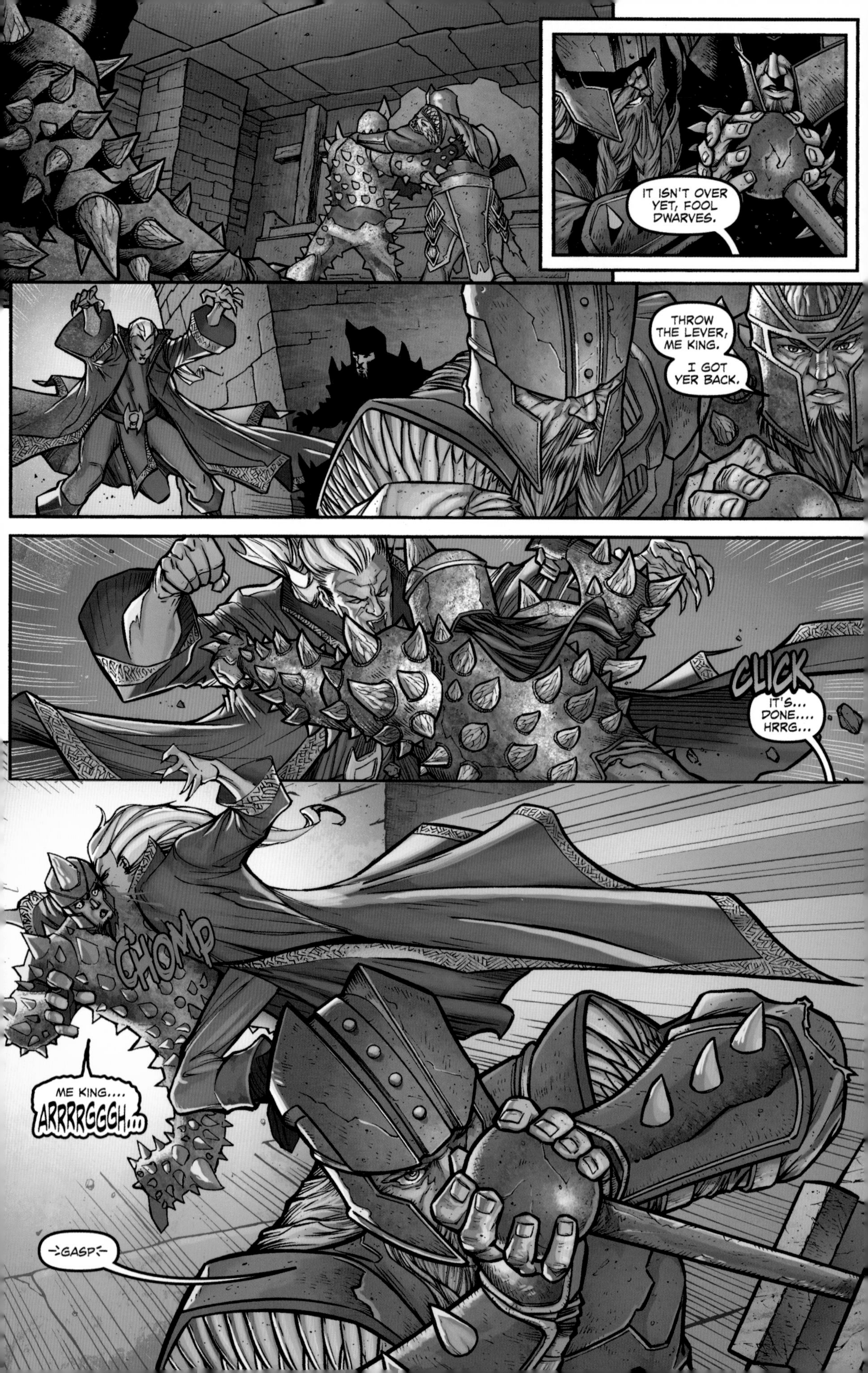
IT ISN'T OVER YET, FOOL DWARVES.
THROW THE LEVER, ME KING.
I GOT YER BACK.
CLICK
IT'S... DONE.... HRRG...
CHOMP
ME KING.... ARRRRGGGH...
-GASP-

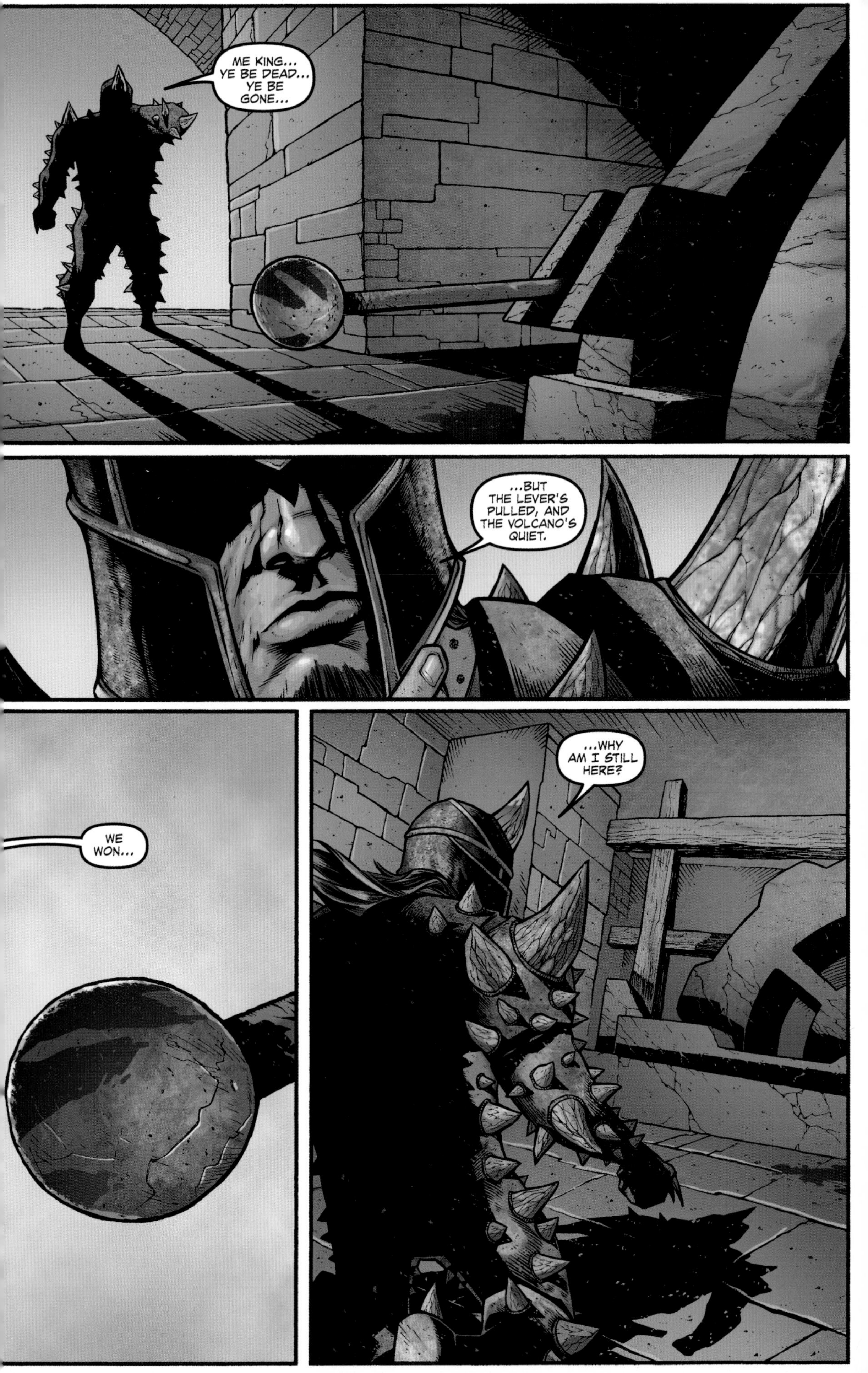
ME KING... YE BE DEAD... YE BE GONE...
...BUT THE LEVER'S PULLED, AND THE VOLCANO'S QUIET.
WE WON...
...WHY AM I STILL HERE?

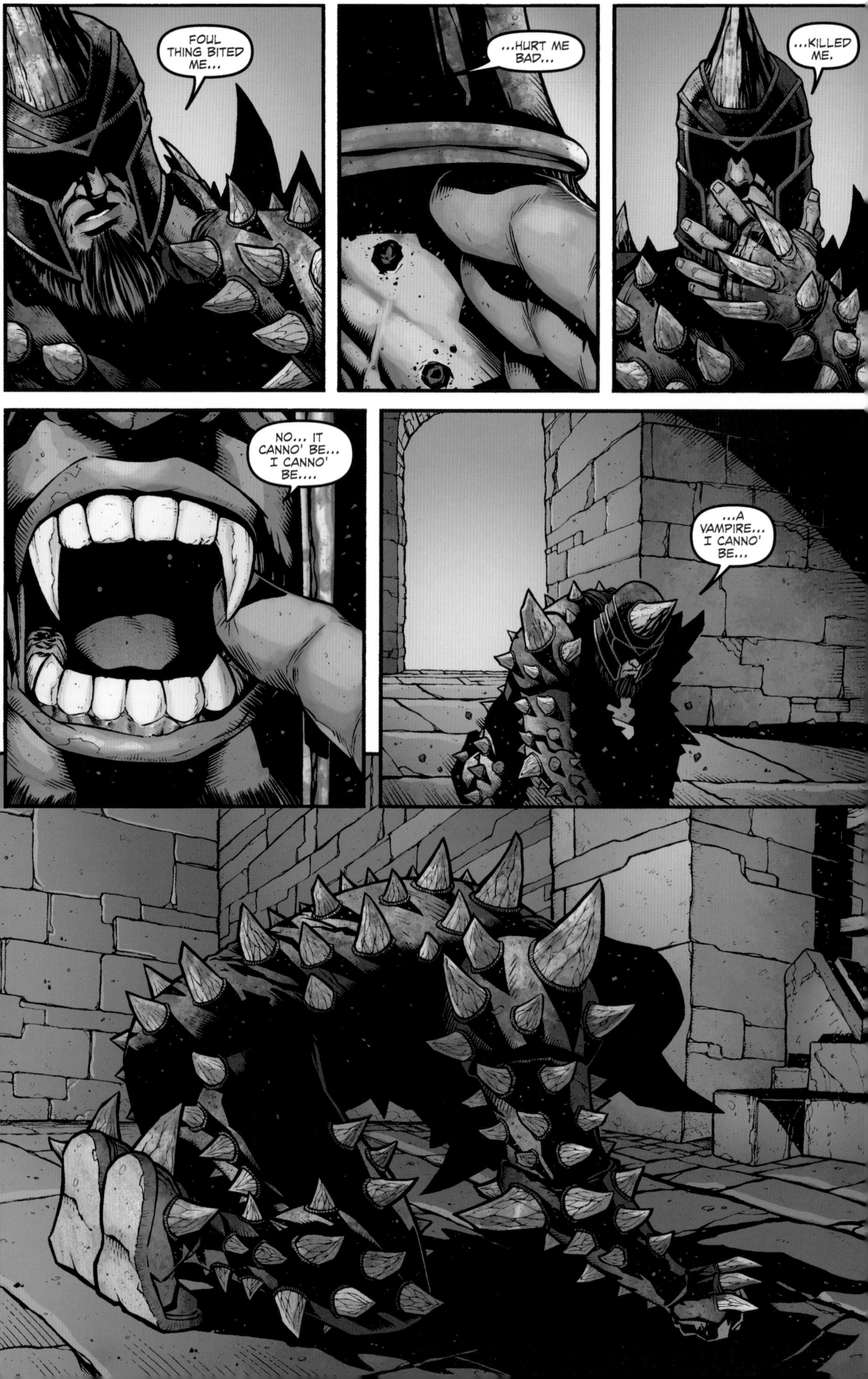
FOUL THING BITED ME...
...HURT ME BAD...
...KILLED ME.
NO... IT CANNO' BE... I CANNO' BE....
...A VAMPIRE... I CANNO' BE...

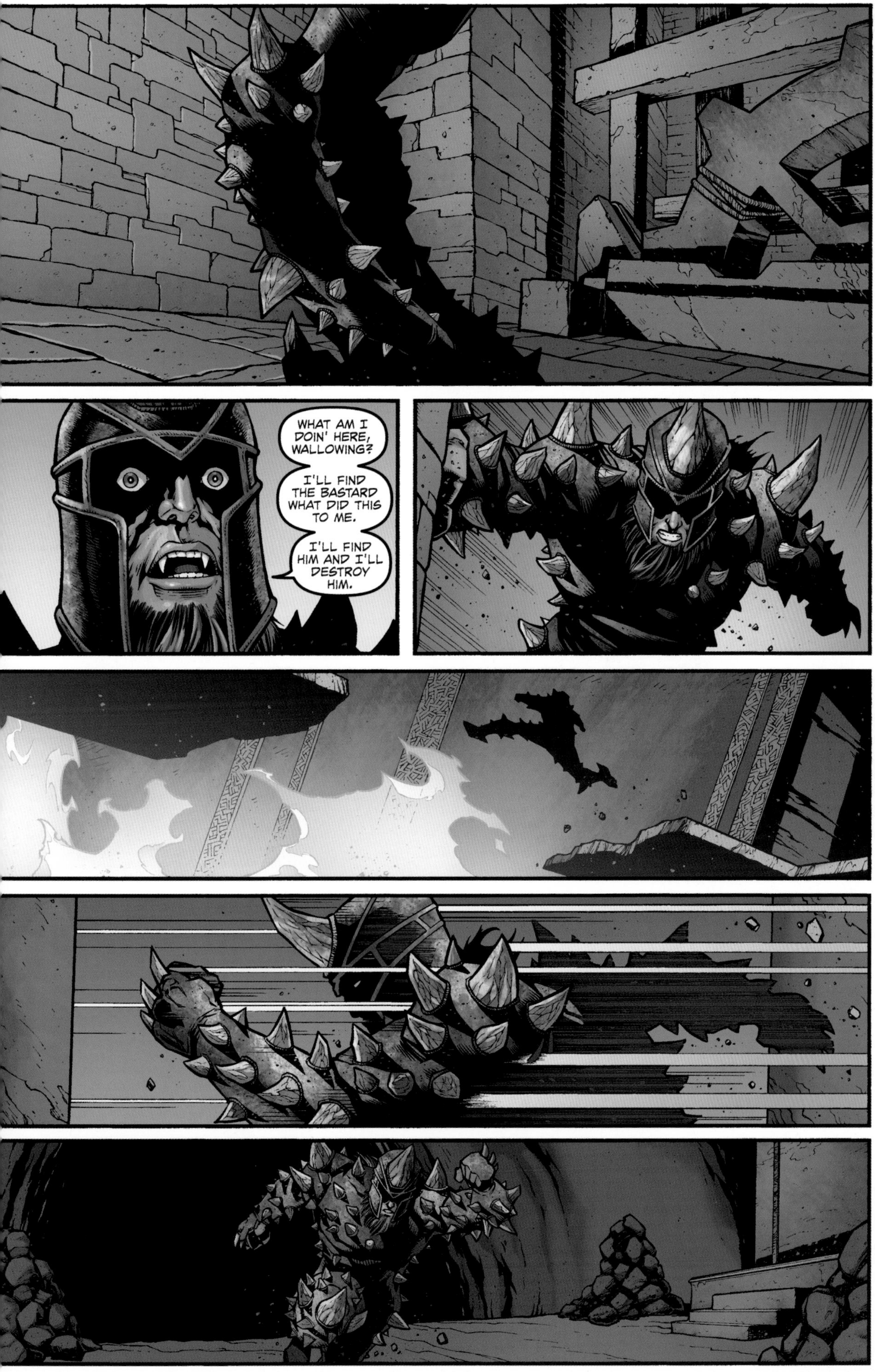
WHAT AM I DOIN' HERE, WALLOWING?
I'LL FIND THE BASTARD WHAT DID THIS TO ME.
I'LL FIND HIM AND I'LL DESTROY HIM.

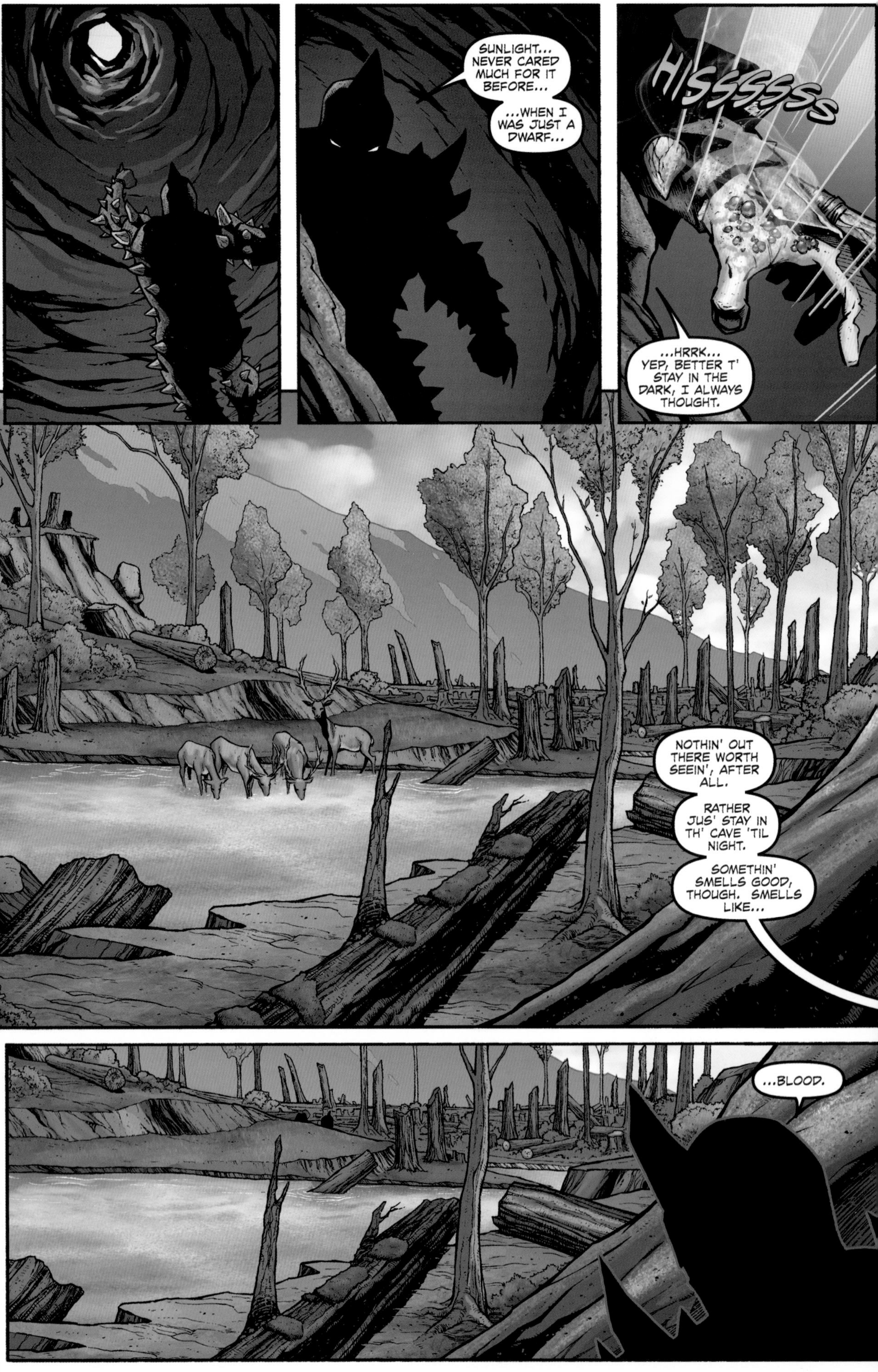
SUNLIGHT... NEVER CARED MUCH FOR IT BEFORE...
...WHEN I WAS JUST A DWARF...
HISSSSSS
...HRRK... YEP, BETTER T' STAY IN THE DARK, I ALWAYS THOUGHT.
NOTHIN' OUT THERE WORTH SEEIN', AFTER ALL.
RATHER JUS' STAY IN TH' CAVE 'TIL NIGHT.
SOMETHIN' SMELLS GOOD, THOUGH. SMELLS LIKE...
...BLOOD.

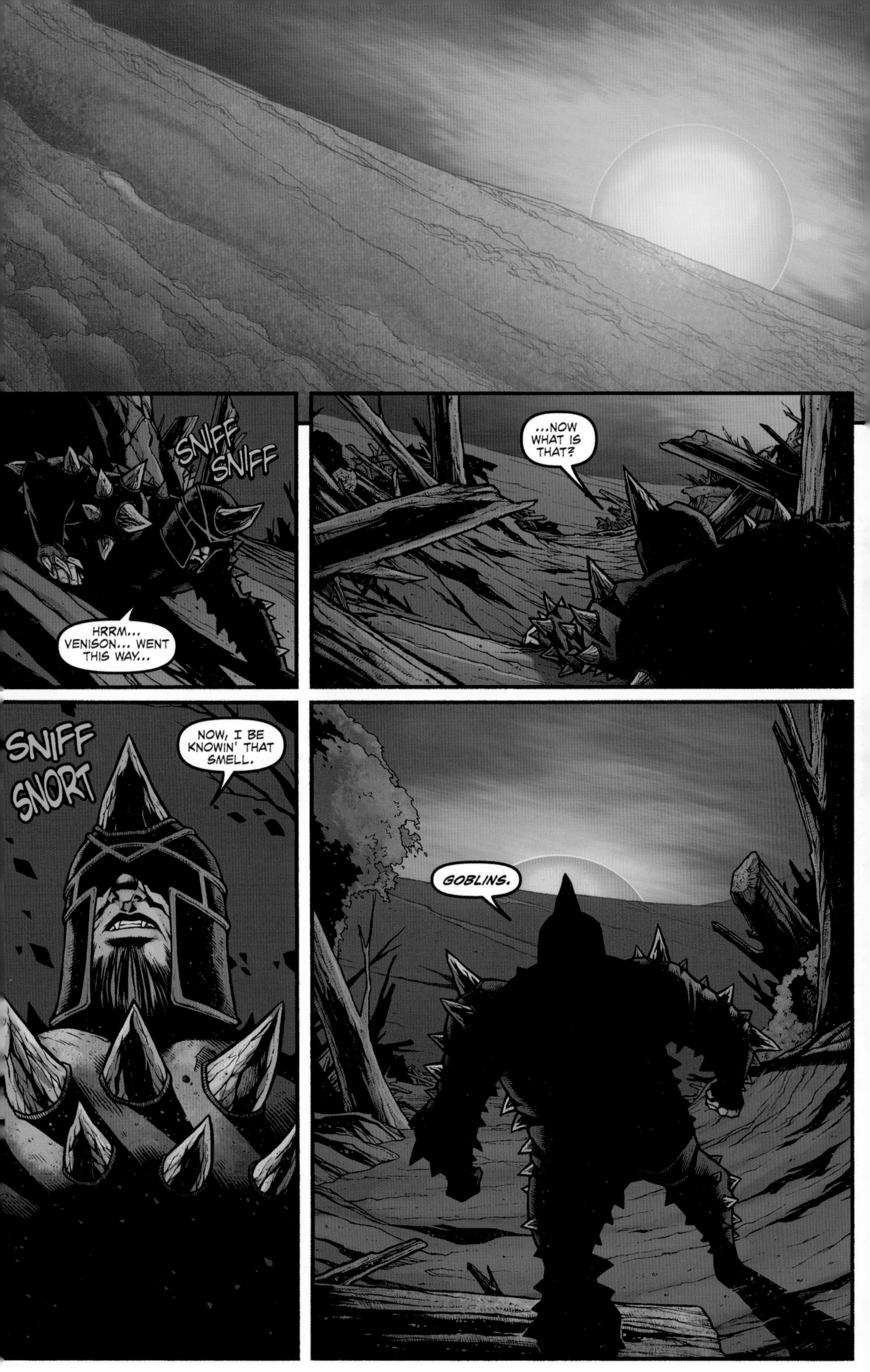
SNIFF SNIFF
HRRM... VENISON... WENT THIS WAY...
...NOW WHAT IS THAT?
SNIFF SNORT
NOW, I BE KNOWIN' THAT SMELL.
GOBLINS.

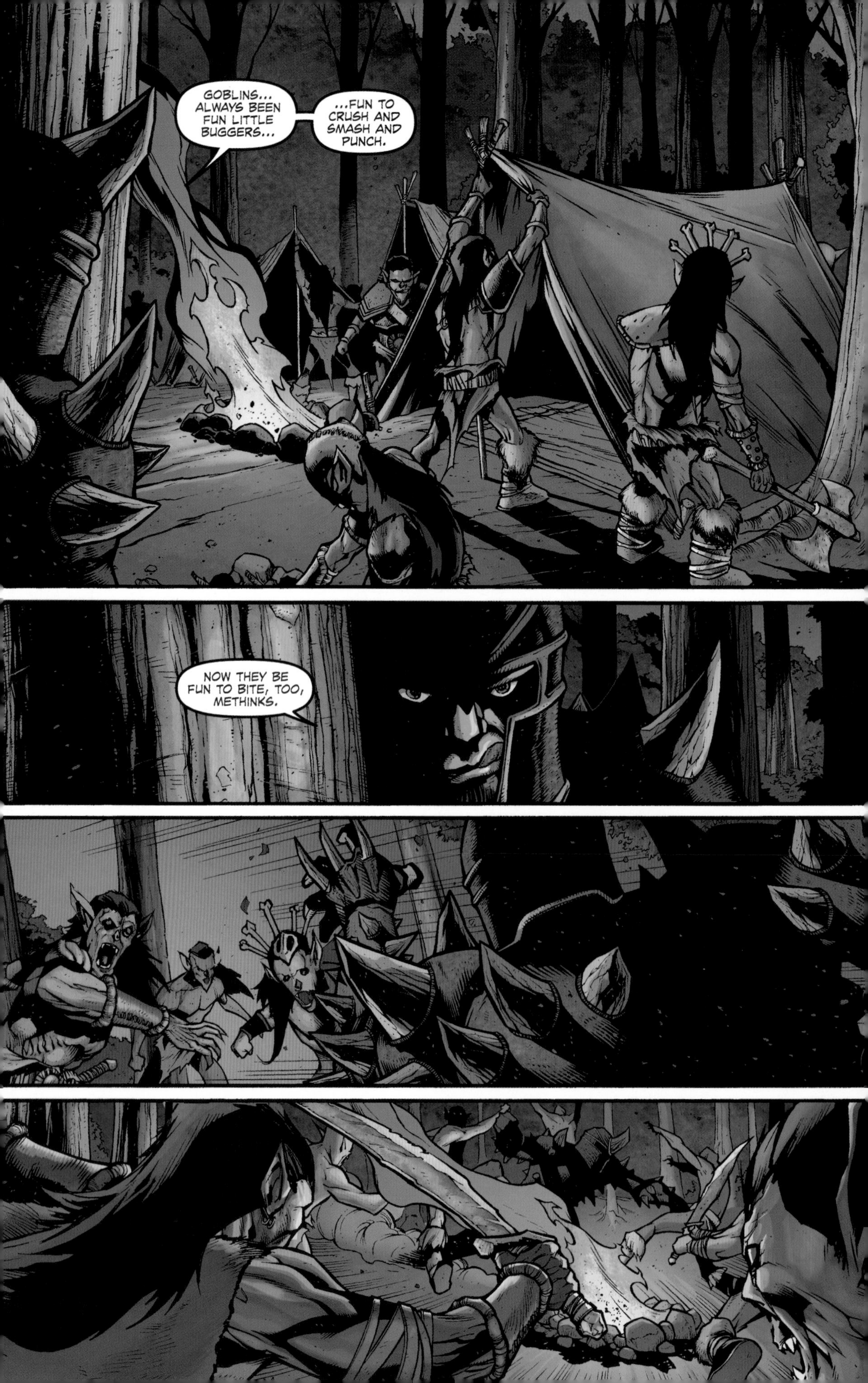
GOBLINS... ALWAYS BEEN FUN LITTLE BUGGERS...
...FUN TO CRUSH AND SMASH AND PUNCH.
NOW THEY BE FUN TO BITE, TOO, METHINKS.

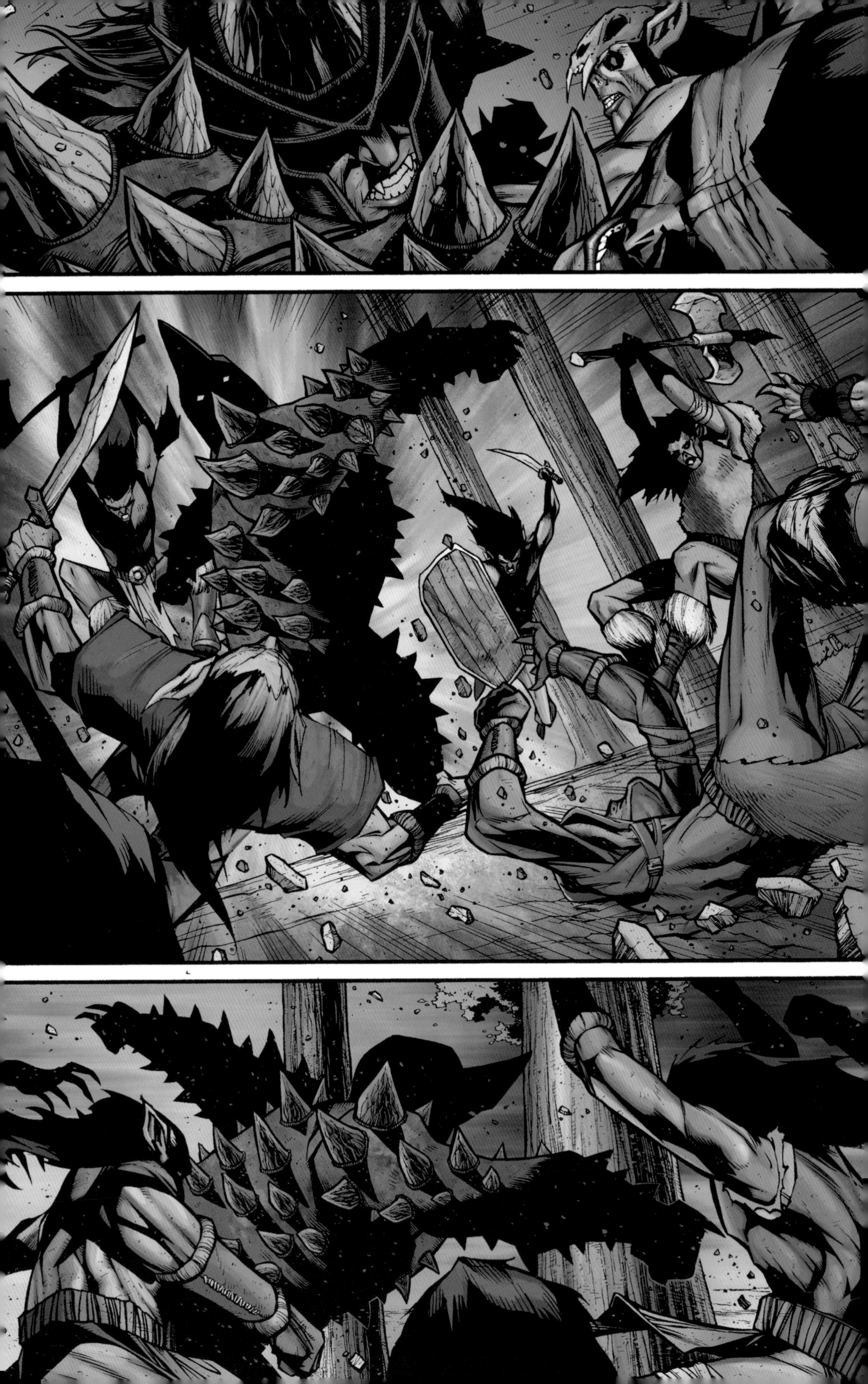

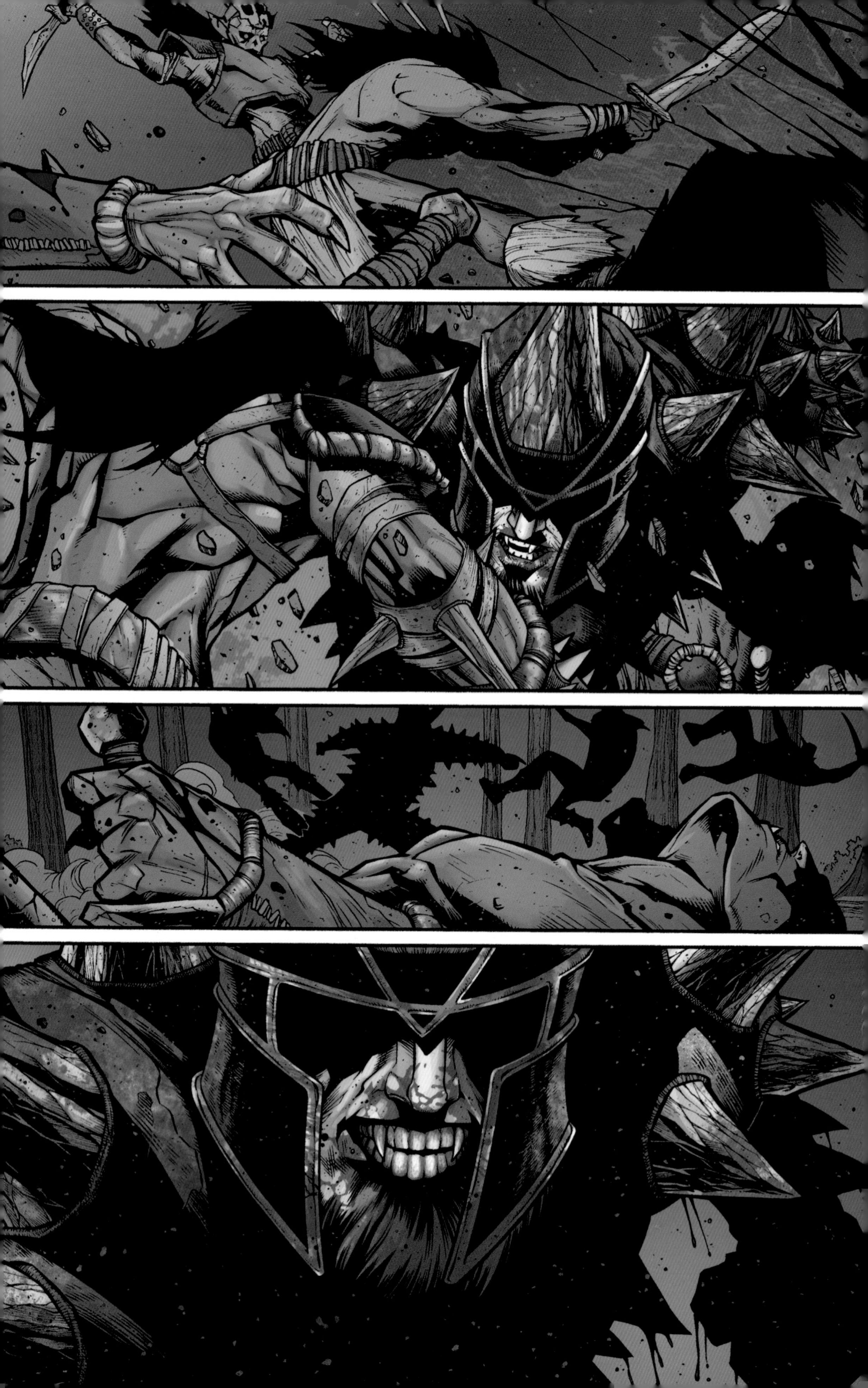

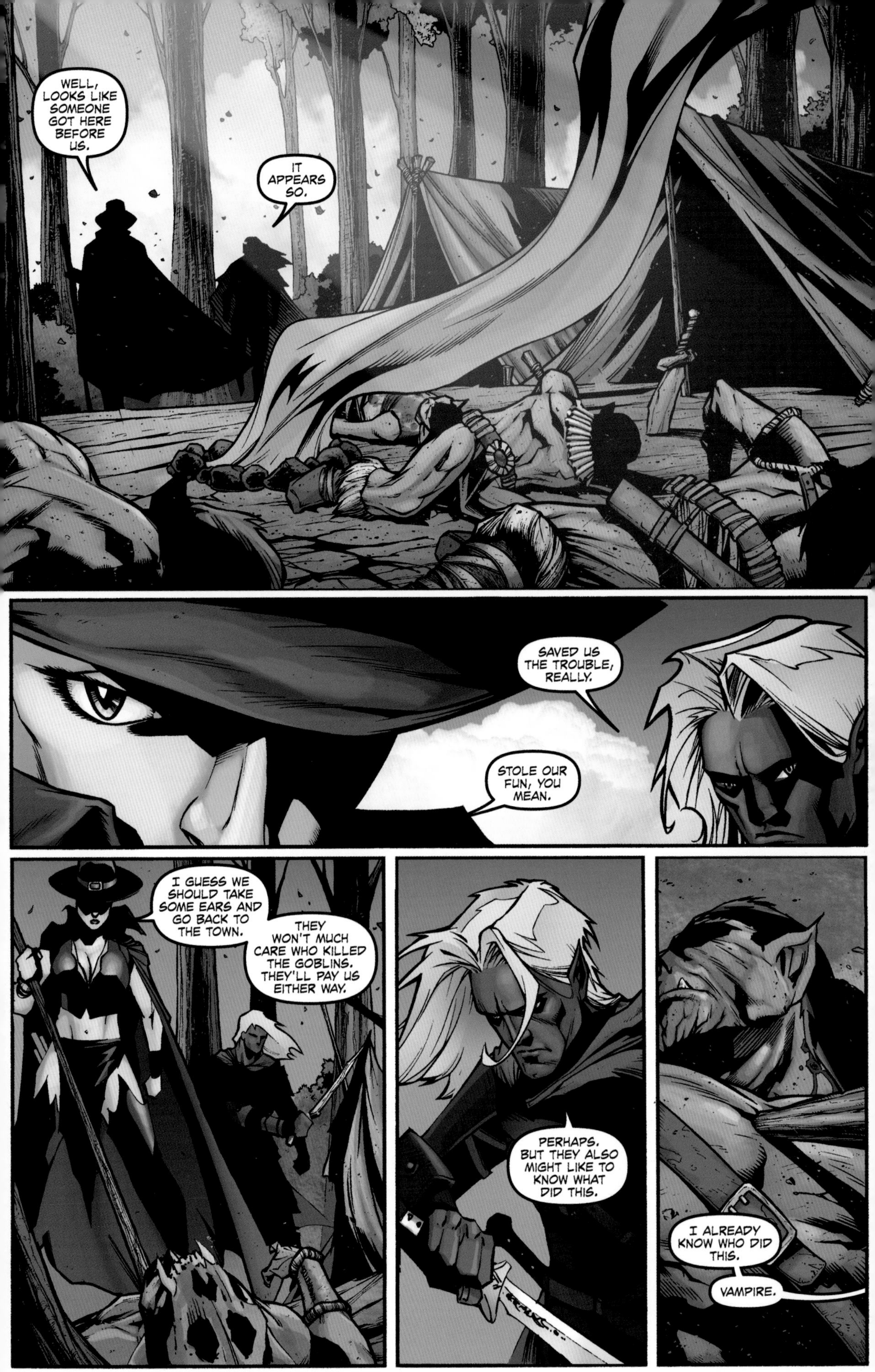
WELL, LOOKS LIKE SOMEONE GOT HERE BEFORE US.
IT APPEARS SO.
SAVED US THE TROUBLE, REALLY.
STOLE OUR FUN, YOU MEAN.
I GUESS WE SHOULD TAKE SOME EARS AND GO BACK TO THE TOWN.
THEY WON'T MUCH CARE WHO KILLED THE GOBLINS. THEY'LL PAY US EITHER WAY.
PERHAPS. BUT THEY ALSO MIGHT LIKE TO KNOW WHAT DID THIS.
I ALREADY KNOW WHO DID THIS.
VAMPIRE.

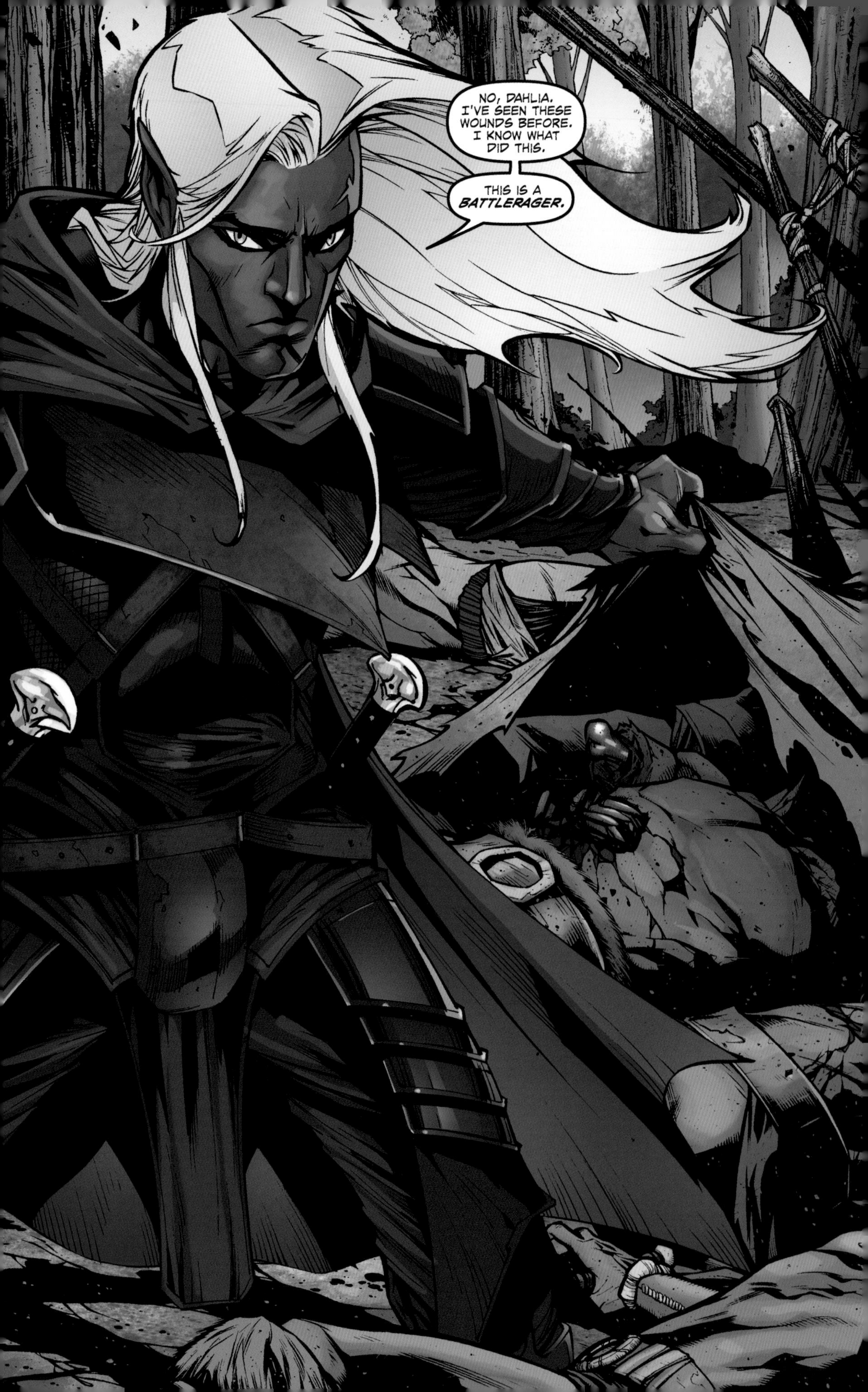
NO, DAHLIA. I'VE SEEN THESE WOUNDS BEFORE. I KNOW WHAT DID THIS.
THIS IS A *BATTLERAGER.*

Art by Tim Seeley • Colors by Leonard O'Grady

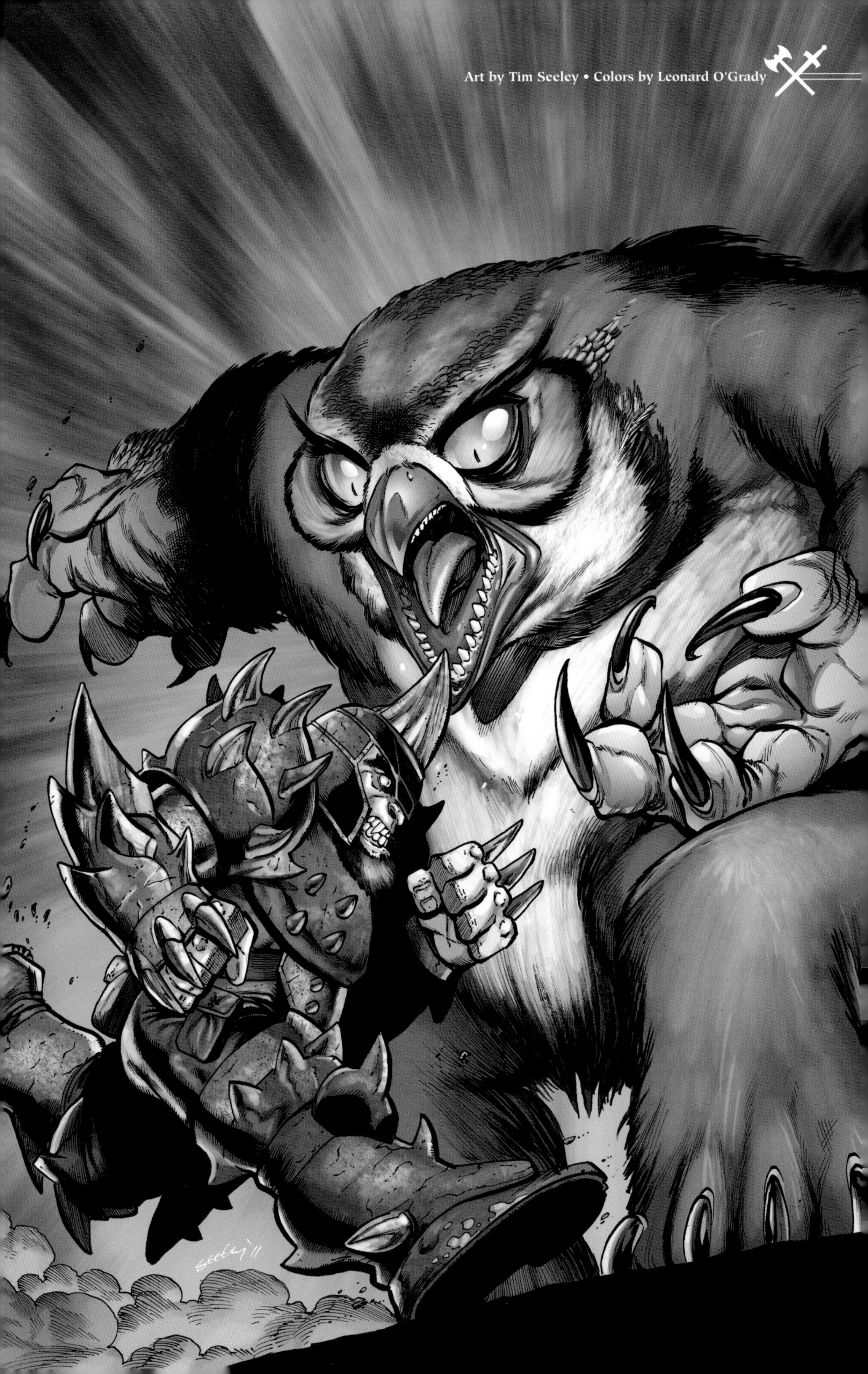

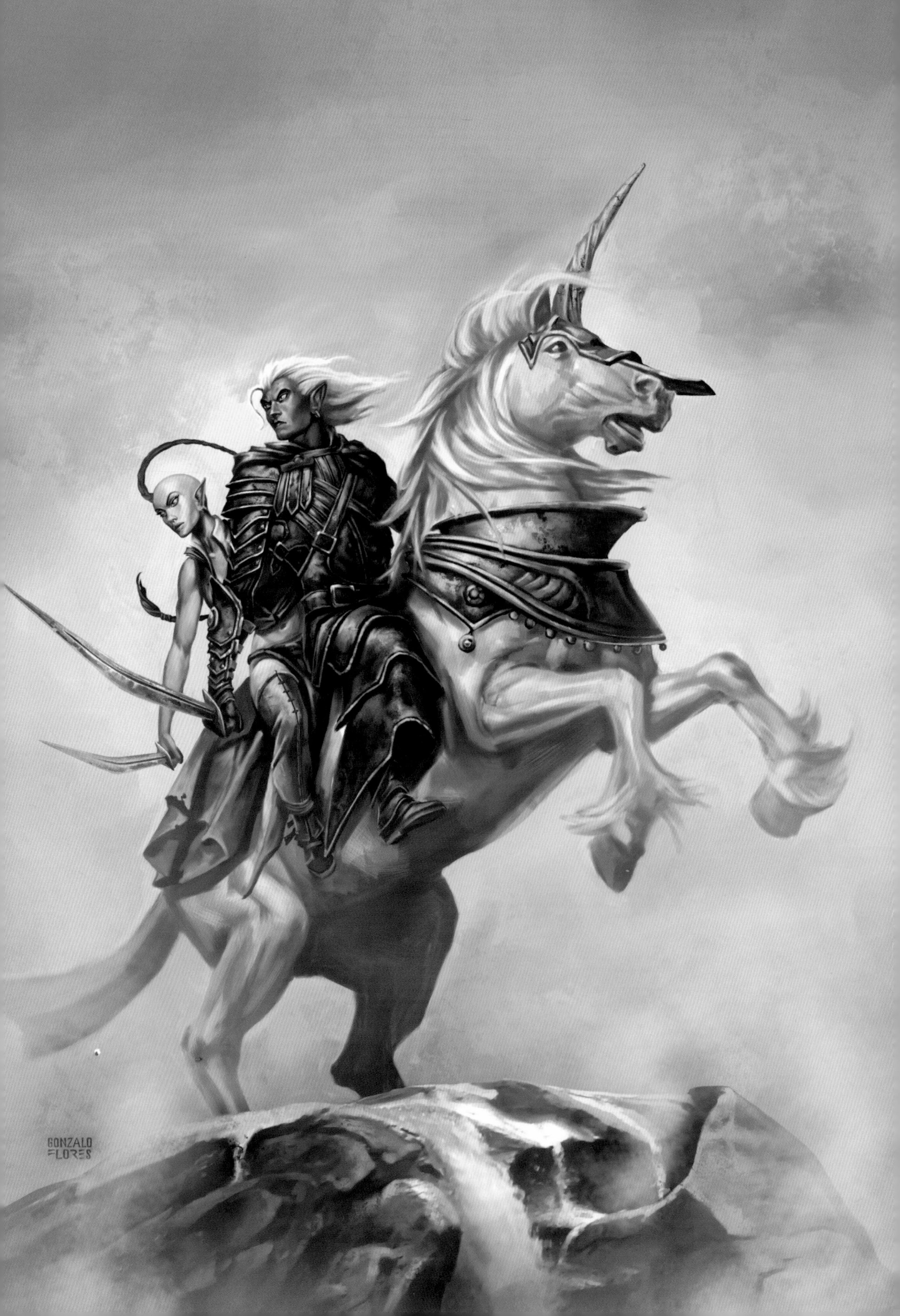
GONZALO
FLORES

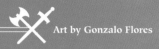

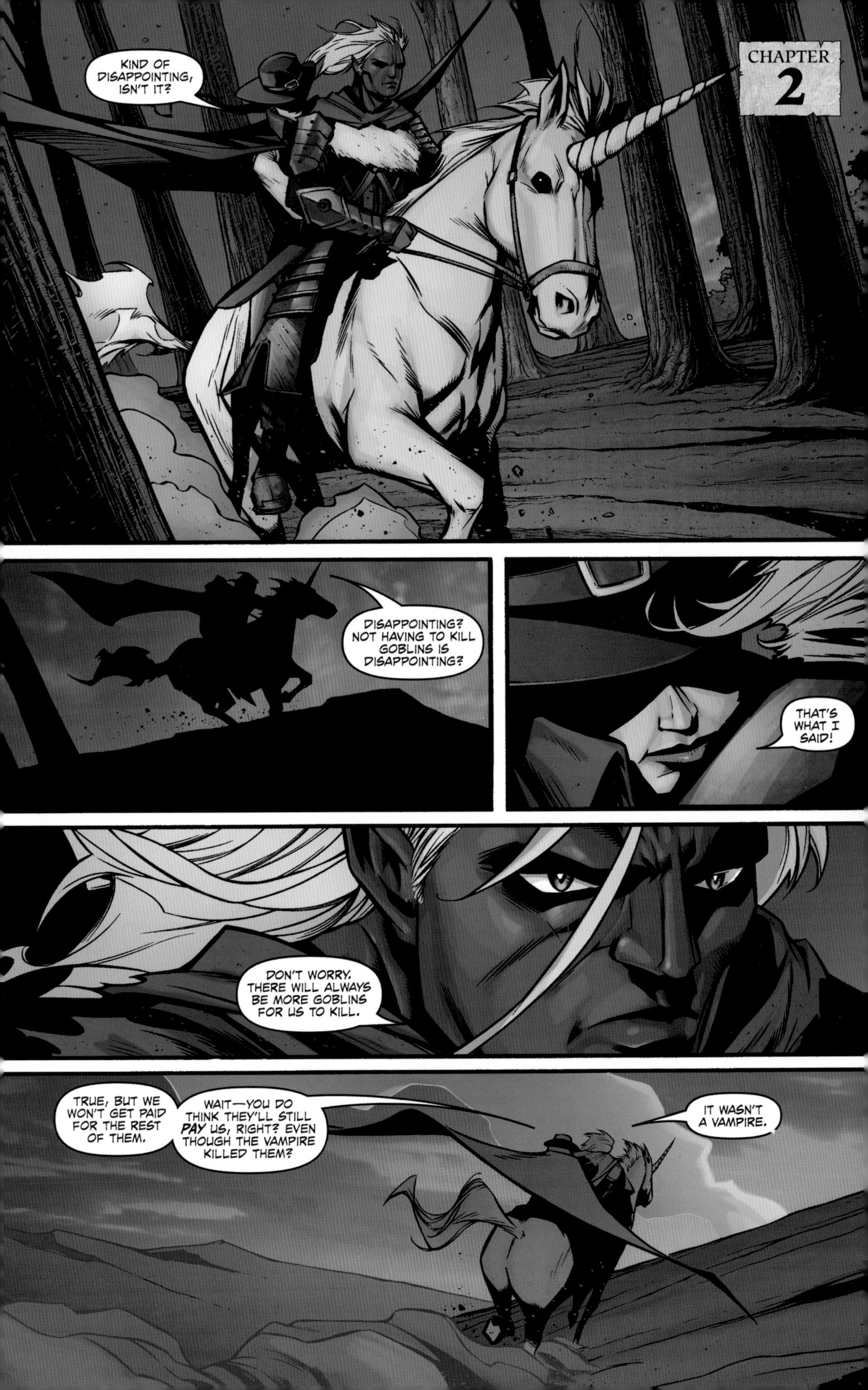
CHAPTER 2
KIND OF DISAPPOINTING, ISN'T IT?
DISAPPOINTING? NOT HAVING TO KILL GOBLINS IS DISAPPOINTING?
THAT'S WHAT I SAID!
DON'T WORRY. THERE WILL ALWAYS BE MORE GOBLINS FOR US TO KILL.
TRUE, BUT WE WON'T GET PAID FOR THE REST OF THEM.
WAIT—YOU DO THINK THEY'LL STILL PAY US, RIGHT? EVEN THOUGH THE VAMPIRE KILLED THEM?
IT WASN'T A VAMPIRE.

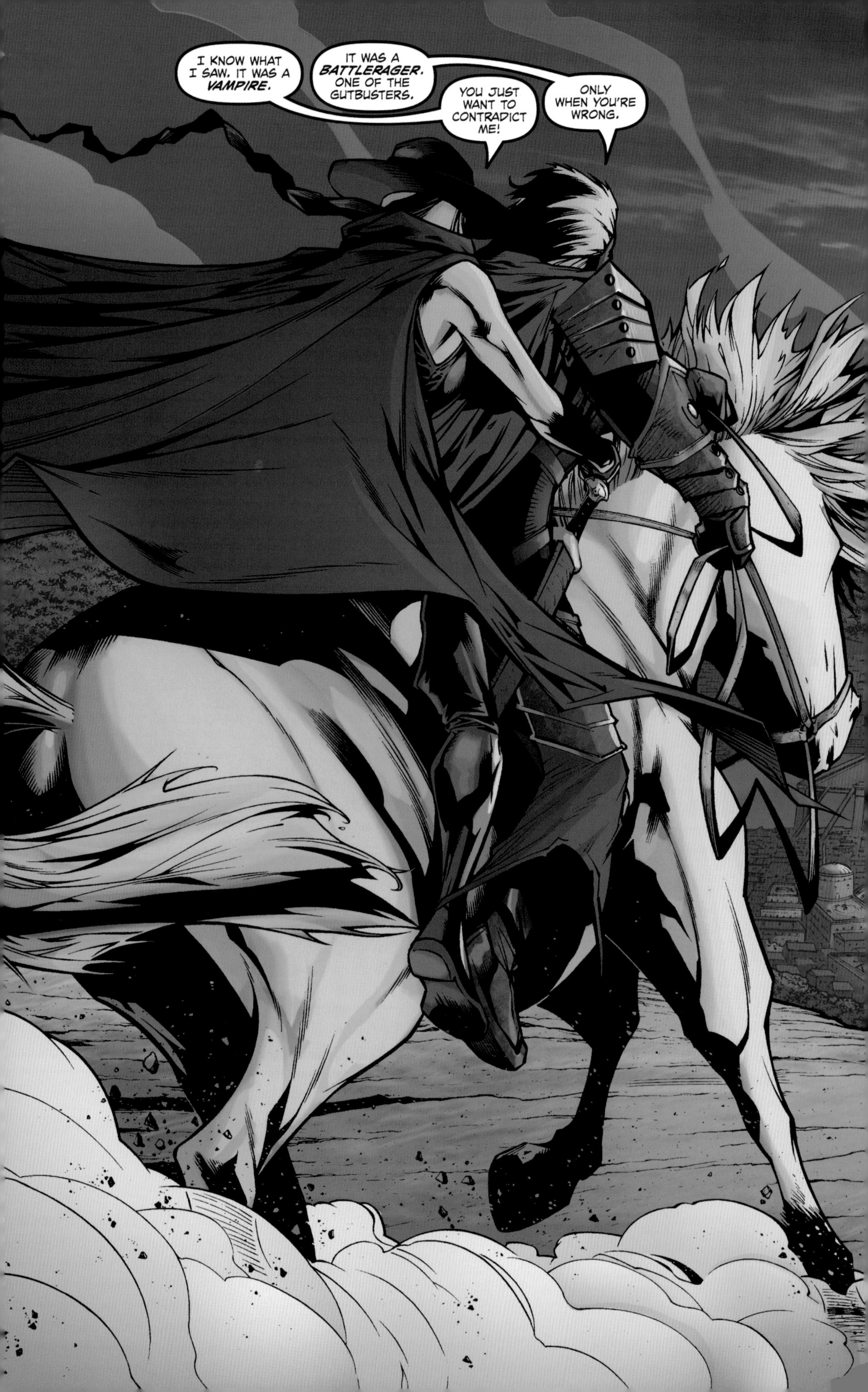
I KNOW WHAT I SAW. IT WAS A *VAMPIRE.*
IT WAS A *BATTLERAGER.* ONE OF THE GUTBUSTERS.
YOU JUST WANT TO CONTRADICT ME!
ONLY WHEN YOU'RE WRONG.

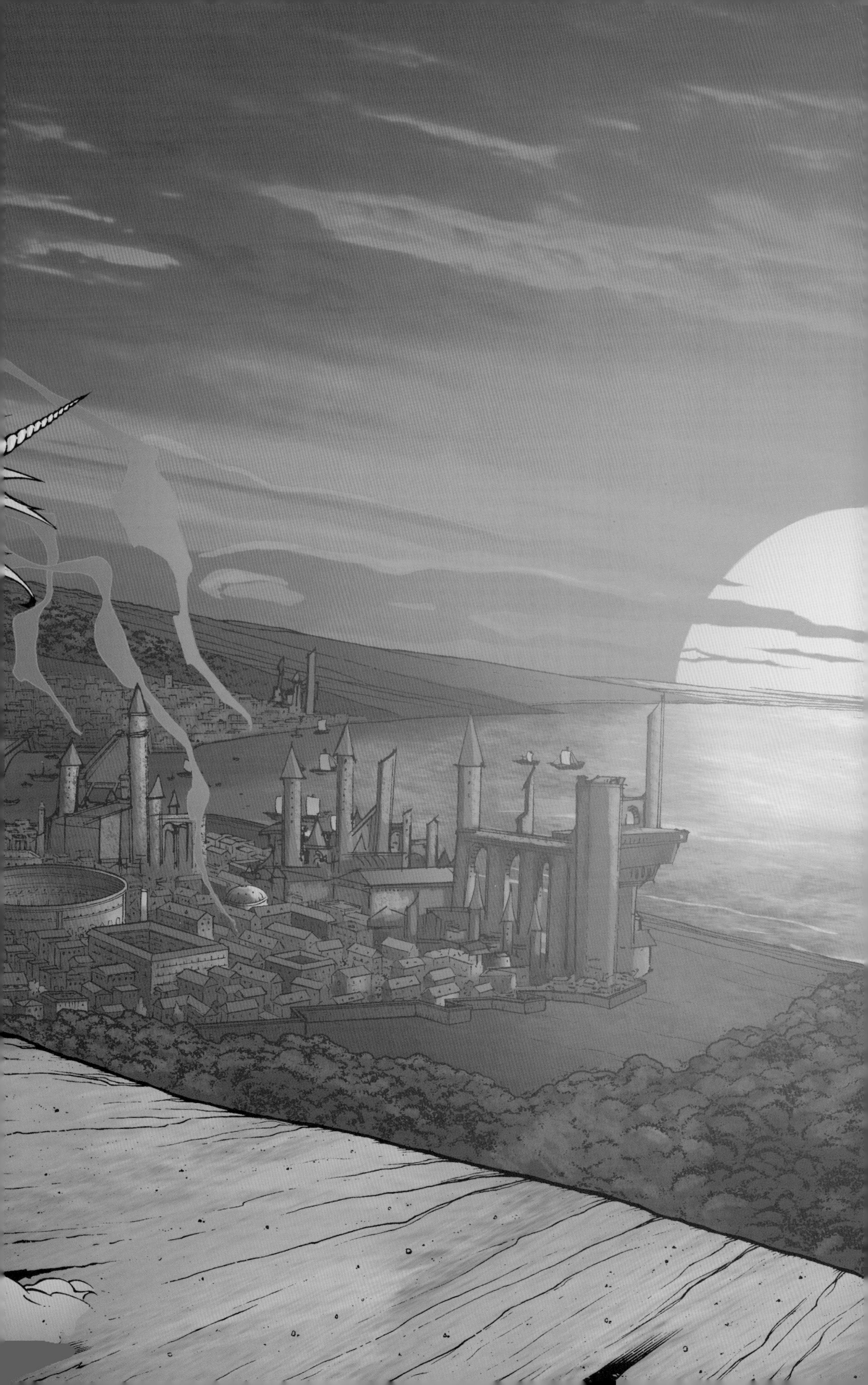

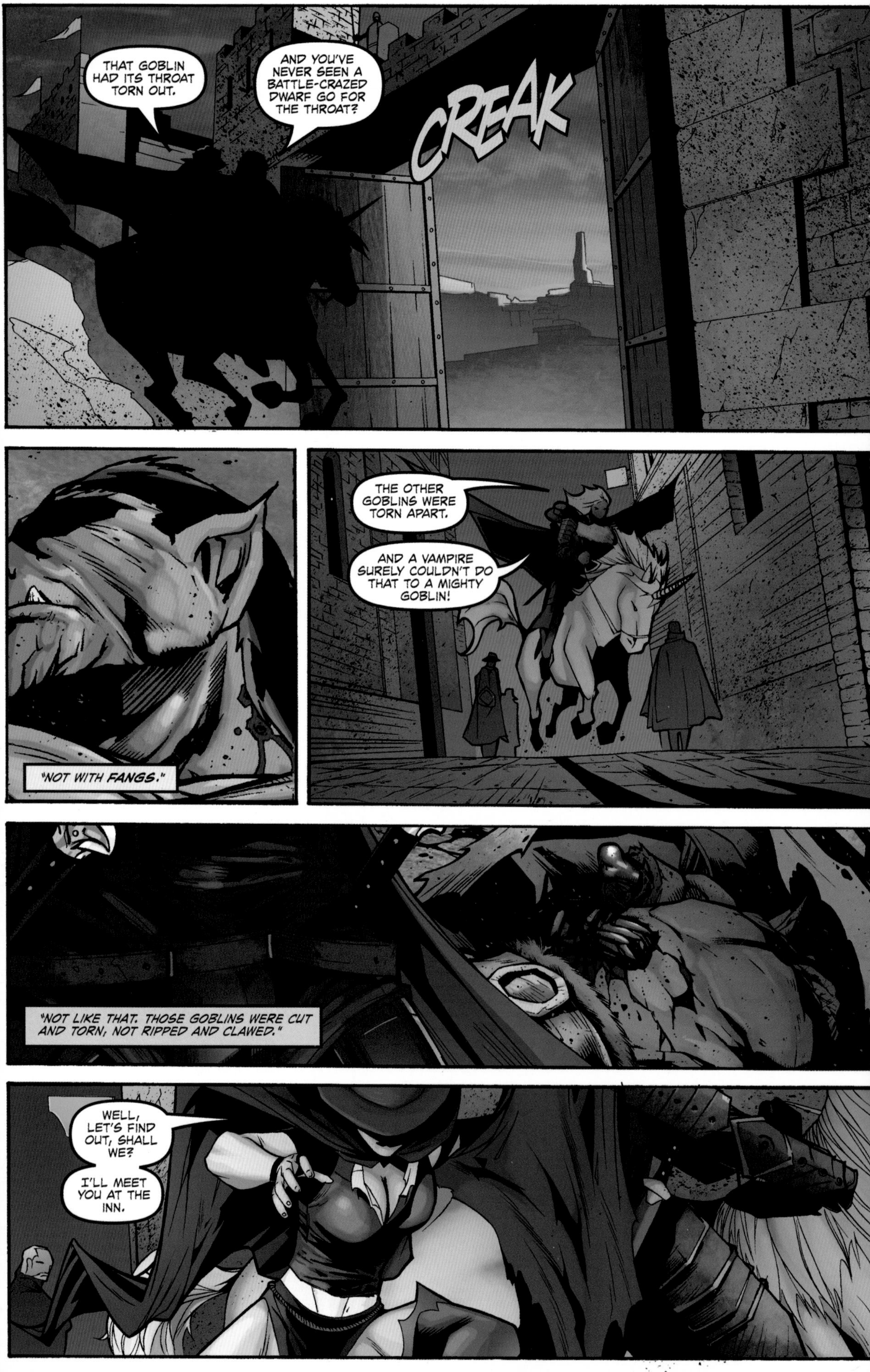
THAT GOBLIN HAD ITS THROAT TORN OUT.
AND YOU'VE NEVER SEEN A BATTLE-CRAZED DWARF GO FOR THE THROAT?
CREAK
"NOT WITH FANGS."
THE OTHER GOBLINS WERE TORN APART.
AND A VAMPIRE SURELY COULDN'T DO THAT TO A MIGHTY GOBLIN!
"NOT LIKE THAT. THOSE GOBLINS WERE CUT AND TORN, NOT RIPPED AND CLAWED."
WELL, LET'S FIND OUT, SHALL WE?
I'LL MEET YOU AT THE INN.

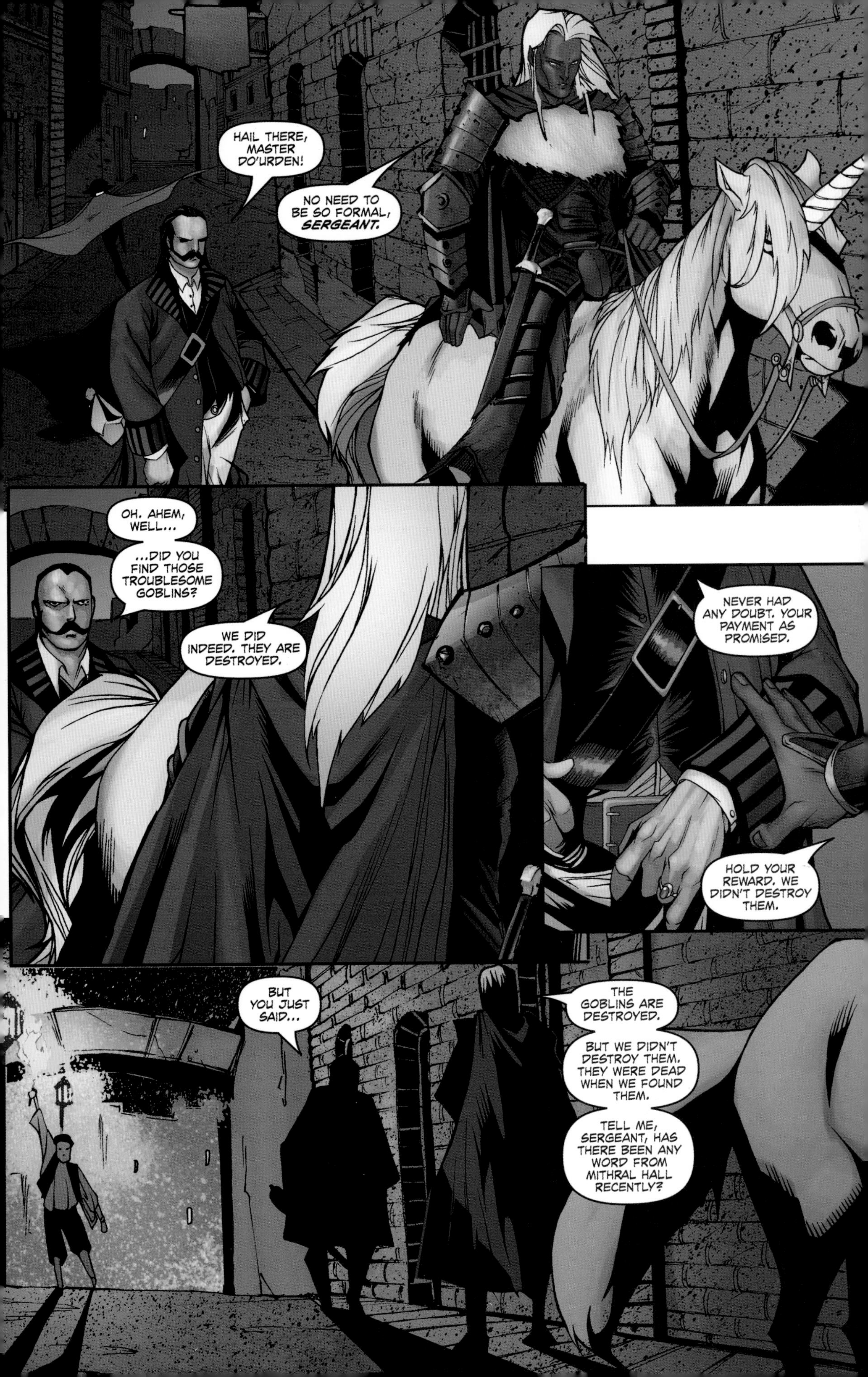
HAIL THERE, MASTER DO'URDEN!
NO NEED TO BE SO FORMAL, ***SERGEANT.***
OH. AHEM, WELL...
...DID YOU FIND THOSE TROUBLESOME GOBLINS?
WE DID INDEED. THEY ARE DESTROYED.
NEVER HAD ANY DOUBT. YOUR PAYMENT AS PROMISED.
HOLD YOUR REWARD. WE DIDN'T DESTROY THEM.
BUT YOU JUST SAID...
THE GOBLINS ARE DESTROYED.
BUT WE DIDN'T DESTROY THEM. THEY WERE DEAD WHEN WE FOUND THEM.
TELL ME, SERGEANT, HAS THERE BEEN ANY WORD FROM MITHRAL HALL RECENTLY?

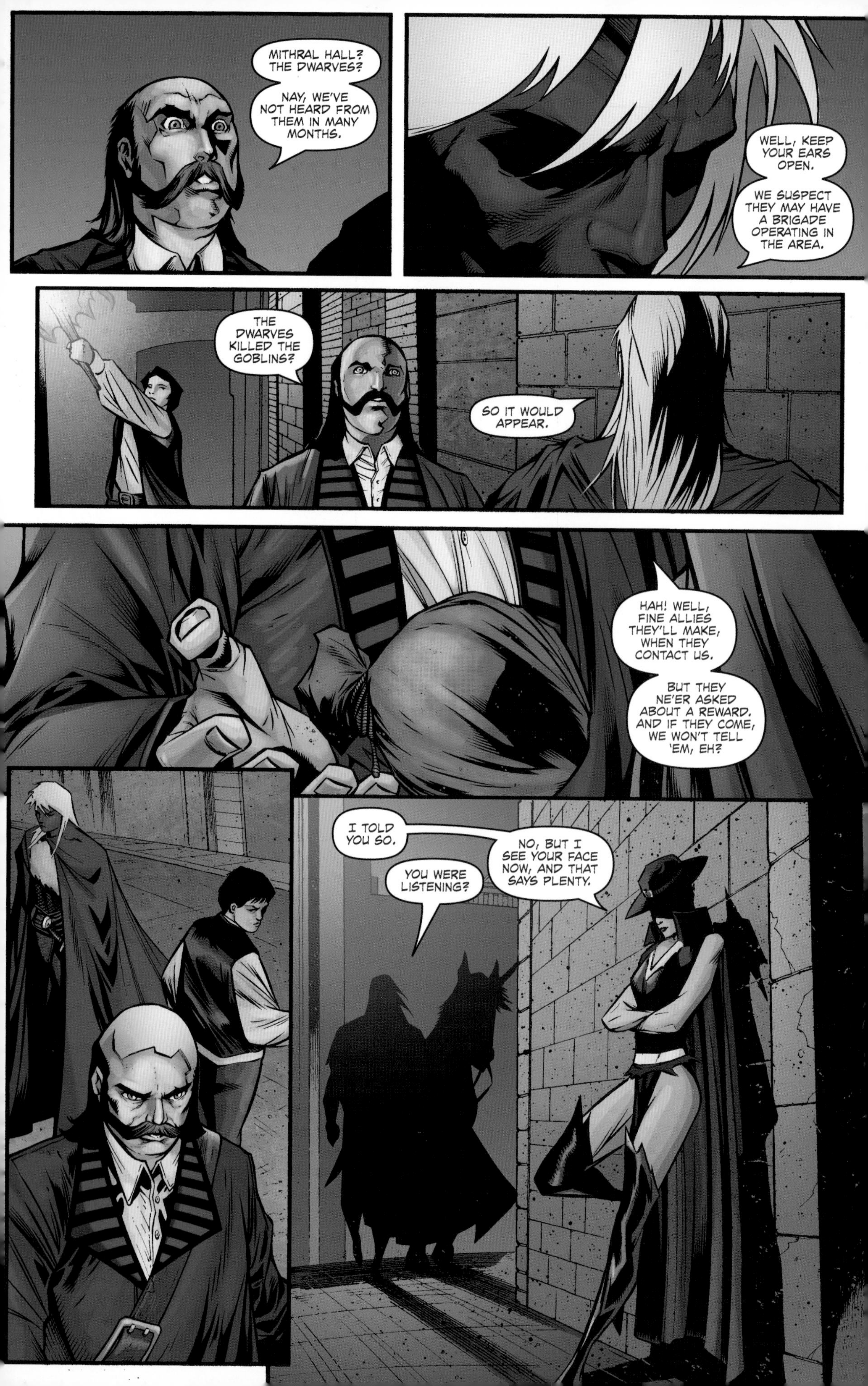
MITHRAL HALL? THE DWARVES?
NAY, WE'VE NOT HEARD FROM THEM IN MANY MONTHS.
WELL, KEEP YOUR EARS OPEN.
WE SUSPECT THEY MAY HAVE A BRIGADE OPERATING IN THE AREA.
THE DWARVES KILLED THE GOBLINS?
SO IT WOULD APPEAR.
HAH! WELL, FINE ALLIES THEY'LL MAKE, WHEN THEY CONTACT US.
BUT THEY NE'ER ASKED ABOUT A REWARD. AND IF THEY COME, WE WON'T TELL 'EM, EH?
I TOLD YOU SO.
YOU WERE LISTENING?
NO, BUT I SEE YOUR FACE NOW, AND THAT SAYS PLENTY.

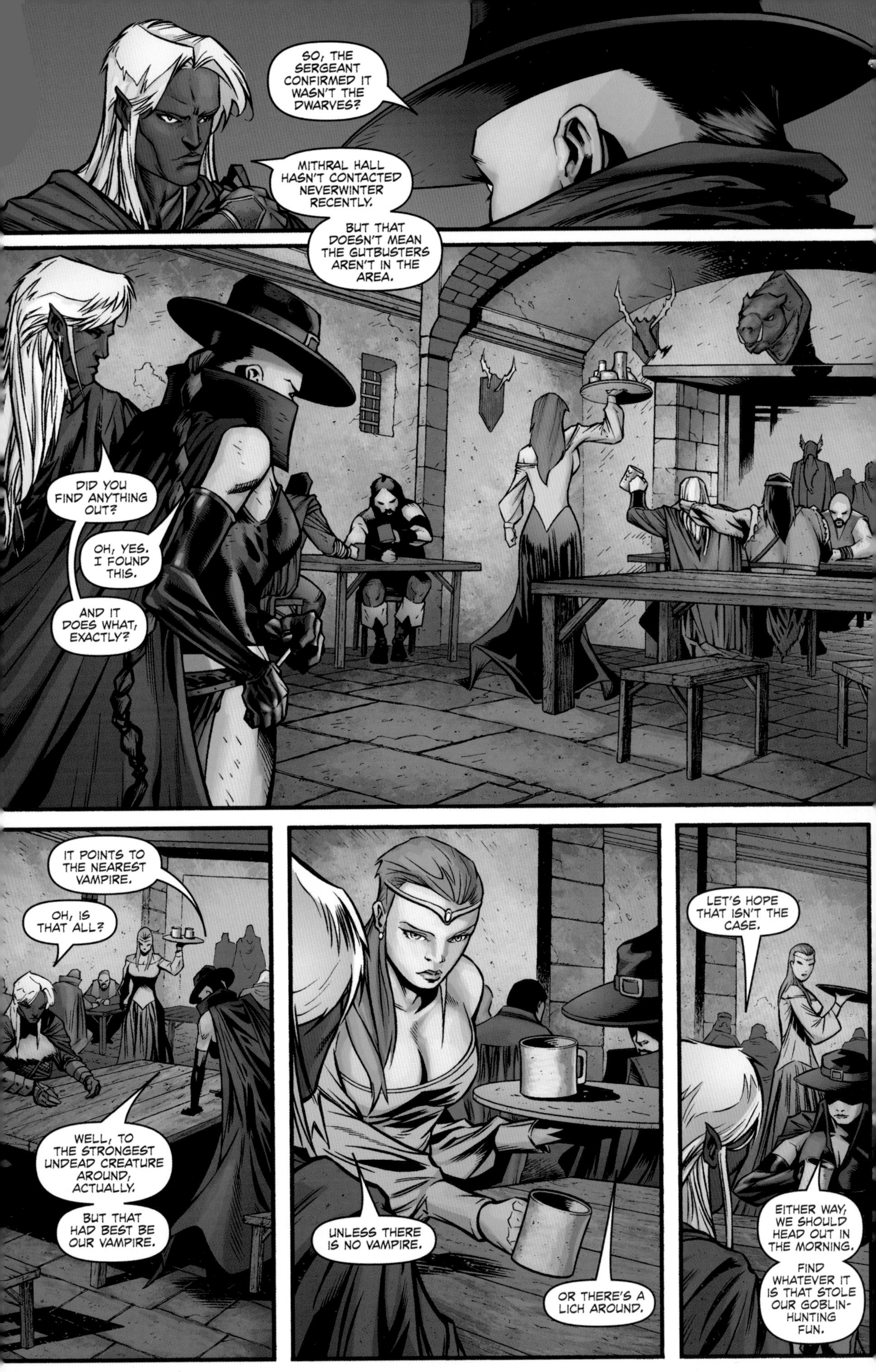
SO, THE SERGEANT CONFIRMED IT WASN'T THE DWARVES?
MITHRAL HALL HASN'T CONTACTED NEVERWINTER RECENTLY.
BUT THAT DOESN'T MEAN THE GUTBUSTERS AREN'T IN THE AREA.
DID YOU FIND ANYTHING OUT?
OH, YES. I FOUND THIS.
AND IT DOES WHAT, EXACTLY?
IT POINTS TO THE NEAREST VAMPIRE.
OH, IS THAT ALL?
WELL, TO THE STRONGEST UNDEAD CREATURE AROUND, ACTUALLY.
BUT THAT HAD BEST BE OUR VAMPIRE.
UNLESS THERE IS NO VAMPIRE.
OR THERE'S A LICH AROUND.
LET'S HOPE THAT ISN'T THE CASE.
EITHER WAY, WE SHOULD HEAD OUT IN THE MORNING.
FIND WHATEVER IT IS THAT STOLE OUR GOBLIN-HUNTING FUN.

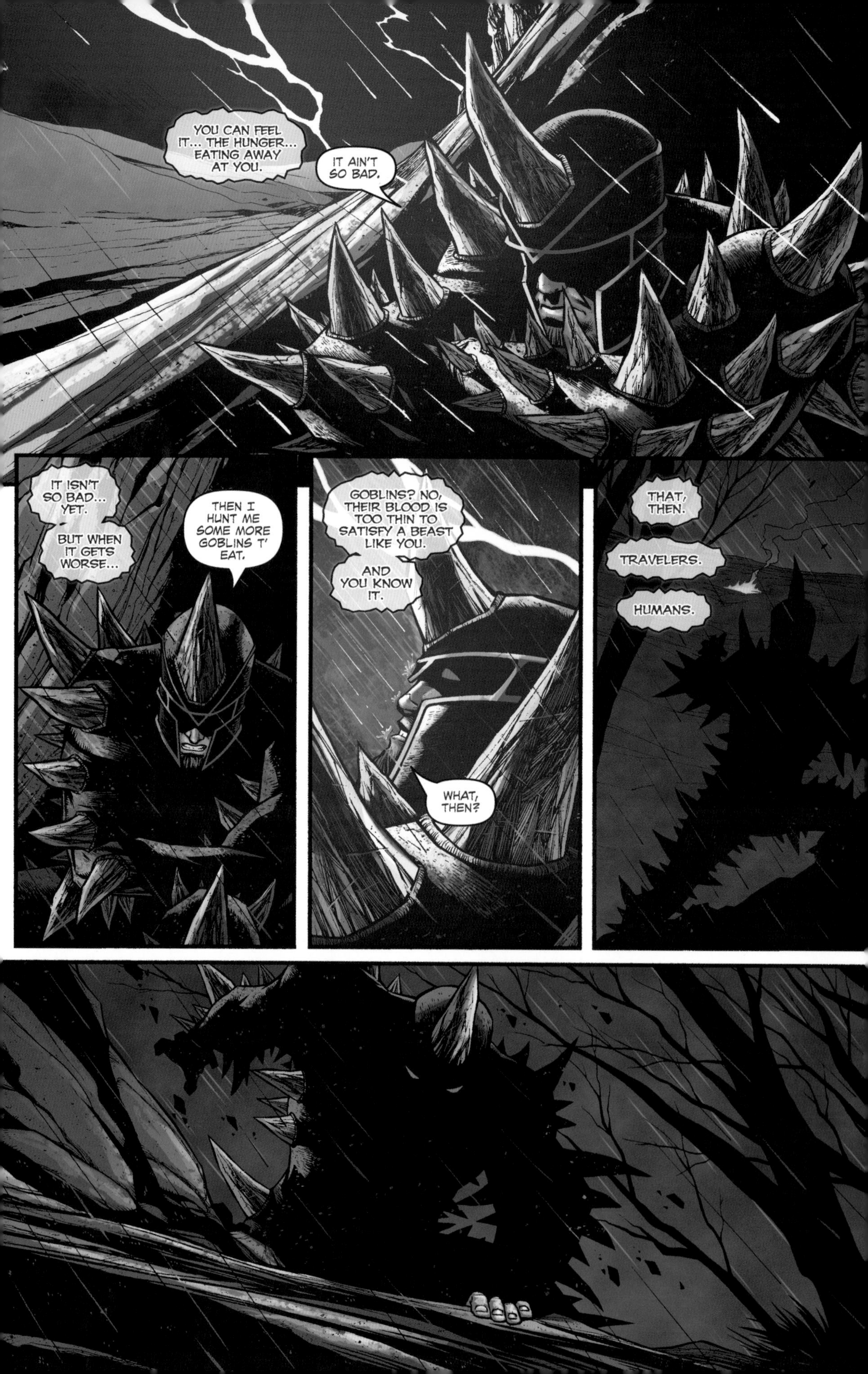
YOU CAN FEEL IT... THE HUNGER... EATING AWAY AT YOU.
IT AIN'T SO BAD.
IT ISN'T SO BAD... YET.
BUT WHEN IT GETS WORSE...
THEN I HUNT ME SOME MORE GOBLINS T' EAT.
GOBLINS? NO, THEIR BLOOD IS TOO THIN TO SATISFY A BEAST LIKE YOU.
AND YOU KNOW IT.
WHAT, THEN?
THAT, THEN.
TRAVELERS.
HUMANS.

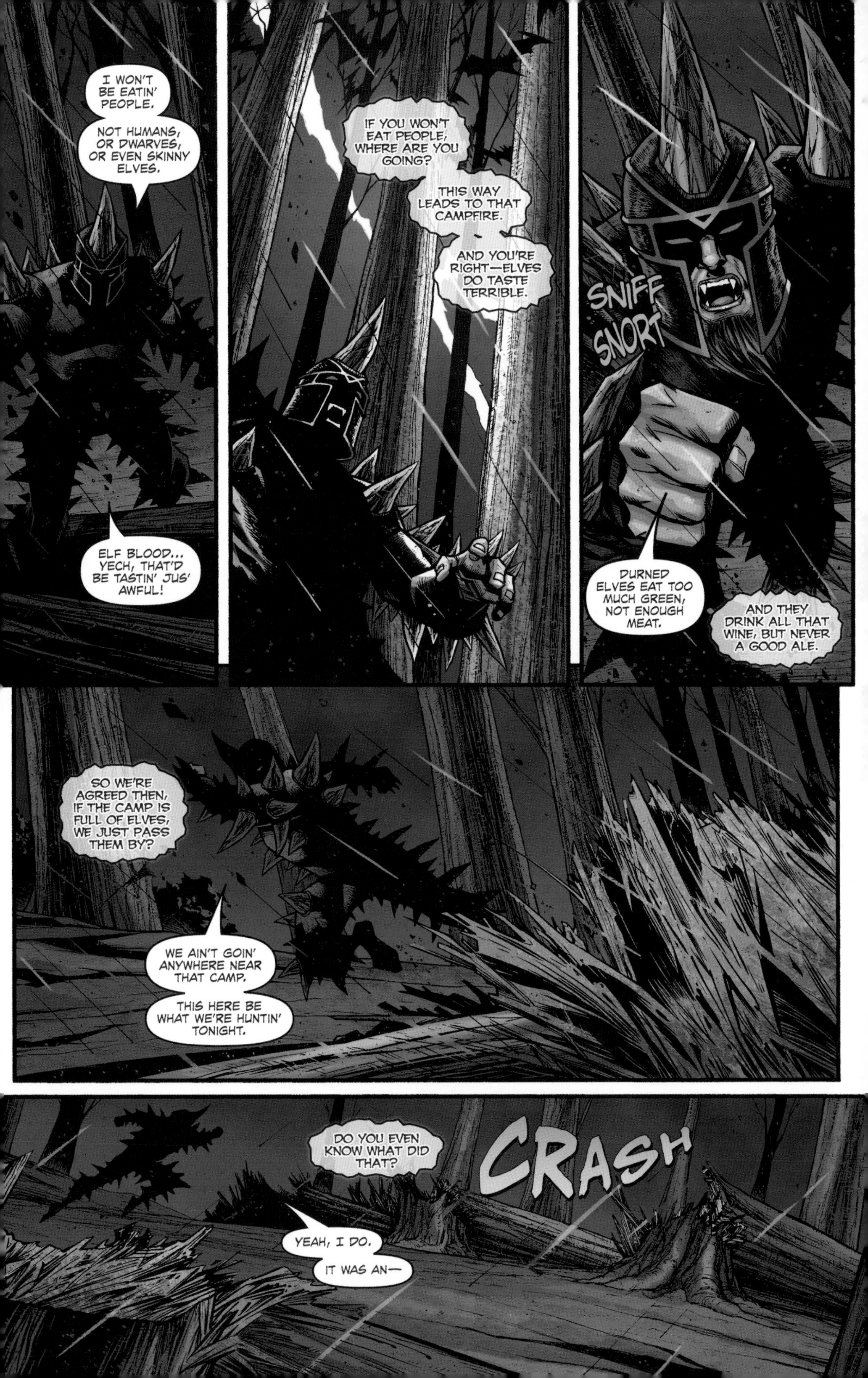
I WON'T BE EATIN' PEOPLE.
NOT HUMANS, OR DWARVES, OR EVEN SKINNY ELVES.
ELF BLOOD... YECH, THAT'D BE TASTIN' JUS' AWFUL!
IF YOU WON'T EAT PEOPLE, WHERE ARE YOU GOING?
THIS WAY LEADS TO THAT CAMPFIRE.
AND YOU'RE RIGHT—ELVES DO TASTE TERRIBLE.
SNIFF
SNORT
DURNED ELVES EAT TOO MUCH GREEN, NOT ENOUGH MEAT.
AND THEY DRINK ALL THAT WINE, BUT NEVER A GOOD ALE.
SO WE'RE AGREED THEN, IF THE CAMP IS FULL OF ELVES, WE JUST PASS THEM BY?
WE AIN'T GOIN' ANYWHERE NEAR THAT CAMP.
THIS HERE BE WHAT WE'RE HUNTIN' TONIGHT.
DO YOU EVEN KNOW WHAT DID THAT?
CRASH
YEAH, I DO.
IT WAS AN—

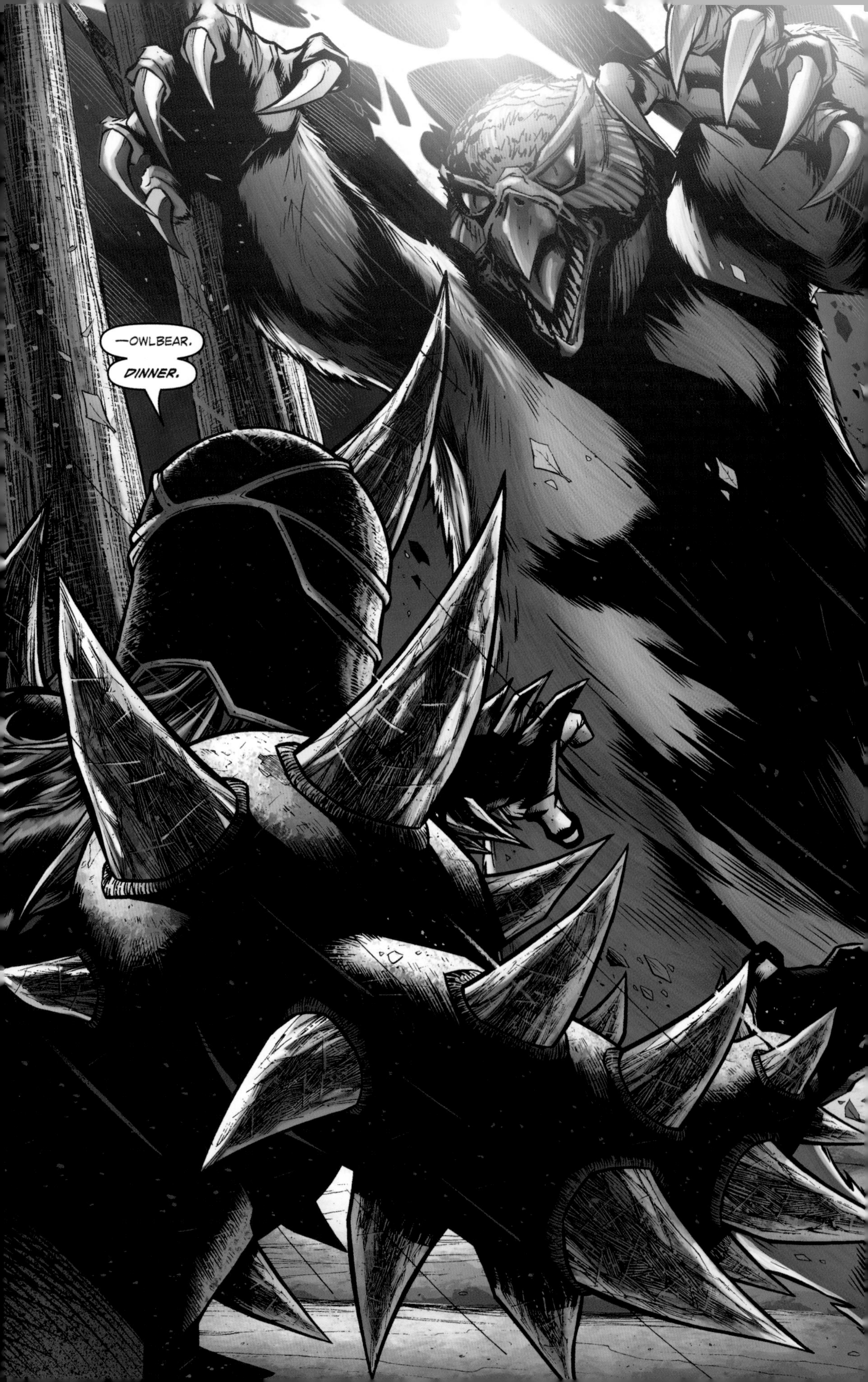
—OWLBEAR.
DINNER.

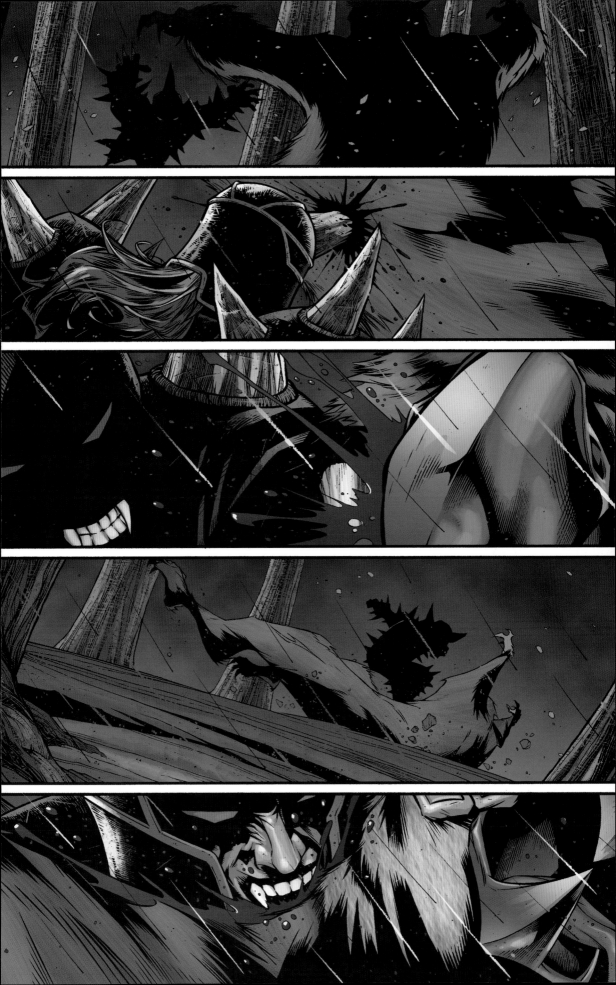

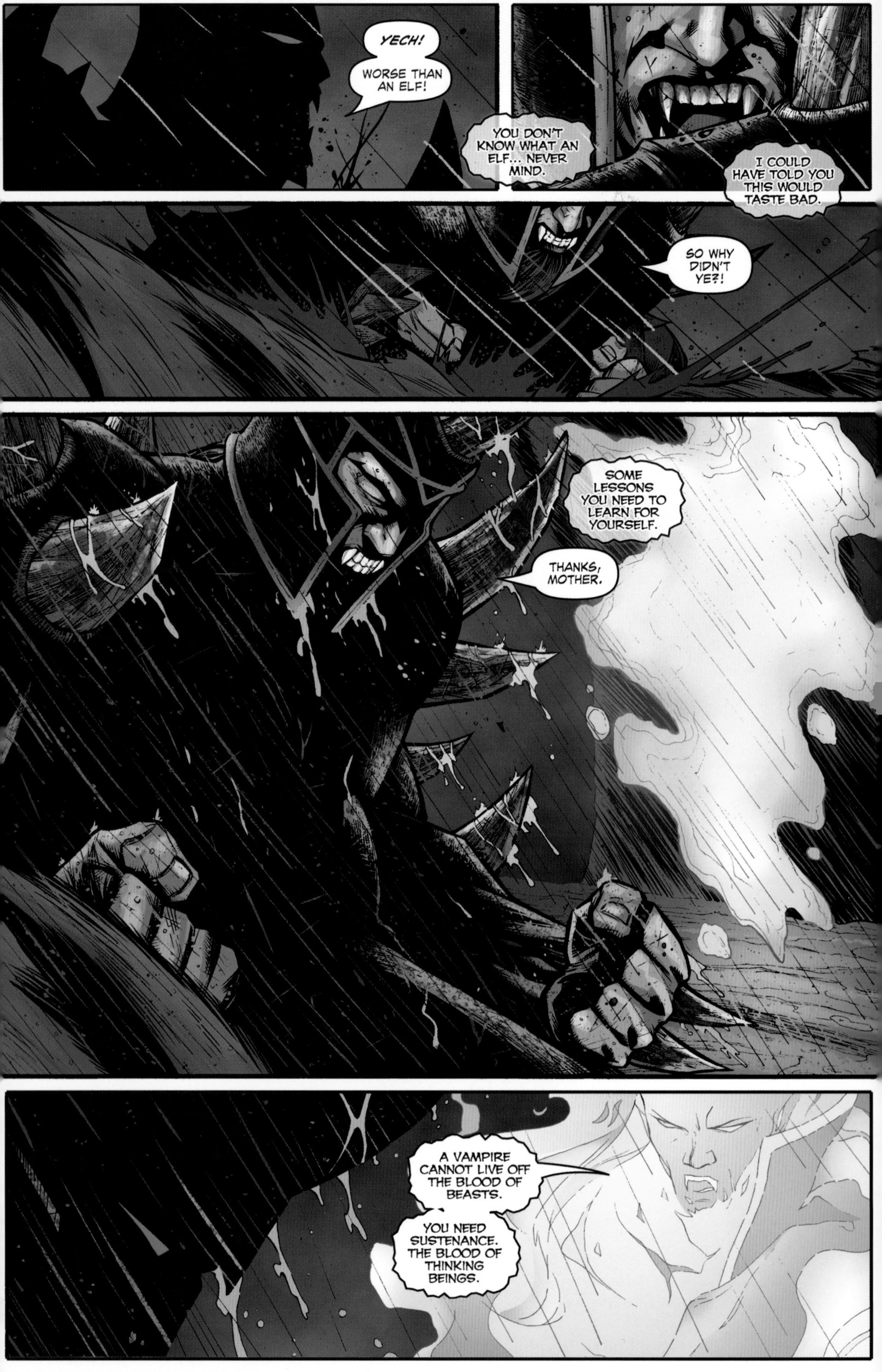
YECH!
WORSE THAN AN ELF!
YOU DON'T KNOW WHAT AN ELF... NEVER MIND.
I COULD HAVE TOLD YOU THIS WOULD TASTE BAD.
SO WHY DIDN'T YE?!
SOME LESSONS YOU NEED TO LEARN FOR YOURSELF.
THANKS, MOTHER.
A VAMPIRE CANNOT LIVE OFF THE BLOOD OF BEASTS.
YOU NEED SUSTENANCE. THE BLOOD OF THINKING BEINGS.

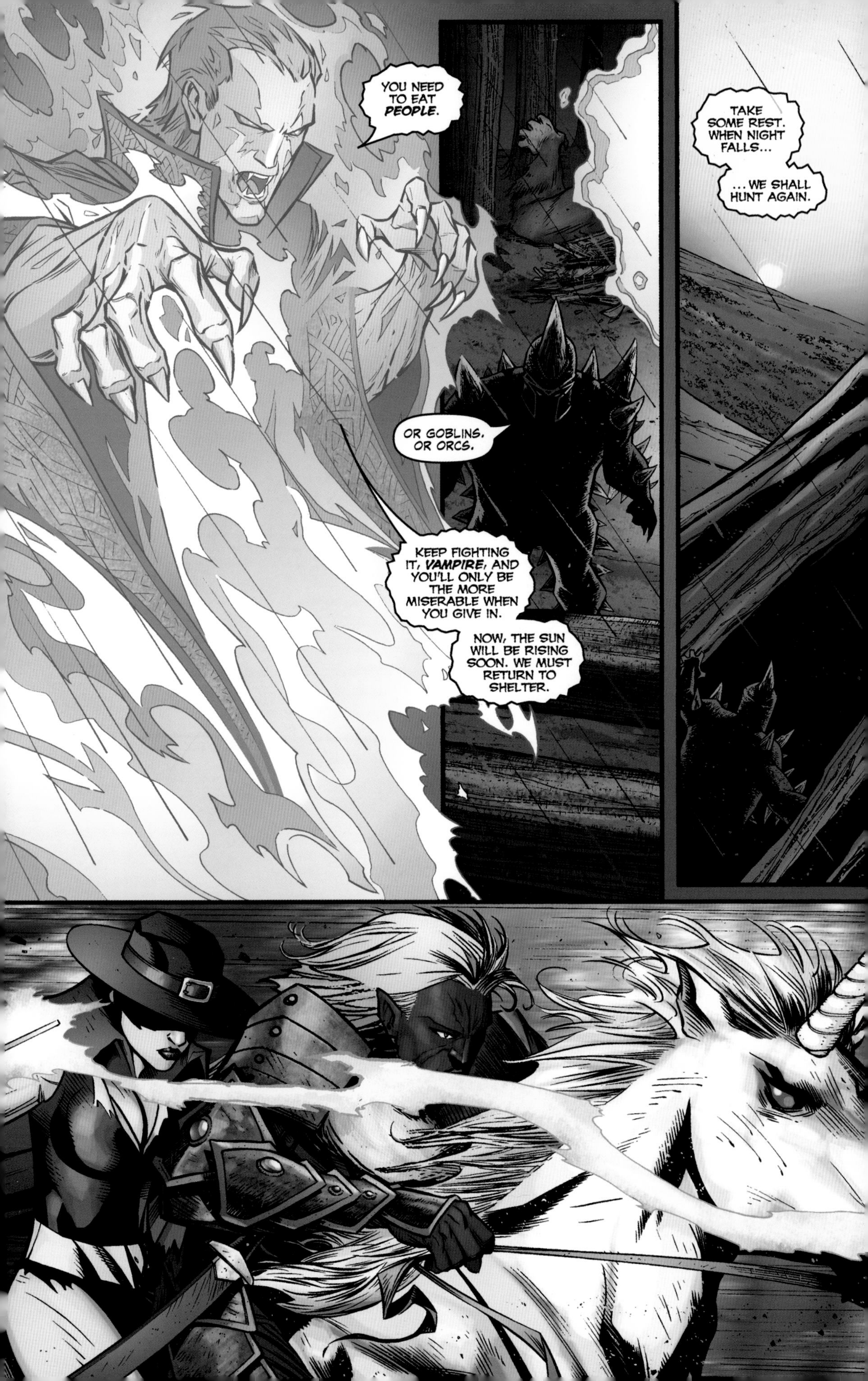
YOU NEED TO EAT *PEOPLE*.
OR GOBLINS. OR ORCS.
KEEP FIGHTING IT, ***VAMPIRE***, AND YOU'LL ONLY BE THE MORE MISERABLE WHEN YOU GIVE IN.
NOW, THE SUN WILL BE RISING SOON. WE MUST RETURN TO SHELTER.
TAKE SOME REST. WHEN NIGHT FALLS...
...WE SHALL HUNT AGAIN.

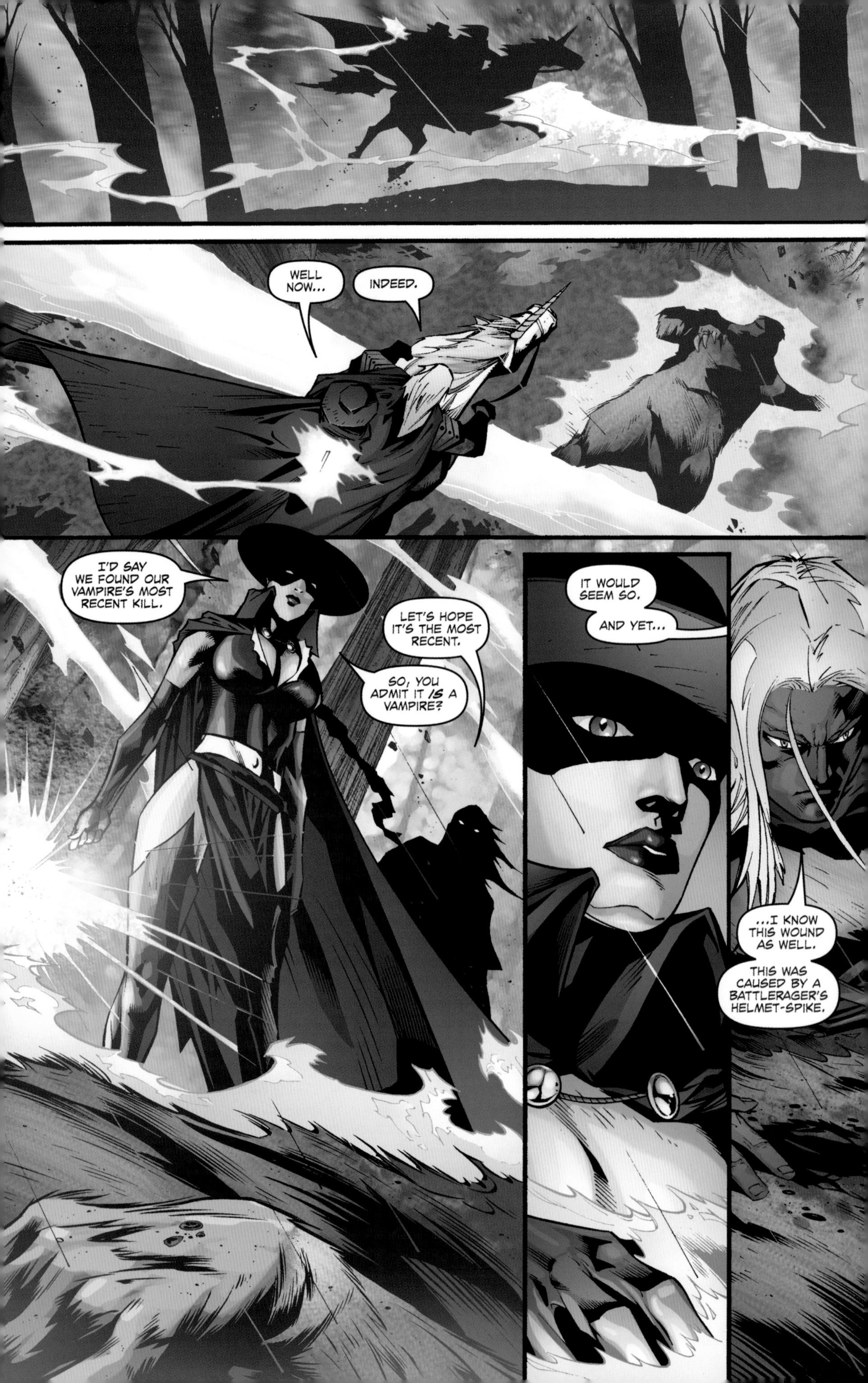
WELL NOW...
INDEED.
I'D SAY WE FOUND OUR VAMPIRE'S MOST RECENT KILL.
LET'S HOPE IT'S THE MOST RECENT.
SO, YOU ADMIT IT IS A VAMPIRE?
IT WOULD SEEM SO.
AND YET...
...I KNOW THIS WOUND AS WELL.
THIS WAS CAUSED BY A BATTLERAGER'S HELMET-SPIKE.

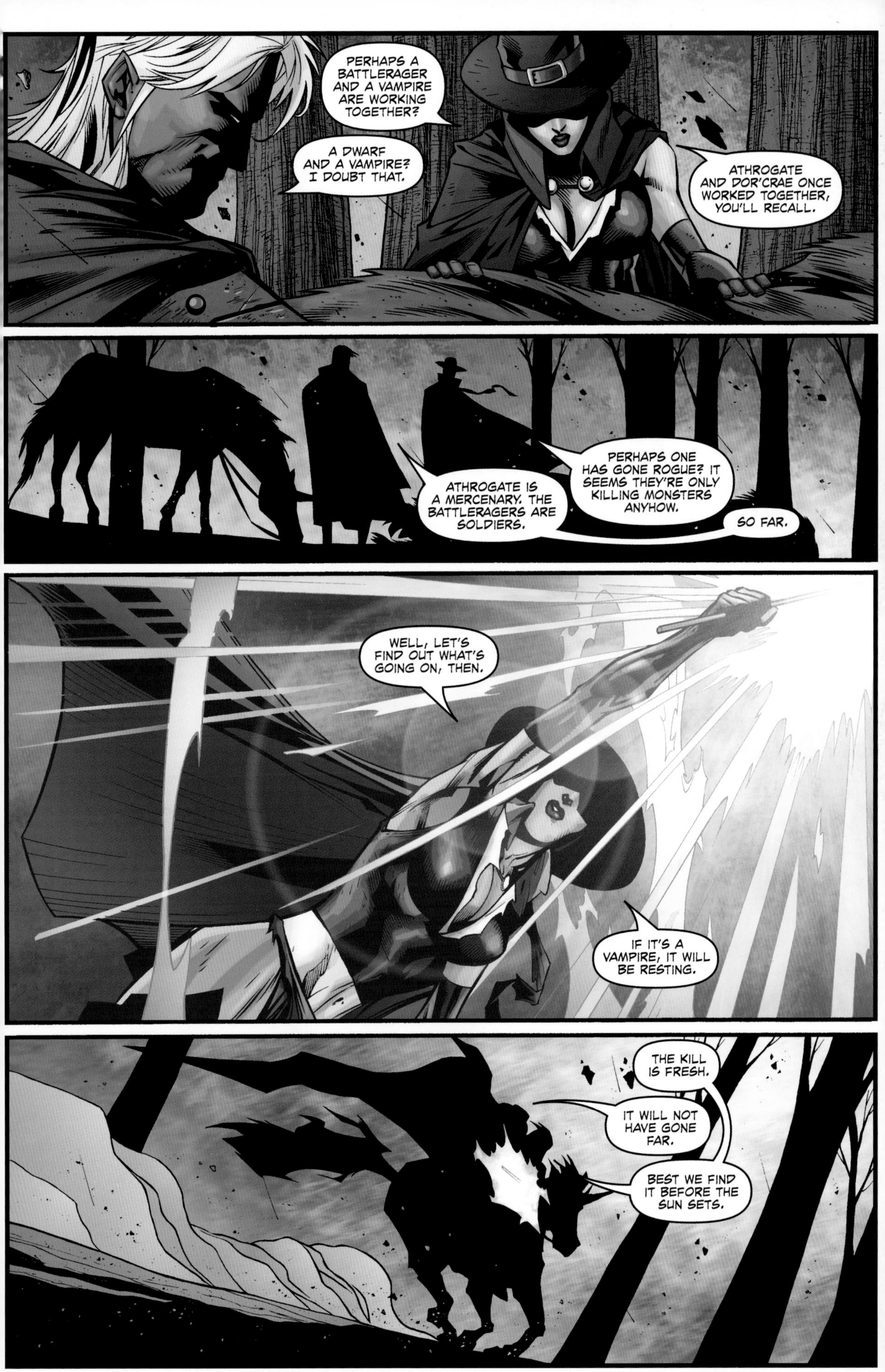
PERHAPS A BATTLERAGER AND A VAMPIRE ARE WORKING TOGETHER?
A DWARF AND A VAMPIRE? I DOUBT THAT.
ATHROGATE AND DOR'CRAE ONCE WORKED TOGETHER, YOU'LL RECALL.
ATHROGATE IS A MERCENARY. THE BATTLERAGERS ARE SOLDIERS.
PERHAPS ONE HAS GONE ROGUE? IT SEEMS THEY'RE ONLY KILLING MONSTERS ANYHOW.
SO FAR.
WELL, LET'S FIND OUT WHAT'S GOING ON, THEN.
IF IT'S A VAMPIRE, IT WILL BE RESTING.
THE KILL IS FRESH.
IT WILL NOT HAVE GONE FAR.
BEST WE FIND IT BEFORE THE SUN SETS.

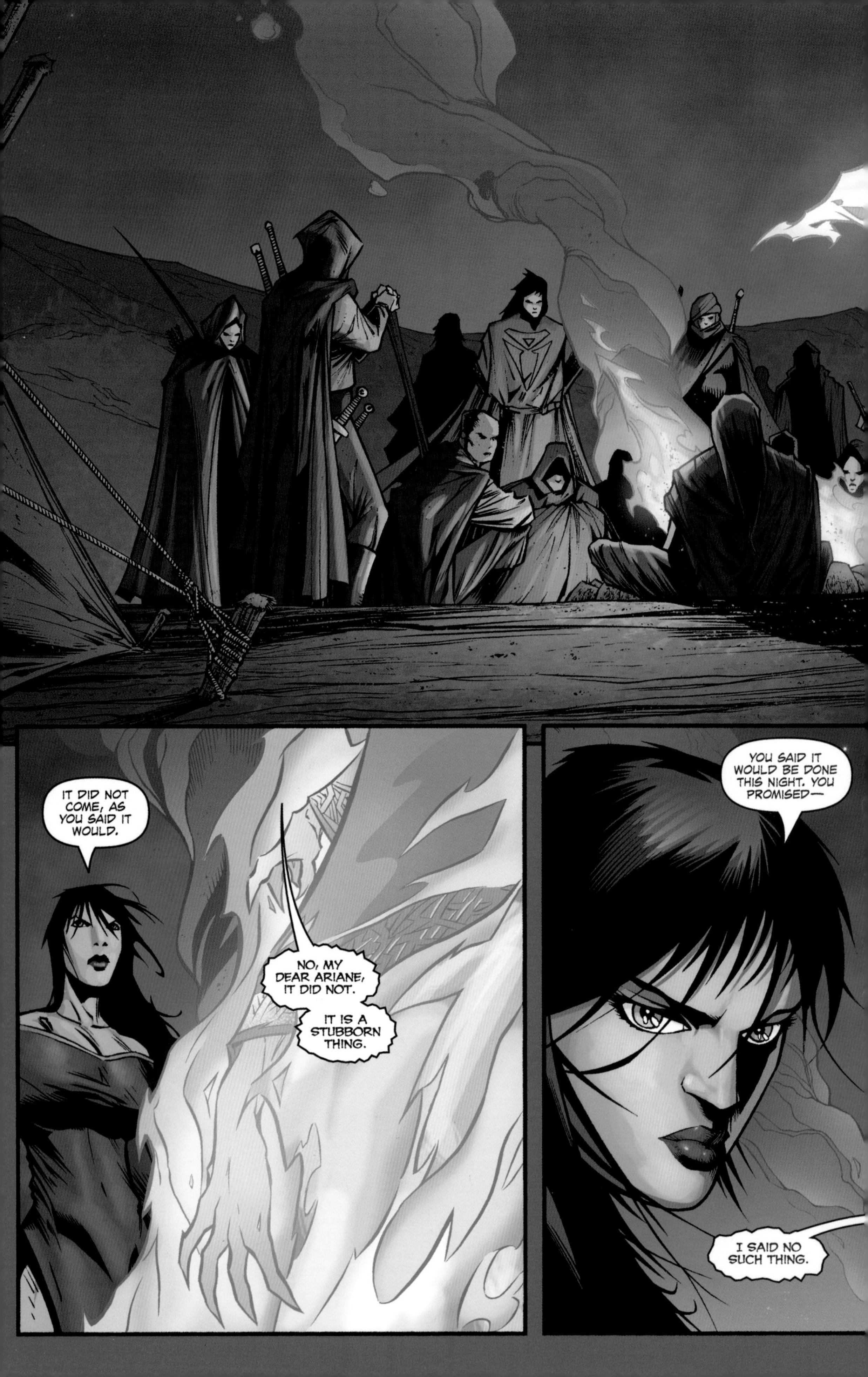
IT DID NOT COME, AS YOU SAID IT WOULD.
NO, MY DEAR ARIANE, IT DID NOT.
IT IS A STUBBORN THING.
YOU SAID IT WOULD BE DONE THIS NIGHT. YOU PROMISED—
I SAID NO SUCH THING.

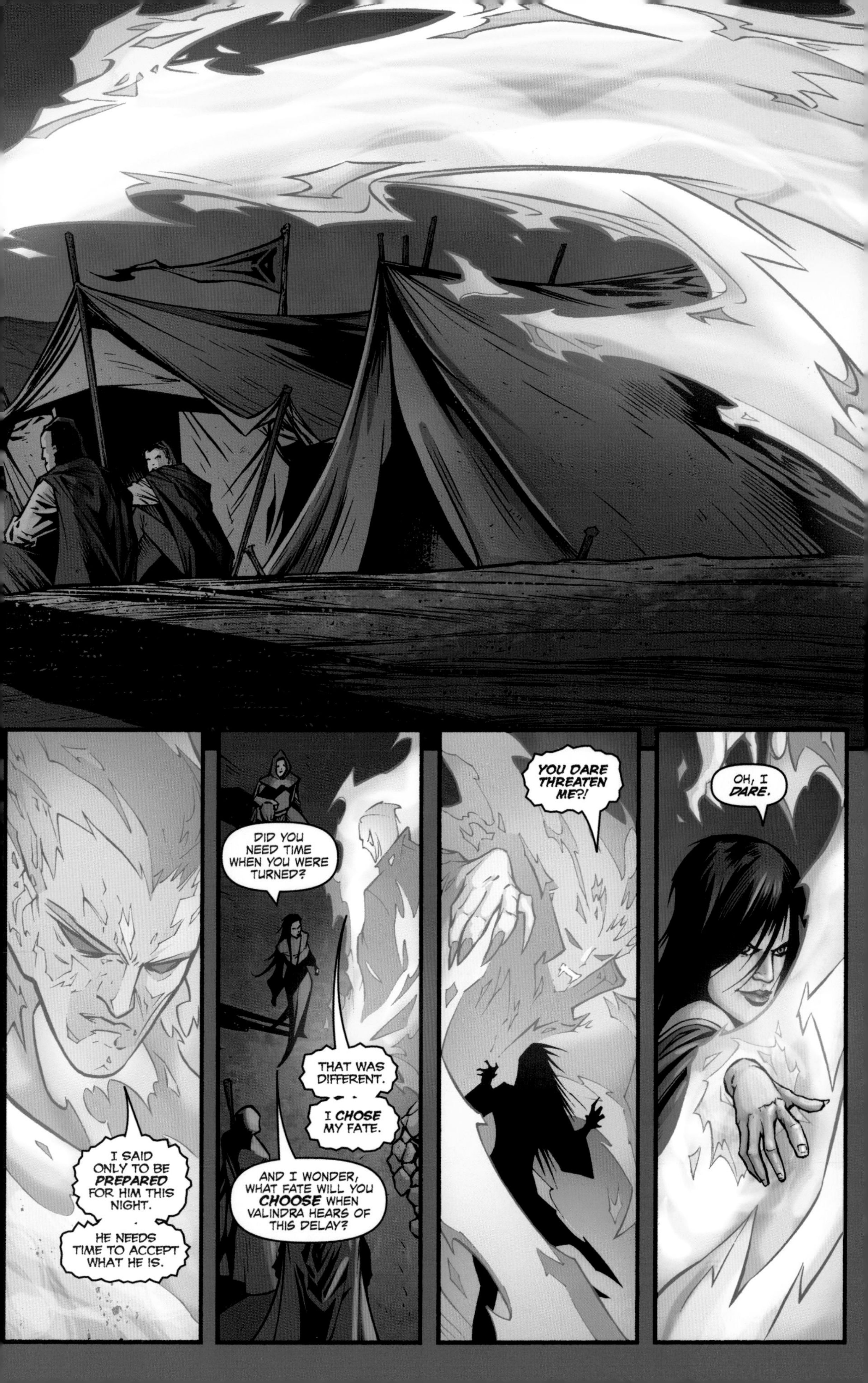
I SAID ONLY TO BE PREPARED FOR HIM THIS NIGHT.
HE NEEDS TIME TO ACCEPT WHAT HE IS.
DID YOU NEED TIME WHEN YOU WERE TURNED?
THAT WAS DIFFERENT.
I CHOSE MY FATE.
AND I WONDER, WHAT FATE WILL YOU CHOOSE WHEN VALINDRA HEARS OF THIS DELAY?
YOU DARE THREATEN ME?!
OH, I DARE.

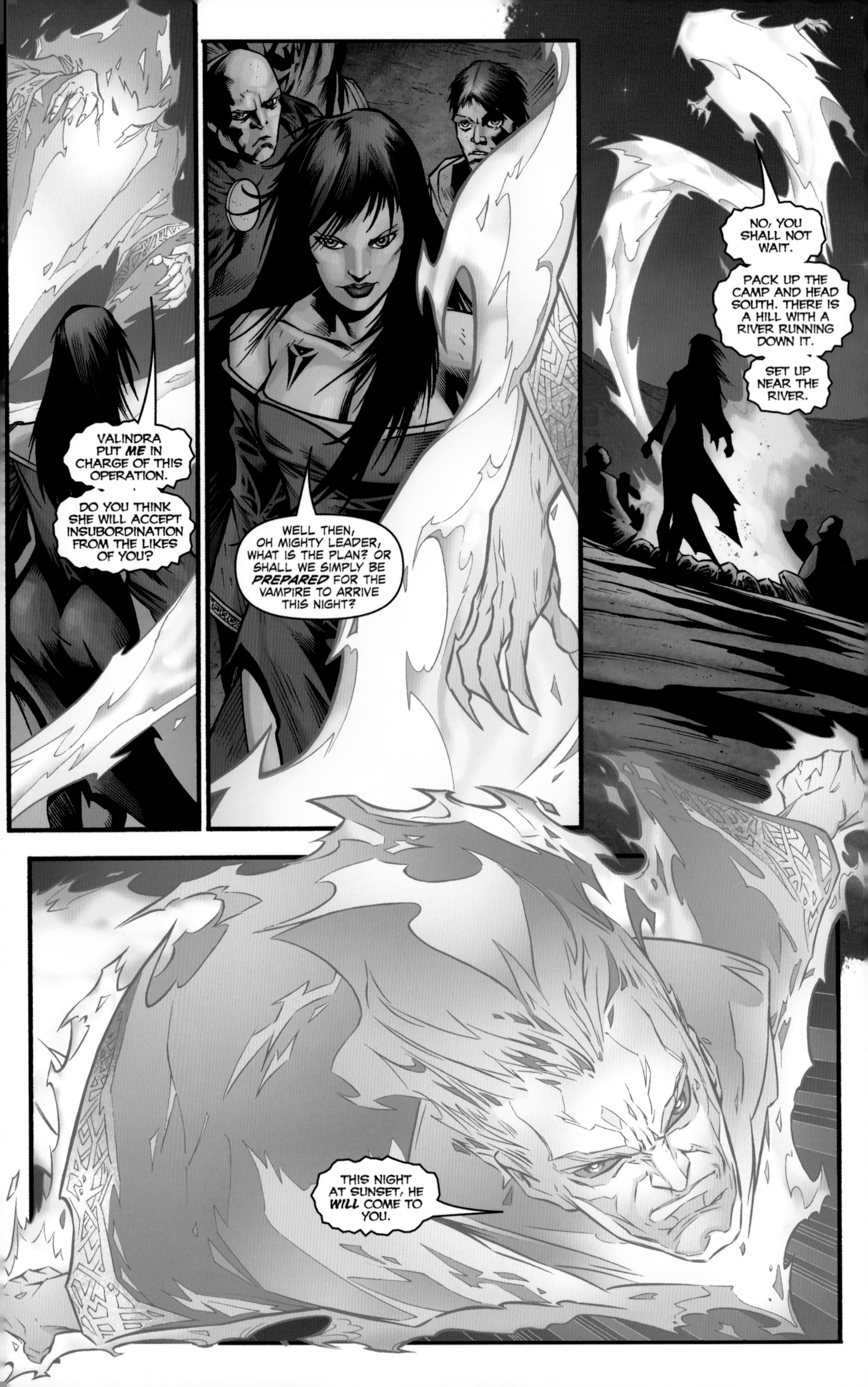
VALINDRA PUT ME IN CHARGE OF THIS OPERATION.
DO YOU THINK SHE WILL ACCEPT INSUBORDINATION FROM THE LIKES OF YOU?
WELL THEN, OH MIGHTY LEADER, WHAT IS THE PLAN? OR SHALL WE SIMPLY BE PREPARED FOR THE VAMPIRE TO ARRIVE THIS NIGHT?
NO, YOU SHALL NOT WAIT.
PACK UP THE CAMP AND HEAD SOUTH. THERE IS A HILL WITH A RIVER RUNNING DOWN IT.
SET UP NEAR THE RIVER.
THIS NIGHT AT SUNSET, HE WILL COME TO YOU.

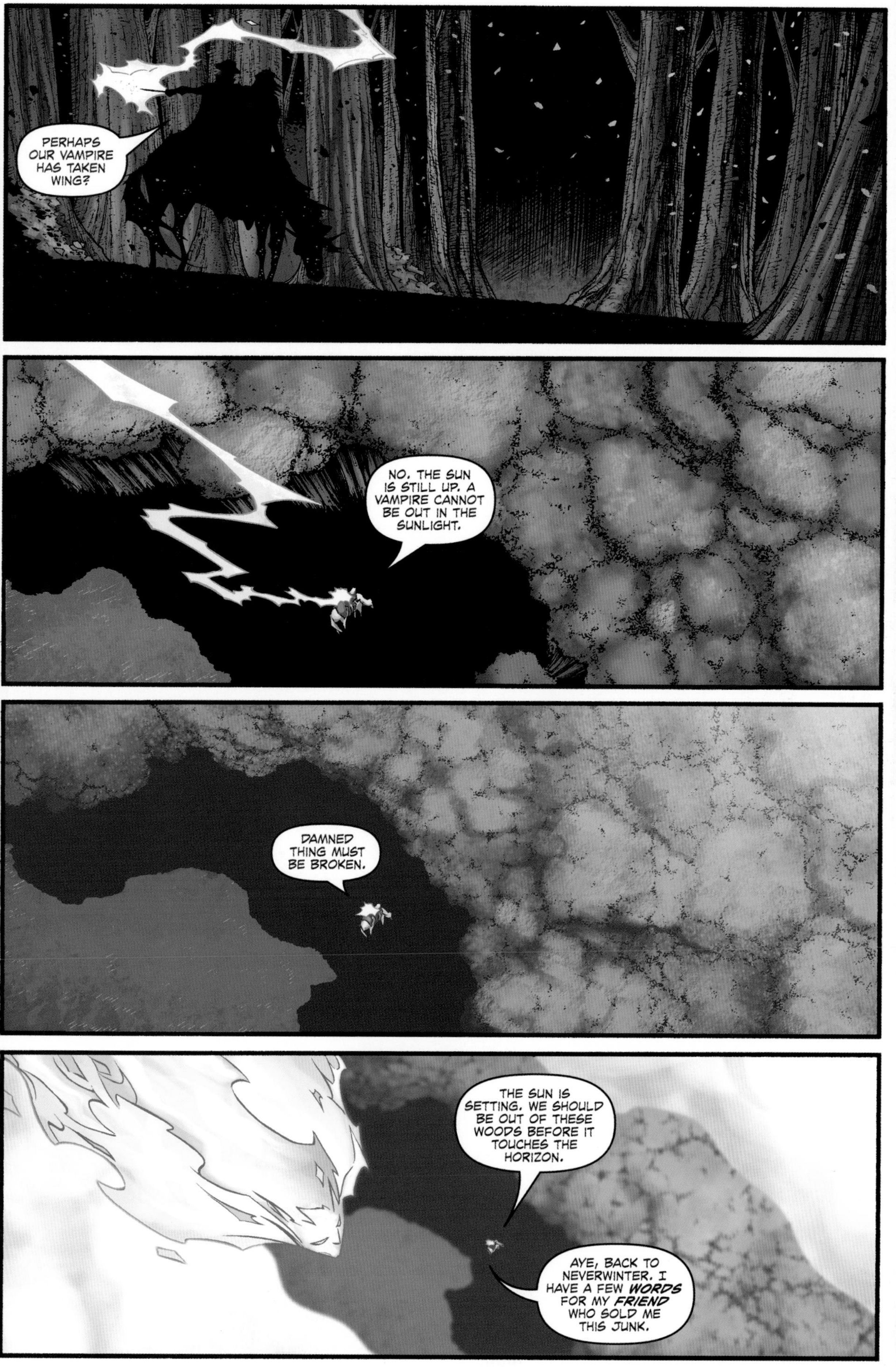
PERHAPS OUR VAMPIRE HAS TAKEN WING?
NO. THE SUN IS STILL UP. A VAMPIRE CANNOT BE OUT IN THE SUNLIGHT.
DAMNED THING MUST BE BROKEN.
THE SUN IS SETTING. WE SHOULD BE OUT OF THESE WOODS BEFORE IT TOUCHES THE HORIZON.
AYE, BACK TO NEVERWINTER. I HAVE A FEW WORDS FOR MY FRIEND WHO SOLD ME THIS JUNK.

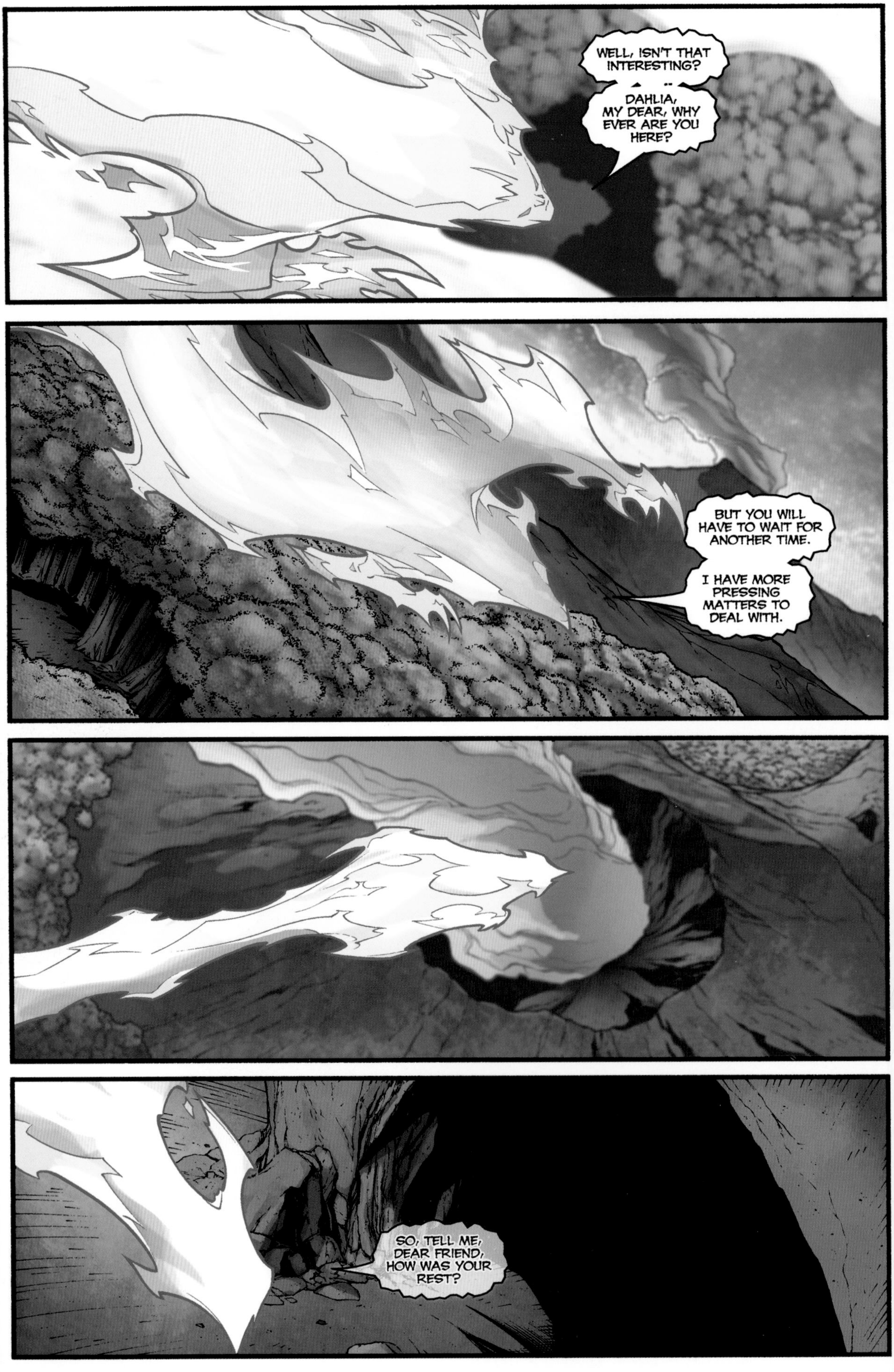
WELL, ISN'T THAT INTERESTING?
DAHLIA, MY DEAR, WHY EVER ARE YOU HERE?
BUT YOU WILL HAVE TO WAIT FOR ANOTHER TIME.
I HAVE MORE PRESSING MATTERS TO DEAL WITH.
SO, TELL ME, DEAR FRIEND, HOW WAS YOUR REST?

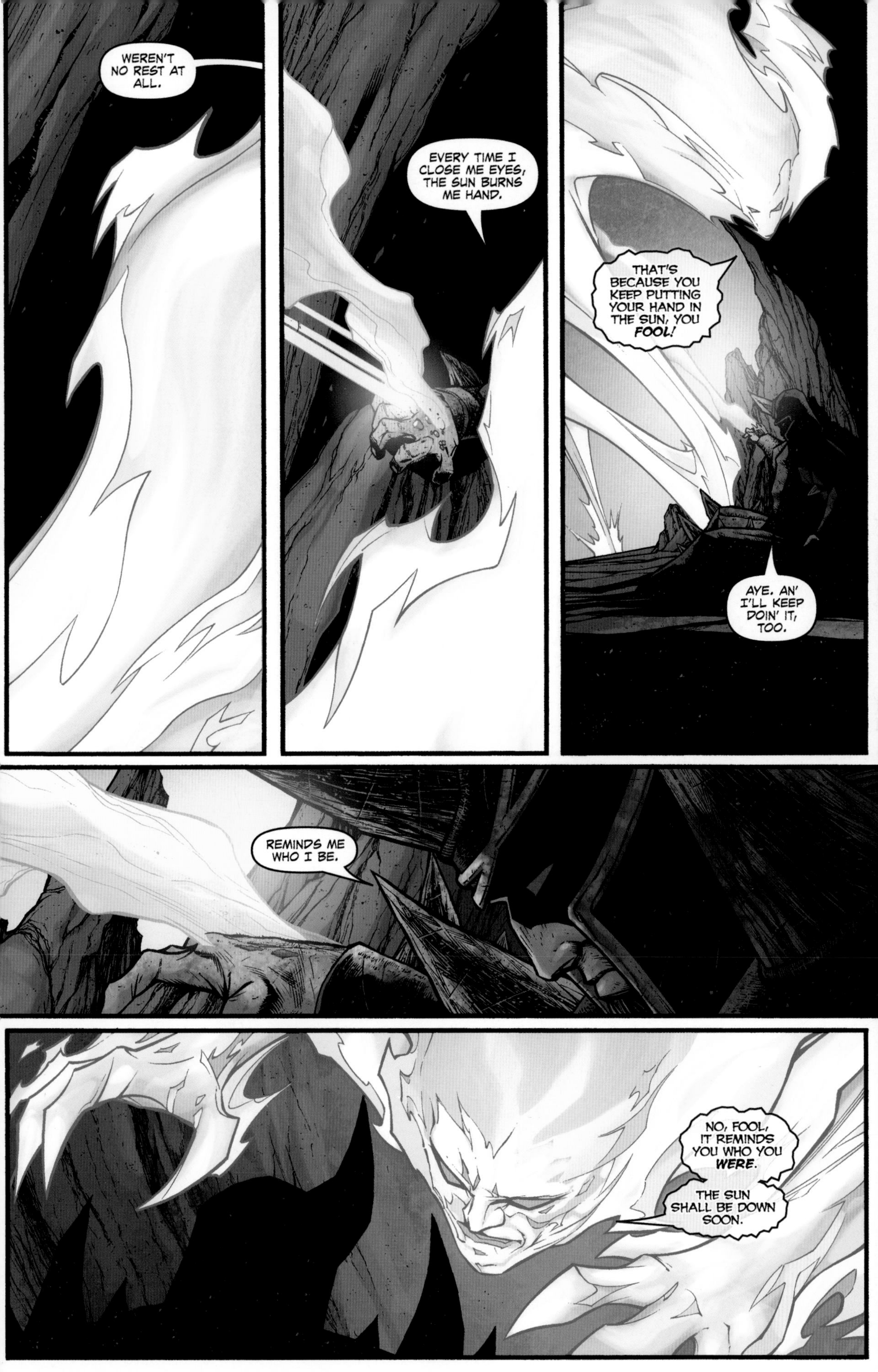
WEREN'T NO REST AT ALL.
EVERY TIME I CLOSE ME EYES, THE SUN BURNS ME HAND.
THAT'S BECAUSE YOU KEEP PUTTING YOUR HAND IN THE SUN, YOU *FOOL!*
AYE. AN' I'LL KEEP DOIN' IT, TOO.
REMINDS ME WHO I BE.
NO, FOOL, IT REMINDS YOU WHO YOU *WERE*.
THE SUN SHALL BE DOWN SOON.

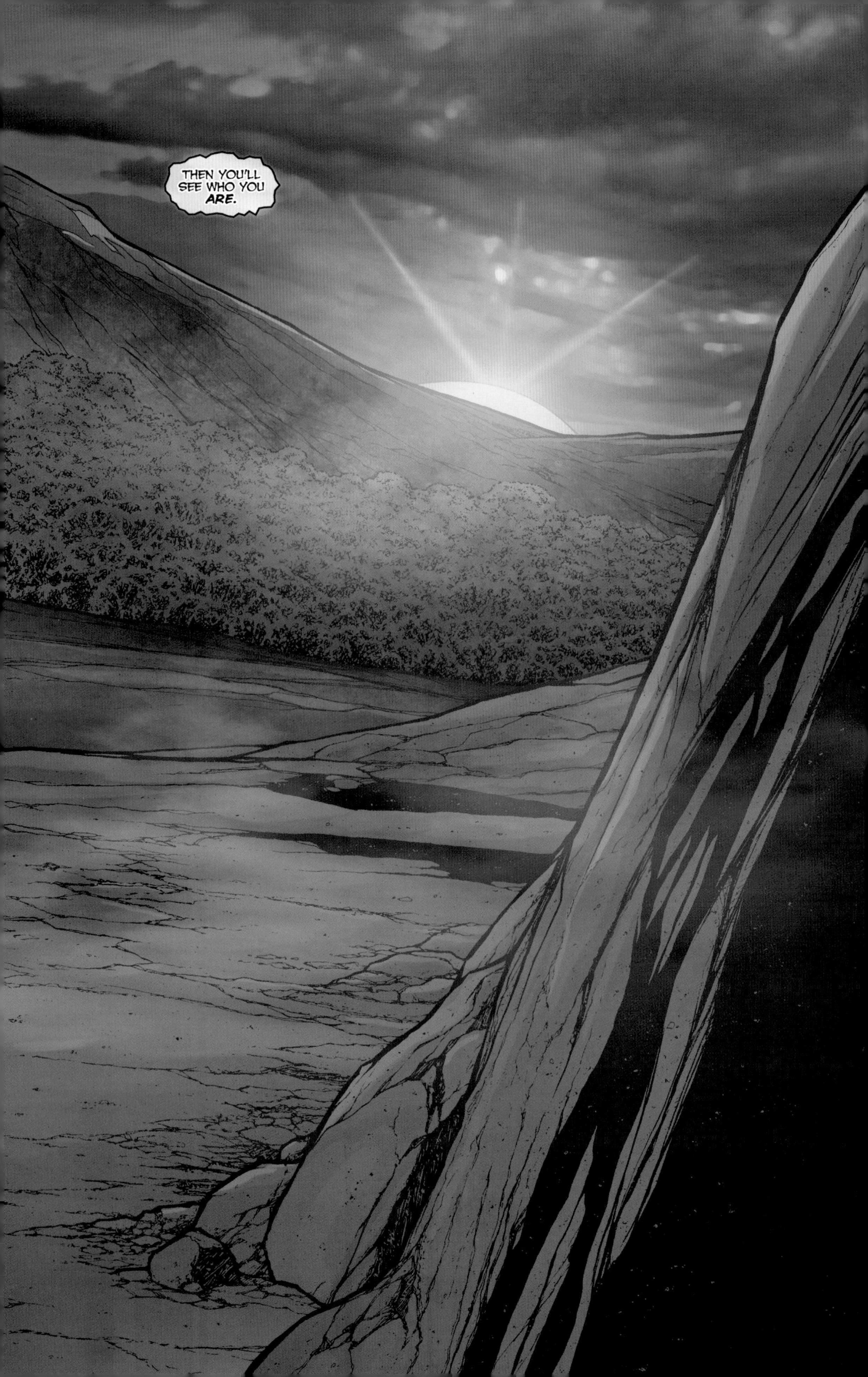
THEN YOU'LL SEE WHO YOU **ARE.**

Art by Tim Seeley • Colors by Leonard O'Grady

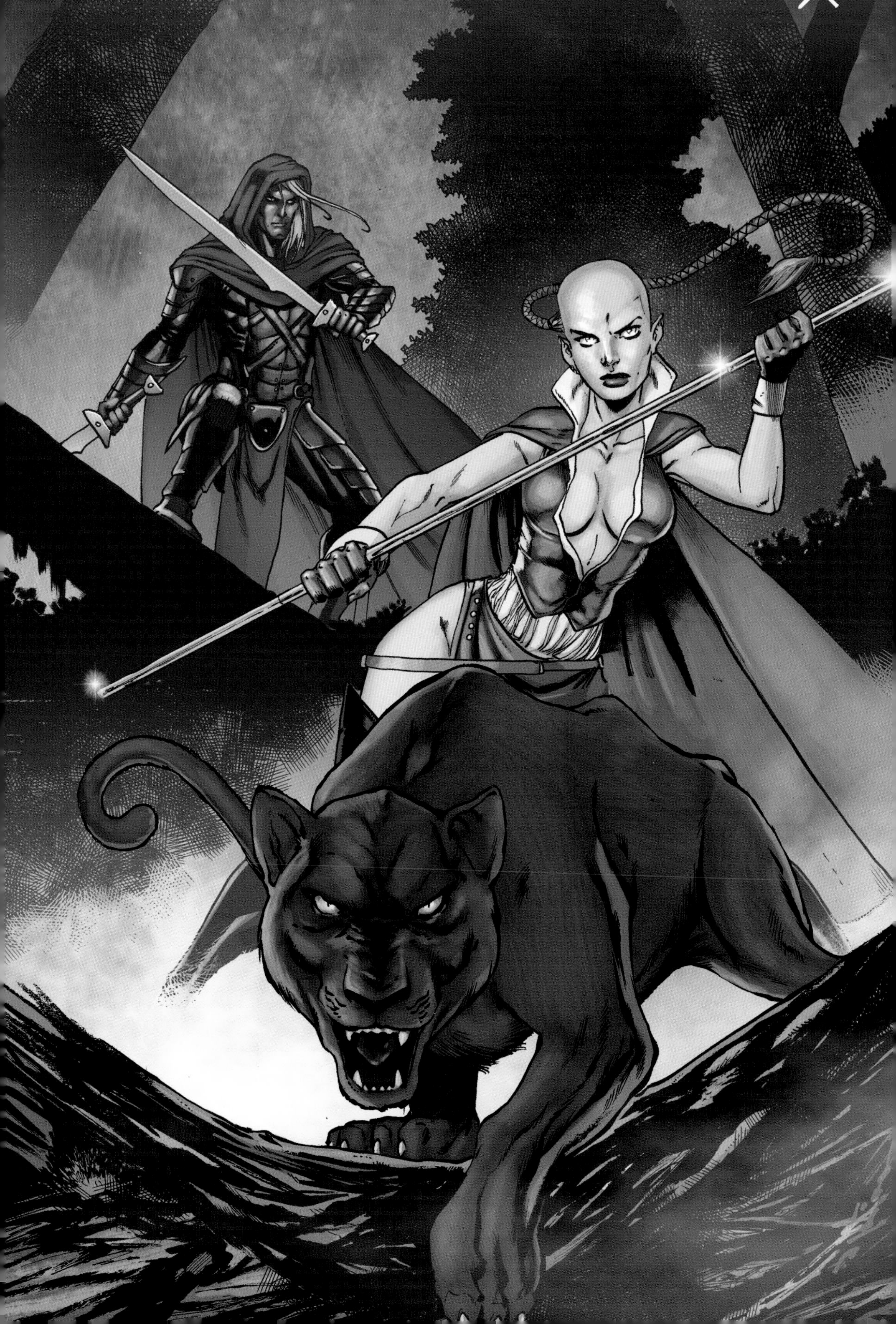

Art by Gonzalo Flores

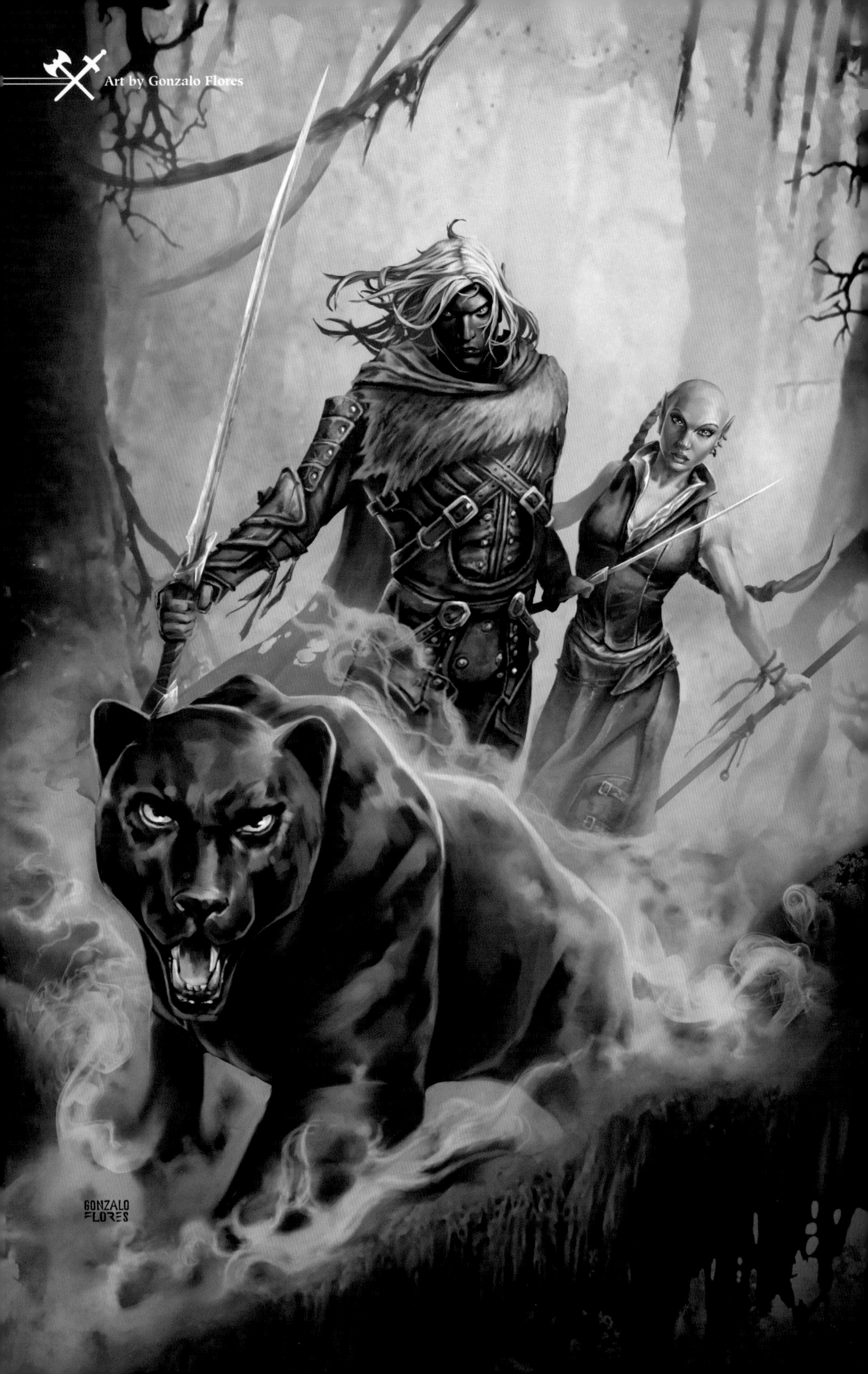
GONZALO
FLORES

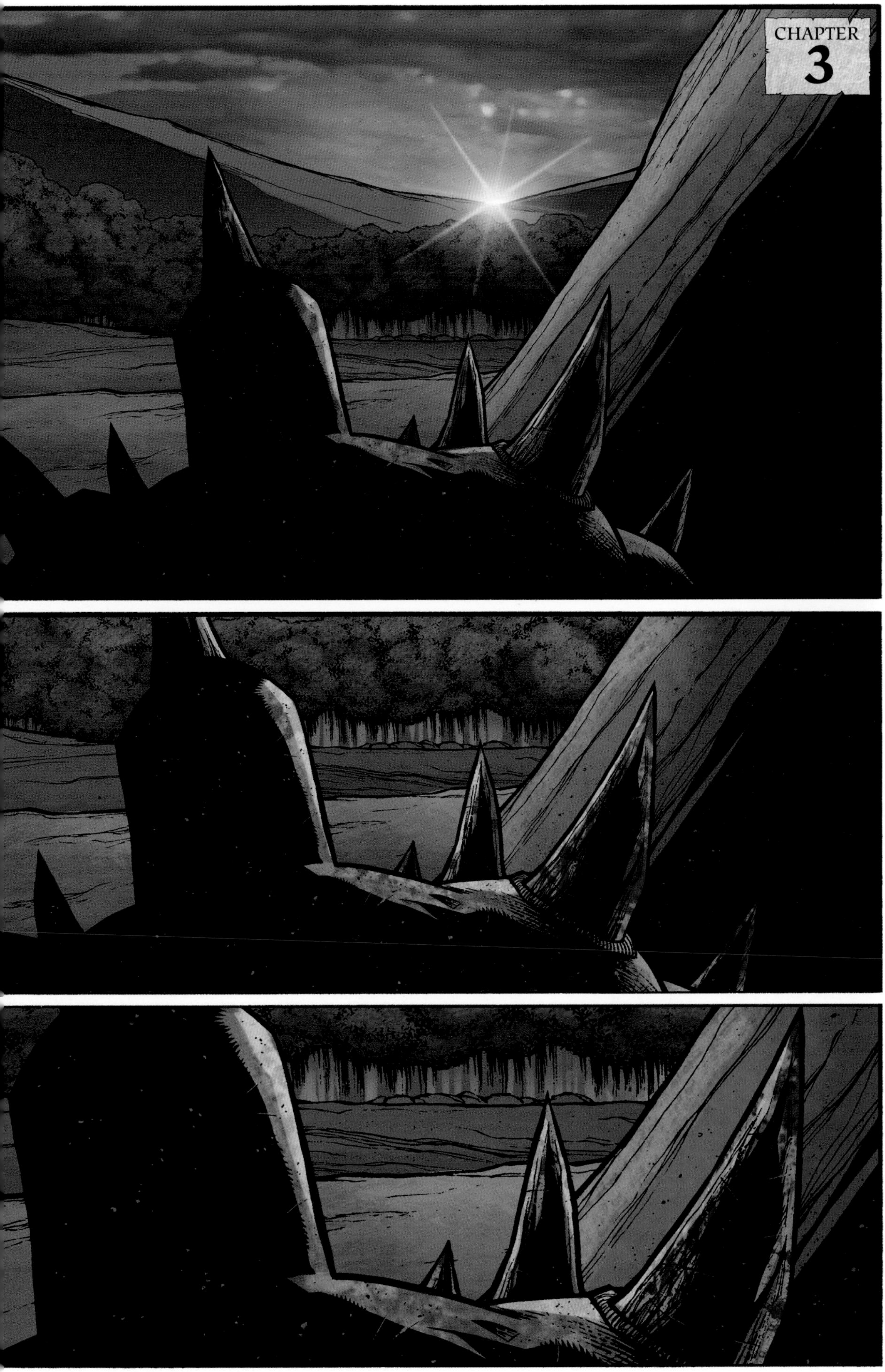
CHAPTER
3

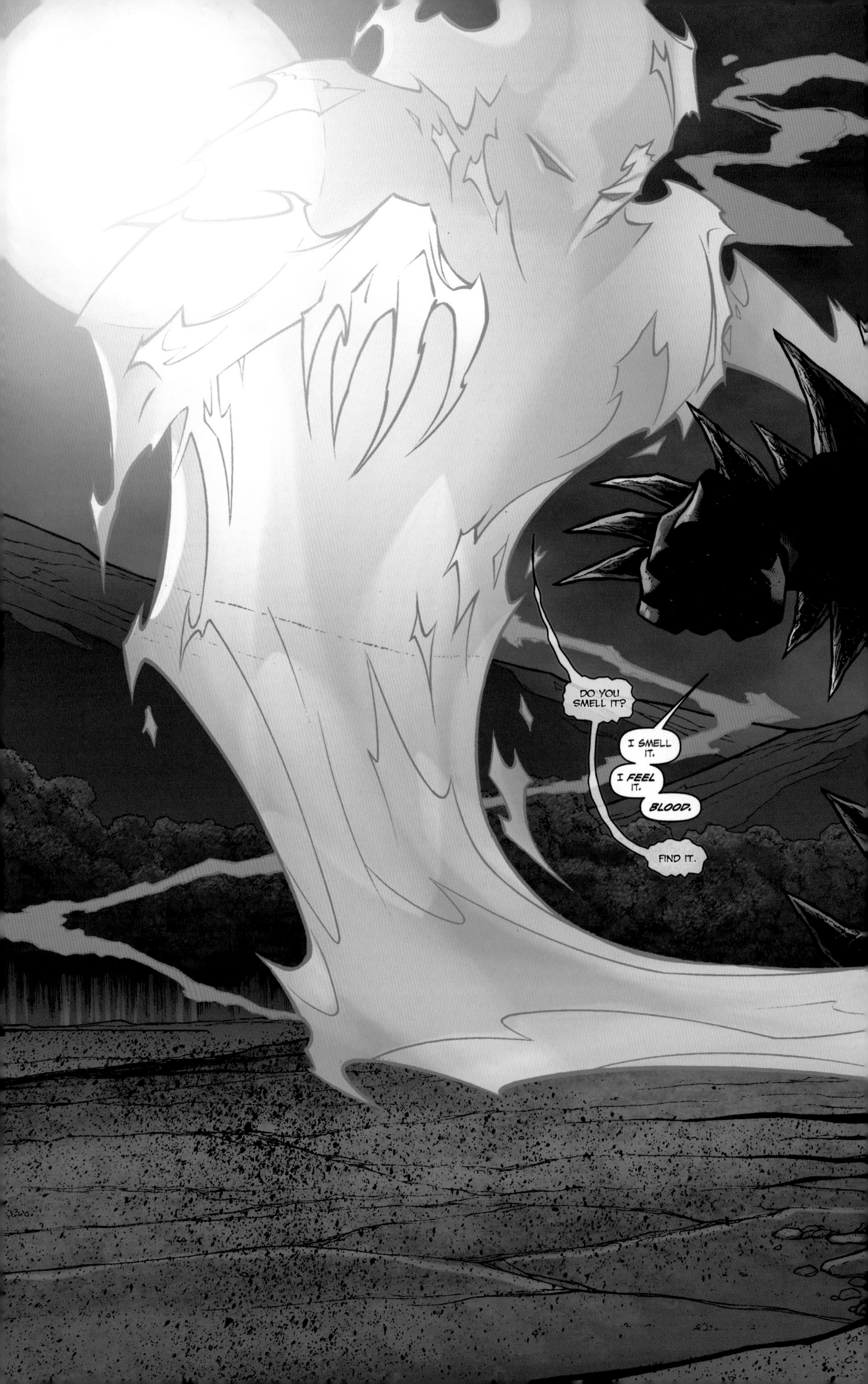

DO YOU SMELL IT?
I SMELL IT.
I FEEL IT.
BLOOD.
FIND IT.

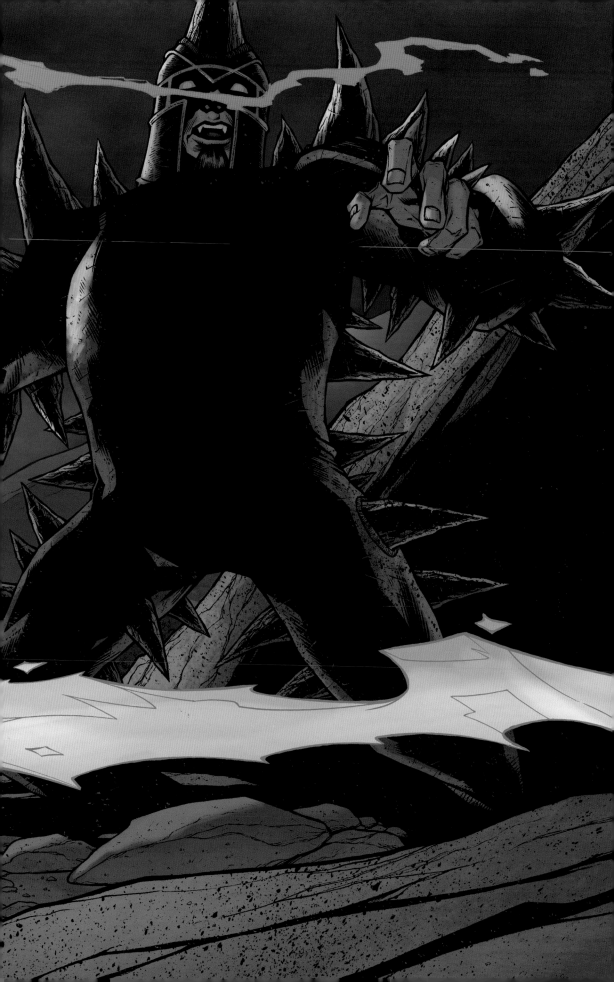

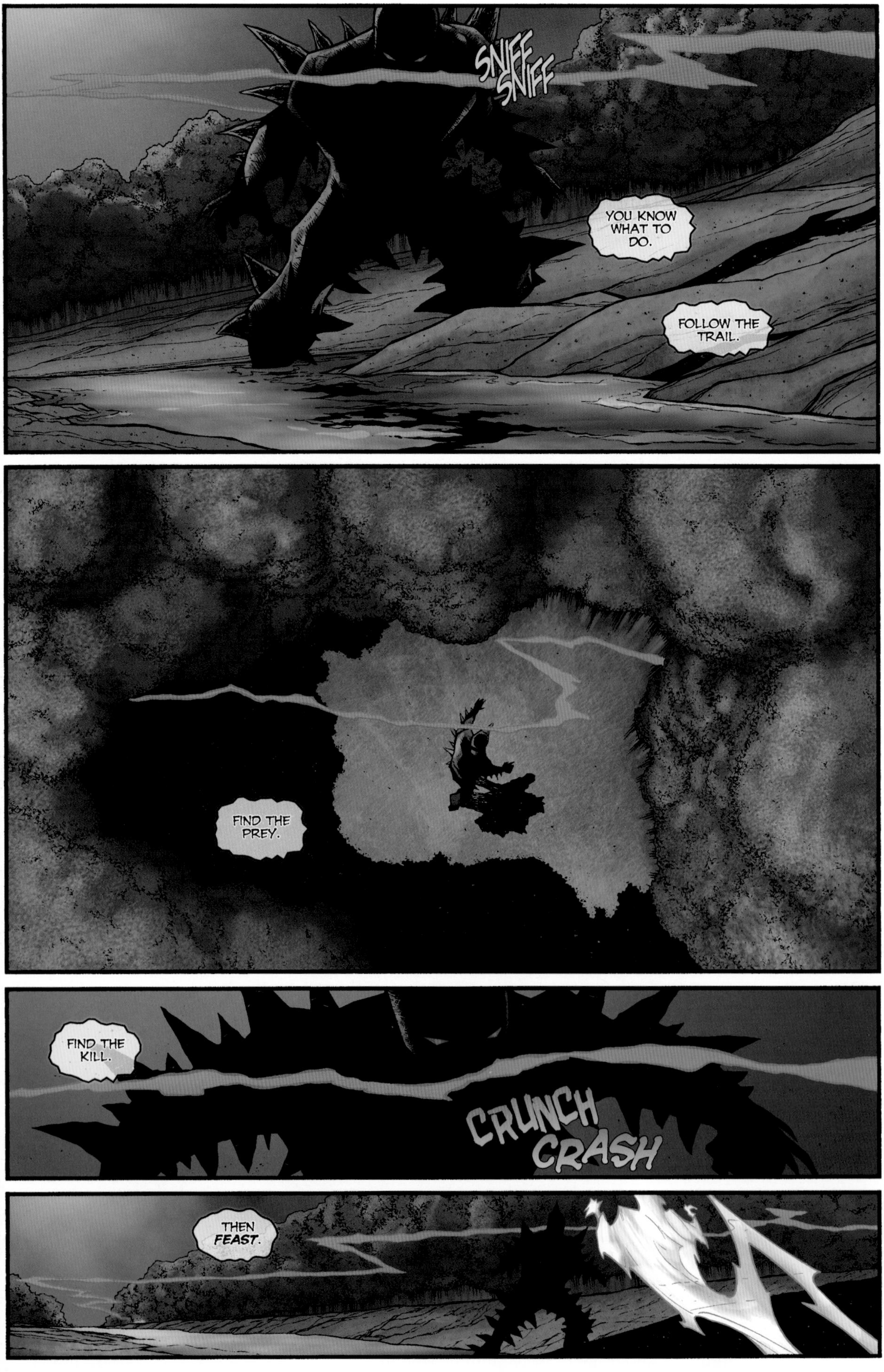
SNIFF SNIFF
YOU KNOW WHAT TO DO.
FOLLOW THE TRAIL.
FIND THE PREY.
FIND THE KILL.
CRUNCH
CRASH
THEN *FEAST*.

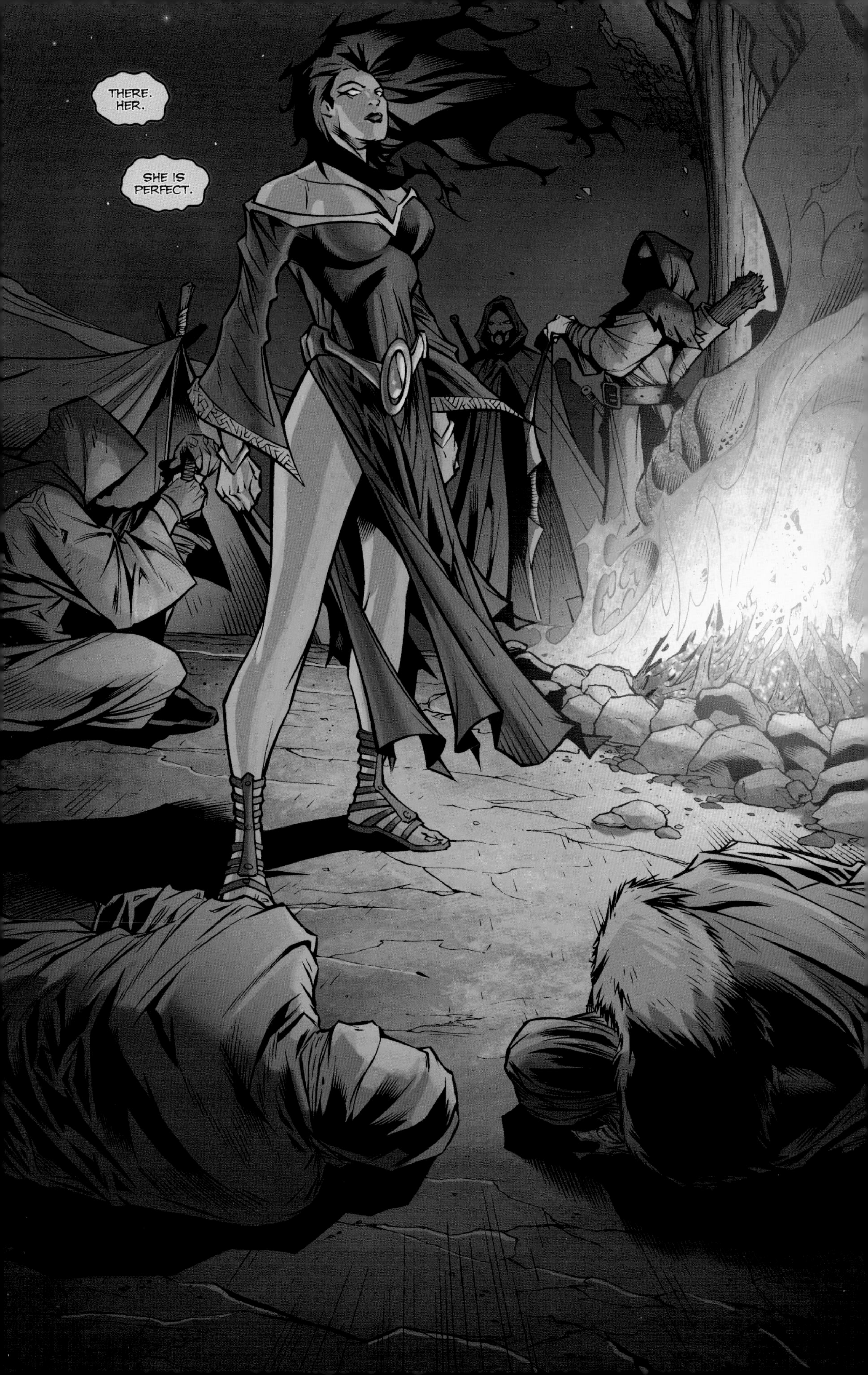
THERE. HER.
SHE IS PERFECT.

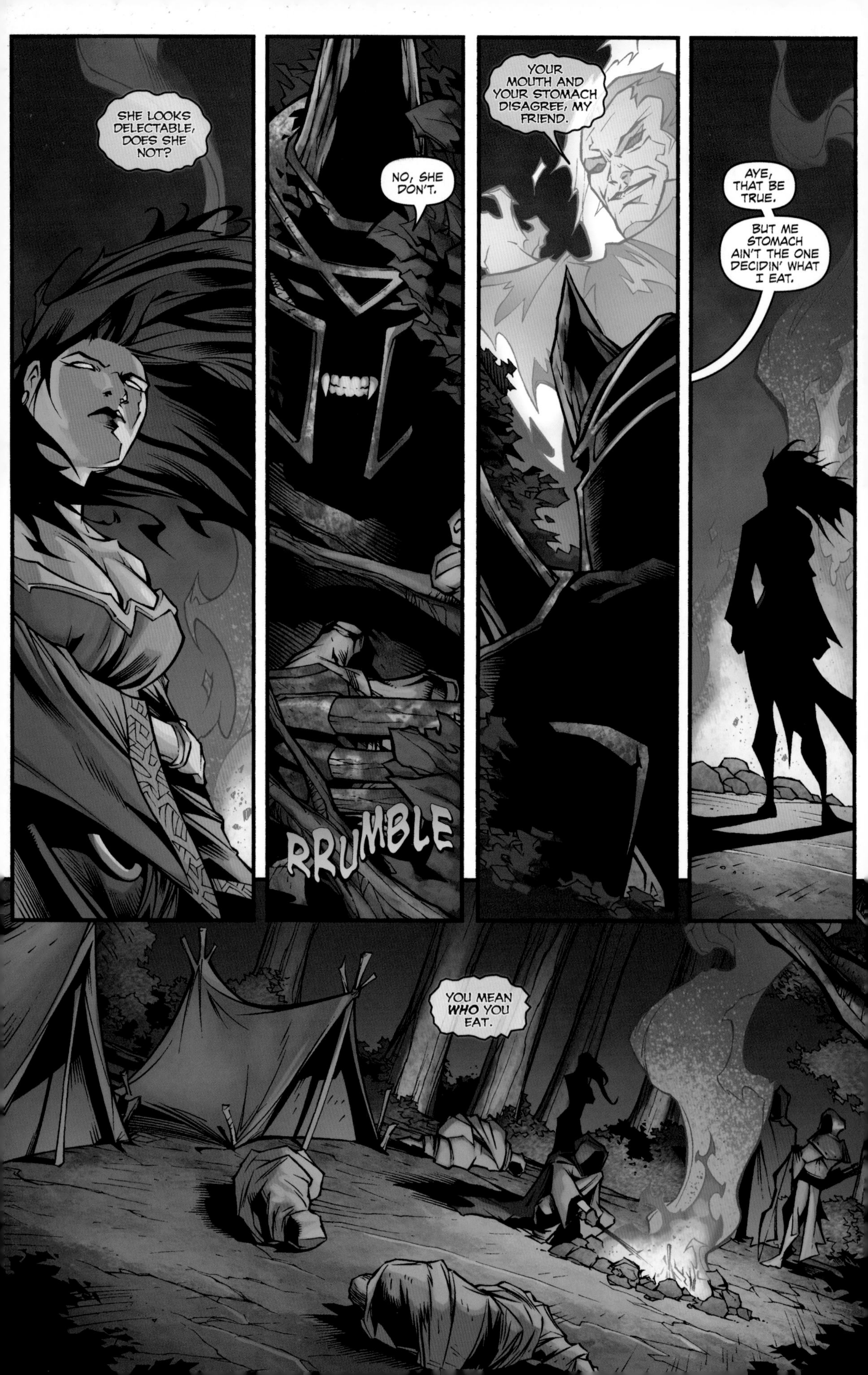
SHE LOOKS DELECTABLE, DOES SHE NOT?
NO, SHE DON'T.
RRUMBLE
YOUR MOUTH AND YOUR STOMACH DISAGREE, MY FRIEND.
AYE, THAT BE TRUE.
BUT ME STOMACH AIN'T THE ONE DECIDIN' WHAT I EAT.
YOU MEAN **WHO** YOU EAT.

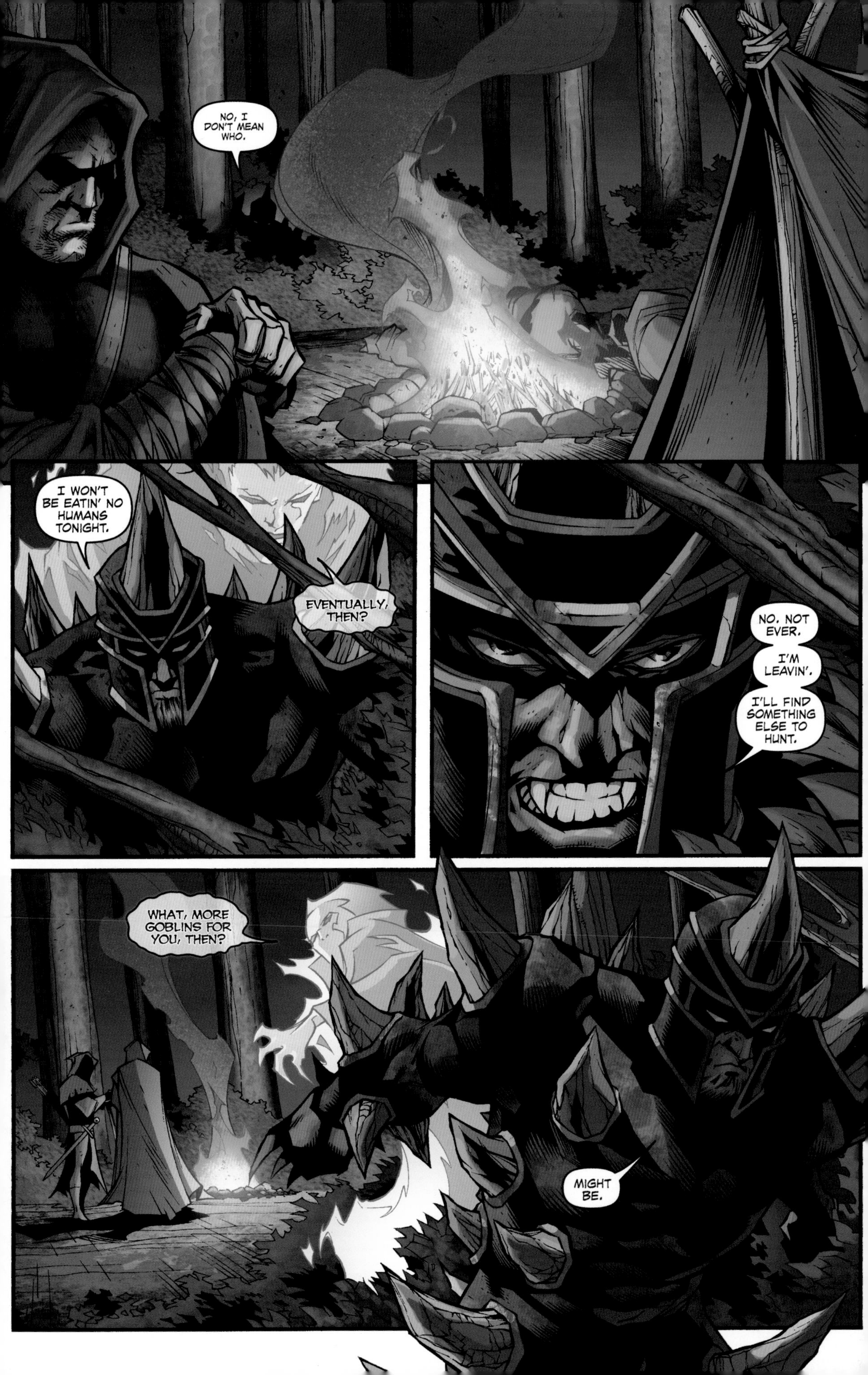
NO, I DON'T MEAN WHO.
I WON'T BE EATIN' NO HUMANS TONIGHT.
EVENTUALLY, THEN?
NO. NOT EVER.
I'M LEAVIN'.
I'LL FIND SOMETHING ELSE TO HUNT.
WHAT, MORE GOBLINS FOR YOU, THEN?
MIGHT BE.

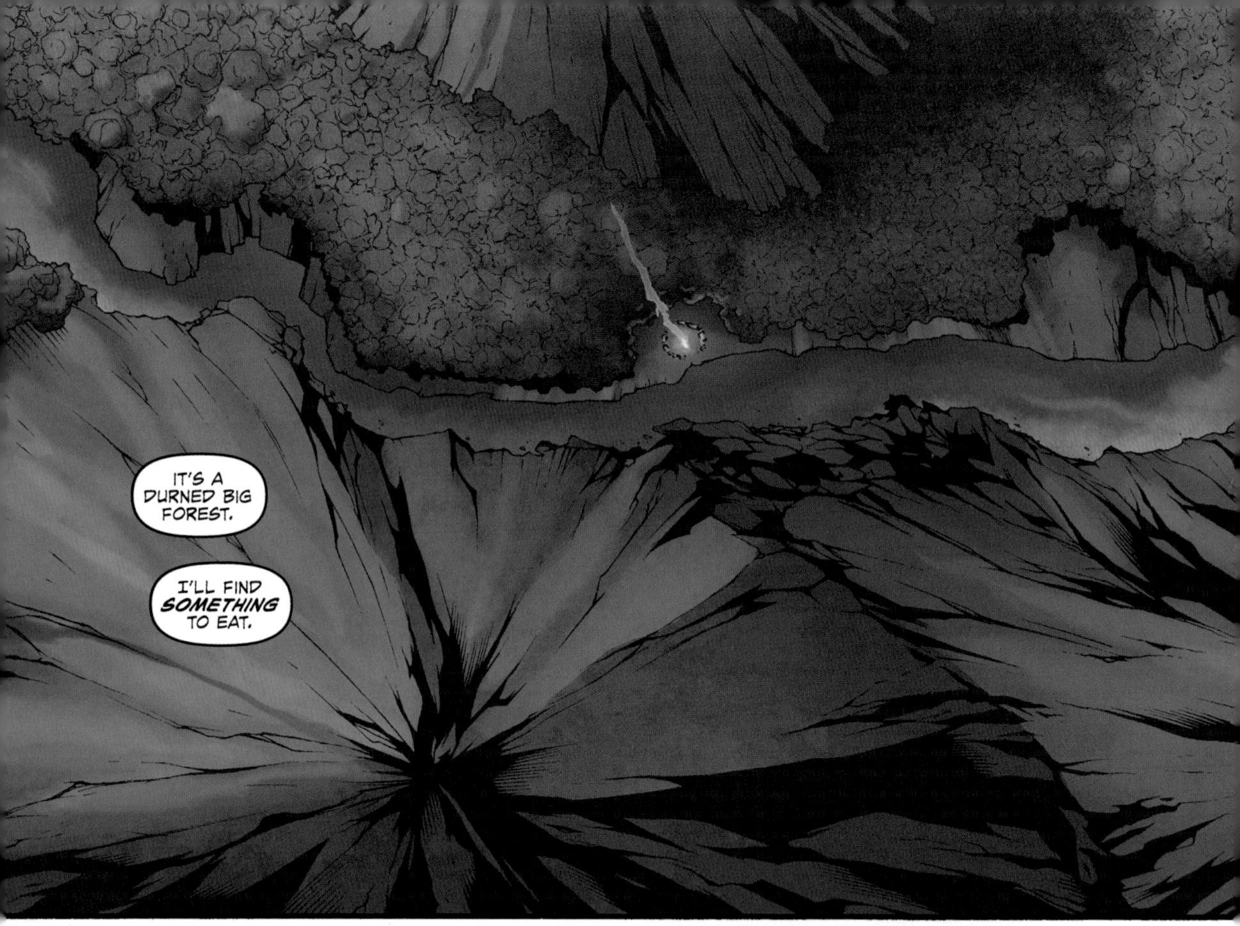
IT'S A DURNED BIG FOREST.
I'LL FIND *SOMETHING* TO EAT.
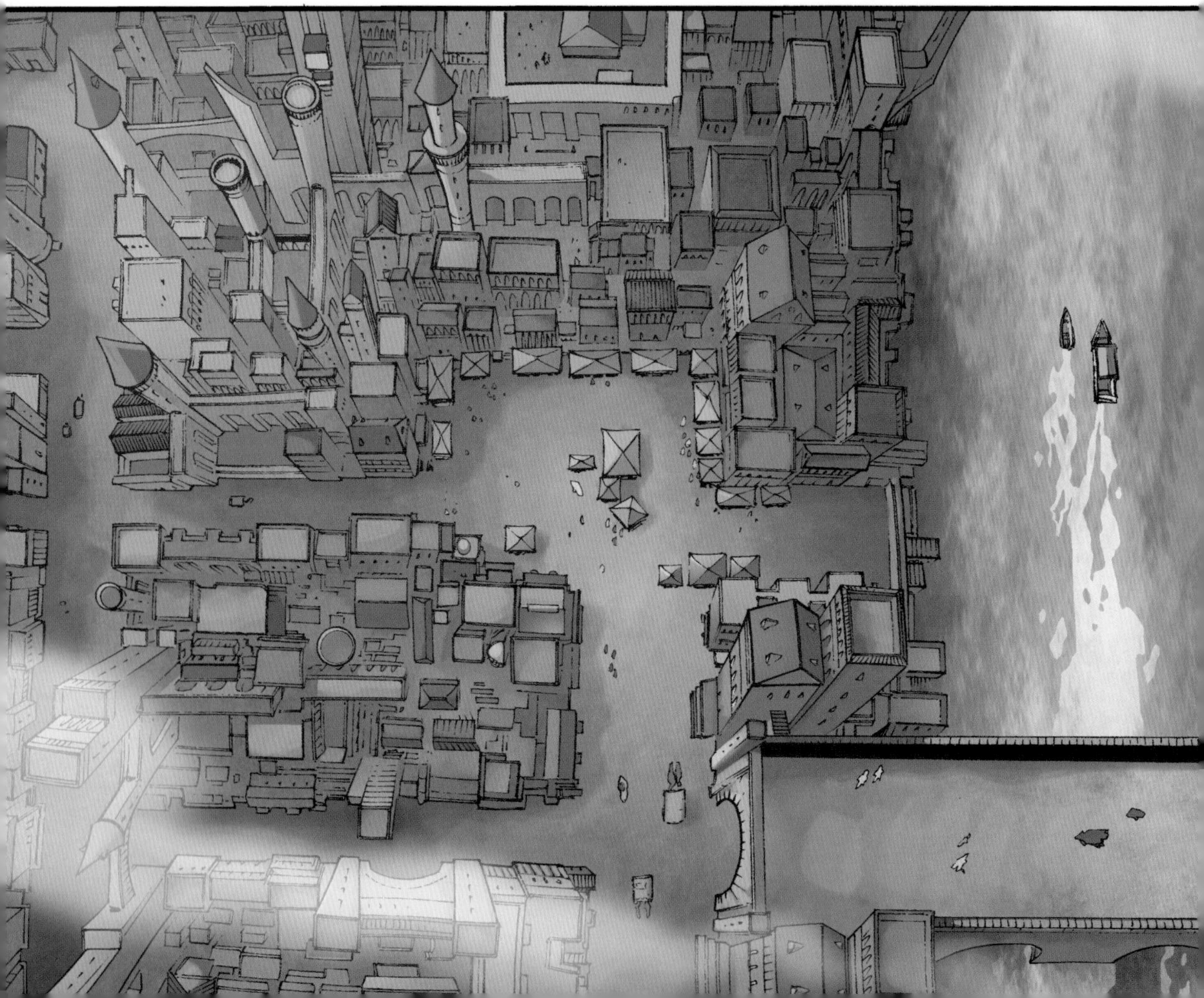

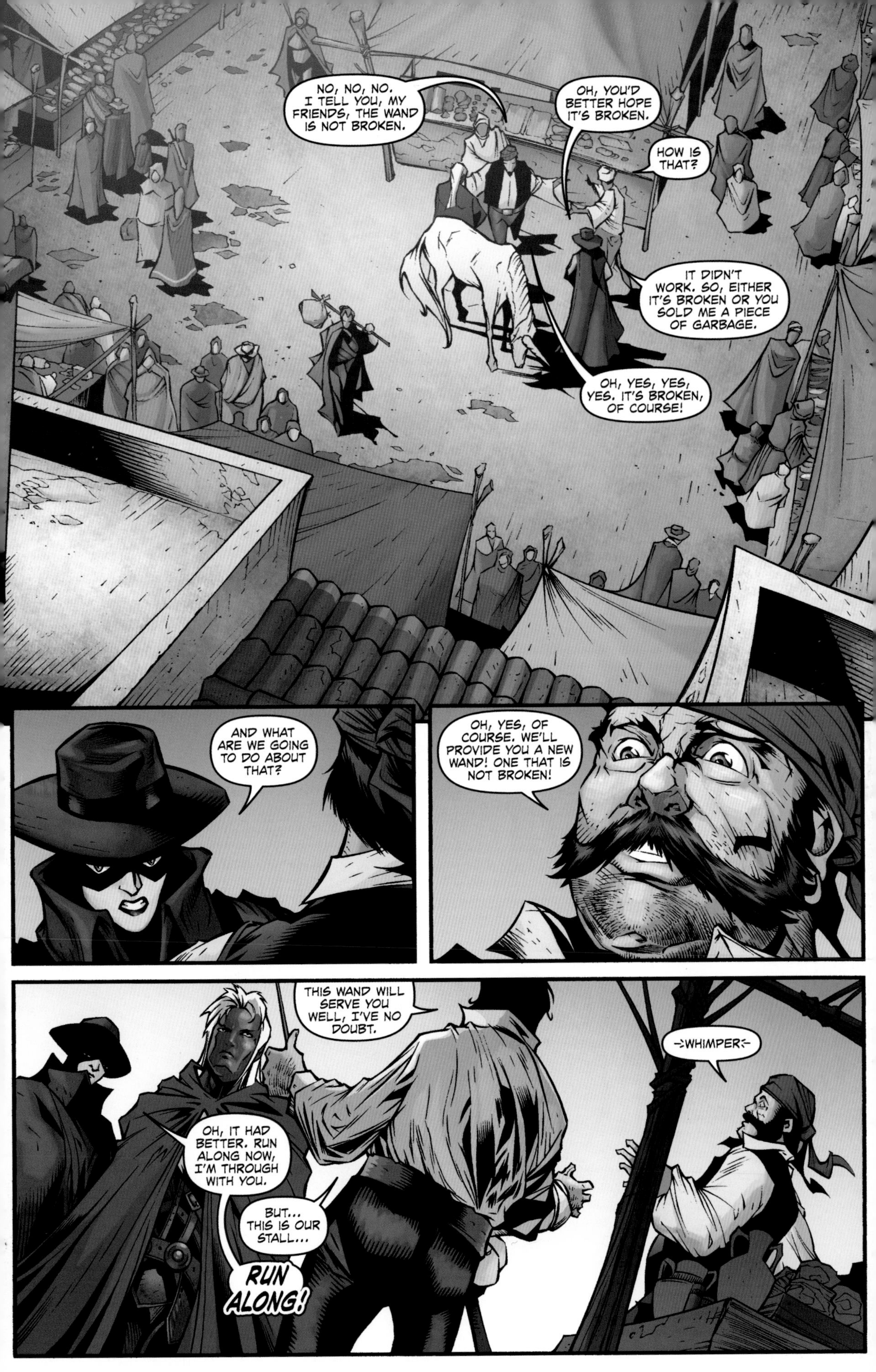
NO, NO, NO. I TELL YOU, MY FRIENDS, THE WAND IS NOT BROKEN.
OH, YOU'D BETTER HOPE IT'S BROKEN.
HOW IS THAT?
IT DIDN'T WORK. SO, EITHER IT'S BROKEN OR YOU SOLD ME A PIECE OF GARBAGE.
OH, YES, YES, YES. IT'S BROKEN, OF COURSE!
AND WHAT ARE WE GOING TO DO ABOUT THAT?
OH, YES, OF COURSE. WE'LL PROVIDE YOU A NEW WAND! ONE THAT IS NOT BROKEN!
THIS WAND WILL SERVE YOU WELL, I'VE NO DOUBT.
WHIMPER
OH, IT HAD BETTER. RUN ALONG NOW, I'M THROUGH WITH YOU.
BUT... THIS IS OUR STALL...
RUN ALONG!

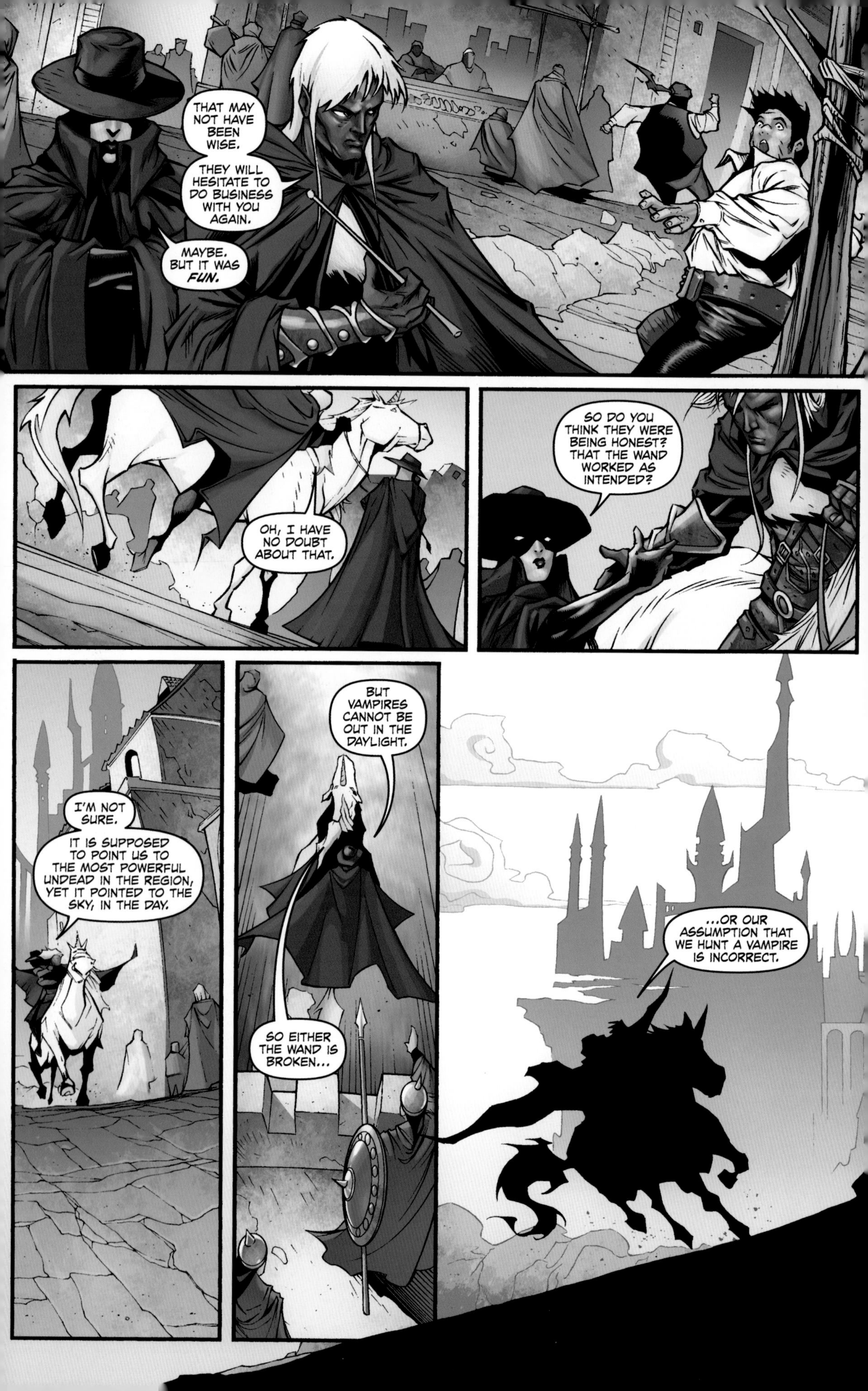
THAT MAY NOT HAVE BEEN WISE.
THEY WILL HESITATE TO DO BUSINESS WITH YOU AGAIN.
MAYBE. BUT IT WAS *FUN*.
OH, I HAVE NO DOUBT ABOUT THAT.
SO DO YOU THINK THEY WERE BEING HONEST? THAT THE WAND WORKED AS INTENDED?
I'M NOT SURE.
IT IS SUPPOSED TO POINT US TO THE MOST POWERFUL UNDEAD IN THE REGION, YET IT POINTED TO THE SKY, IN THE DAY.
BUT VAMPIRES CANNOT BE OUT IN THE DAYLIGHT.
SO EITHER THE WAND IS BROKEN...
...OR OUR ASSUMPTION THAT WE HUNT A VAMPIRE IS INCORRECT.

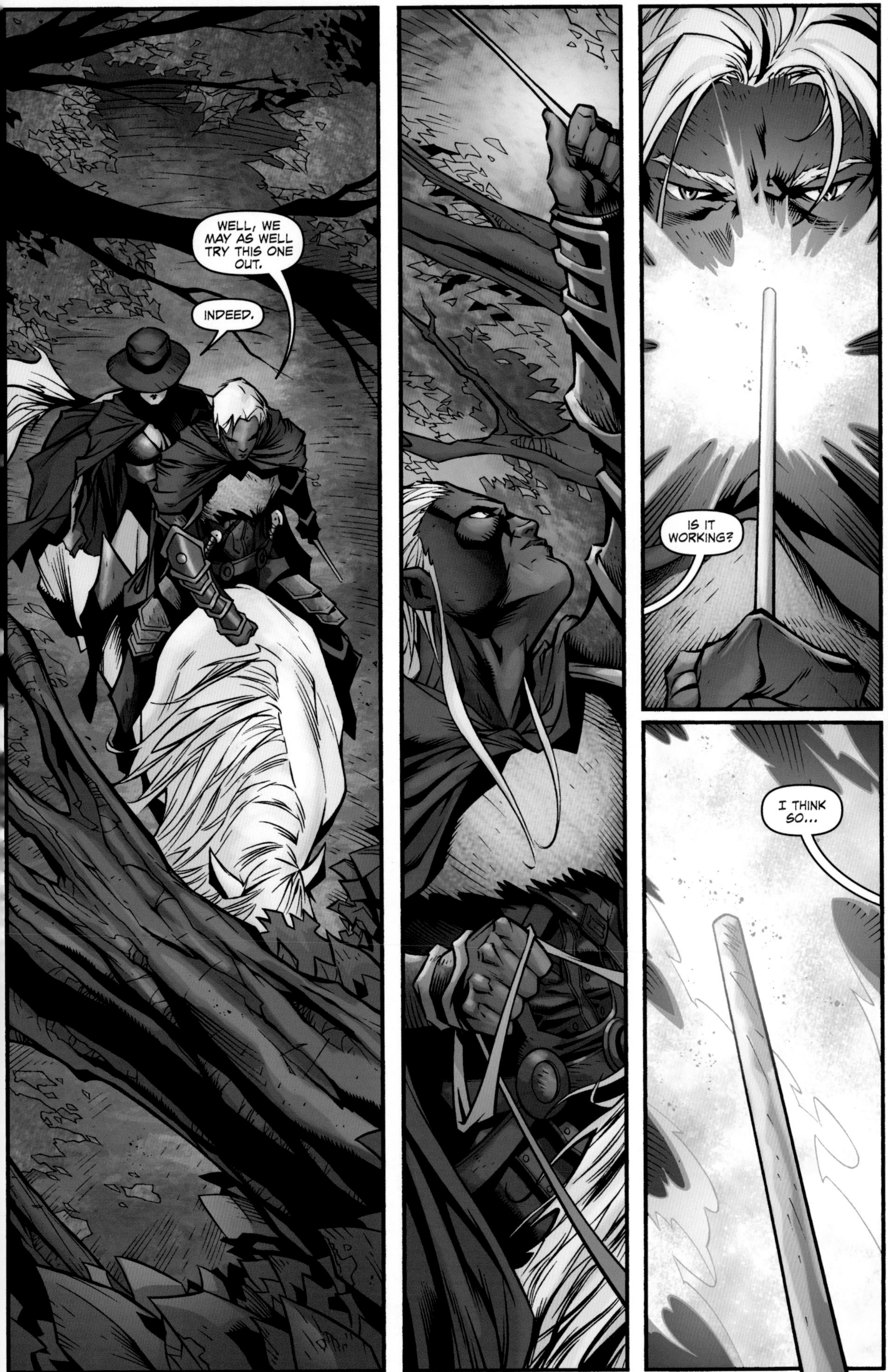
WELL, WE MAY AS WELL TRY THIS ONE OUT.
INDEED.
IS IT WORKING?
I THINK SO...

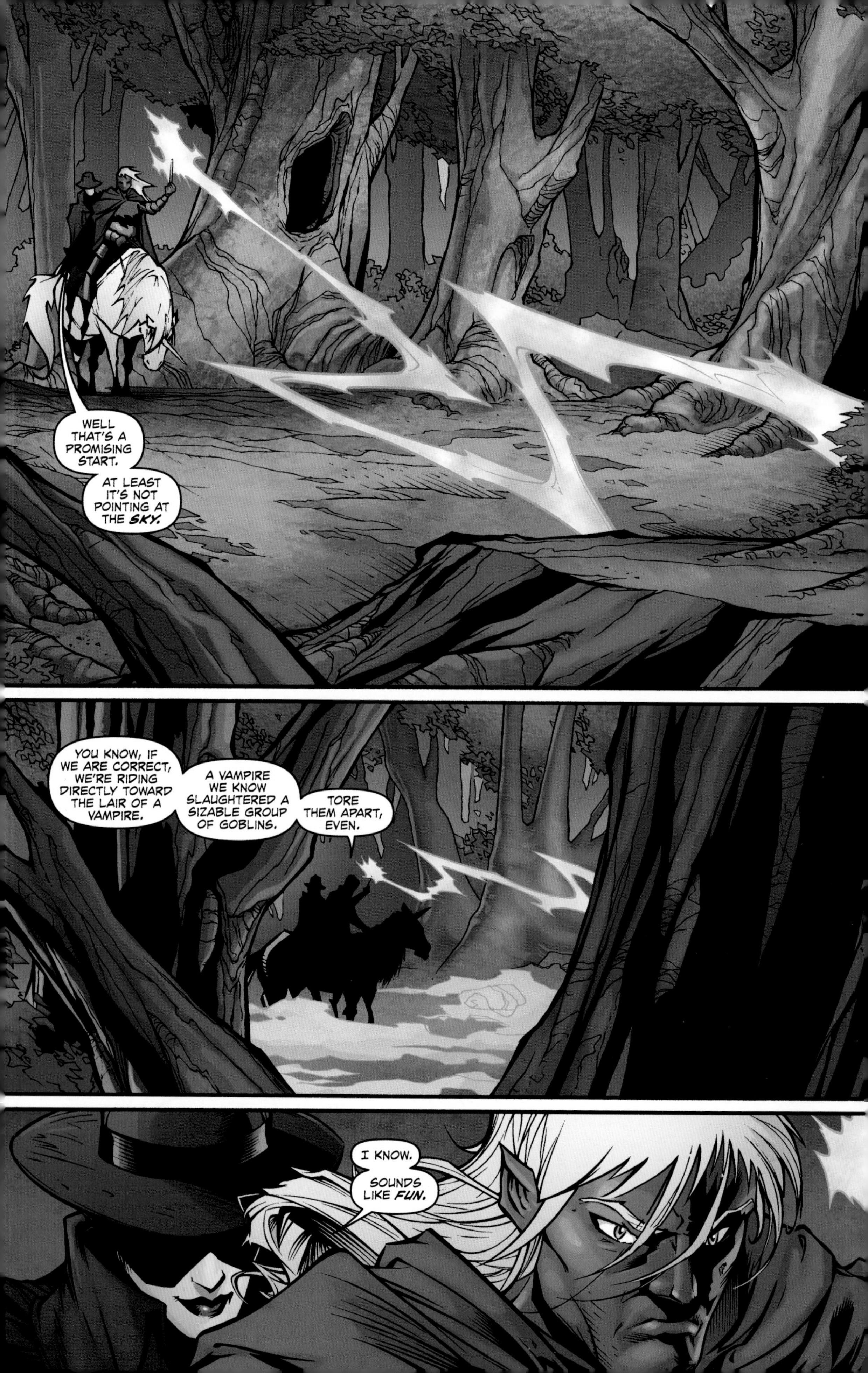
WELL THAT'S A PROMISING START.
AT LEAST IT'S NOT POINTING AT THE *SKY.*
YOU KNOW, IF WE ARE CORRECT, WE'RE RIDING DIRECTLY TOWARD THE LAIR OF A VAMPIRE.
A VAMPIRE WE KNOW SLAUGHTERED A SIZABLE GROUP OF GOBLINS.
TORE THEM APART, EVEN.
I KNOW.
SOUNDS LIKE *FUN.*

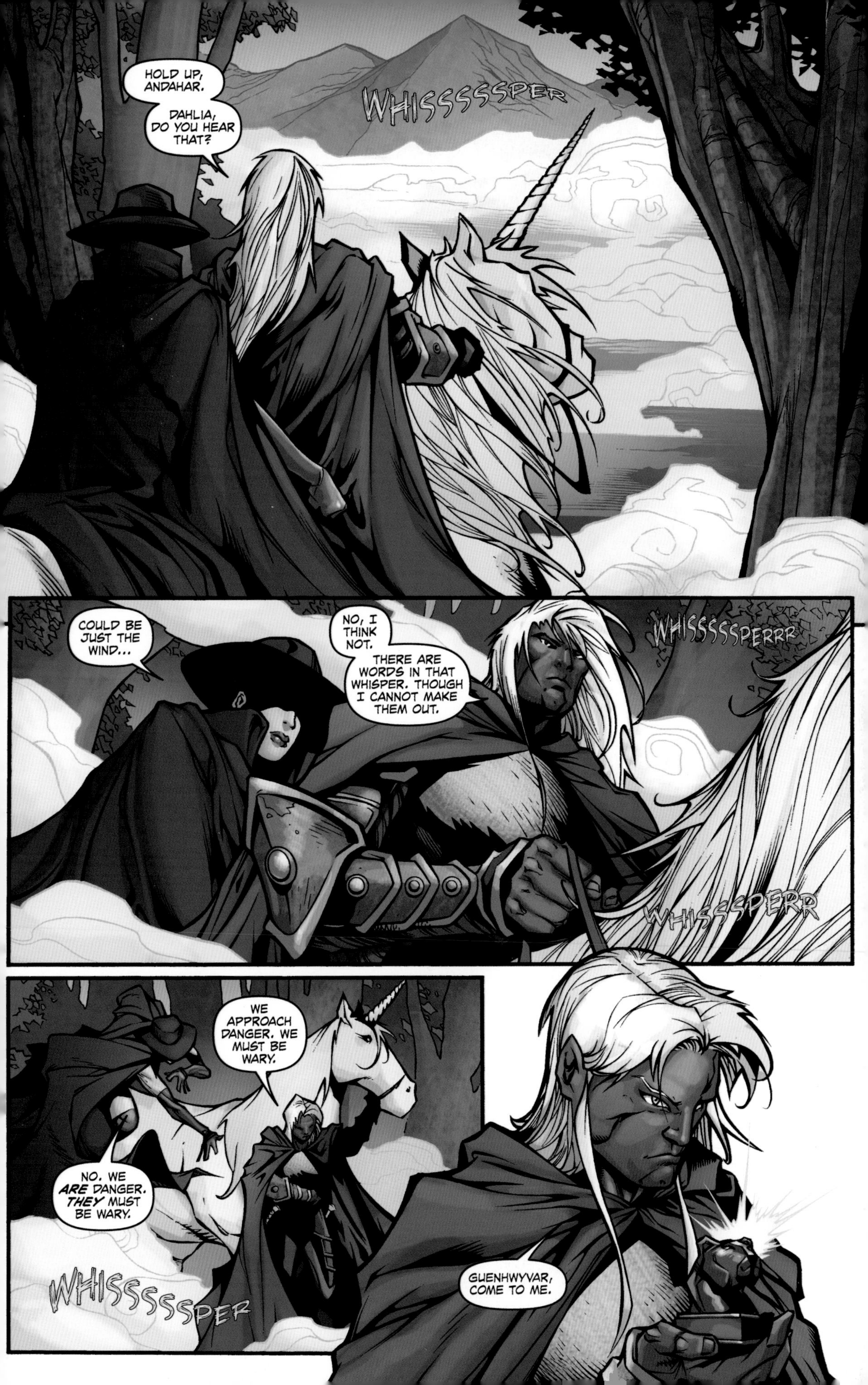
HOLD UP, ANDAHAR.
DAHLIA, DO YOU HEAR THAT?
WHISSSSSSPER
COULD BE JUST THE WIND...
NO, I THINK NOT.
THERE ARE WORDS IN THAT WHISPER. THOUGH I CANNOT MAKE THEM OUT.
WHISSSSSPERRR
WHISSSSPERR
WE APPROACH DANGER. WE MUST BE WARY.
NO. WE *ARE* DANGER. *THEY* MUST BE WARY.
WHISSSSSSPER
GUENHWYVAR, COME TO ME.

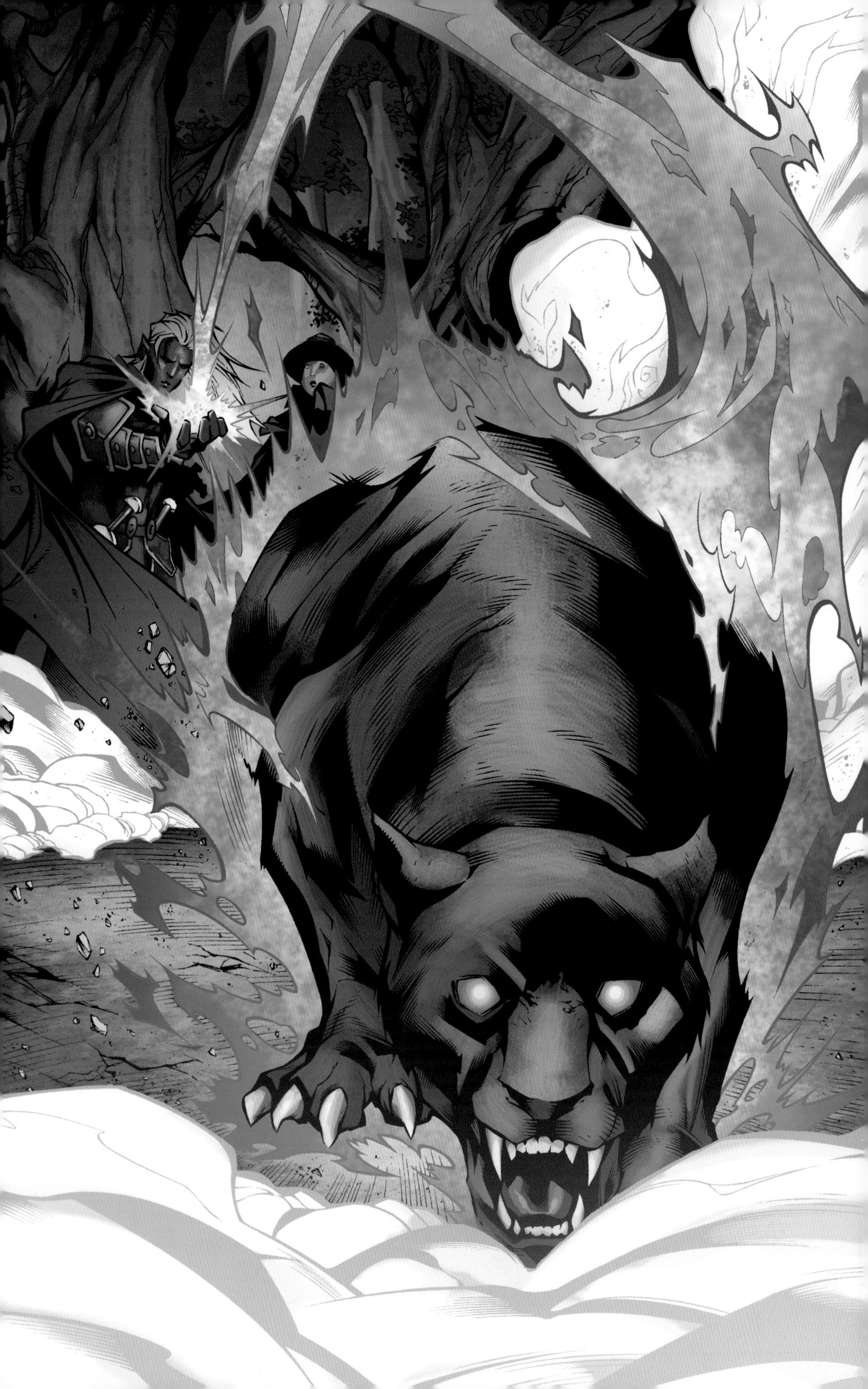

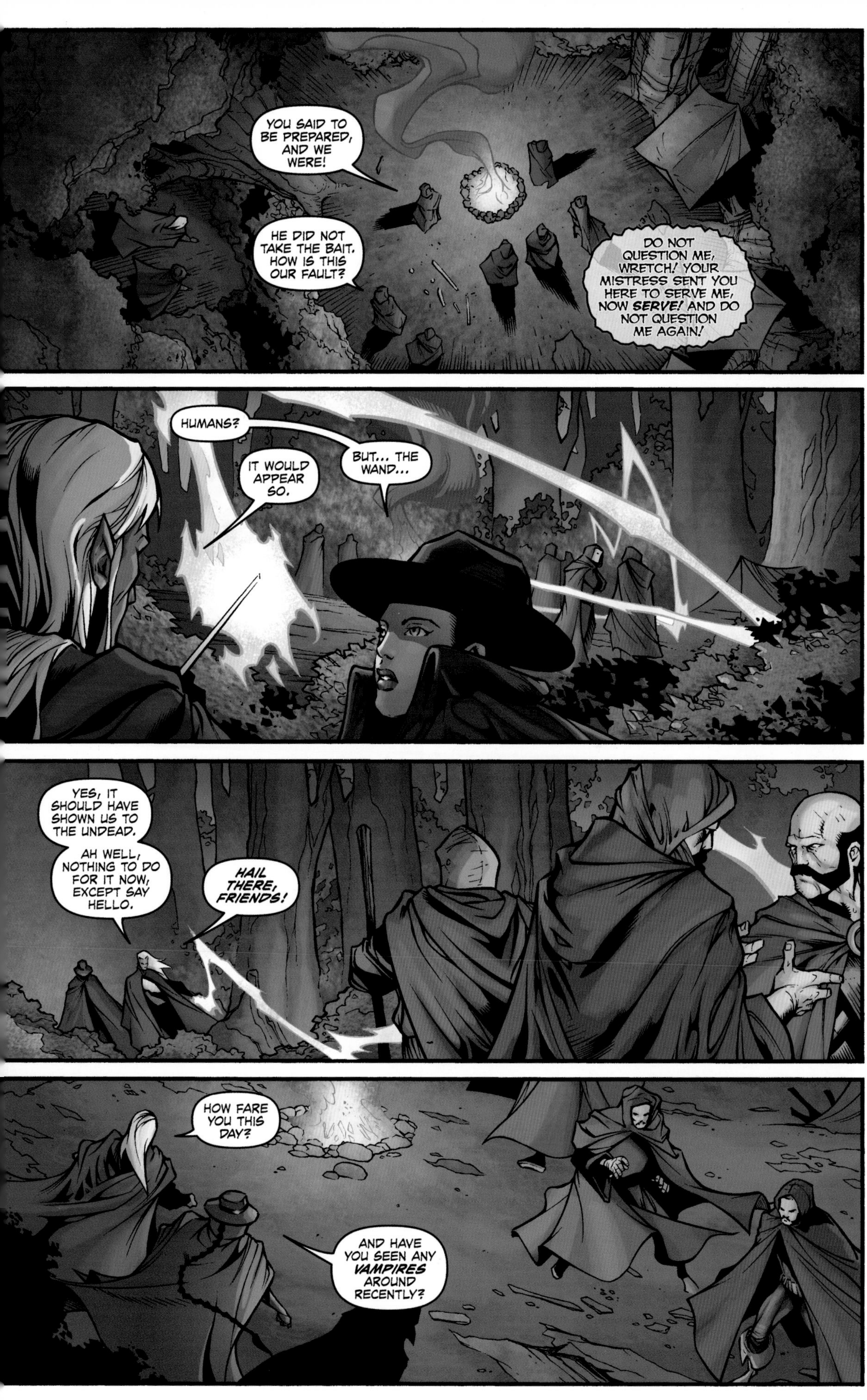
YOU SAID TO BE PREPARED, AND WE WERE!
HE DID NOT TAKE THE BAIT. HOW IS THIS OUR FAULT?
DO NOT QUESTION ME, WRETCH! YOUR MISTRESS SENT YOU HERE TO SERVE ME, NOW SERVE! AND DO NOT QUESTION ME AGAIN!
HUMANS?
IT WOULD APPEAR SO.
BUT... THE WAND...
YES, IT SHOULD HAVE SHOWN US TO THE UNDEAD.
AH WELL, NOTHING TO DO FOR IT NOW, EXCEPT SAY HELLO.
HAIL THERE, FRIENDS!
HOW FARE YOU THIS DAY?
AND HAVE YOU SEEN ANY VAMPIRES AROUND RECENTLY?

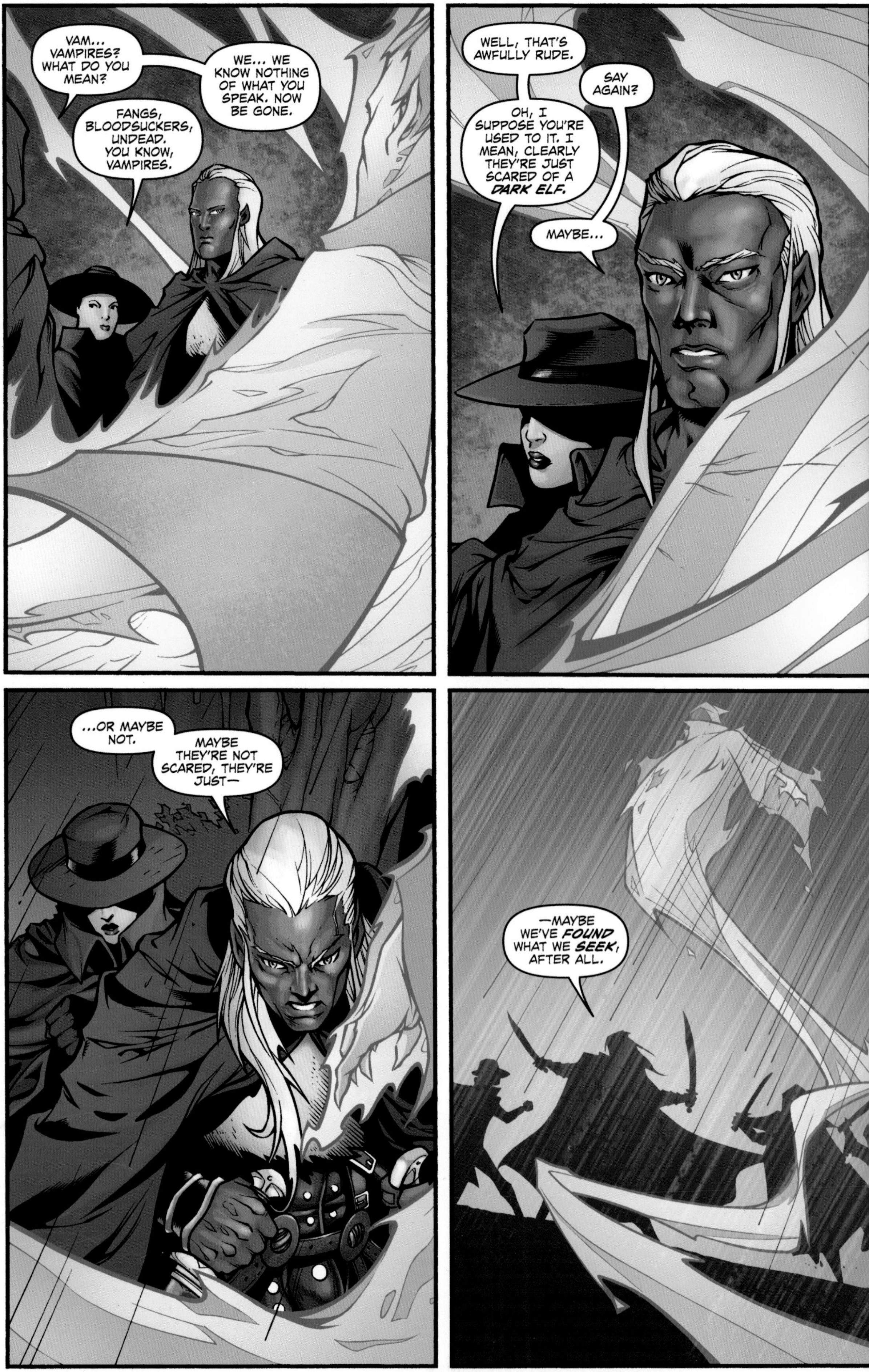
VAM... VAMPIRES? WHAT DO YOU MEAN?
WE... WE KNOW NOTHING OF WHAT YOU SPEAK. NOW BE GONE.
FANGS, BLOODSUCKERS, UNDEAD. YOU KNOW, VAMPIRES.
WELL, THAT'S AWFULLY RUDE.
SAY AGAIN?
OH, I SUPPOSE YOU'RE USED TO IT. I MEAN, CLEARLY THEY'RE JUST SCARED OF A DARK ELF.
MAYBE...
...OR MAYBE NOT.
MAYBE THEY'RE NOT SCARED, THEY'RE JUST—
—MAYBE WE'VE FOUND WHAT WE SEEK, AFTER ALL.

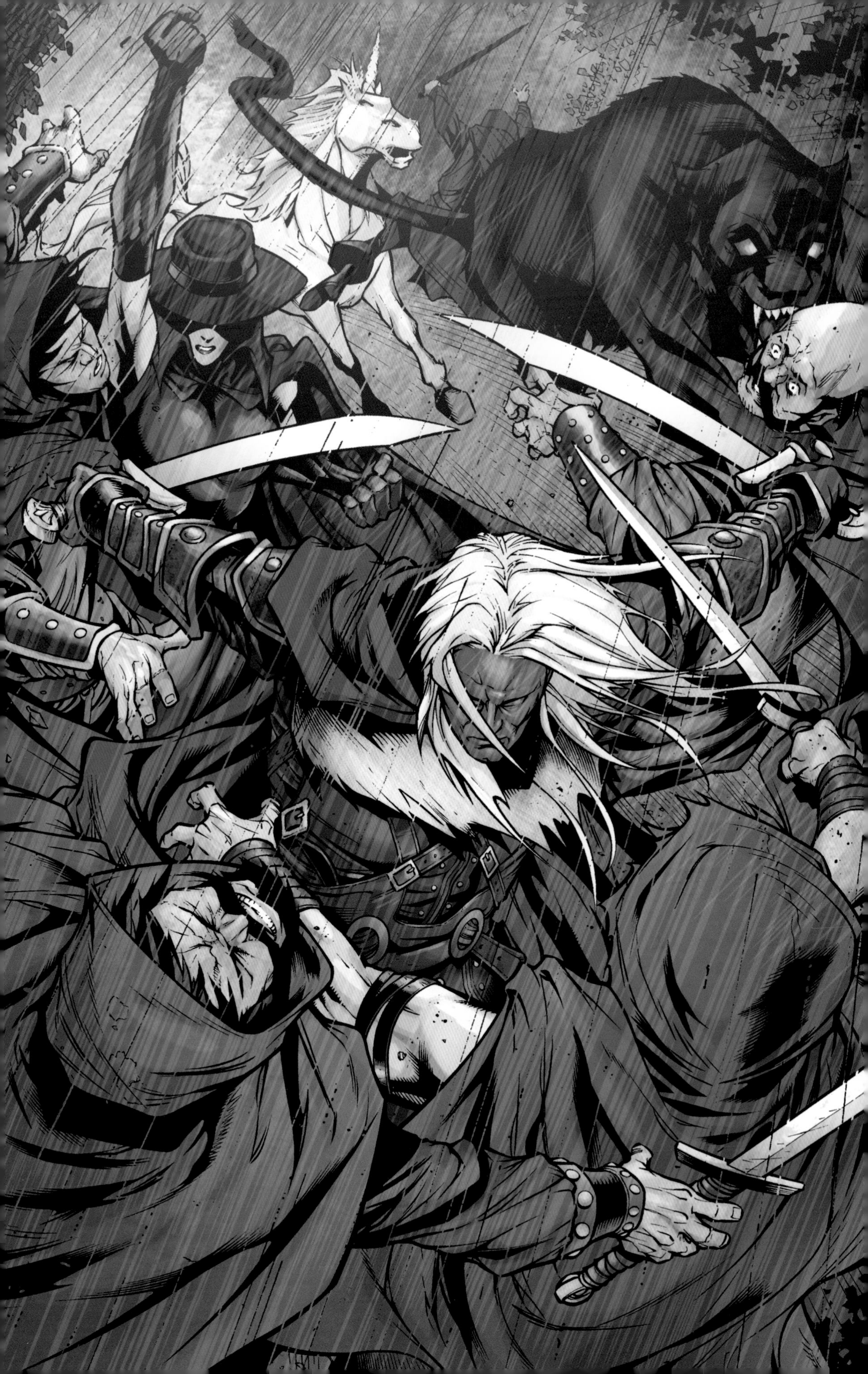

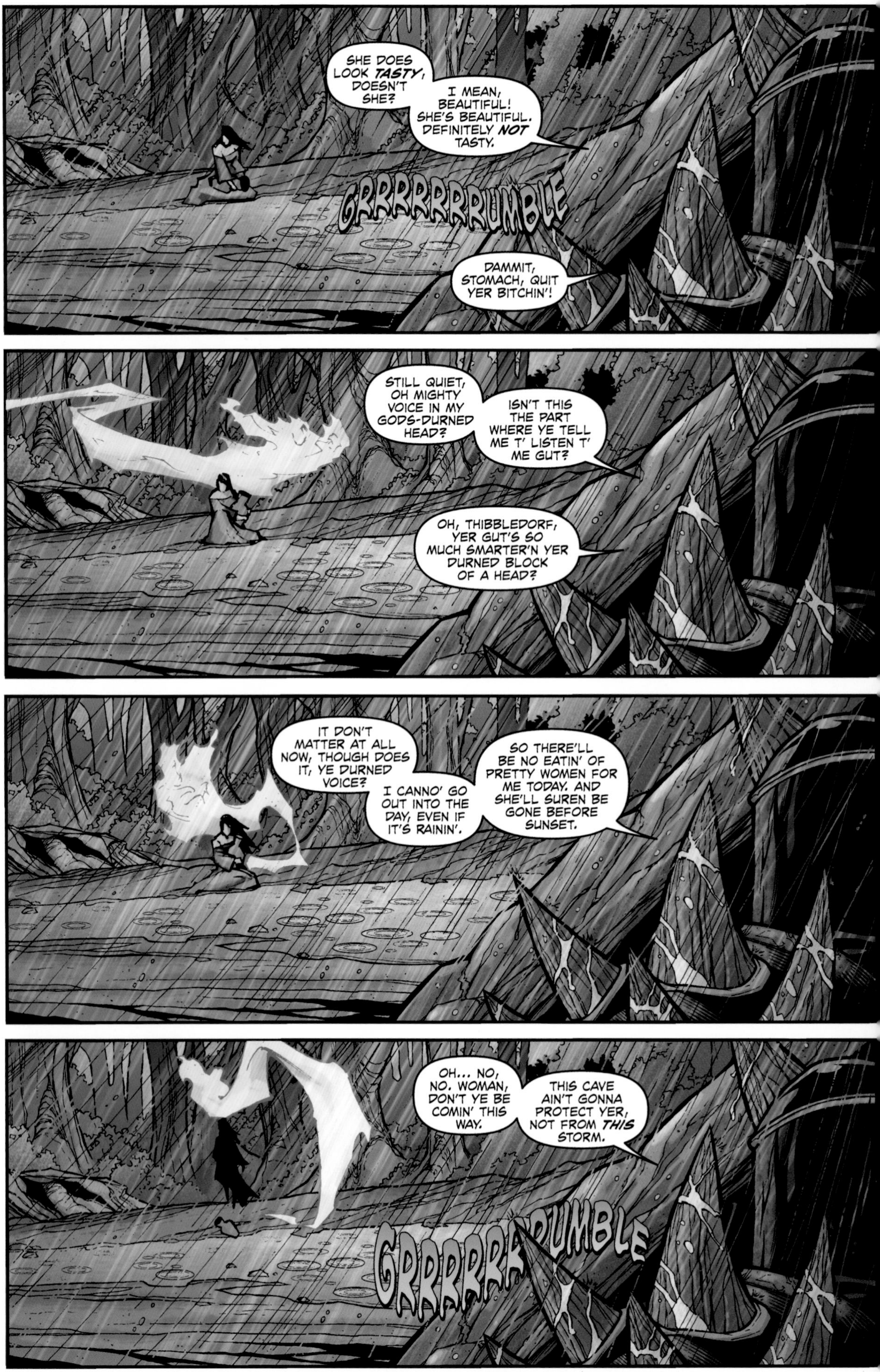
SHE DOES LOOK TASTY, DOESN'T SHE?
I MEAN, BEAUTIFUL! SHE'S BEAUTIFUL. DEFINITELY NOT TASTY.
GRRRRRRRUMBLE
DAMMIT, STOMACH, QUIT YER BITCHIN'!
STILL QUIET, OH MIGHTY VOICE IN MY GODS-DURNED HEAD?
ISN'T THIS THE PART WHERE YE TELL ME T' LISTEN T' ME GUT?
OH, THIBBLEDORF, YER GUT'S SO MUCH SMARTER'N YER DURNED BLOCK OF A HEAD?
IT DON'T MATTER AT ALL NOW, THOUGH DOES IT, YE DURNED VOICE?
I CANNO' GO OUT INTO THE DAY, EVEN IF IT'S RAININ'.
SO THERE'LL BE NO EATIN' OF PRETTY WOMEN FOR ME TODAY. AND SHE'LL SUREN BE GONE BEFORE SUNSET.
OH... NO, NO. WOMAN, DON'T YE BE COMIN' THIS WAY.
THIS CAVE AIN'T GONNA PROTECT YER, NOT FROM THIS STORM.
GRRRRRRRUMBLE

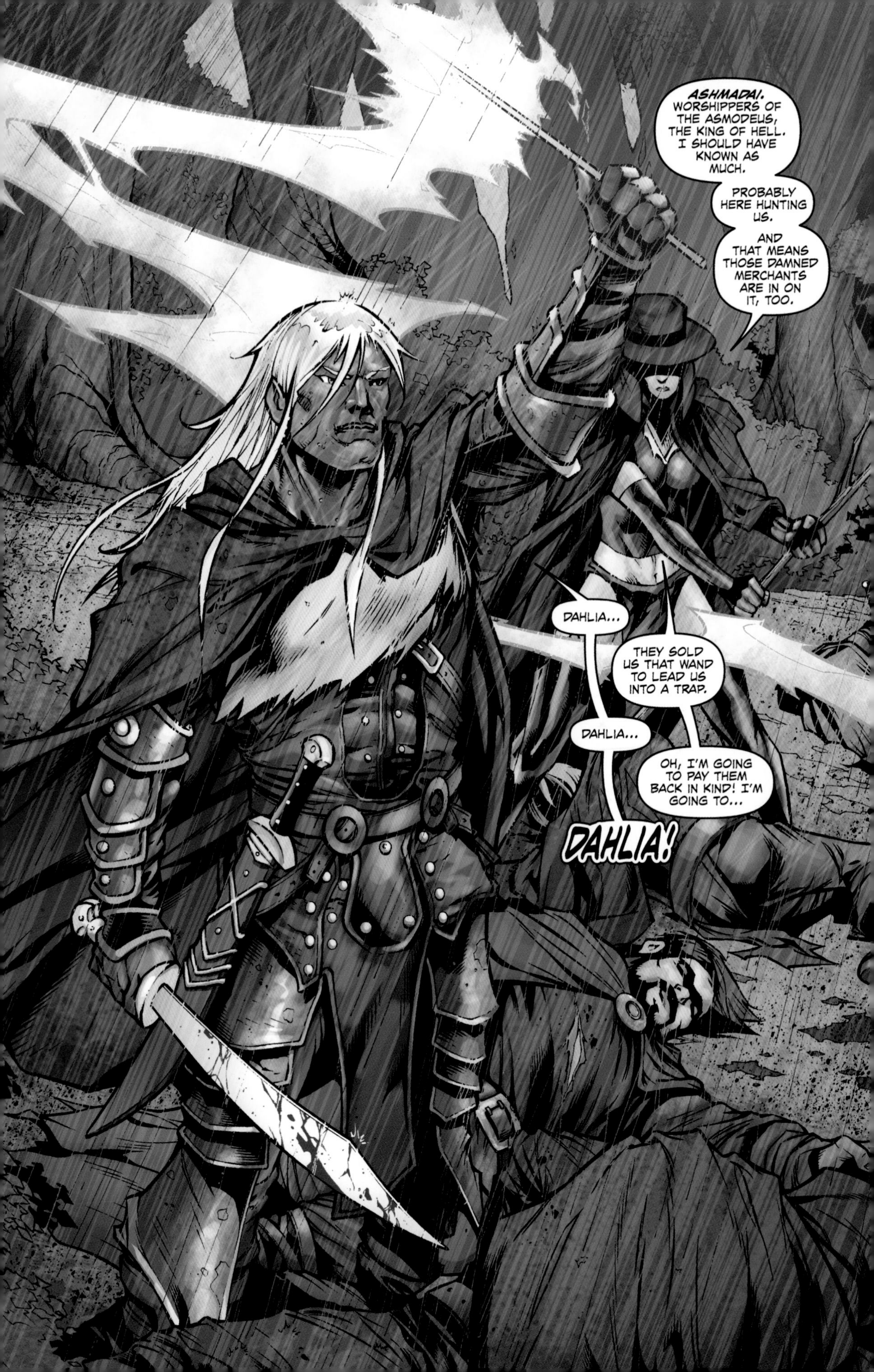
ASHMADAI. WORSHIPPERS OF THE ASMODEUS, THE KING OF HELL. I SHOULD HAVE KNOWN AS MUCH.
PROBABLY HERE HUNTING US.
AND THAT MEANS THOSE DAMNED MERCHANTS ARE IN ON IT, TOO.
DAHLIA...
THEY SOLD US THAT WAND TO LEAD US INTO A TRAP.
DAHLIA...
OH, I'M GOING TO PAY THEM BACK IN KIND! I'M GOING TO...
DAHLIA!

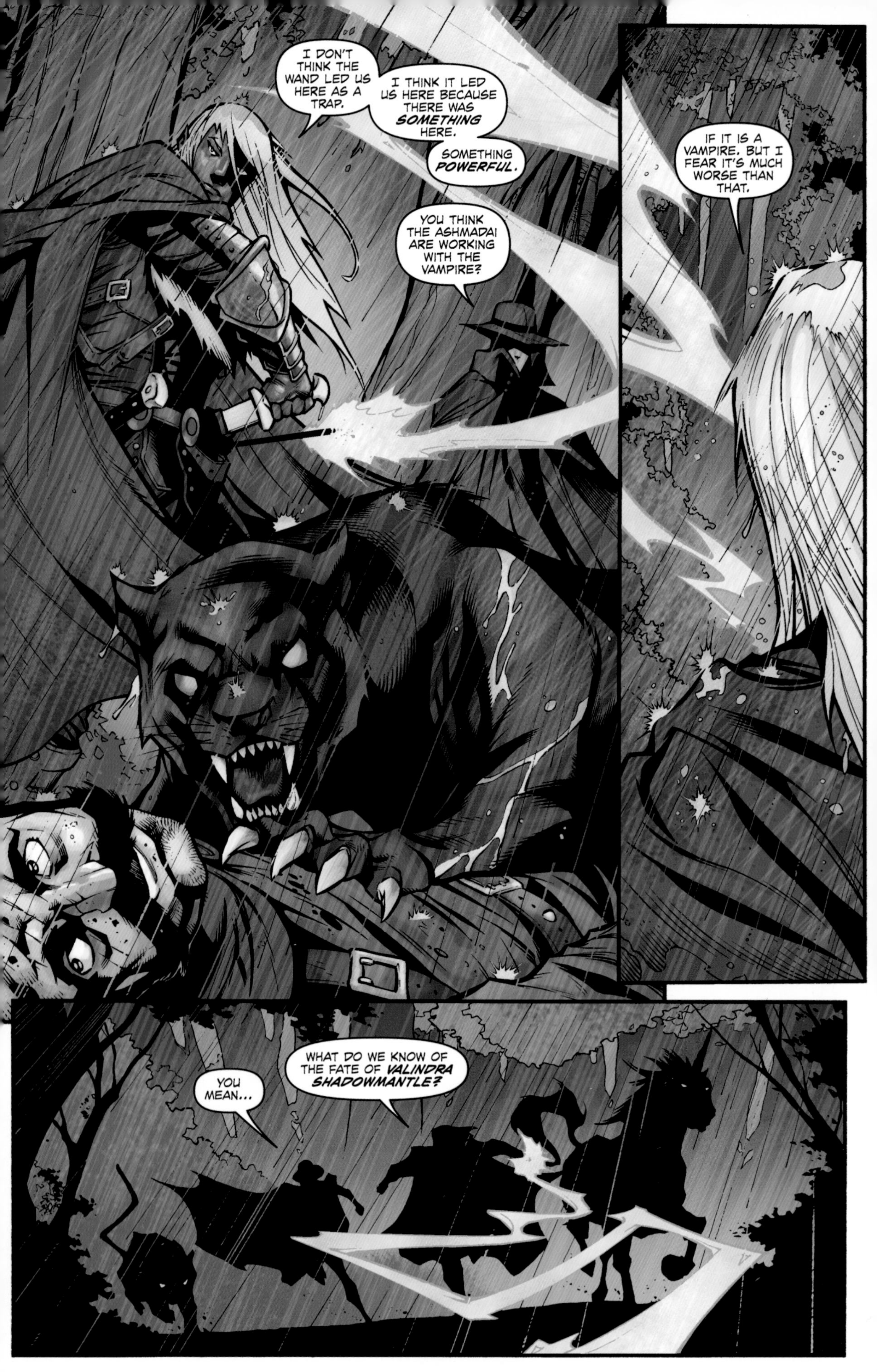
I DON'T THINK THE WAND LED US HERE AS A TRAP.
I THINK IT LED US HERE BECAUSE THERE WAS SOMETHING HERE.
SOMETHING POWERFUL.
YOU THINK THE ASHMADAI ARE WORKING WITH THE VAMPIRE?
IF IT IS A VAMPIRE. BUT I FEAR IT'S MUCH WORSE THAN THAT.
WHAT DO WE KNOW OF THE FATE OF VALINDRA SHADOWMANTLE?
YOU MEAN...

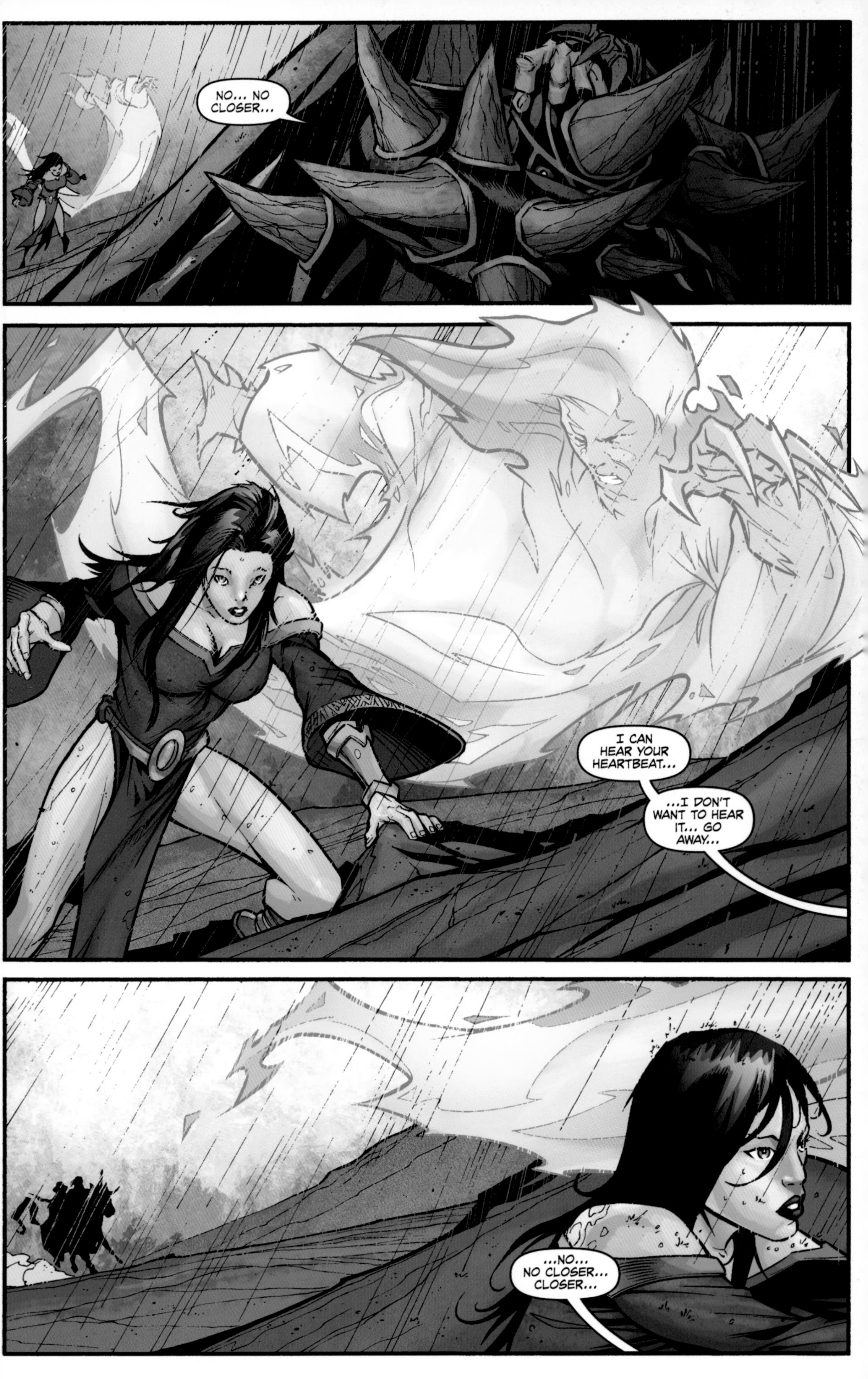
NO... NO CLOSER...
I CAN HEAR YOUR HEARTBEAT...
...I DON'T WANT TO HEAR IT... GO AWAY...
...NO... NO CLOSER... CLOSER...

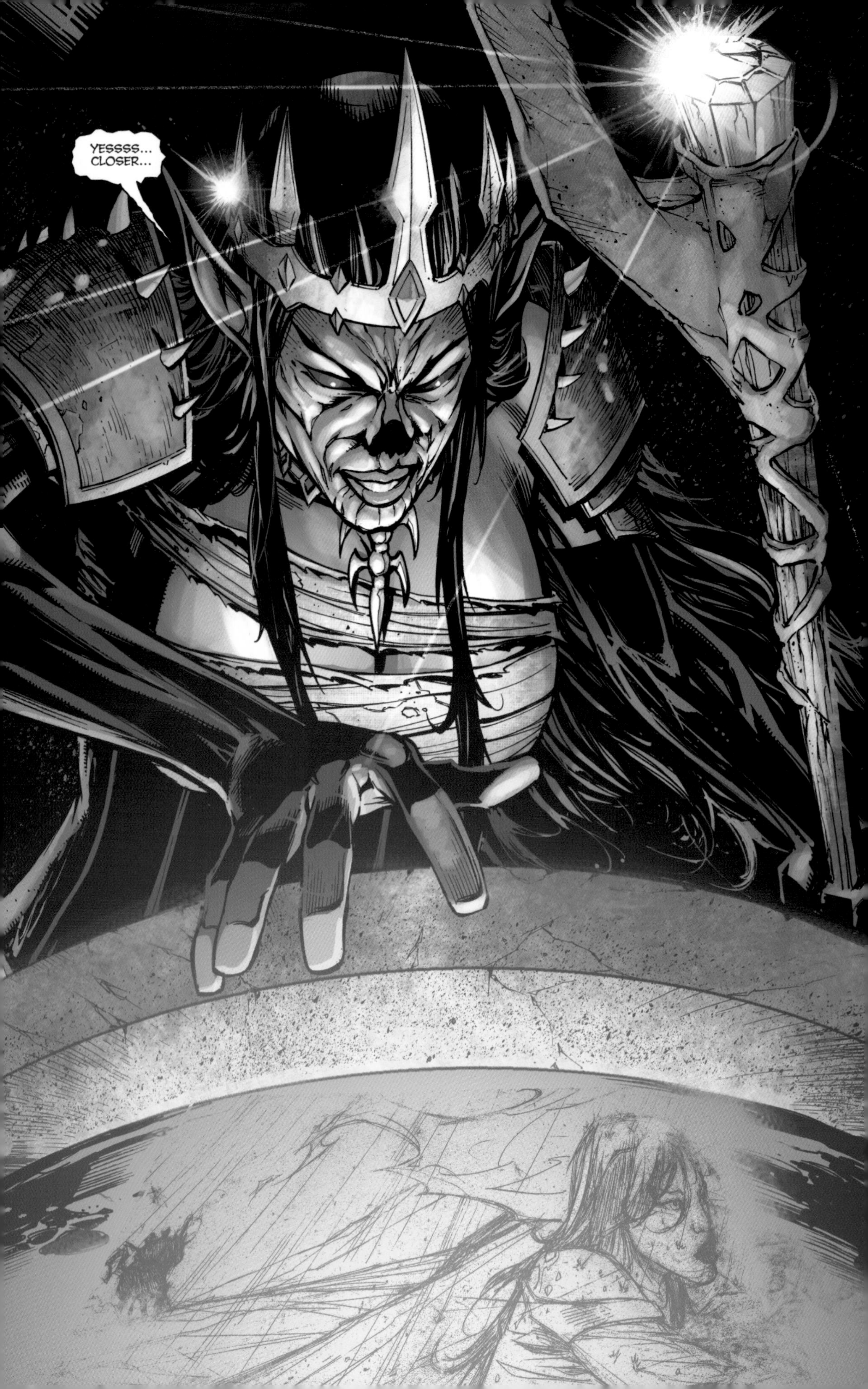
YESSSS... CLOSER...

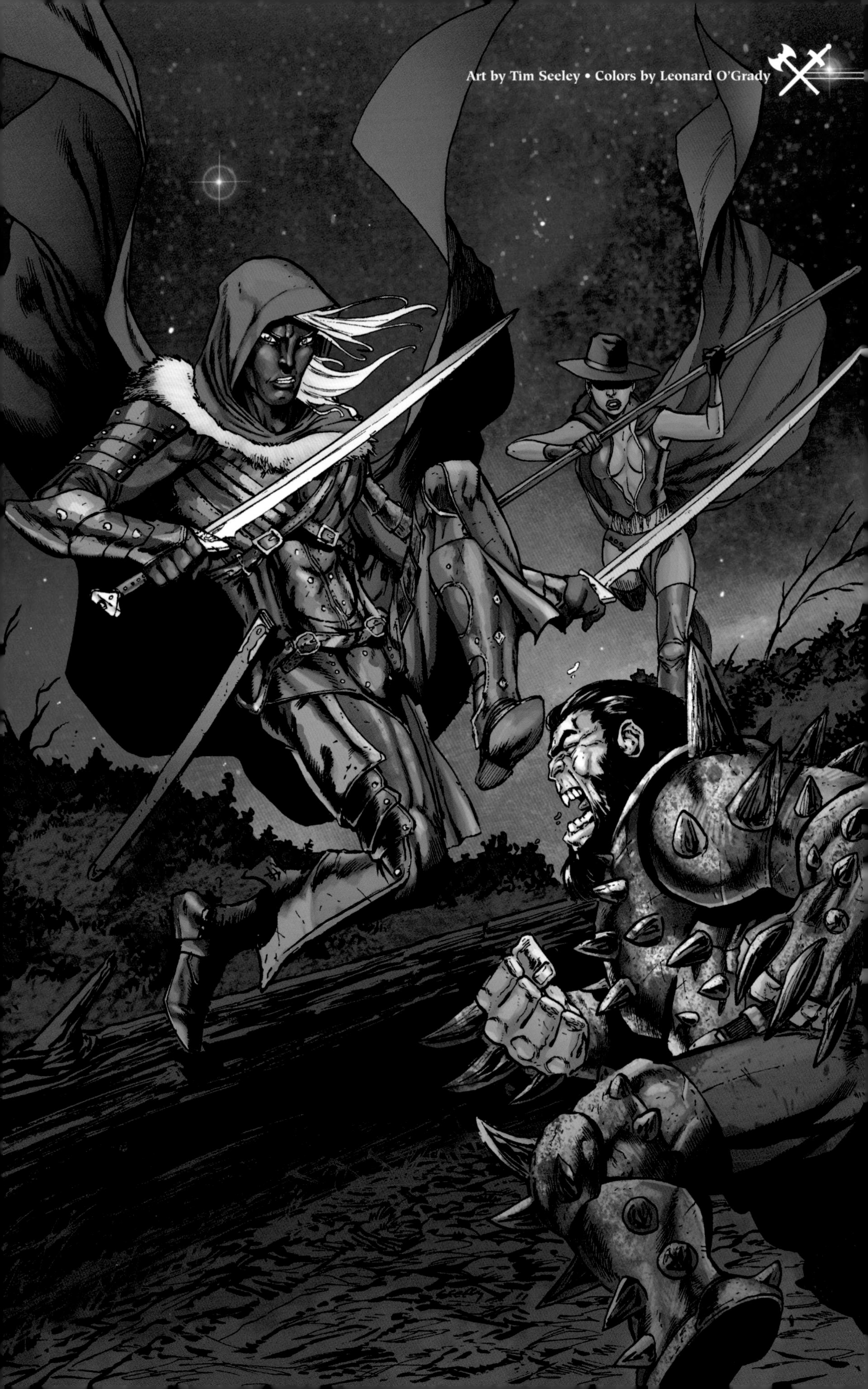

Art by Tim Seeley • Colors by Leonard O'Grady

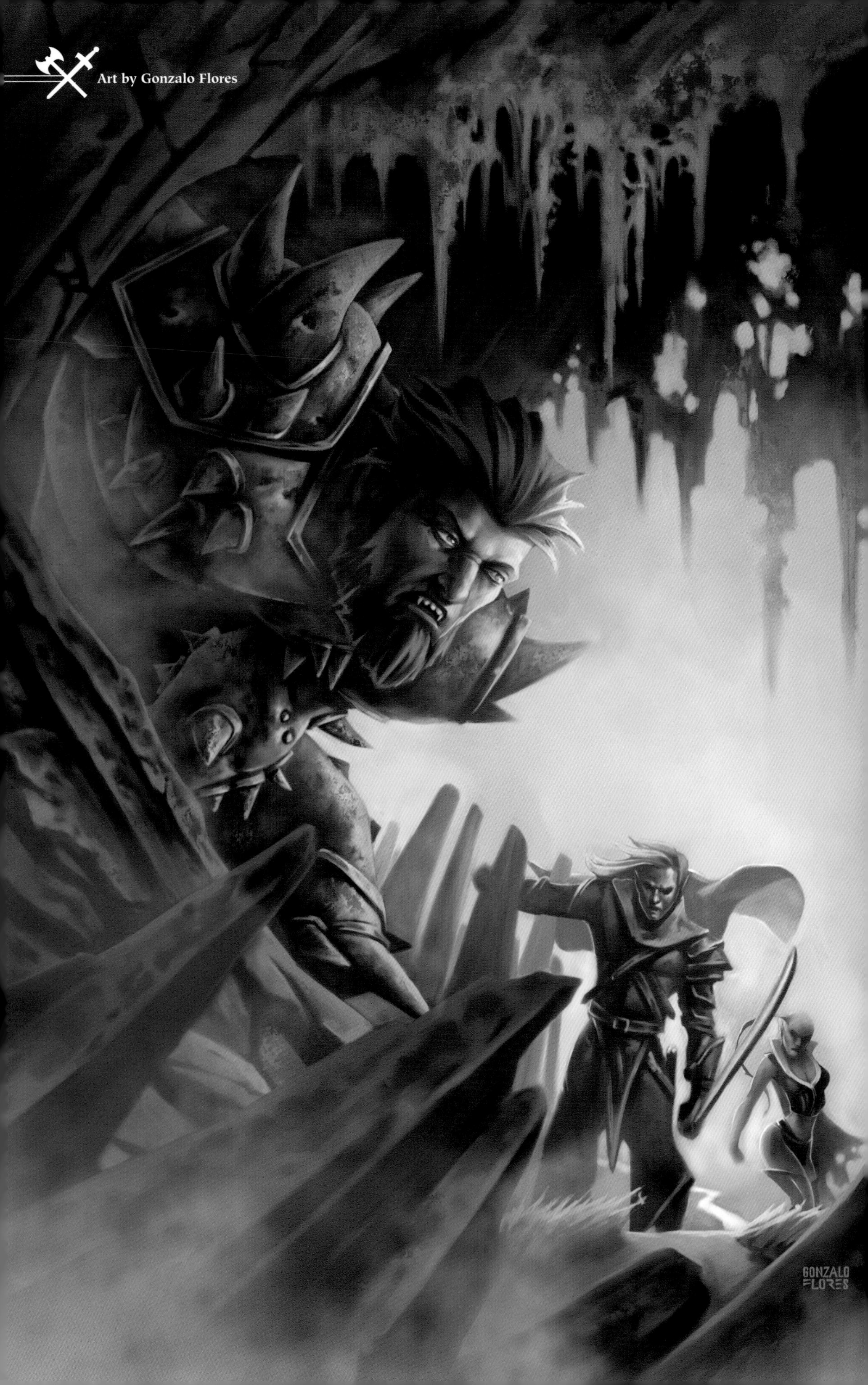
GONZALO
FLORES
Art by Gonzalo Flores

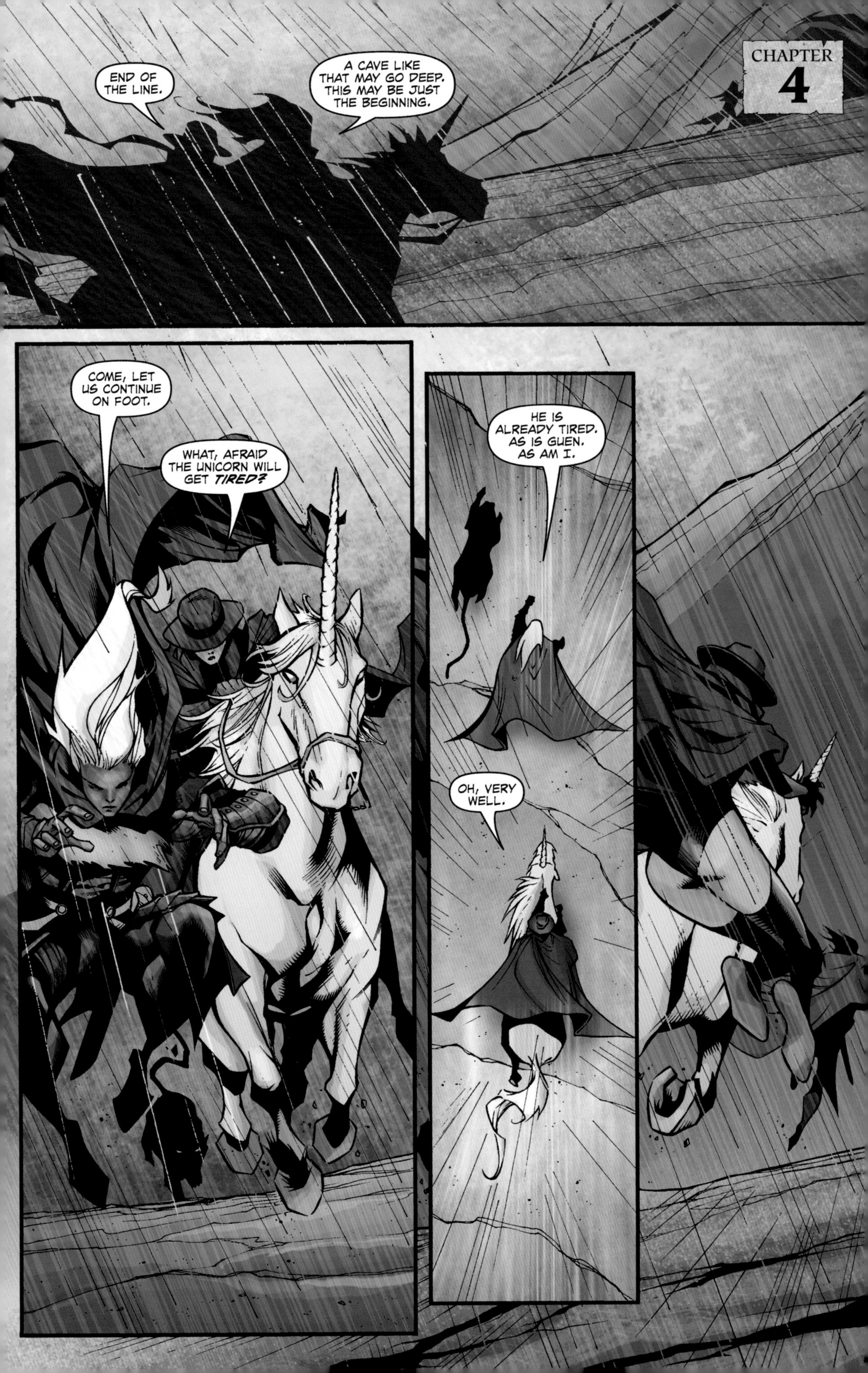
CHAPTER 4
END OF THE LINE.
A CAVE LIKE THAT MAY GO DEEP. THIS MAY BE JUST THE BEGINNING.
COME, LET US CONTINUE ON FOOT.
WHAT, AFRAID THE UNICORN WILL GET *TIRED?*
HE IS ALREADY TIRED. AS IS GUEN. AS AM I.
OH, VERY WELL.

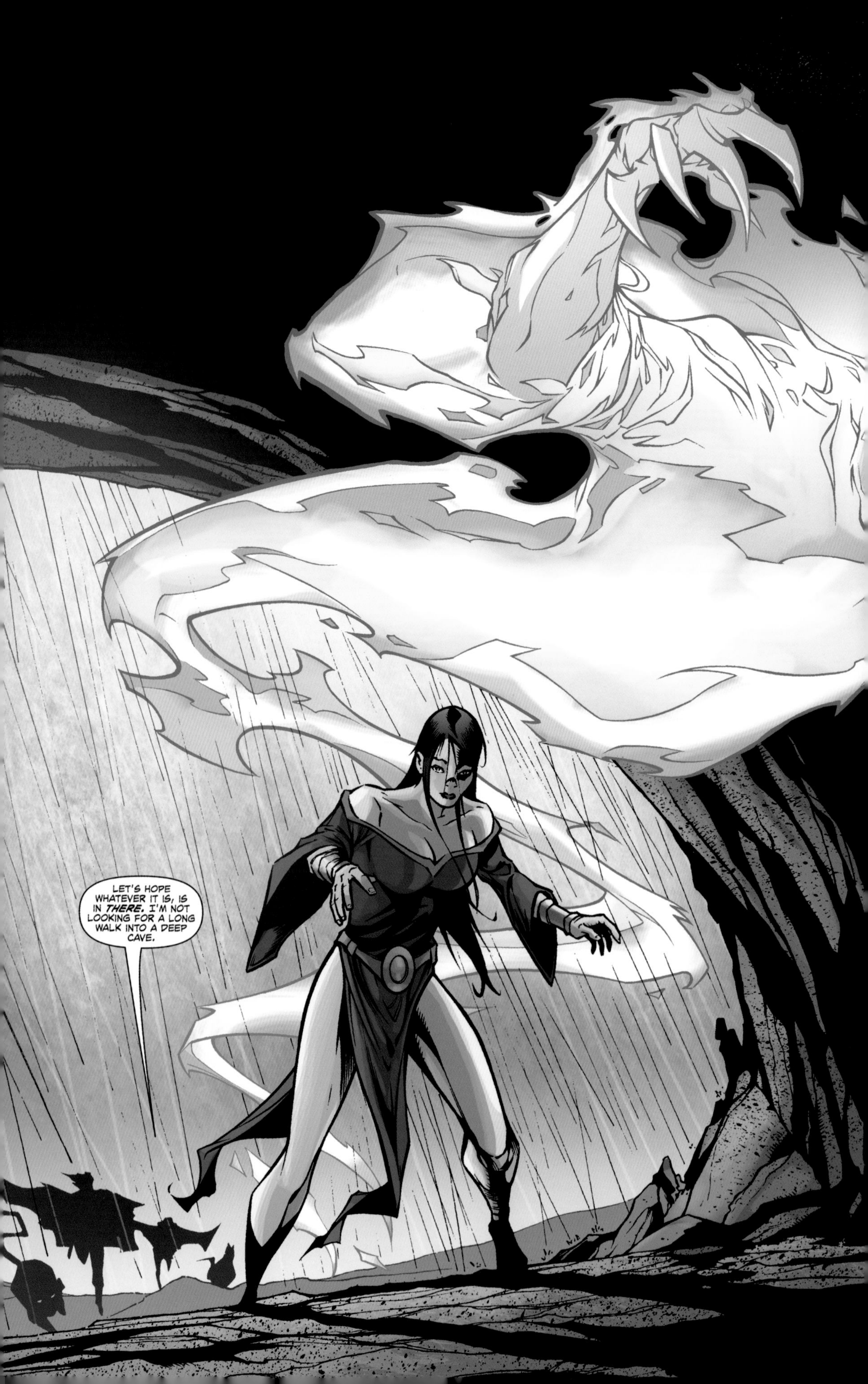
LET'S HOPE WHATEVER IT IS, IS IN *THERE.* I'M NOT LOOKING FOR A LONG WALK INTO A DEEP CAVE.

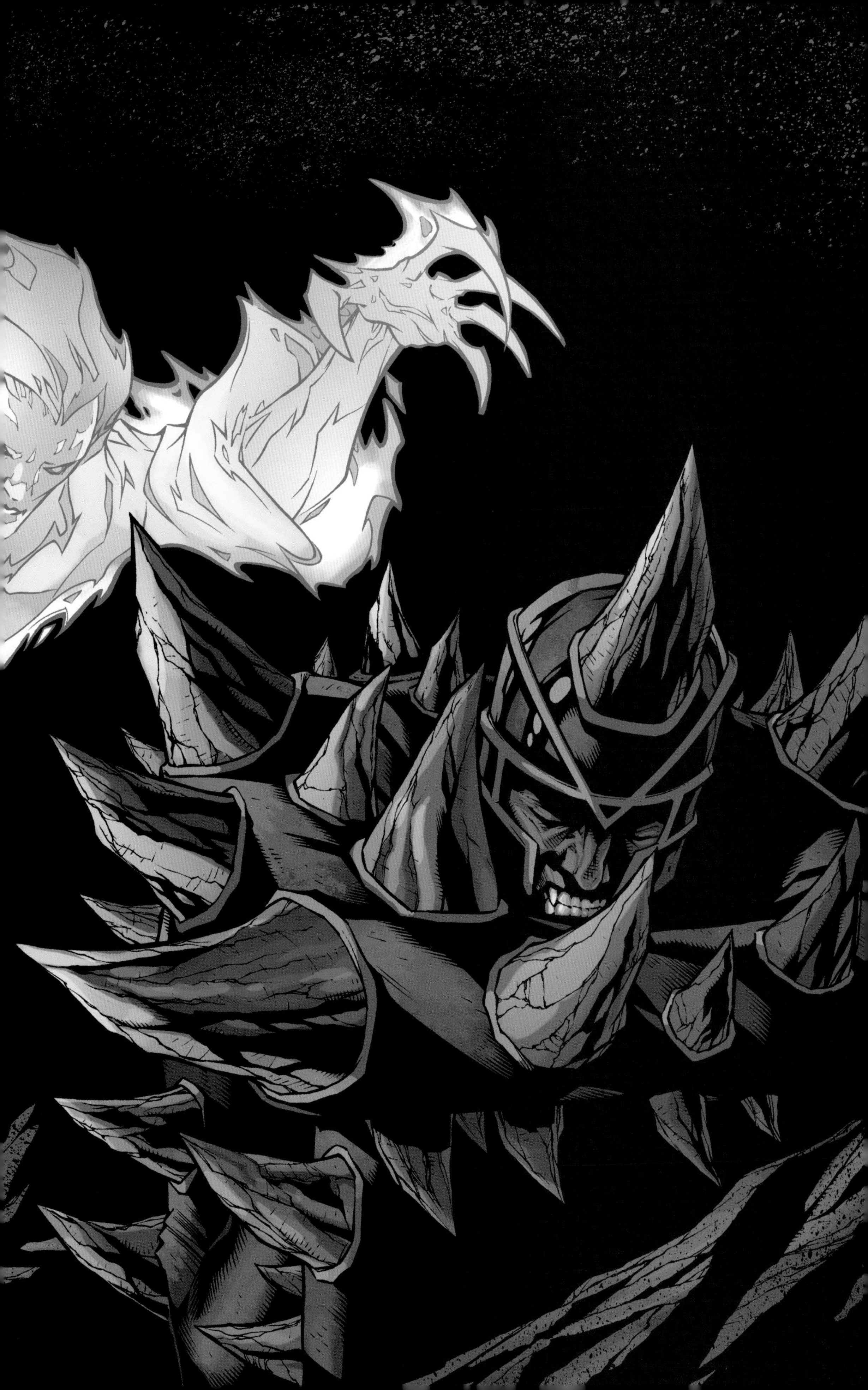

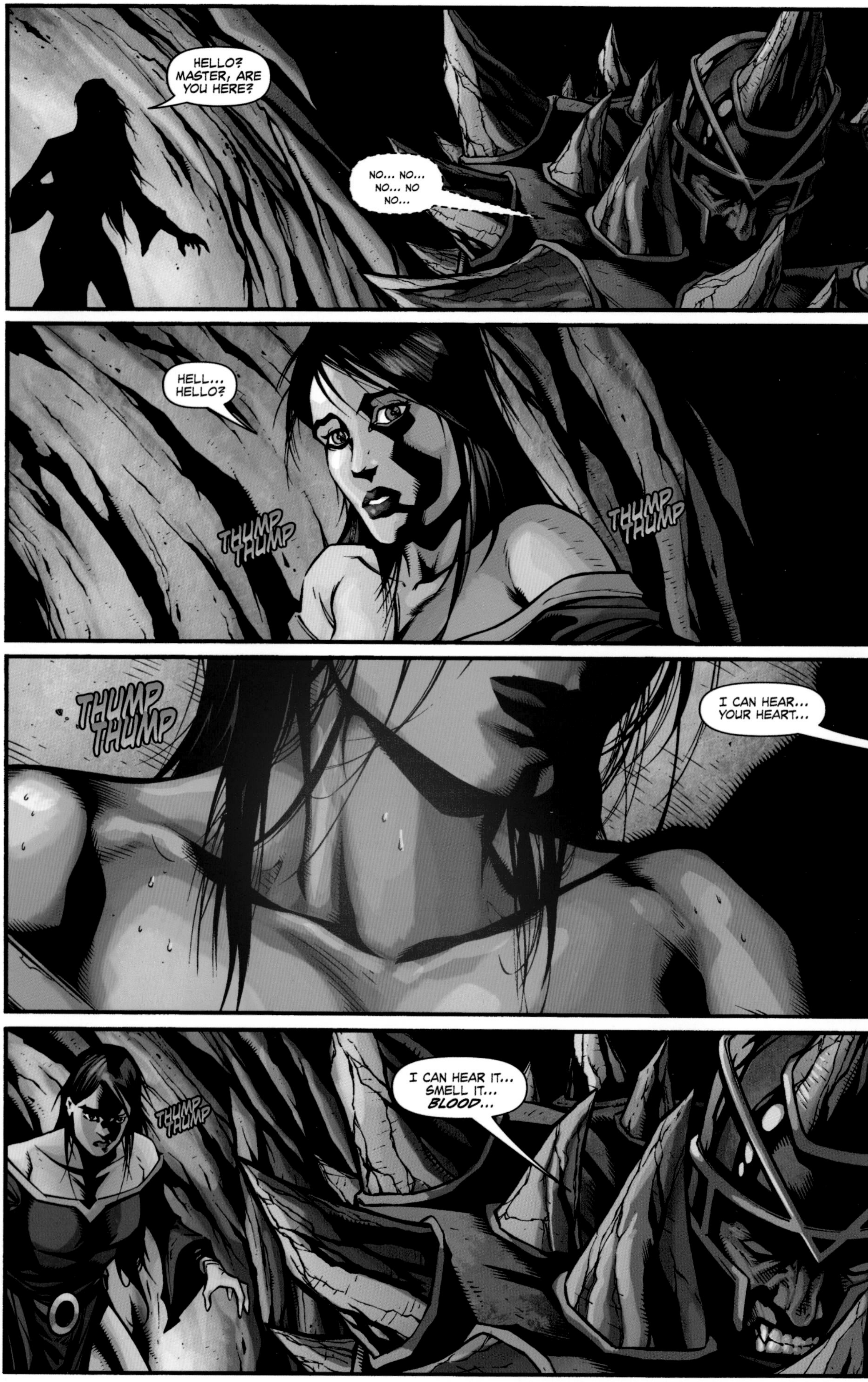
HELLO? MASTER, ARE YOU HERE?
NO... NO... NO... NO NO...
HELL... HELLO?
THUMP THUMP
THUMP THUMP
THUMP THUMP
I CAN HEAR... YOUR HEART...
THUMP THUMP
I CAN HEAR IT... SMELL IT... *BLOOD*...

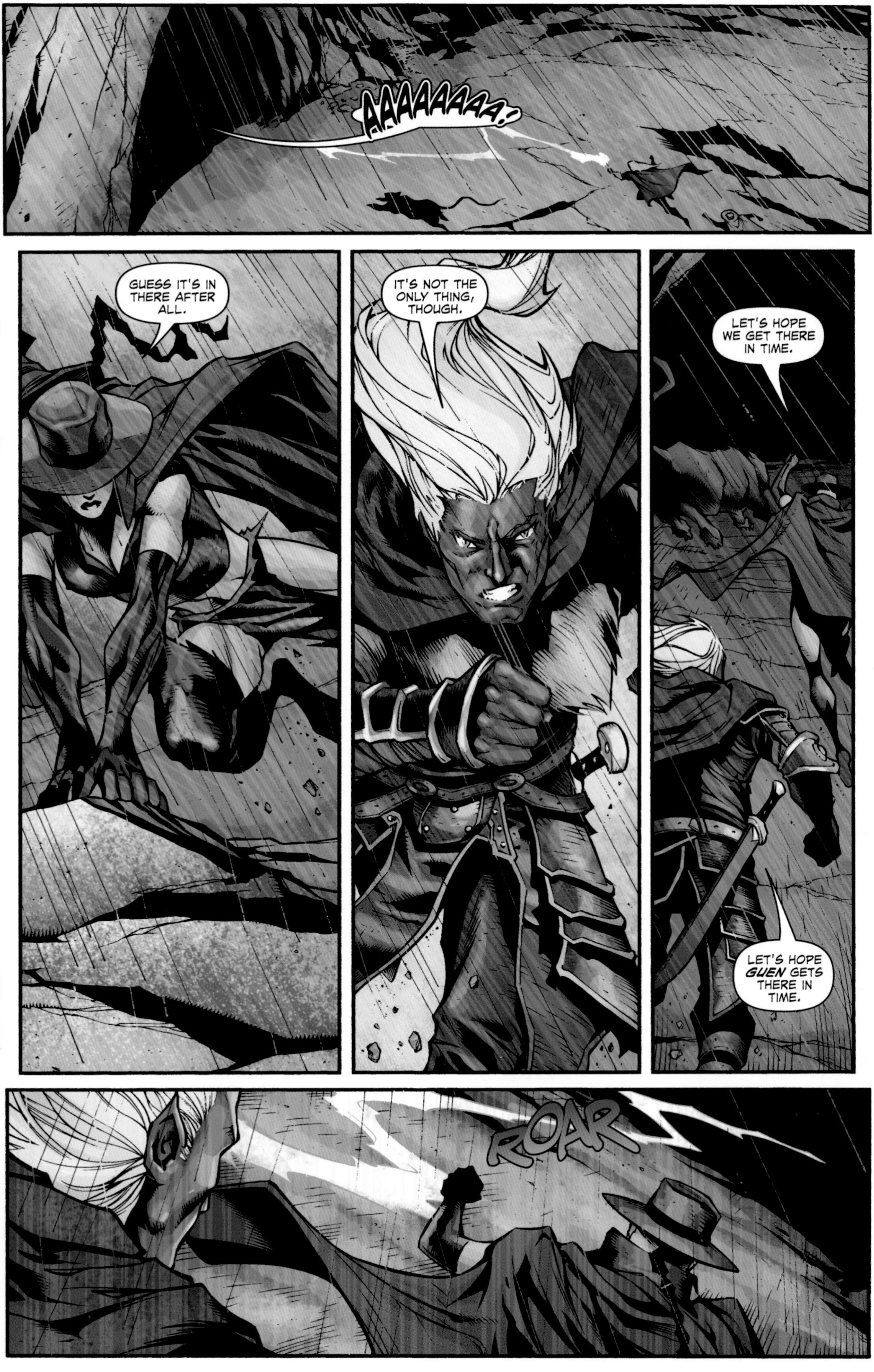
AAAAAAAA!
GUESS IT'S IN THERE AFTER ALL.
IT'S NOT THE ONLY THING, THOUGH.
LET'S HOPE WE GET THERE IN TIME.
LET'S HOPE GUEN GETS THERE IN TIME.
ROAR

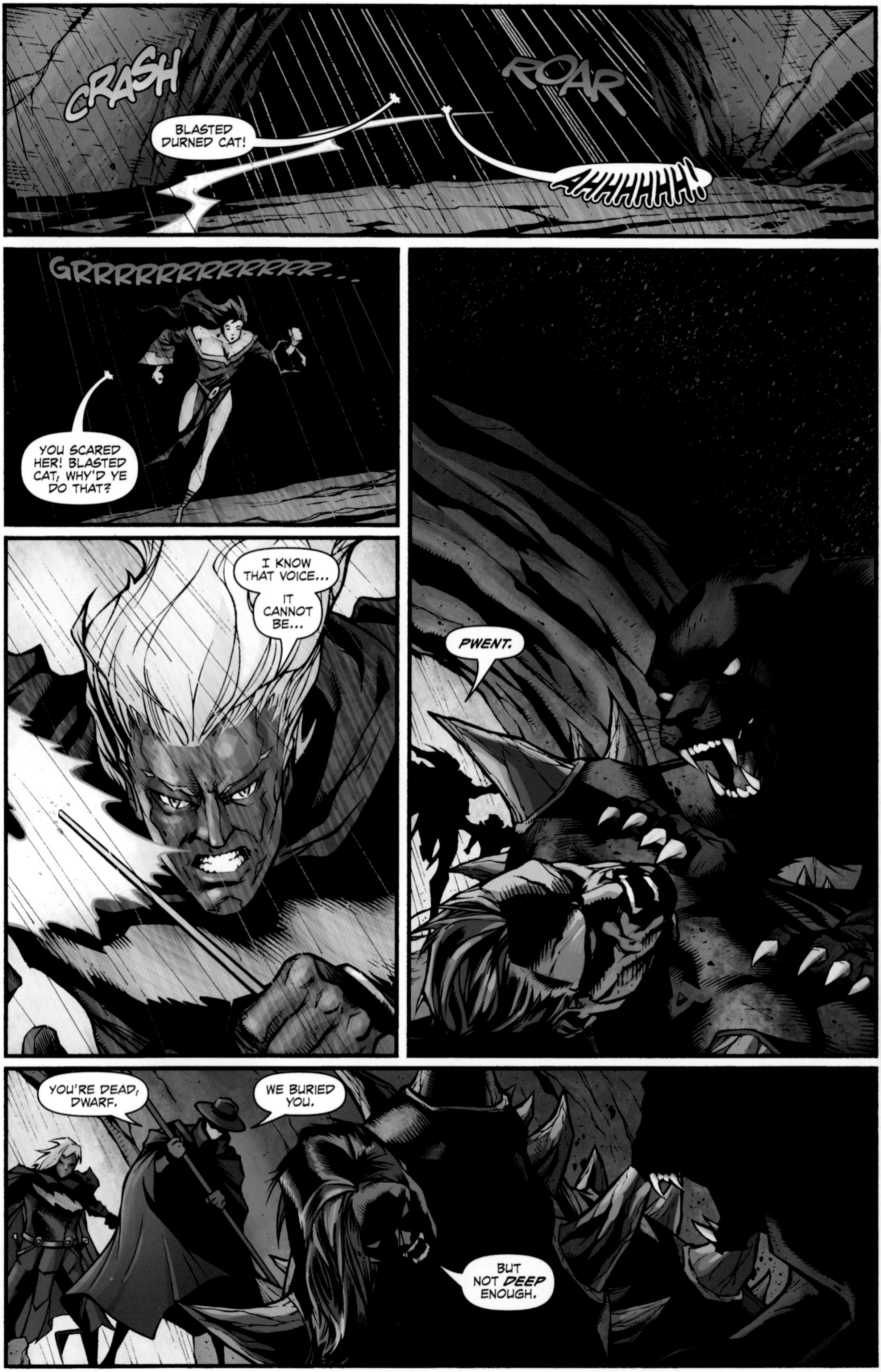
CRASH
ROAR
BLASTED DURNED CAT!
AHHHHHH!
GRRRRRRRRRRRR...
YOU SCARED HER! BLASTED CAT, WHY'D YE DO THAT?
I KNOW THAT VOICE...
IT CANNOT BE...
PWENT.
YOU'RE DEAD, DWARF.
WE BURIED YOU.
BUT NOT *DEEP* ENOUGH.

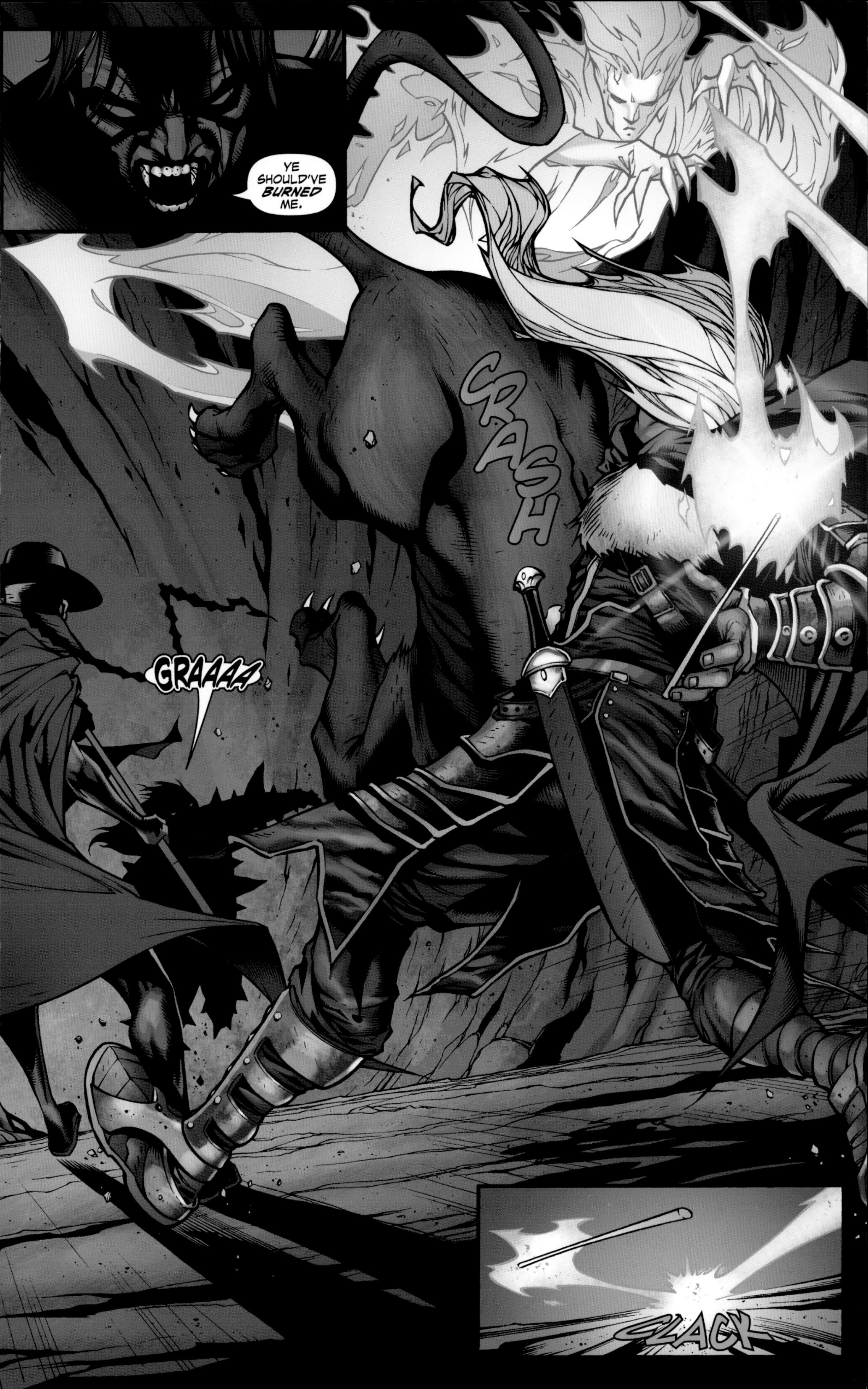
YE SHOULD'VE *BURNED* ME.
CRASH
GRAAAA
CLACK

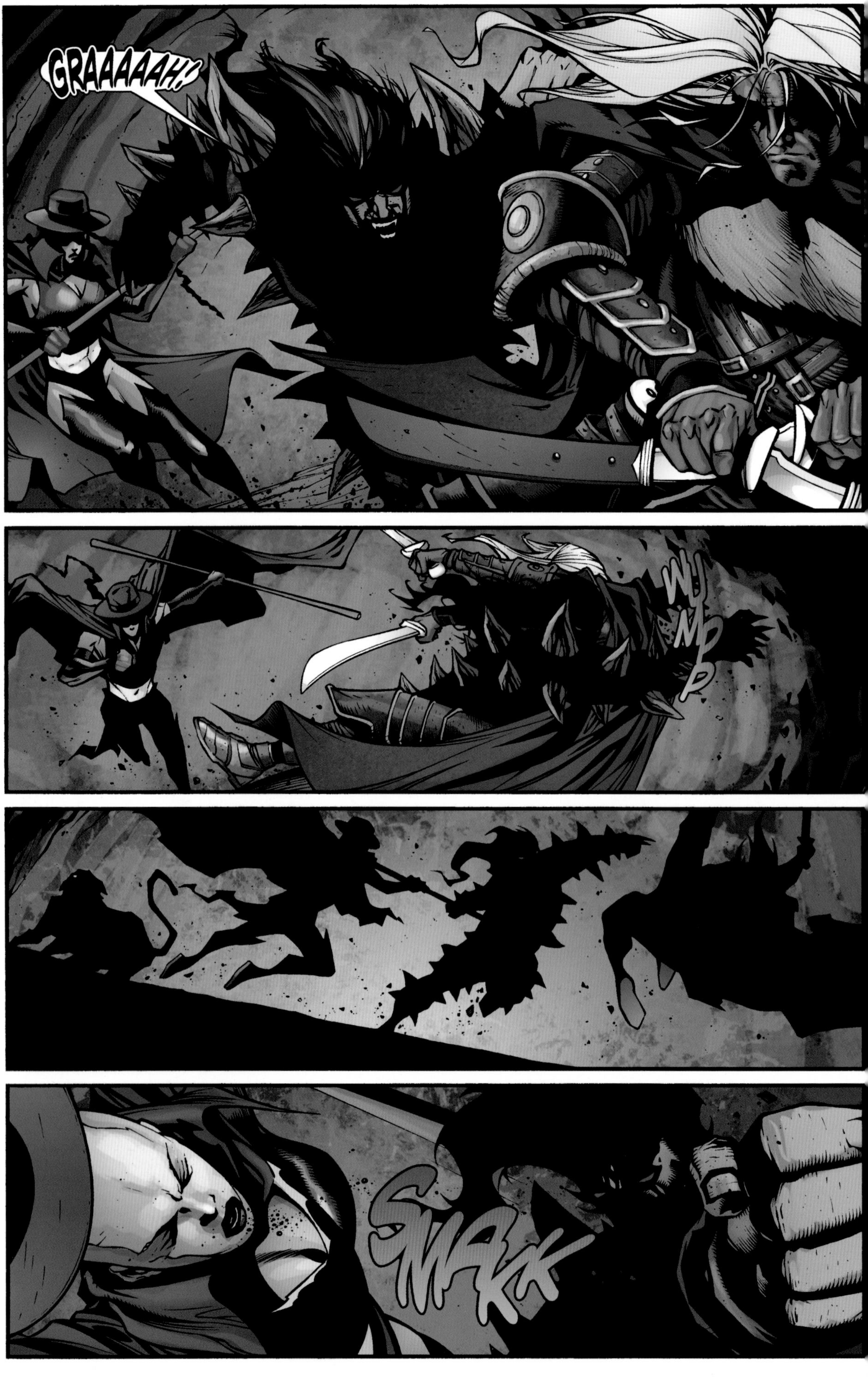
GRAAAAAH!
WUMP
SMACK

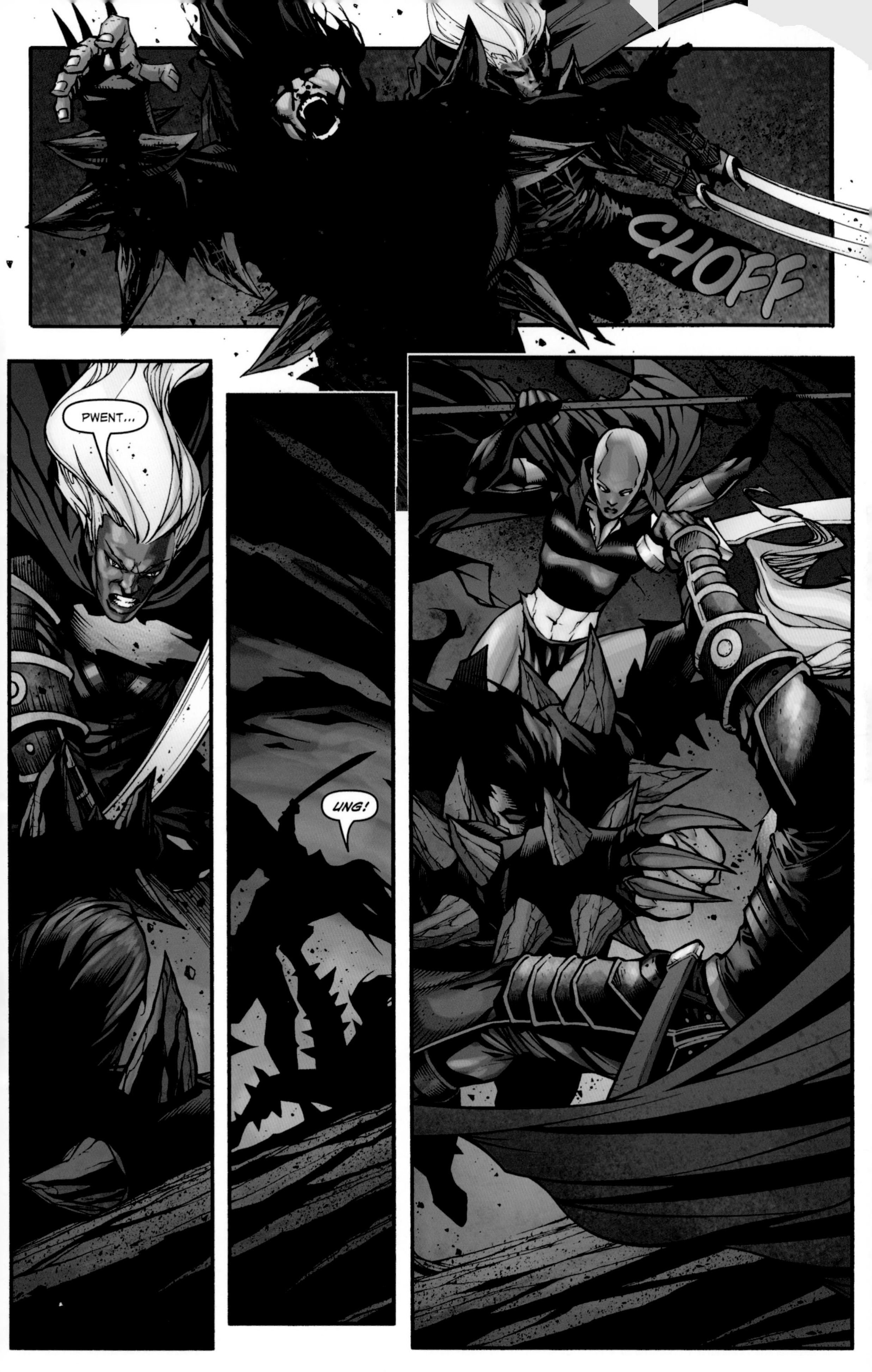
CHOFF
PWENT...
UNG!

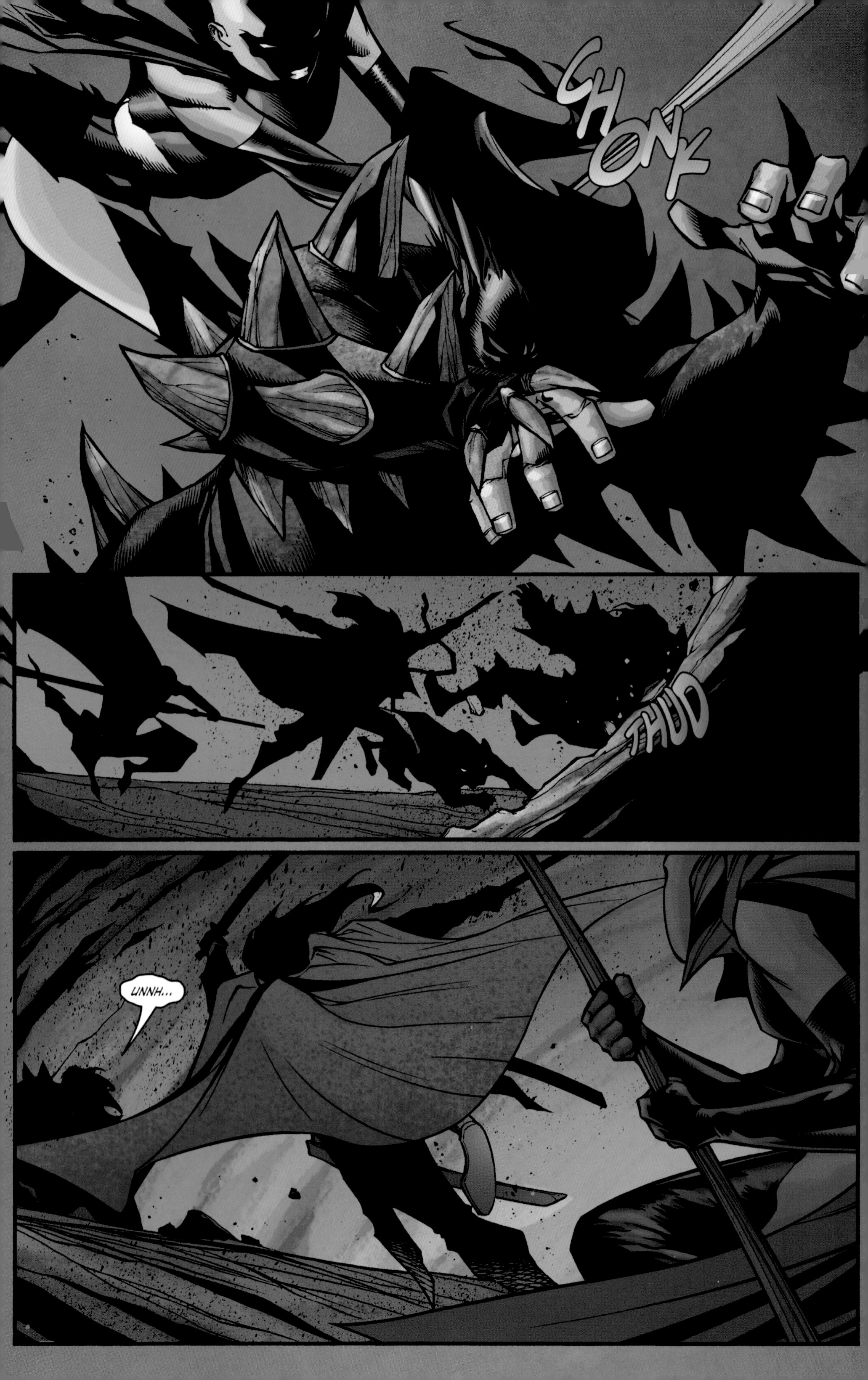
CHONK
THUD
UNNH...

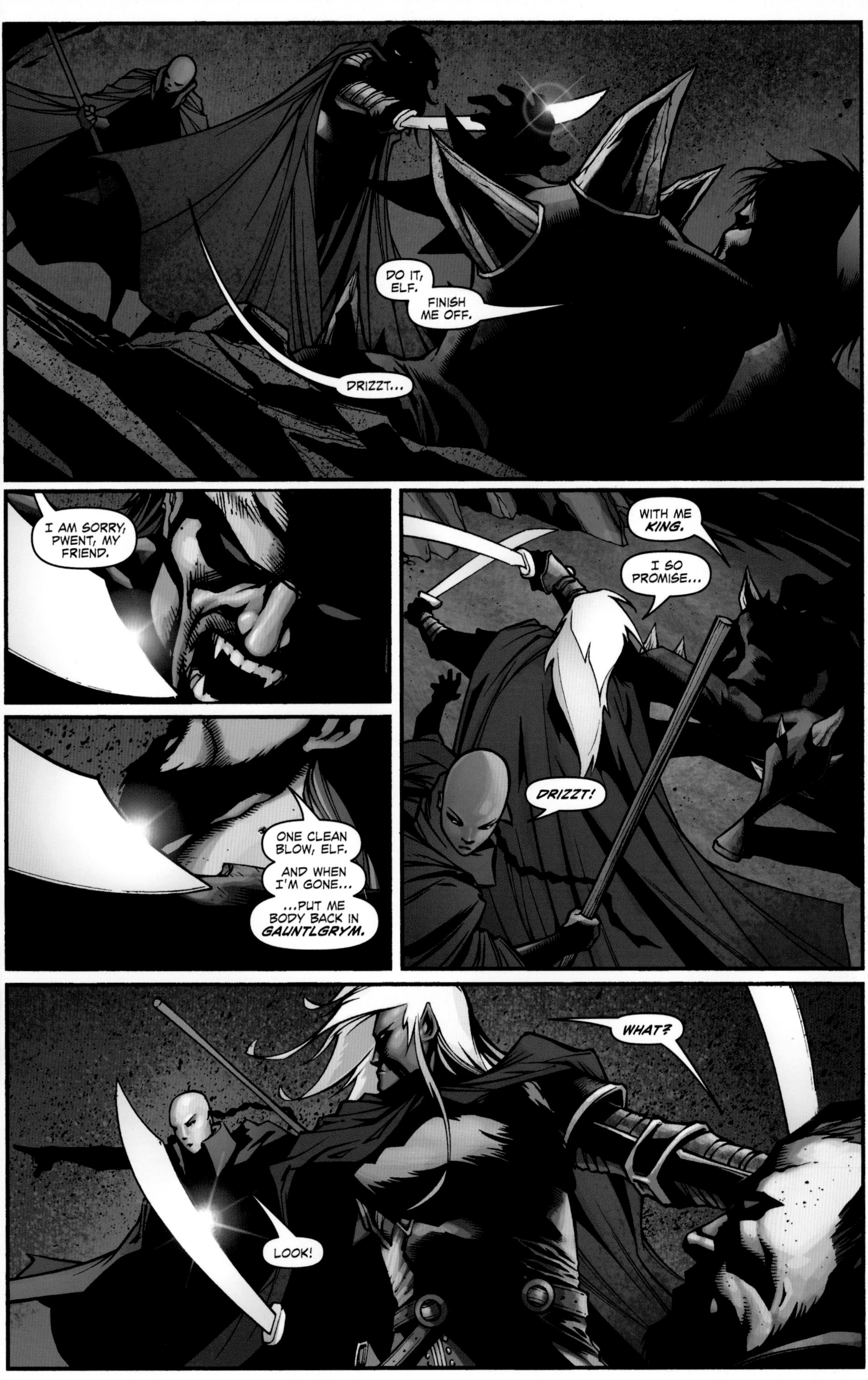
DO IT, ELF.
FINISH ME OFF.
DRIZZT...
I AM SORRY, PWENT, MY FRIEND.
ONE CLEAN BLOW, ELF.
AND WHEN I'M GONE...
...PUT ME BODY BACK IN GAUNTLGRYM.
WITH ME KING.
I SO PROMISE...
DRIZZT!
WHAT?
LOOK!

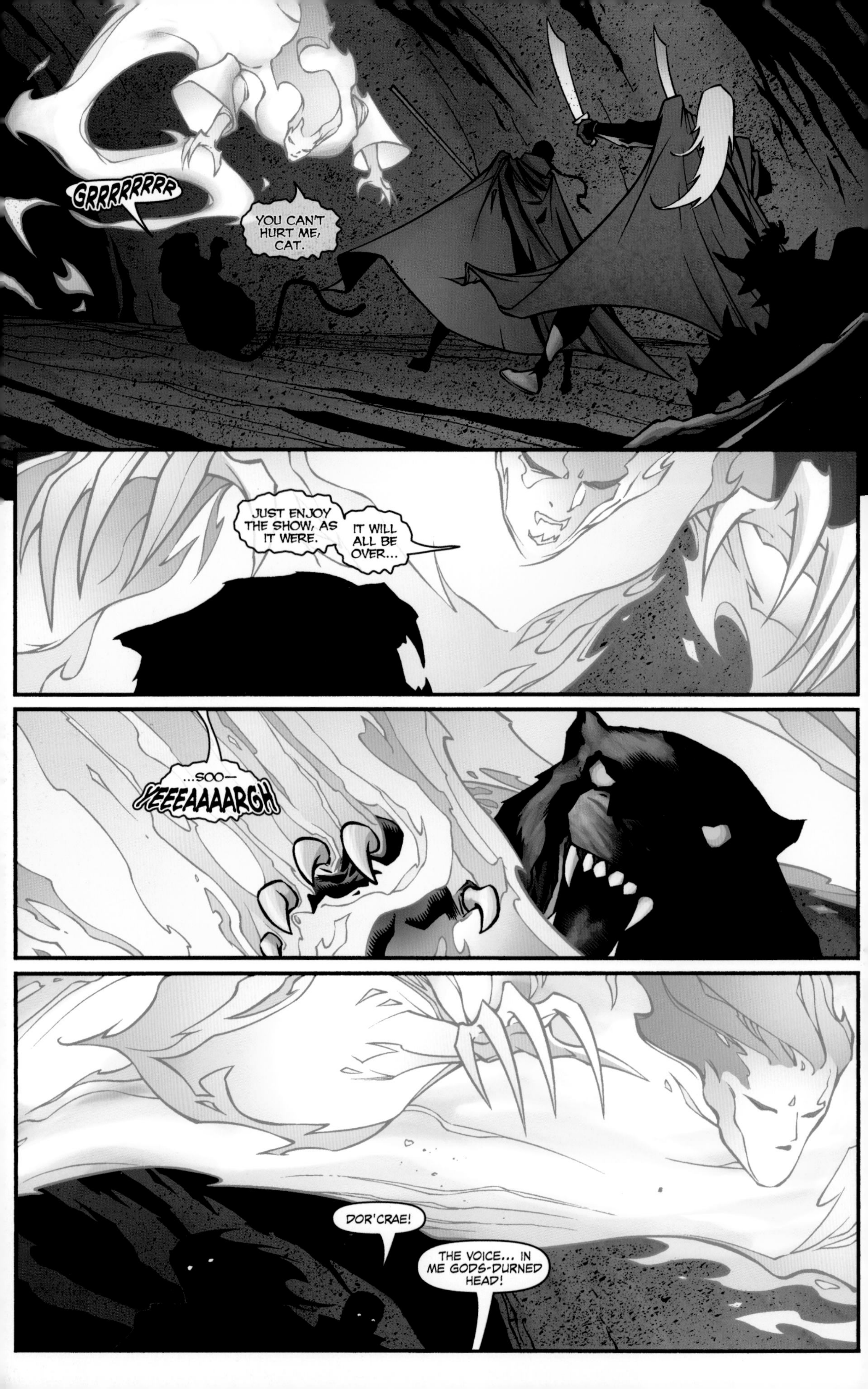
GRRRRRRR
YOU CAN'T HURT ME, CAT.
JUST ENJOY THE SHOW, AS IT WERE.
IT WILL ALL BE OVER...
...SOO—
YEEEAAAARGH
DOR'CRAE!
THE VOICE... IN ME GODS-DURNED HEAD!

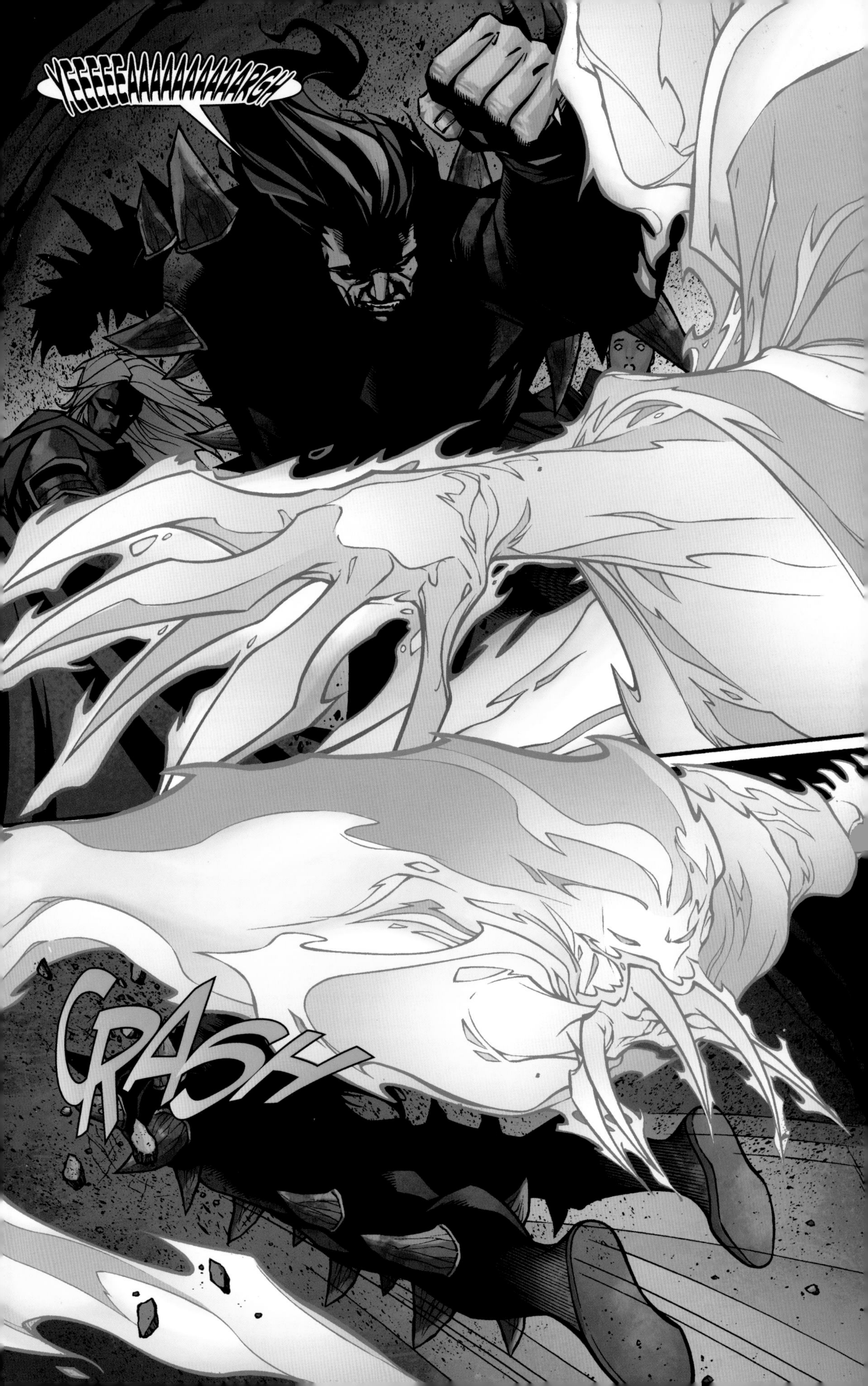
YEEEEEAAAAAAAAARGH
CRASH

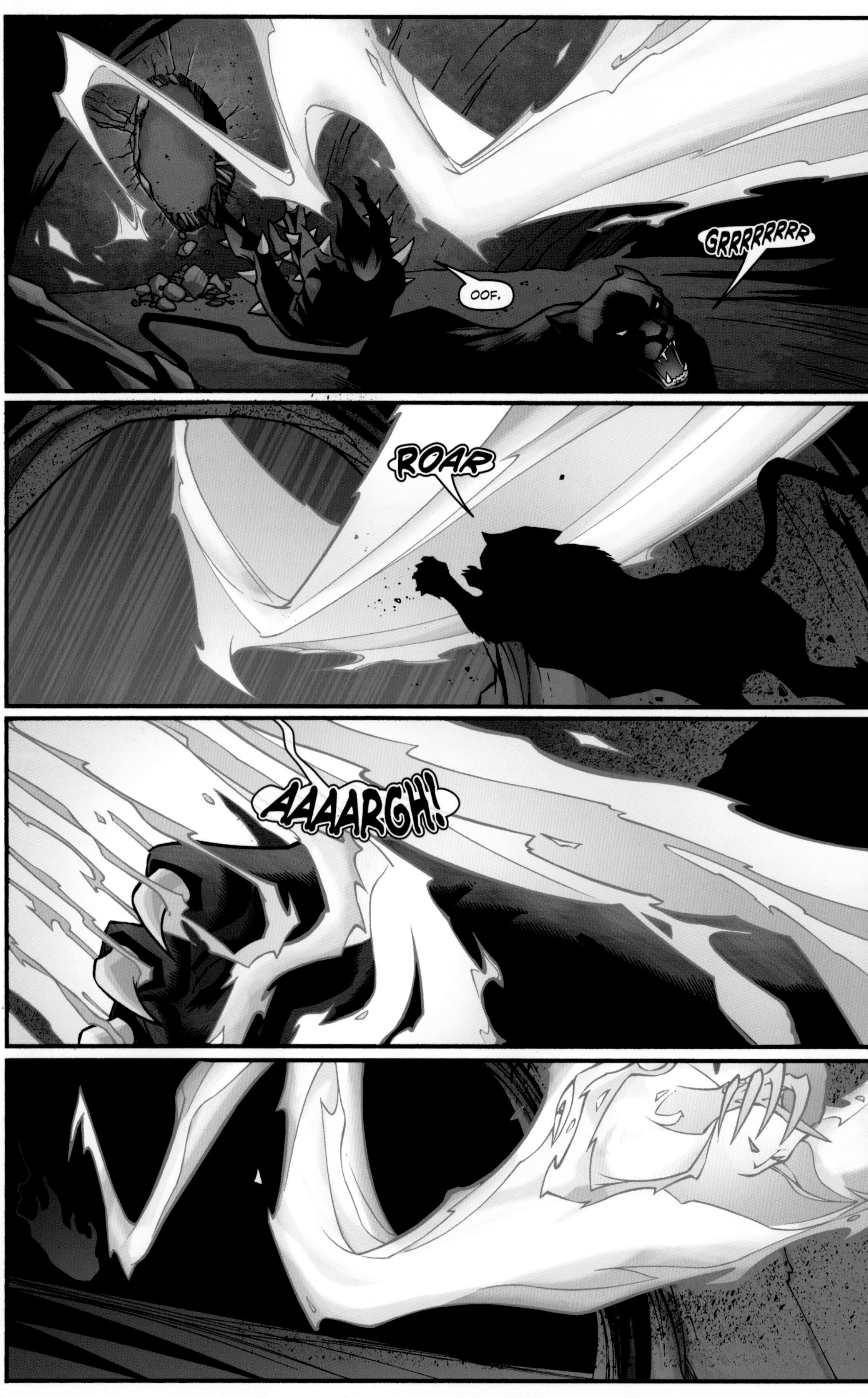
OOF.
GRRRRRRRR
ROAR
AAAARGH!

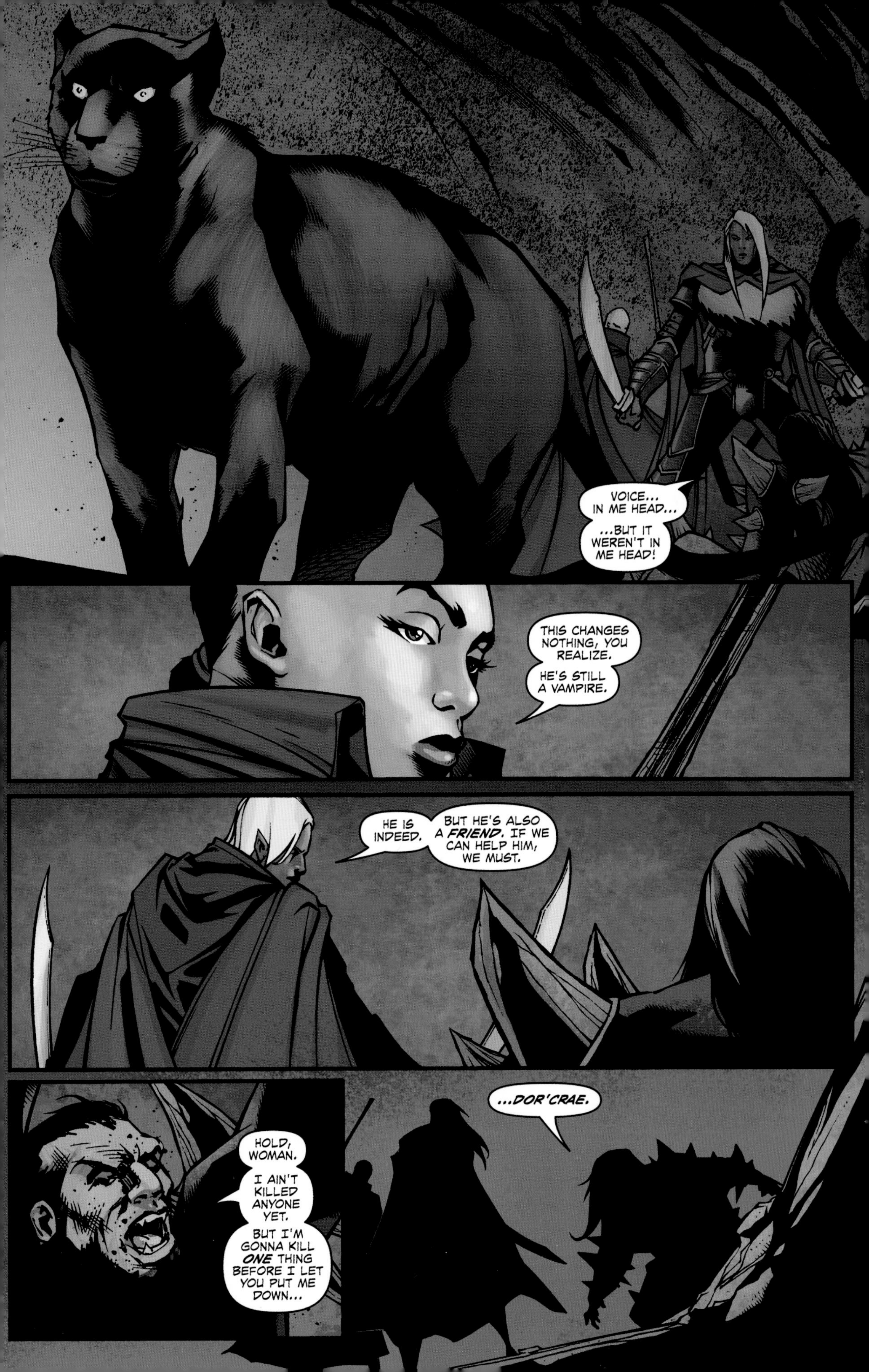
VOICE... IN ME HEAD...
...BUT IT WEREN'T IN ME HEAD!
THIS CHANGES NOTHING, YOU REALIZE.
HE'S STILL A VAMPIRE.
HE IS INDEED.
BUT HE'S ALSO A *FRIEND*. IF WE CAN HELP HIM, WE MUST.
...*DOR'CRAE.*
HOLD, WOMAN.
I AIN'T KILLED ANYONE YET.
BUT I'M GONNA KILL *ONE* THING BEFORE I LET YOU PUT ME DOWN...

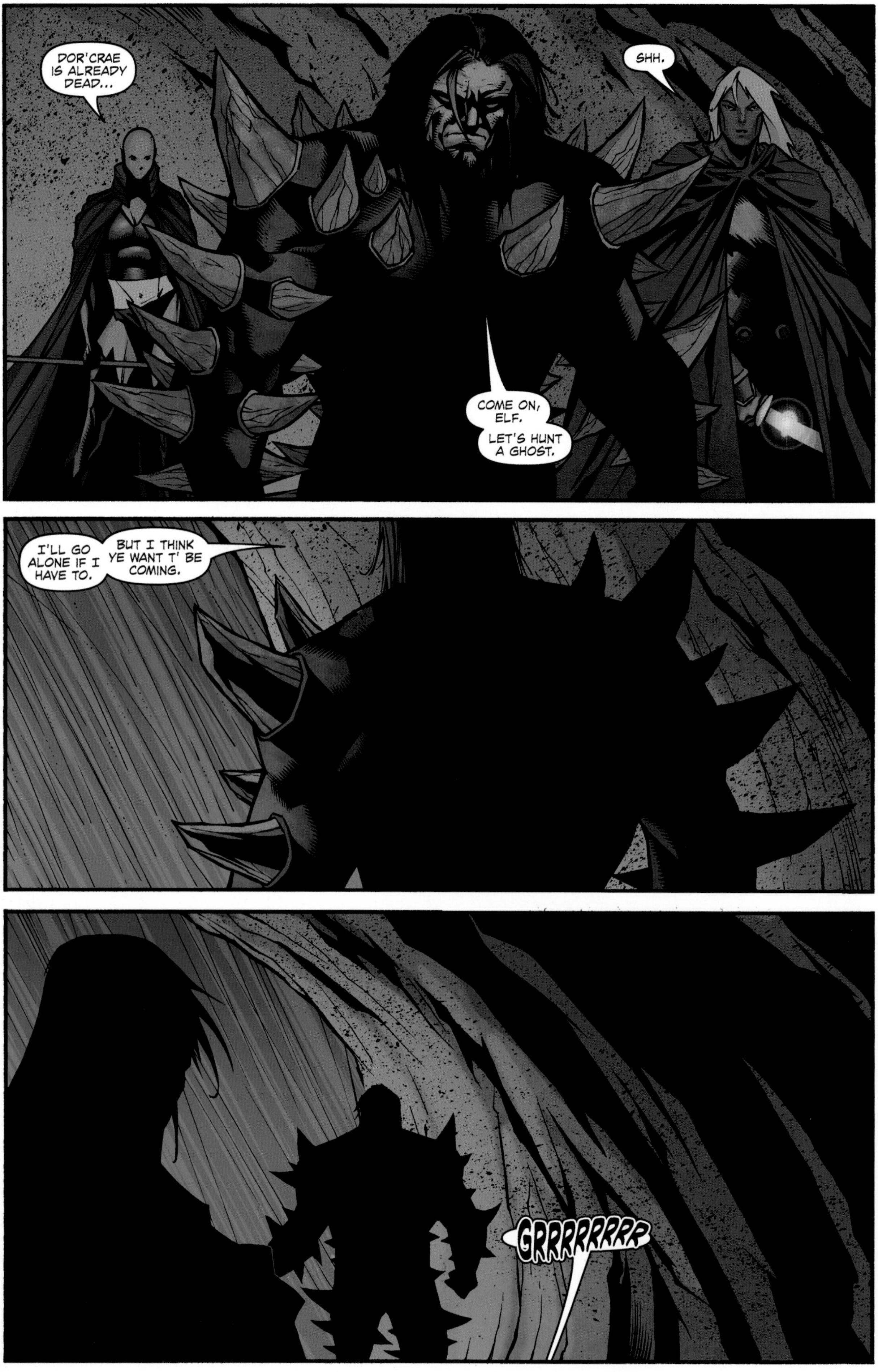
DOR'CRAE IS ALREADY DEAD...
SHH.
COME ON, ELF.
LET'S HUNT A GHOST.
I'LL GO ALONE IF I HAVE TO.
BUT I THINK YE WANT T' BE COMING.
GRRRRRRRR

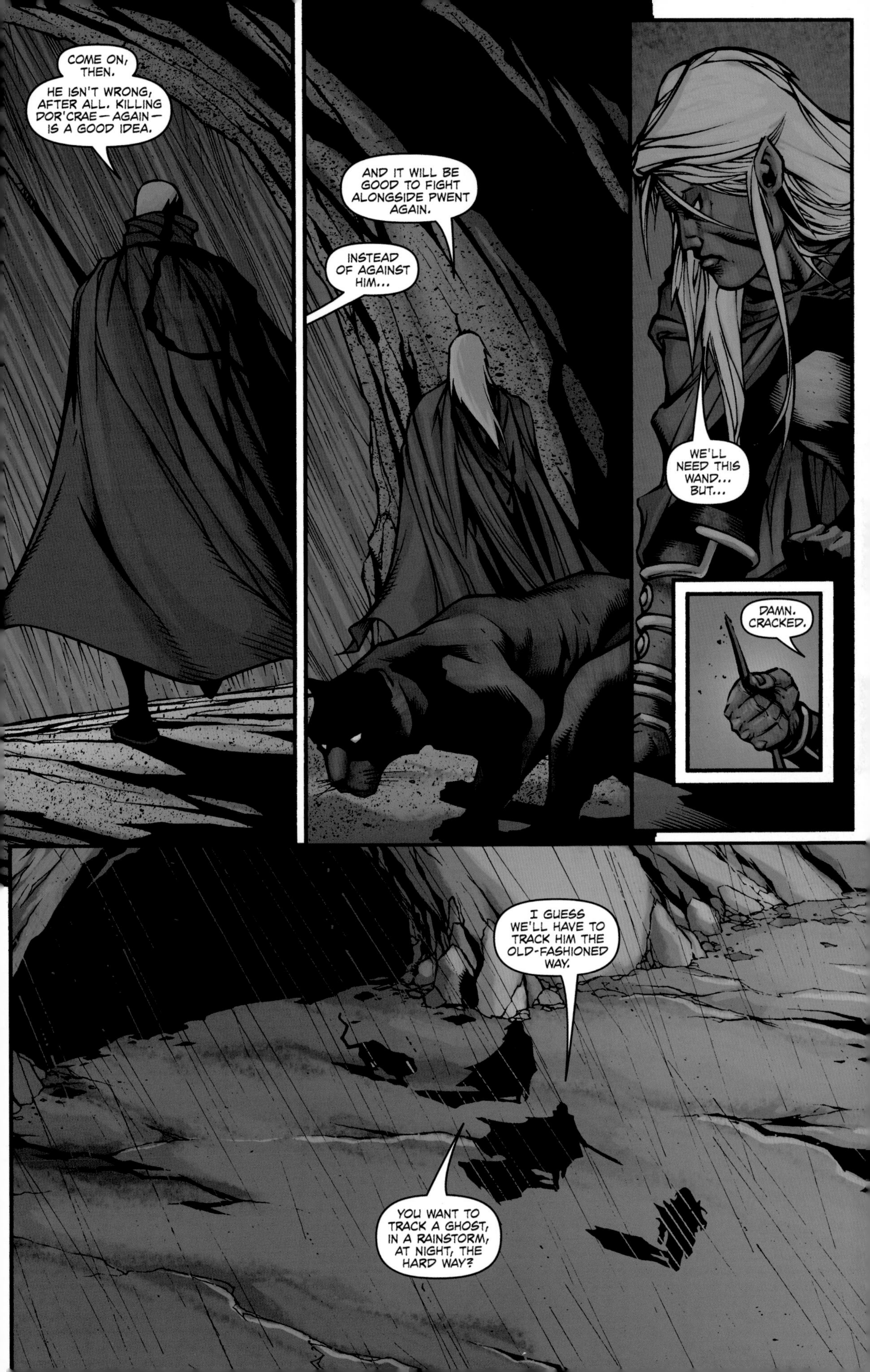
COME ON, THEN.
HE ISN'T WRONG, AFTER ALL. KILLING DOR'CRAE—AGAIN—IS A GOOD IDEA.
AND IT WILL BE GOOD TO FIGHT ALONGSIDE PWENT AGAIN.
INSTEAD OF AGAINST HIM...
WE'LL NEED THIS WAND... BUT...
DAMN. CRACKED.
I GUESS WE'LL HAVE TO TRACK HIM THE OLD-FASHIONED WAY.
YOU WANT TO TRACK A GHOST, IN A RAINSTORM, AT NIGHT, THE HARD WAY?

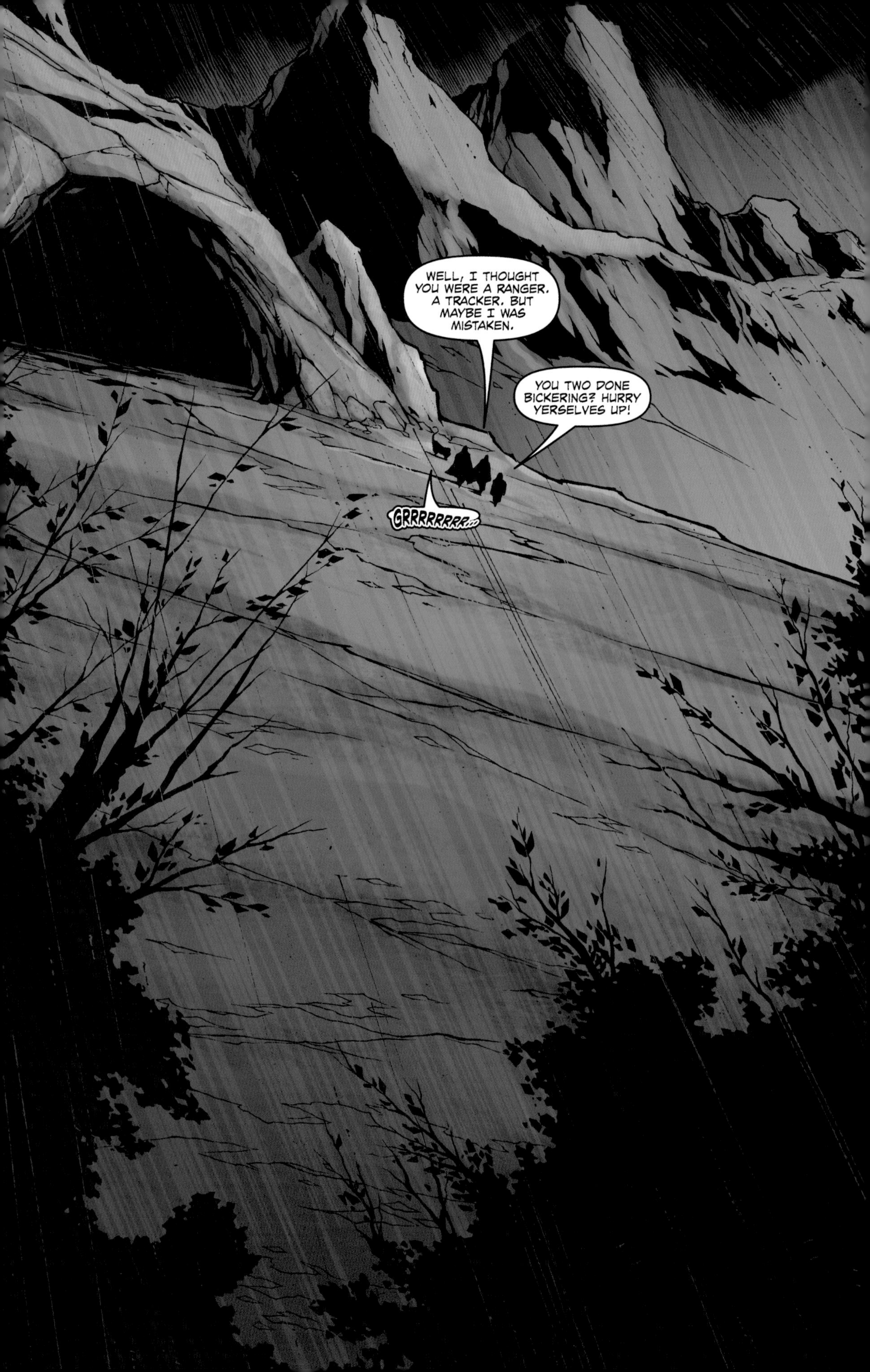
WELL, I THOUGHT YOU WERE A RANGER. A TRACKER. BUT MAYBE I WAS MISTAKEN.
YOU TWO DONE BICKERING? HURRY YERSELVES UP!
GRRRRRRRR...

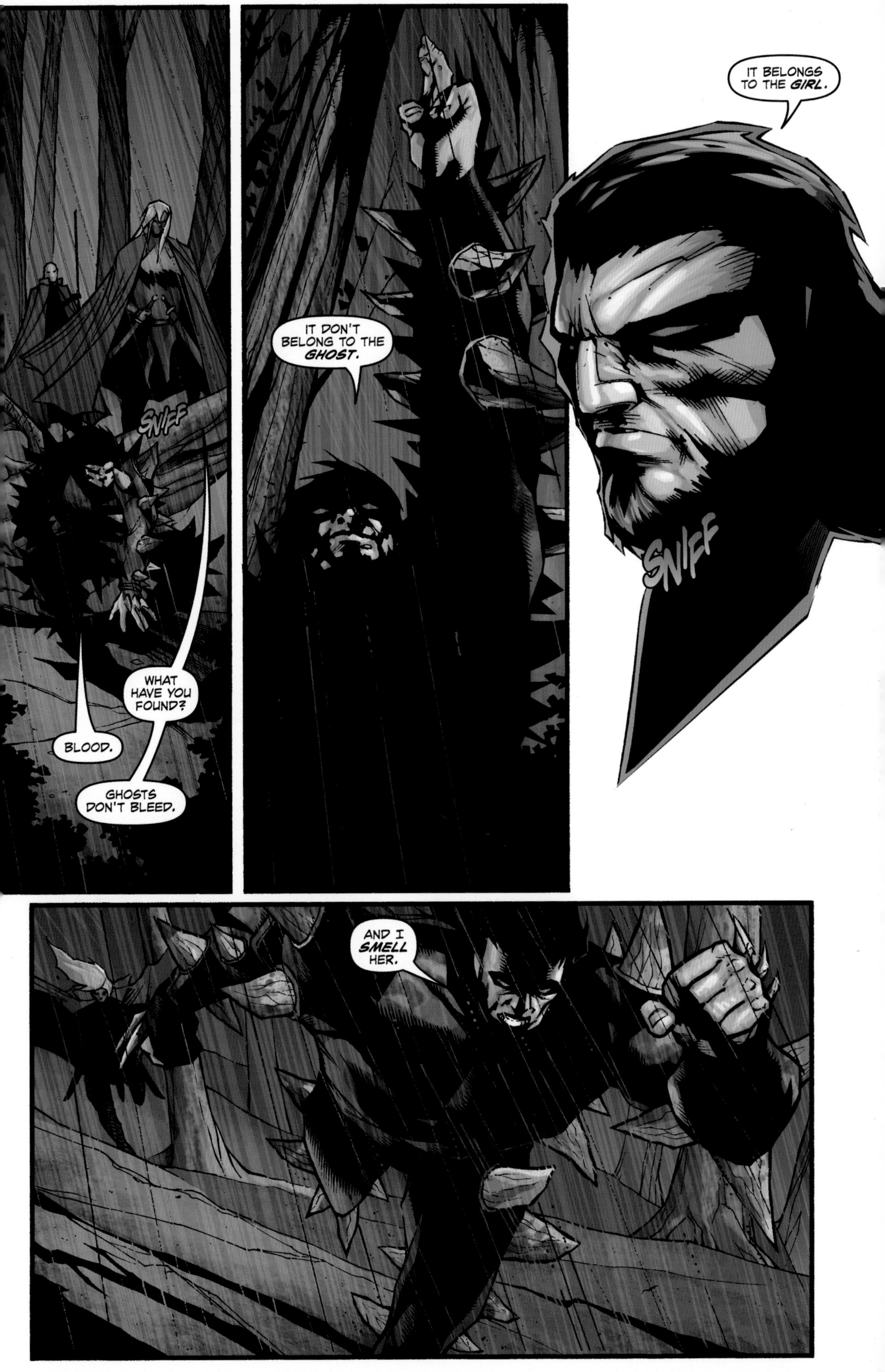
SNIFF
WHAT HAVE YOU FOUND?
BLOOD.
GHOSTS DON'T BLEED.
IT DON'T BELONG TO THE GHOST.
IT BELONGS TO THE GIRL.
SNIFF
AND I SMELL HER.

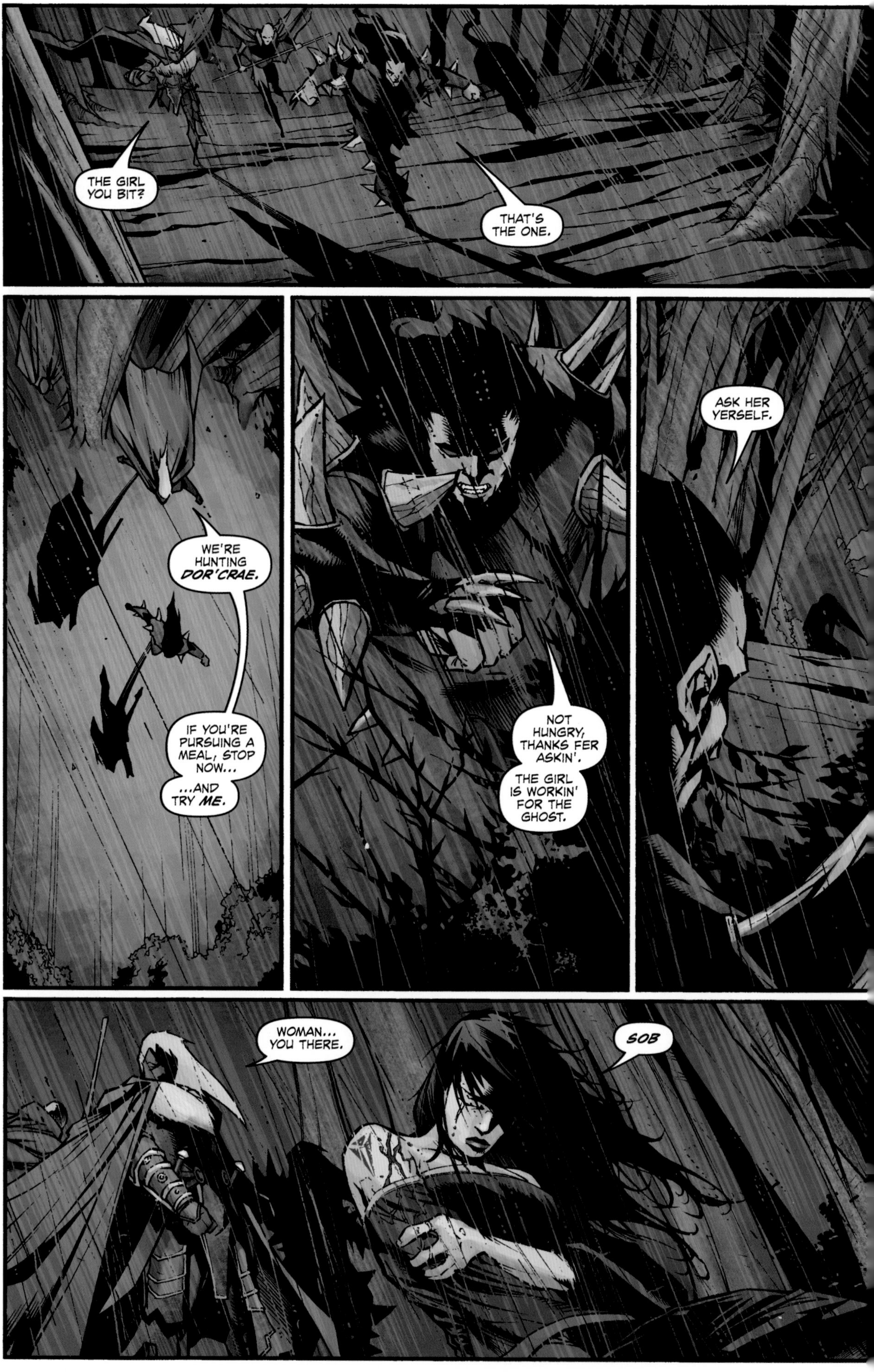
THE GIRL YOU BIT?
THAT'S THE ONE.
WE'RE HUNTING *DOR'CRAE.*
IF YOU'RE PURSUING A MEAL, STOP NOW...
...AND TRY *ME.*
NOT HUNGRY, THANKS FER ASKIN'.
THE GIRL IS WORKIN' FOR THE GHOST.
ASK HER YERSELF.
WOMAN... YOU THERE.
SOB

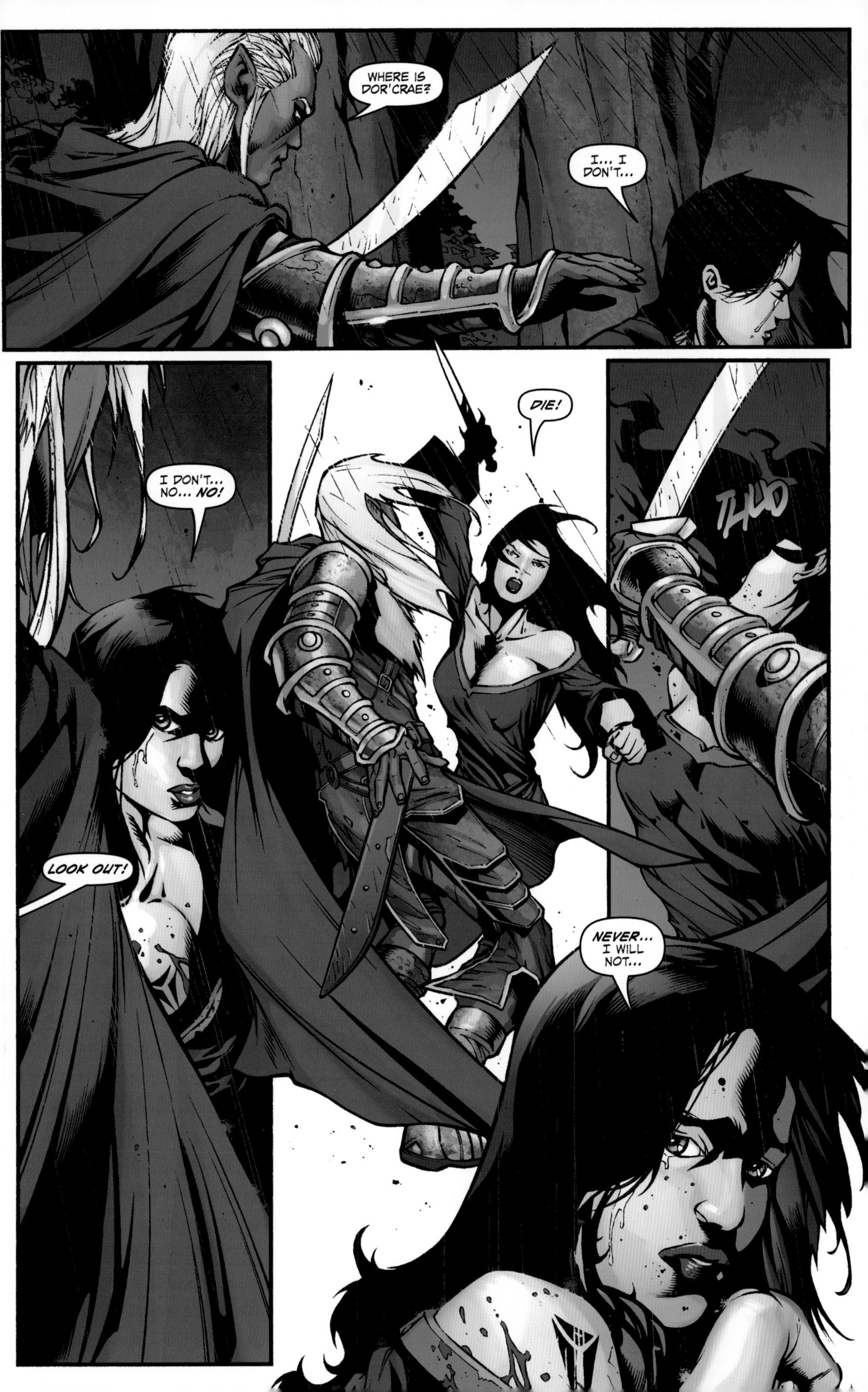
WHERE IS DOR'CRAE?
I... I DON'T...
I DON'T... NO... NO!
DIE!
THUD
LOOK OUT!
NEVER... I WILL NOT...

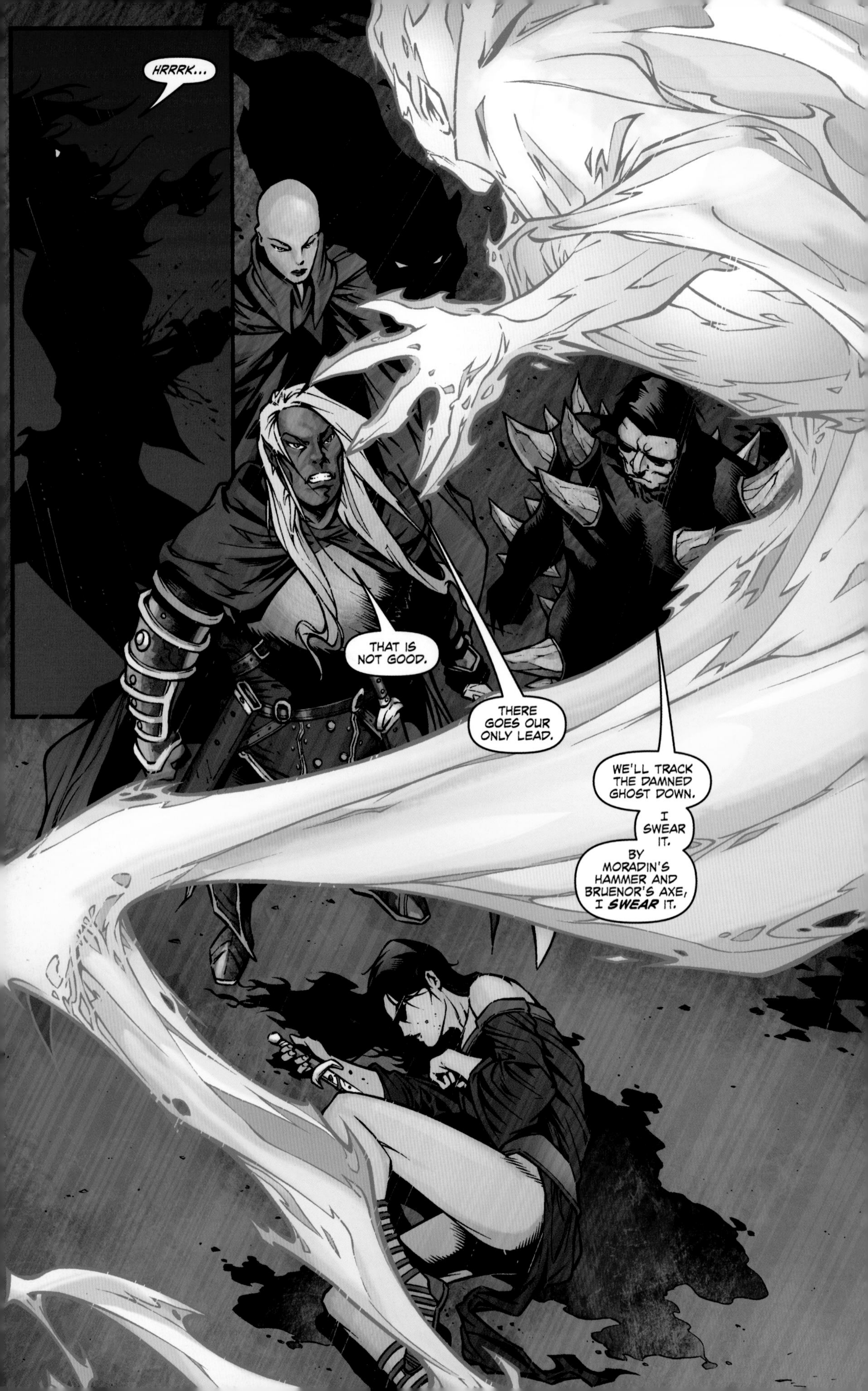
HRRRK...
THAT IS NOT GOOD.
THERE GOES OUR ONLY LEAD.
WE'LL TRACK THE DAMNED GHOST DOWN.
I SWEAR IT.
BY MORADIN'S HAMMER AND BRUENOR'S AXE, I **SWEAR** IT.

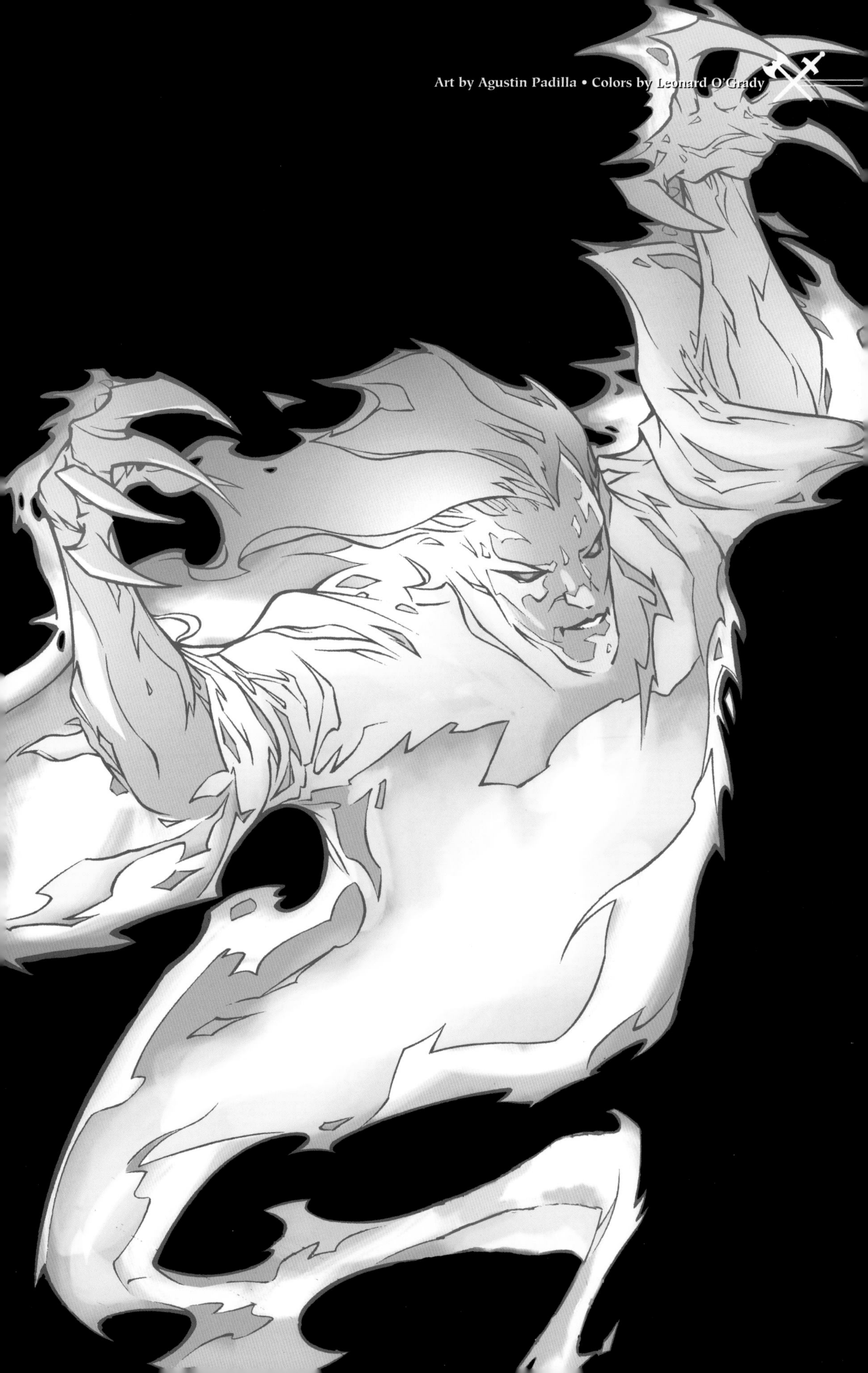

Art by Agustin Padilla • Colors by Leonard O'Grady

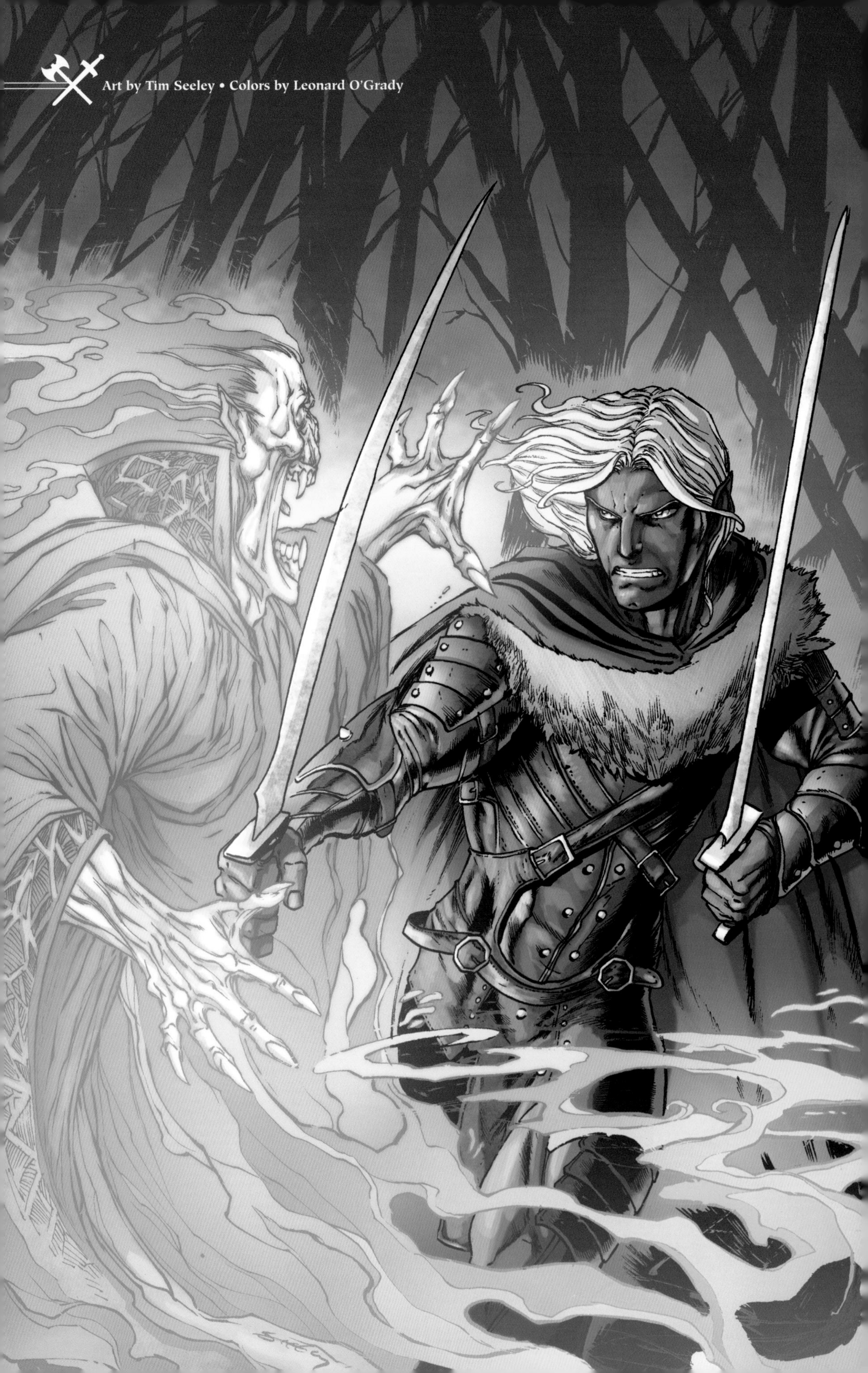

Art by Tim Seeley • Colors by Leonard O'Grady

CHAPTER 5

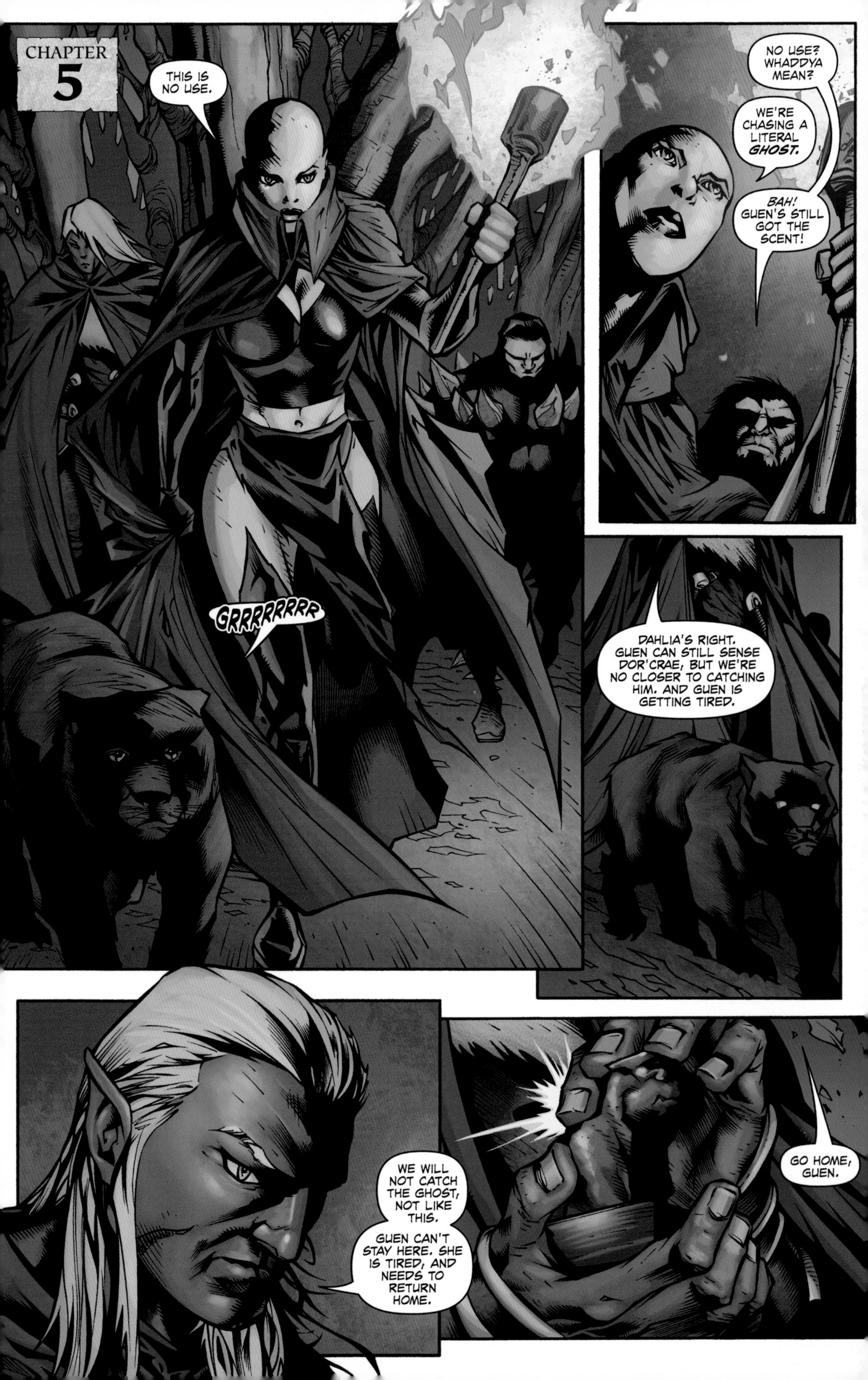
THIS IS NO USE.
GRRRRRRRR
NO USE? WHADDYA MEAN?
WE'RE CHASING A LITERAL GHOST.
BAH! GUEN'S STILL GOT THE SCENT!
DAHLIA'S RIGHT. GUEN CAN STILL SENSE DOR'CRAE, BUT WE'RE NO CLOSER TO CATCHING HIM. AND GUEN IS GETTING TIRED.
WE WILL NOT CATCH THE GHOST, NOT LIKE THIS.
GUEN CAN'T STAY HERE. SHE IS TIRED, AND NEEDS TO RETURN HOME.
GO HOME, GUEN.

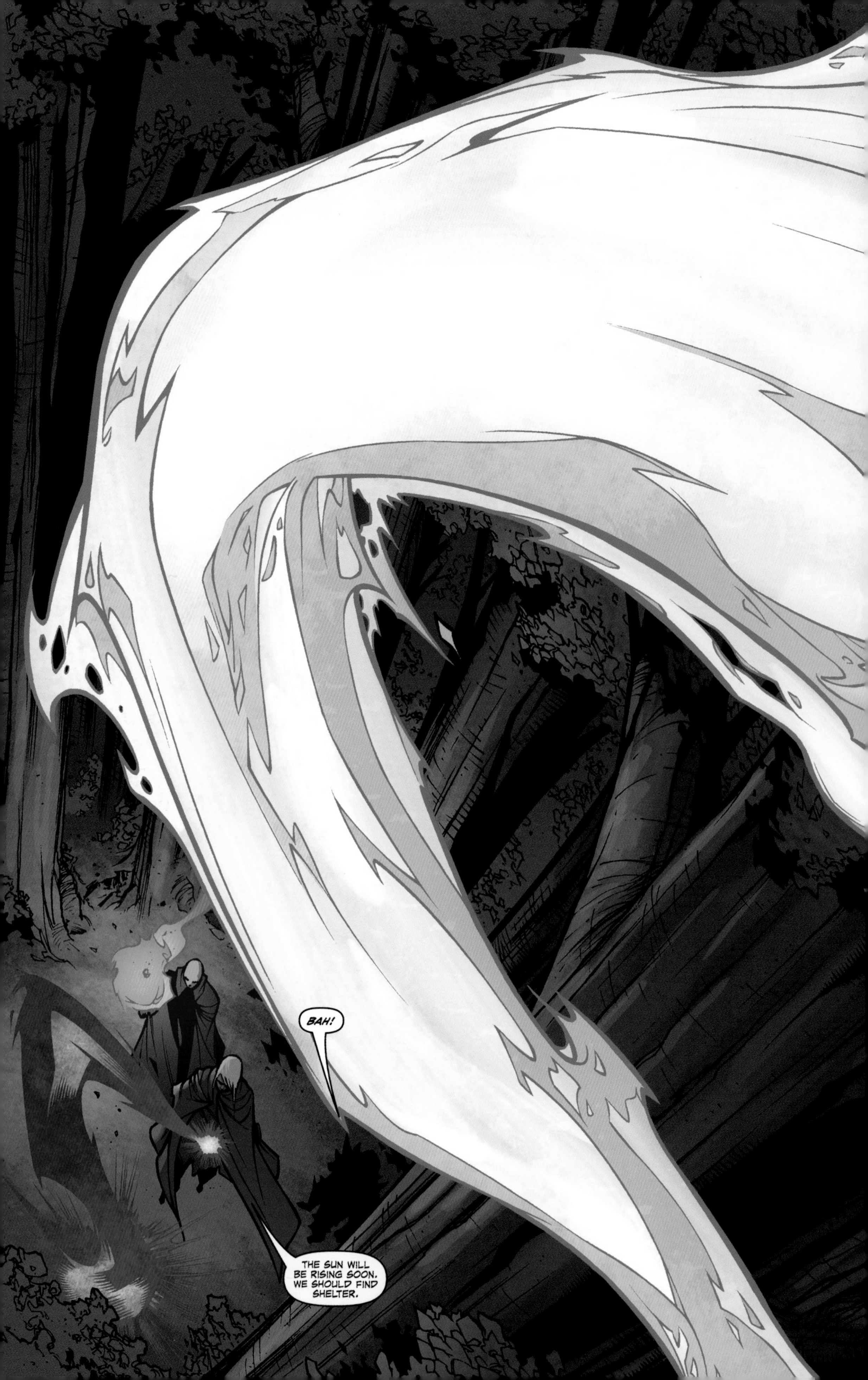
BAH!
THE SUN WILL BE RISING SOON. WE SHOULD FIND SHELTER.

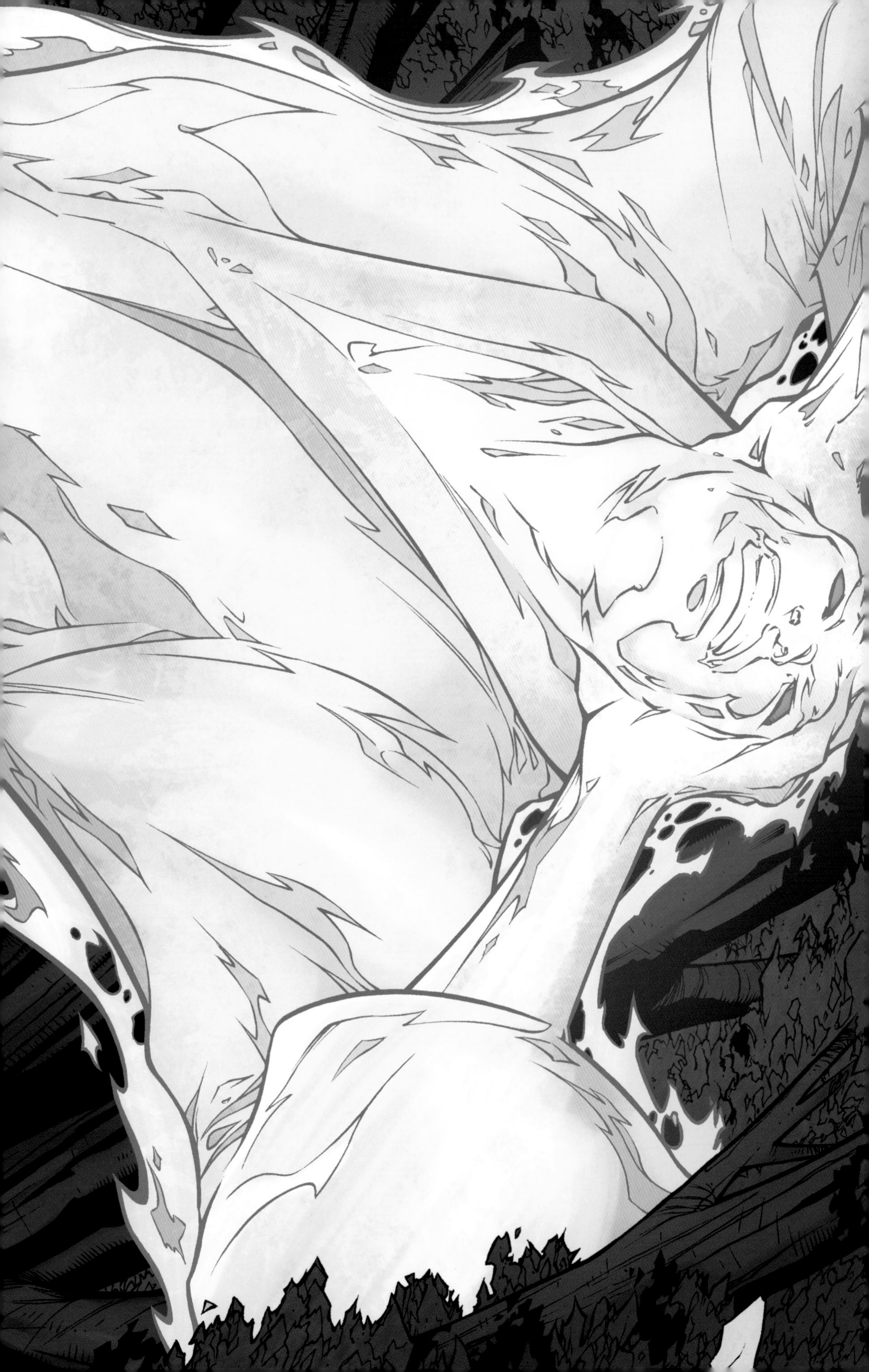

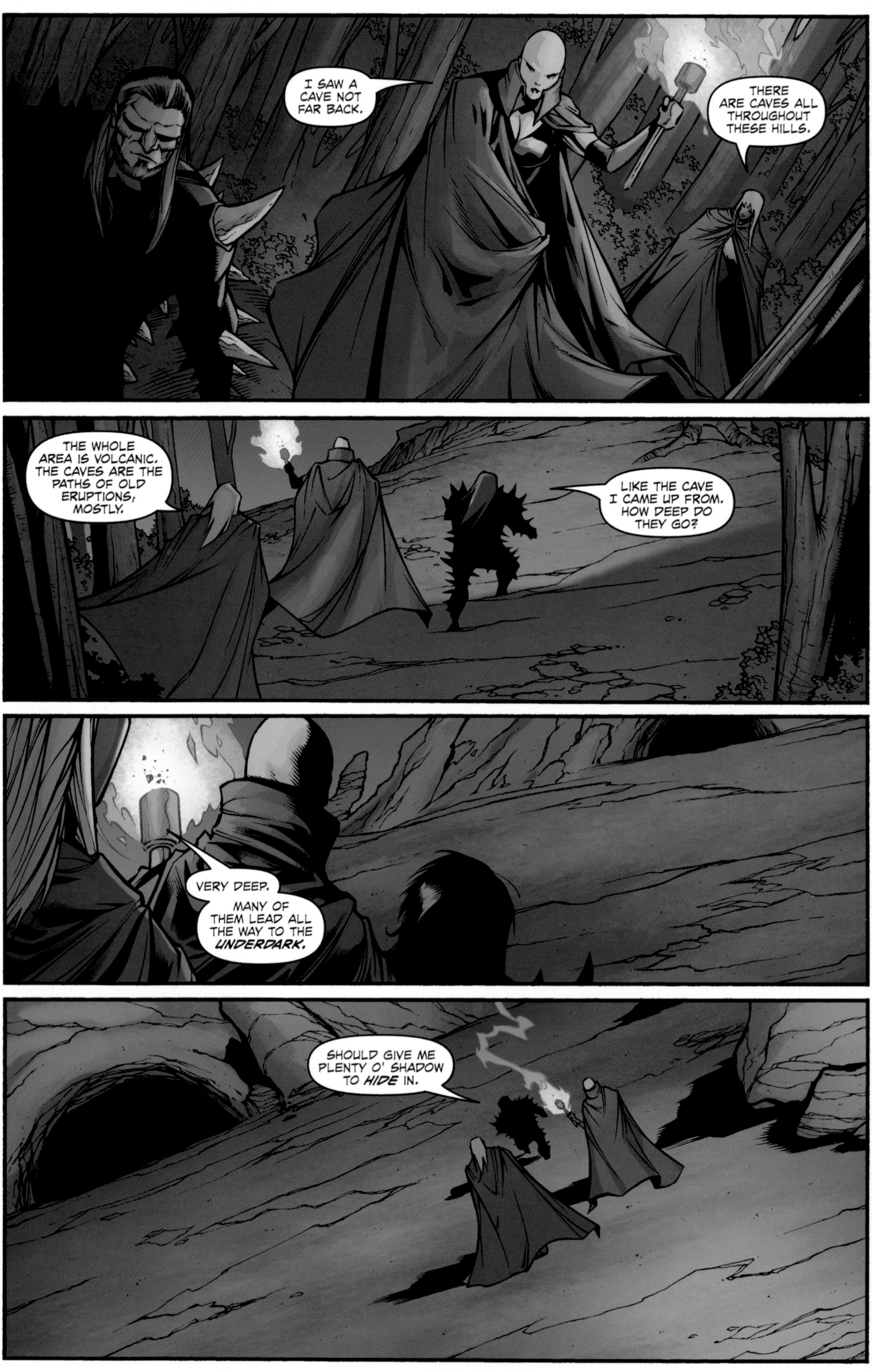
I SAW A CAVE NOT FAR BACK.
THERE ARE CAVES ALL THROUGHOUT THESE HILLS.
THE WHOLE AREA IS VOLCANIC. THE CAVES ARE THE PATHS OF OLD ERUPTIONS, MOSTLY.
LIKE THE CAVE I CAME UP FROM. HOW DEEP DO THEY GO?
VERY DEEP.
MANY OF THEM LEAD ALL THE WAY TO THE UNDERDARK.
SHOULD GIVE ME PLENTY O' SHADOW TO HIDE IN.

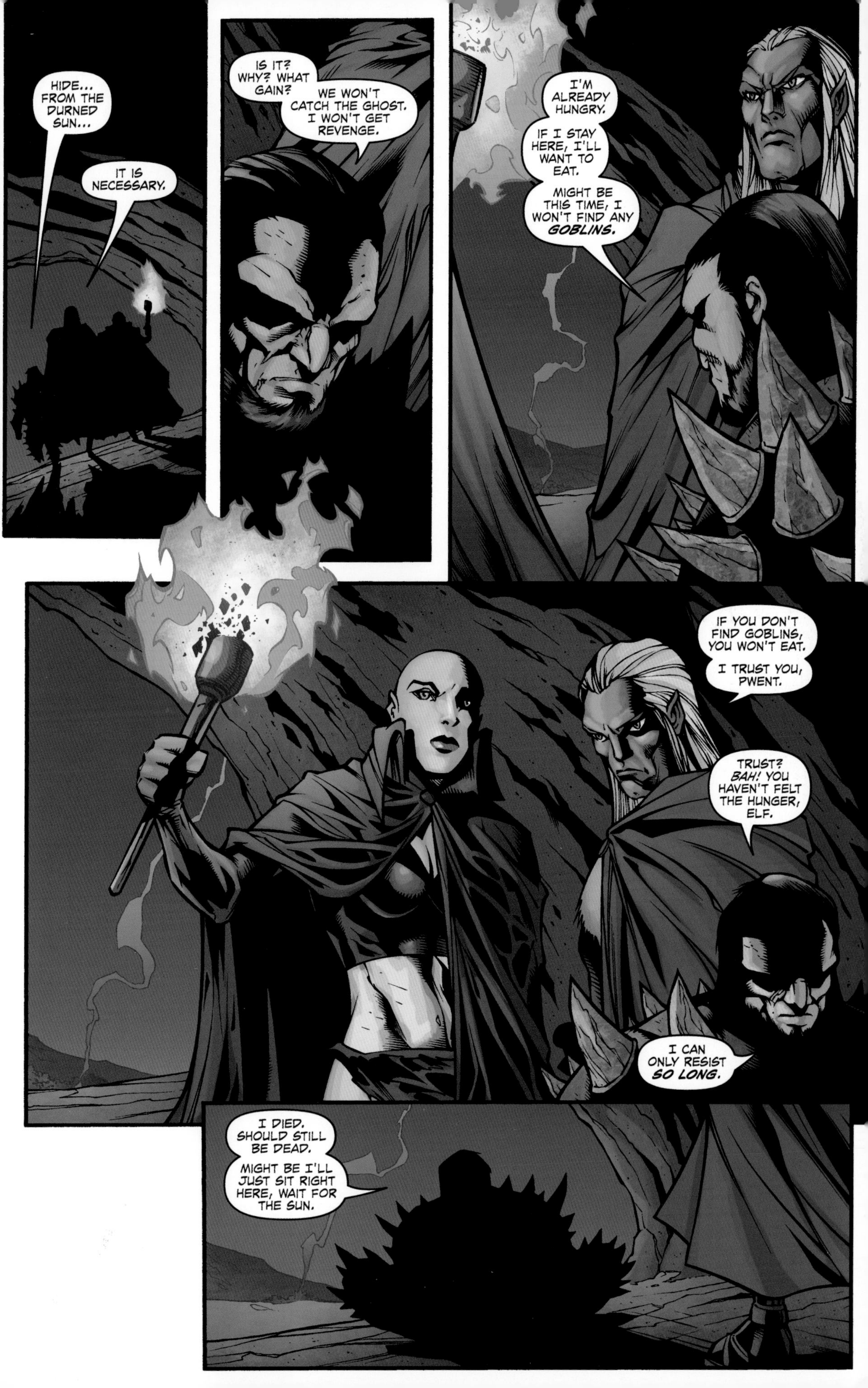
HIDE... FROM THE DURNED SUN...
IT IS NECESSARY.
IS IT? WHY? WHAT GAIN?
WE WON'T CATCH THE GHOST. I WON'T GET REVENGE.
I'M ALREADY HUNGRY.
IF I STAY HERE, I'LL WANT TO EAT.
MIGHT BE THIS TIME, I WON'T FIND ANY ***GOBLINS.***
IF YOU DON'T FIND GOBLINS, YOU WON'T EAT.
I TRUST YOU, PWENT.
TRUST? *BAH!* YOU HAVEN'T FELT THE HUNGER, ELF.
I CAN ONLY RESIST ***SO LONG.***
I DIED. SHOULD STILL BE DEAD.
MIGHT BE I'LL JUST SIT RIGHT HERE, WAIT FOR THE SUN.

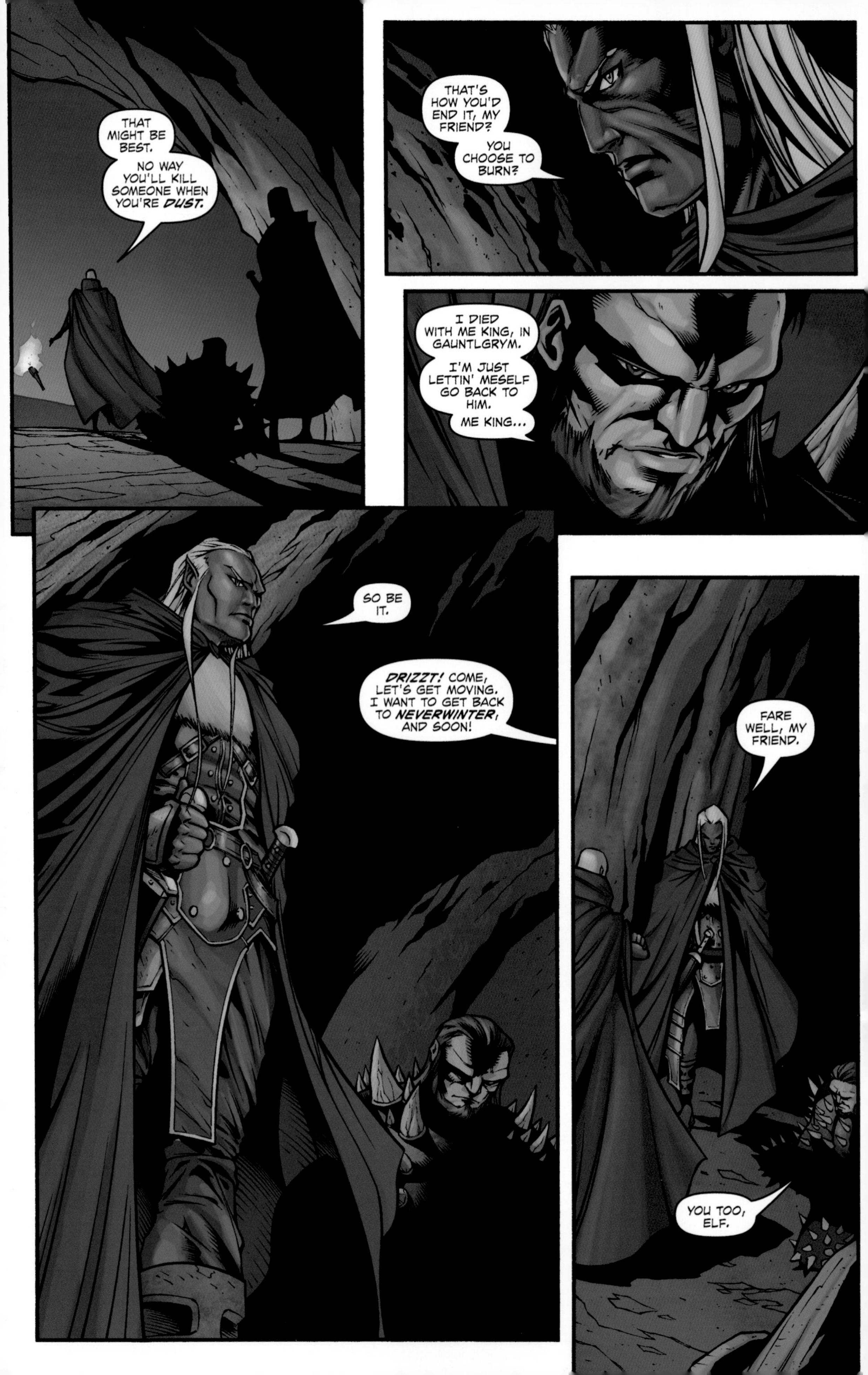
THAT MIGHT BE BEST.
NO WAY YOU'LL KILL SOMEONE WHEN YOU'RE *DUST.*
THAT'S HOW YOU'D END IT, MY FRIEND?
YOU CHOOSE TO BURN?
I DIED WITH ME KING, IN GAUNTLGRYM.
I'M JUST LETTIN' MESELF GO BACK TO HIM.
ME KING...
SO BE IT.
DRIZZT! COME, LET'S GET MOVING. I WANT TO GET BACK TO *NEVERWINTER*, AND SOON!
FARE WELL, MY FRIEND.
YOU TOO, ELF.

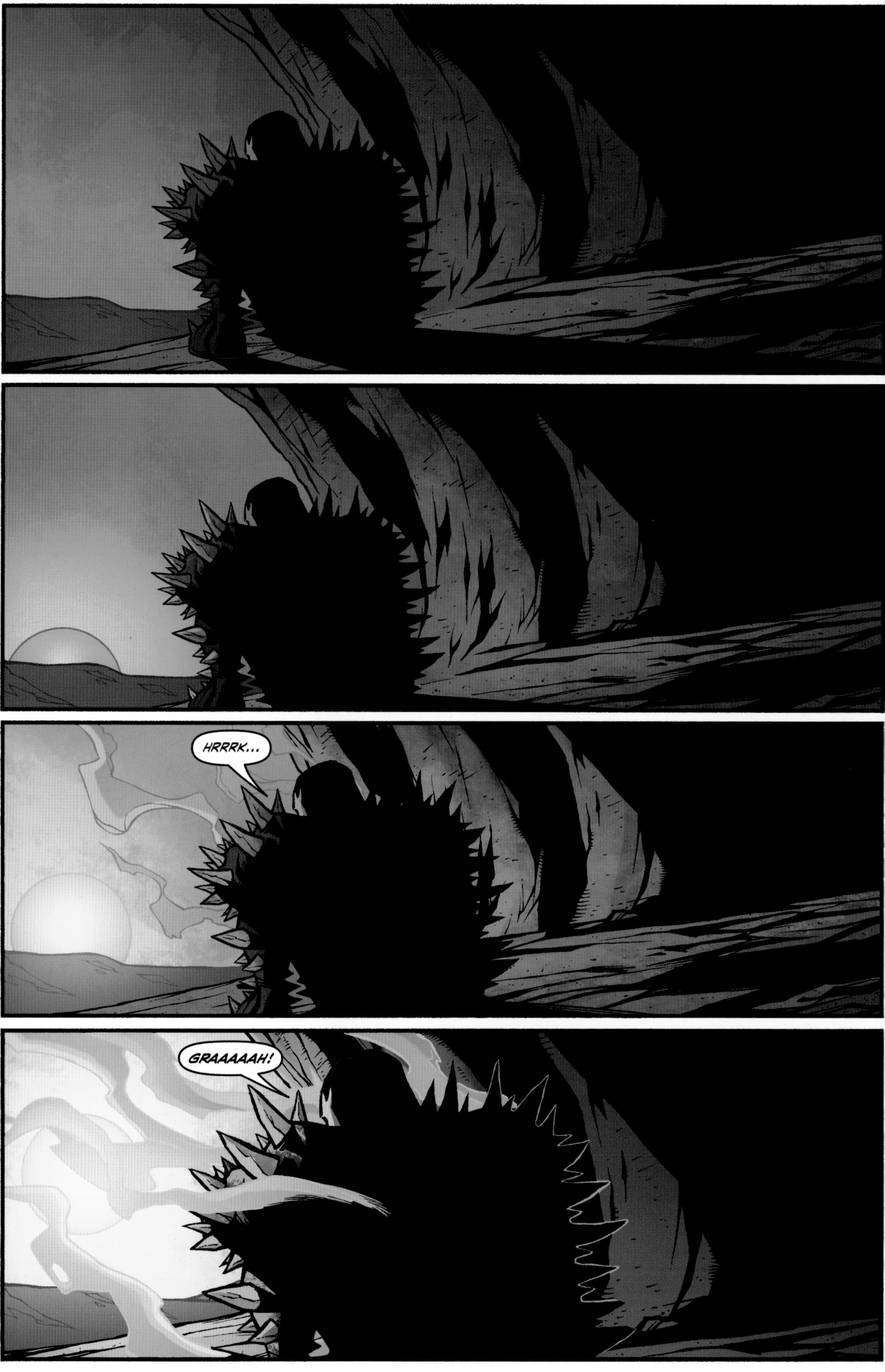
HRRRK...
GRAAAAAH!

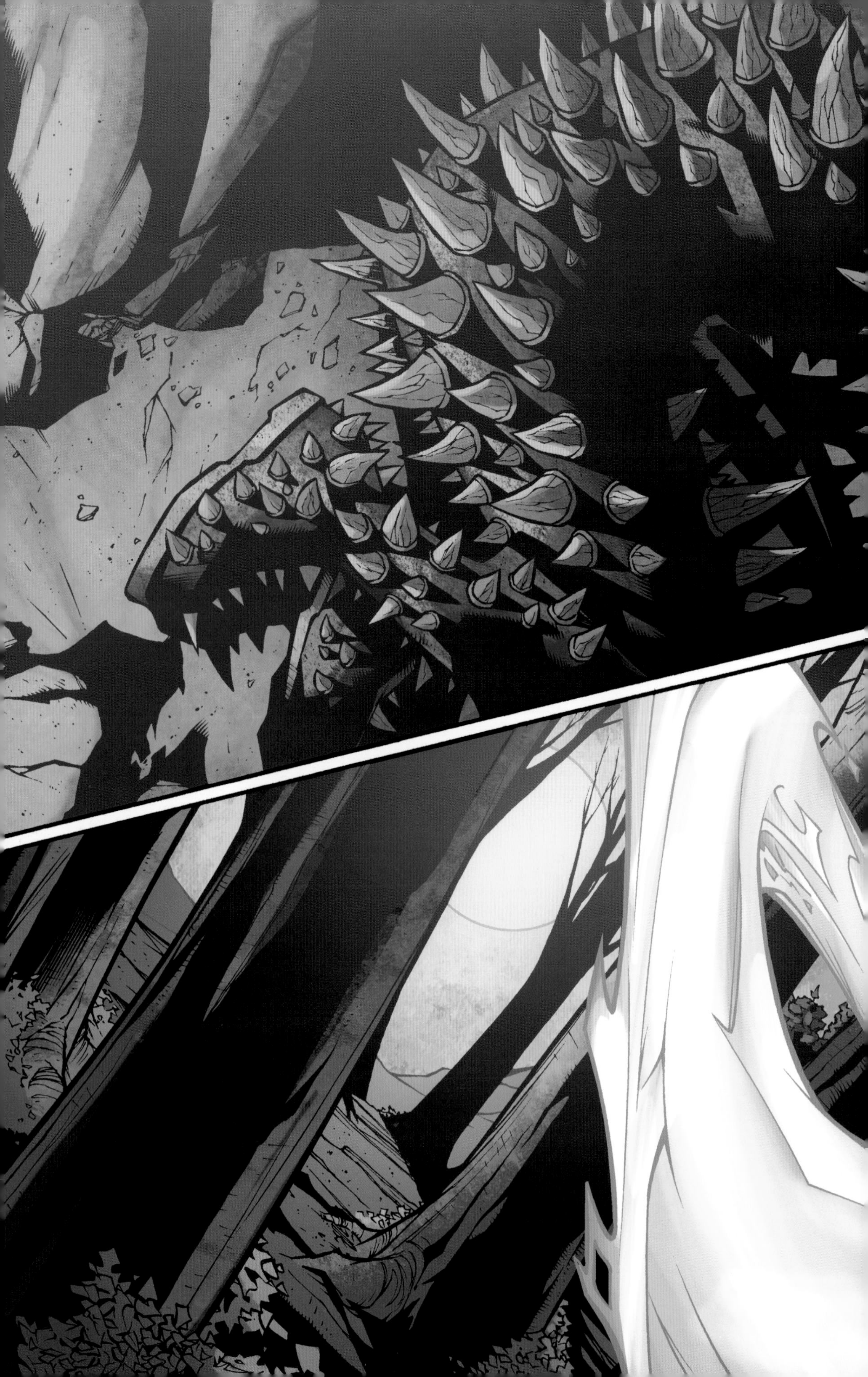

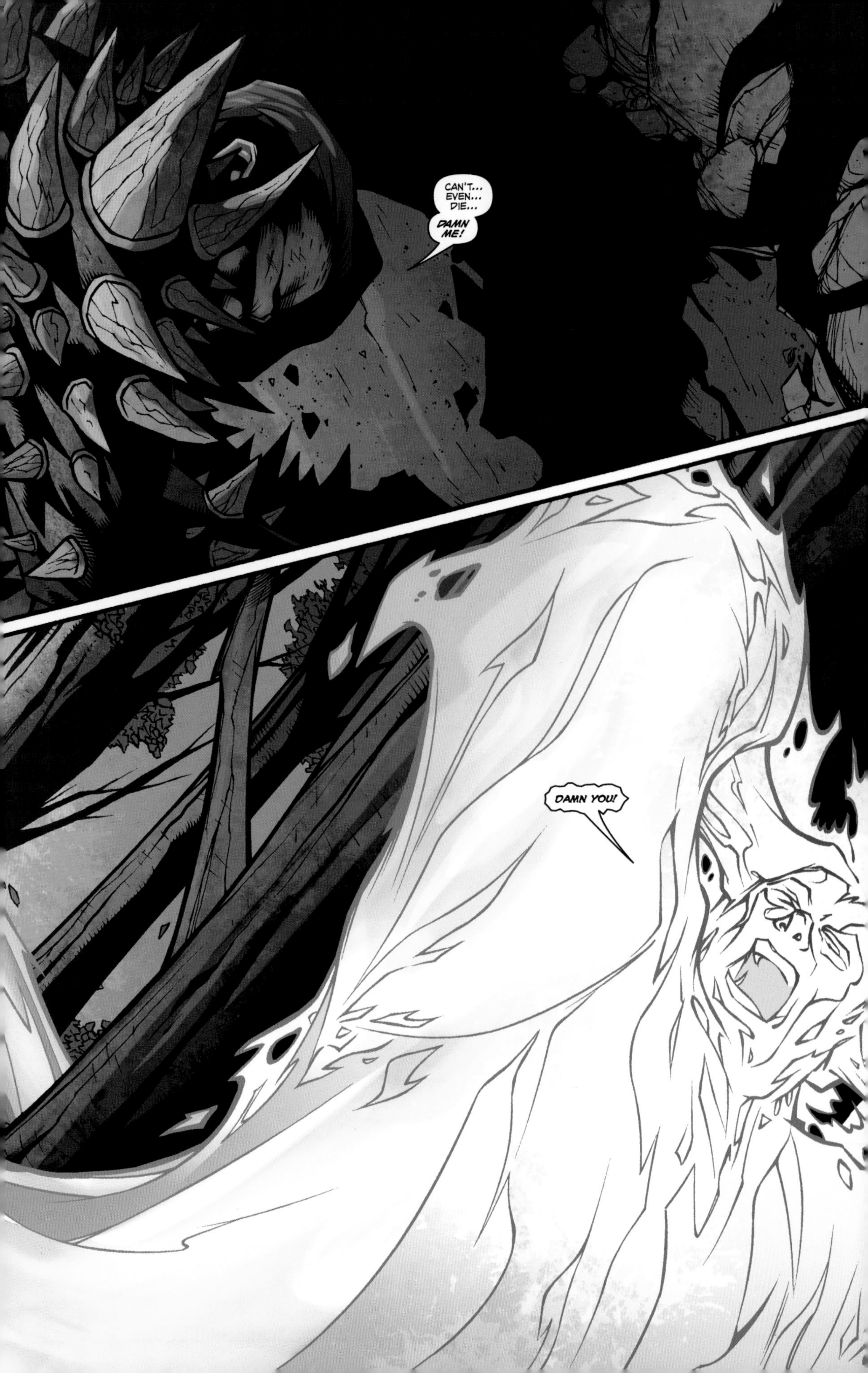
CAN'T... EVEN... DIE...
DAMN ME!
DAMN YOU!

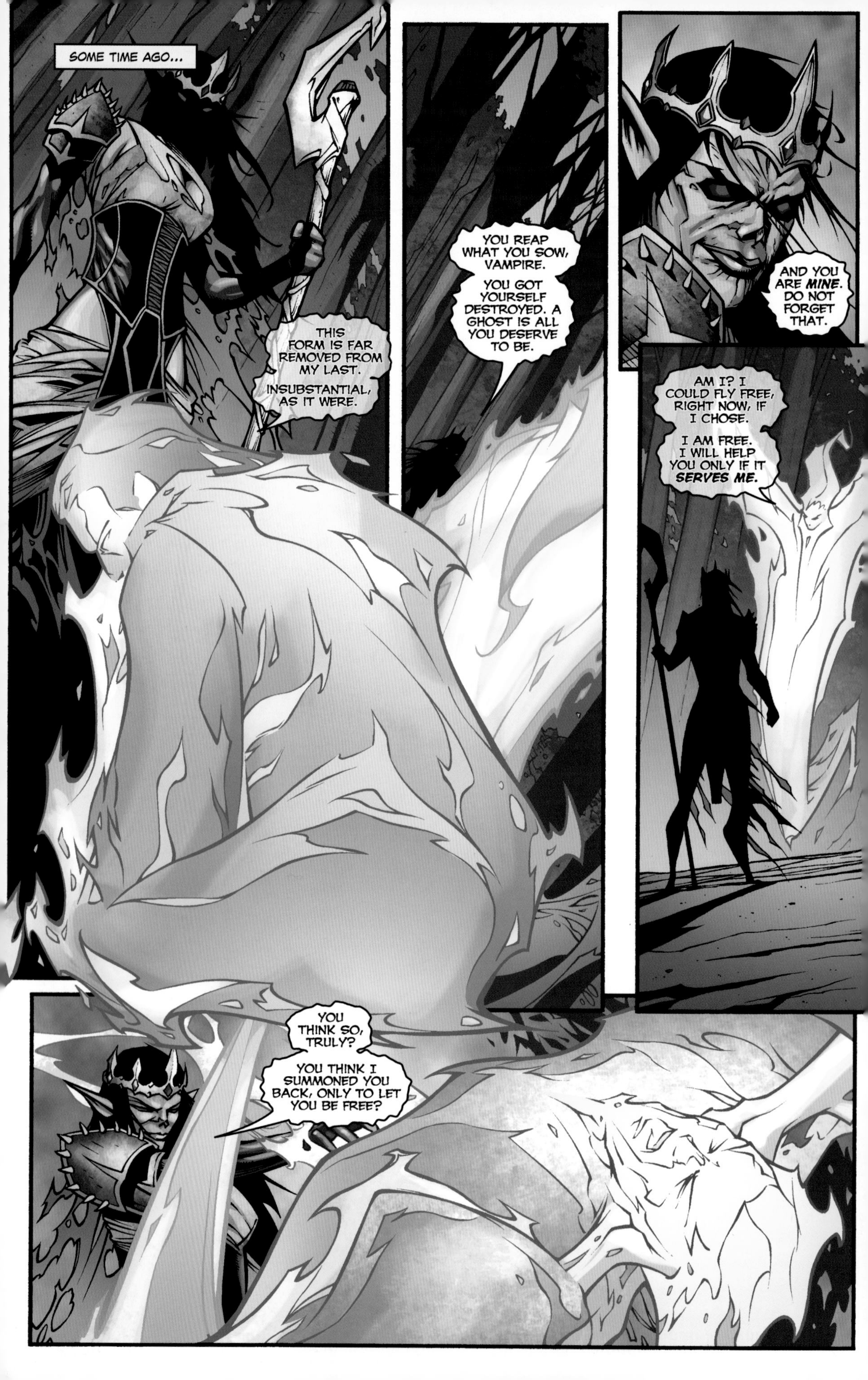

SOME TIME AGO...
THIS FORM IS FAR REMOVED FROM MY LAST.
INSUBSTANTIAL, AS IT WERE.
YOU REAP WHAT YOU SOW, VAMPIRE.
YOU GOT YOURSELF DESTROYED. A GHOST IS ALL YOU DESERVE TO BE.
AND YOU ARE MINE. DO NOT FORGET THAT.
AM I? I COULD FLY FREE, RIGHT NOW, IF I CHOSE.
I AM FREE. I WILL HELP YOU ONLY IF IT SERVES ME.
YOU THINK SO, TRULY?
YOU THINK I SUMMONED YOU BACK, ONLY TO LET YOU BE FREE?

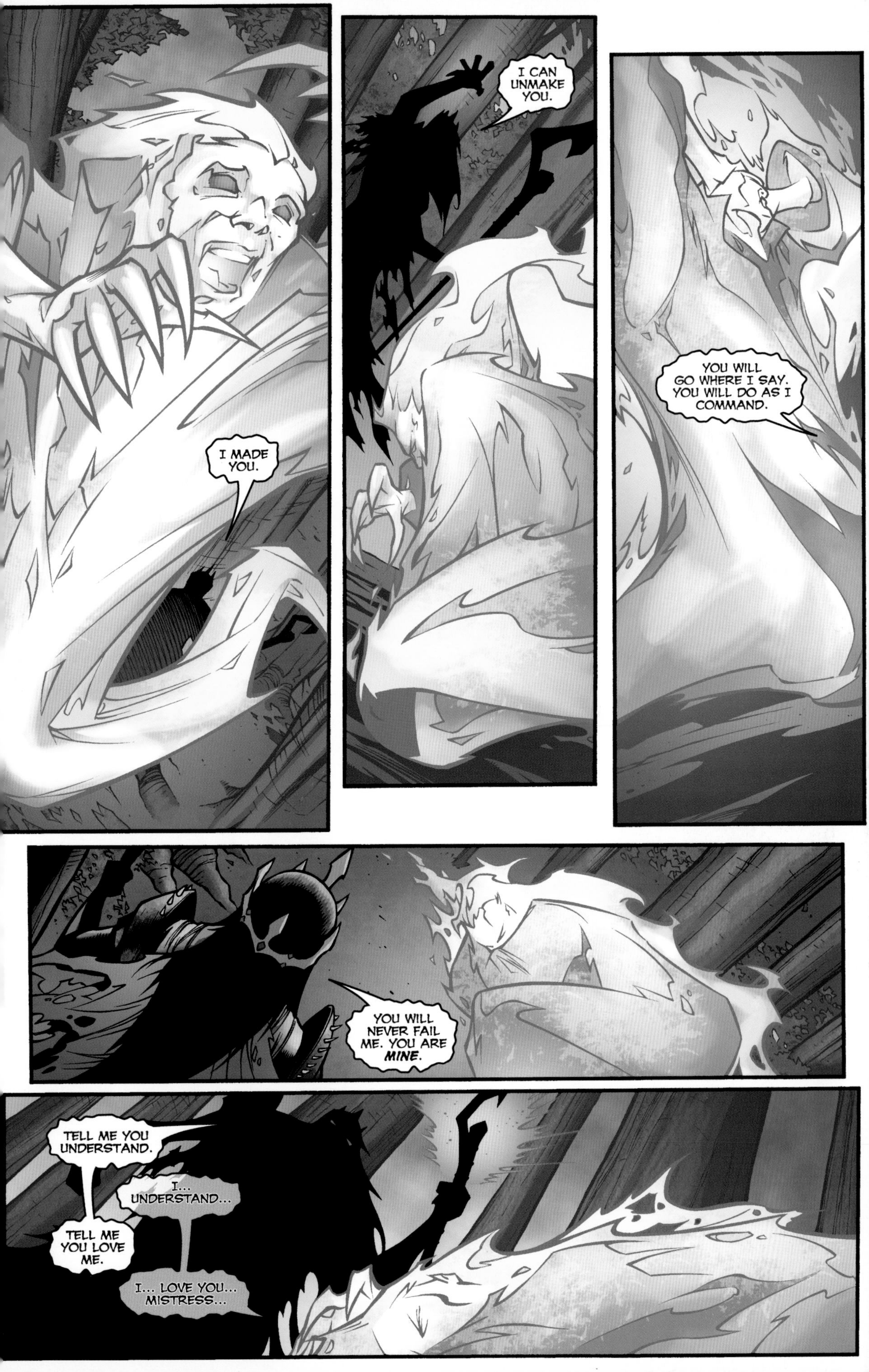
I MADE YOU.
I CAN UNMAKE YOU.
YOU WILL GO WHERE I SAY. YOU WILL DO AS I COMMAND.
YOU WILL NEVER FAIL ME. YOU ARE *MINE*.
TELL ME YOU UNDERSTAND.
I... UNDERSTAND...
TELL ME YOU LOVE ME.
I... LOVE YOU... MISTRESS...

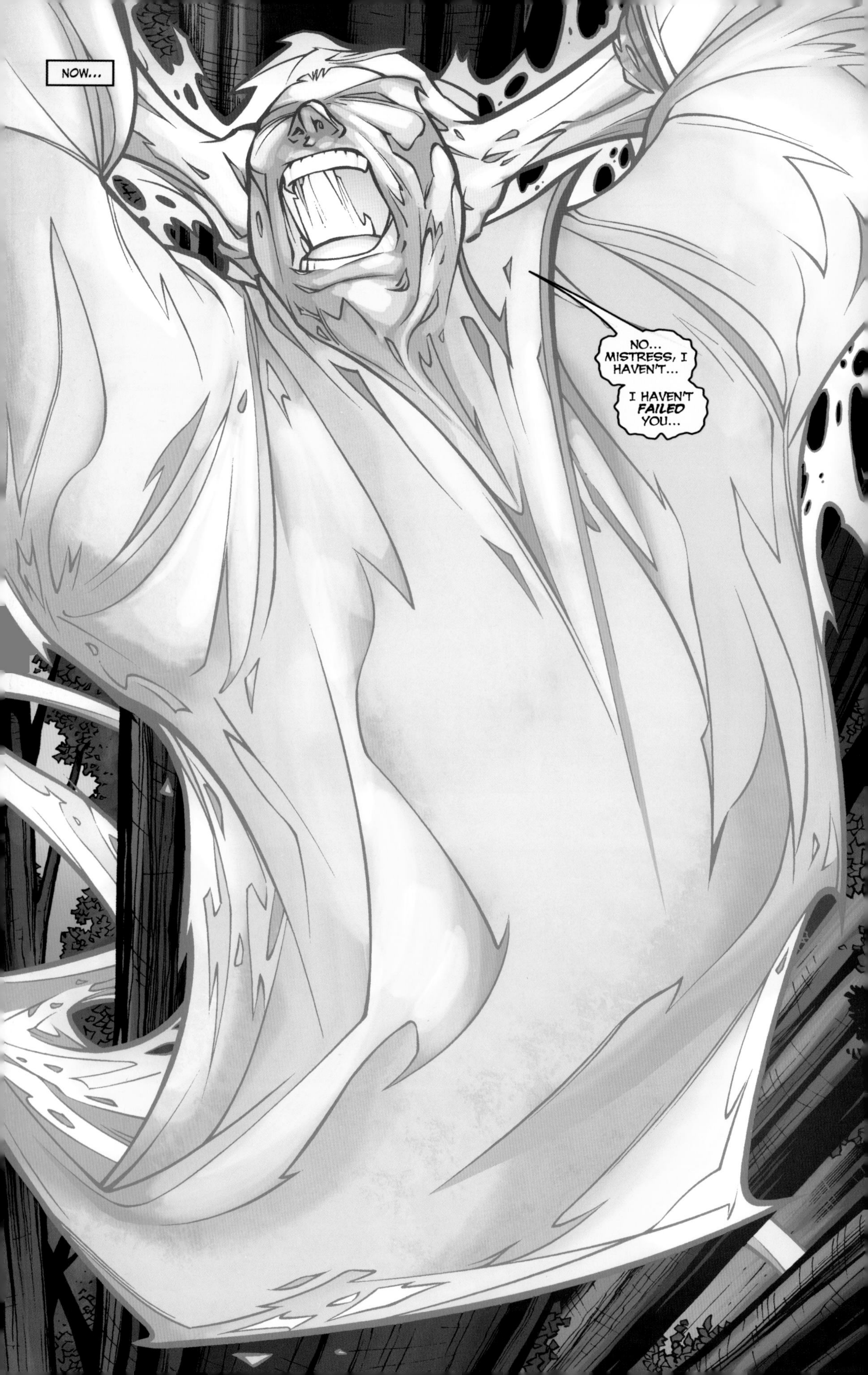
NOW...
NO... MISTRESS, I HAVEN'T...
I HAVEN'T *FAILED* YOU...

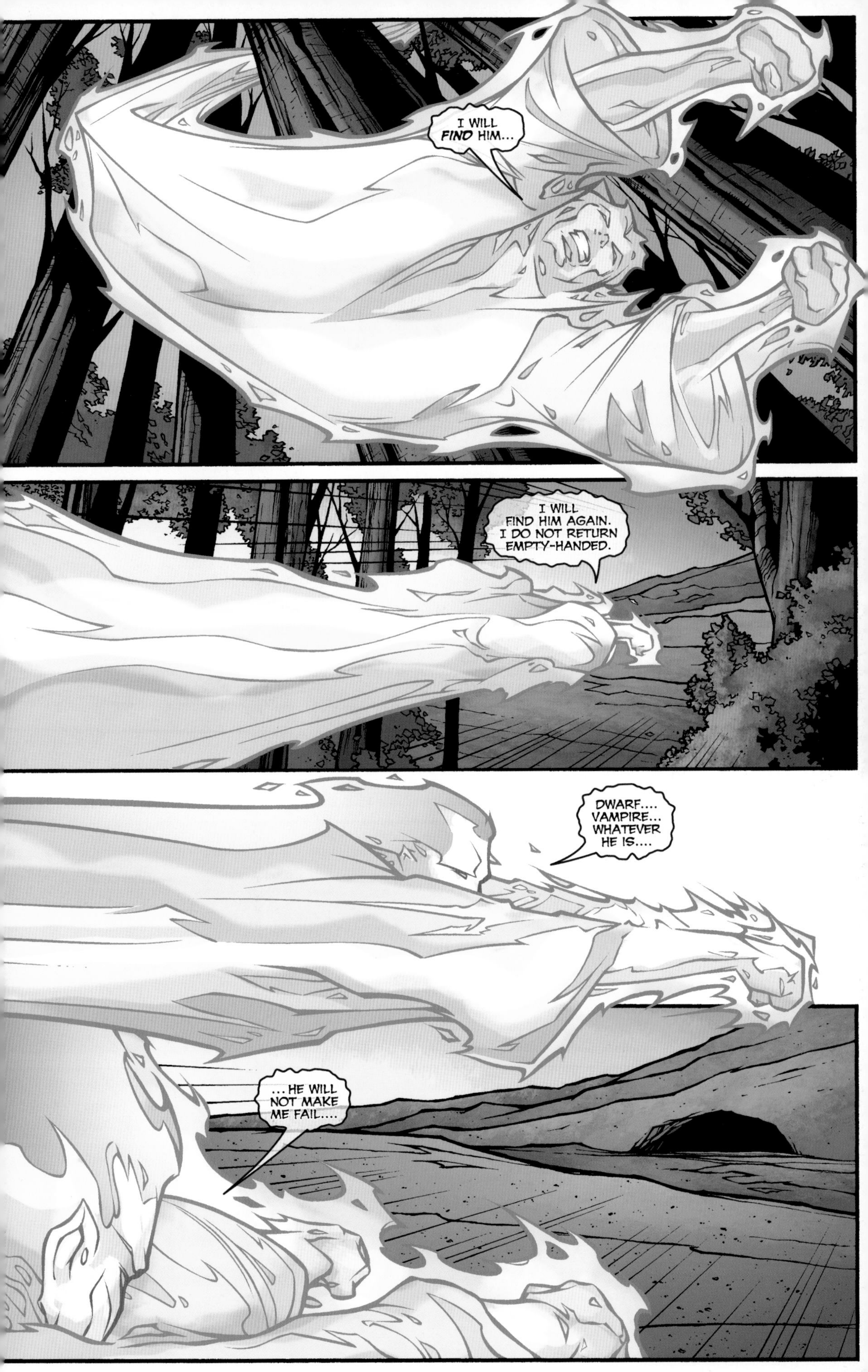
I WILL *FIND* HIM...
I WILL FIND HIM AGAIN. I DO NOT RETURN EMPTY-HANDED.
DWARF.... VAMPIRE... WHATEVER HE IS....
...HE WILL NOT MAKE ME FAIL....

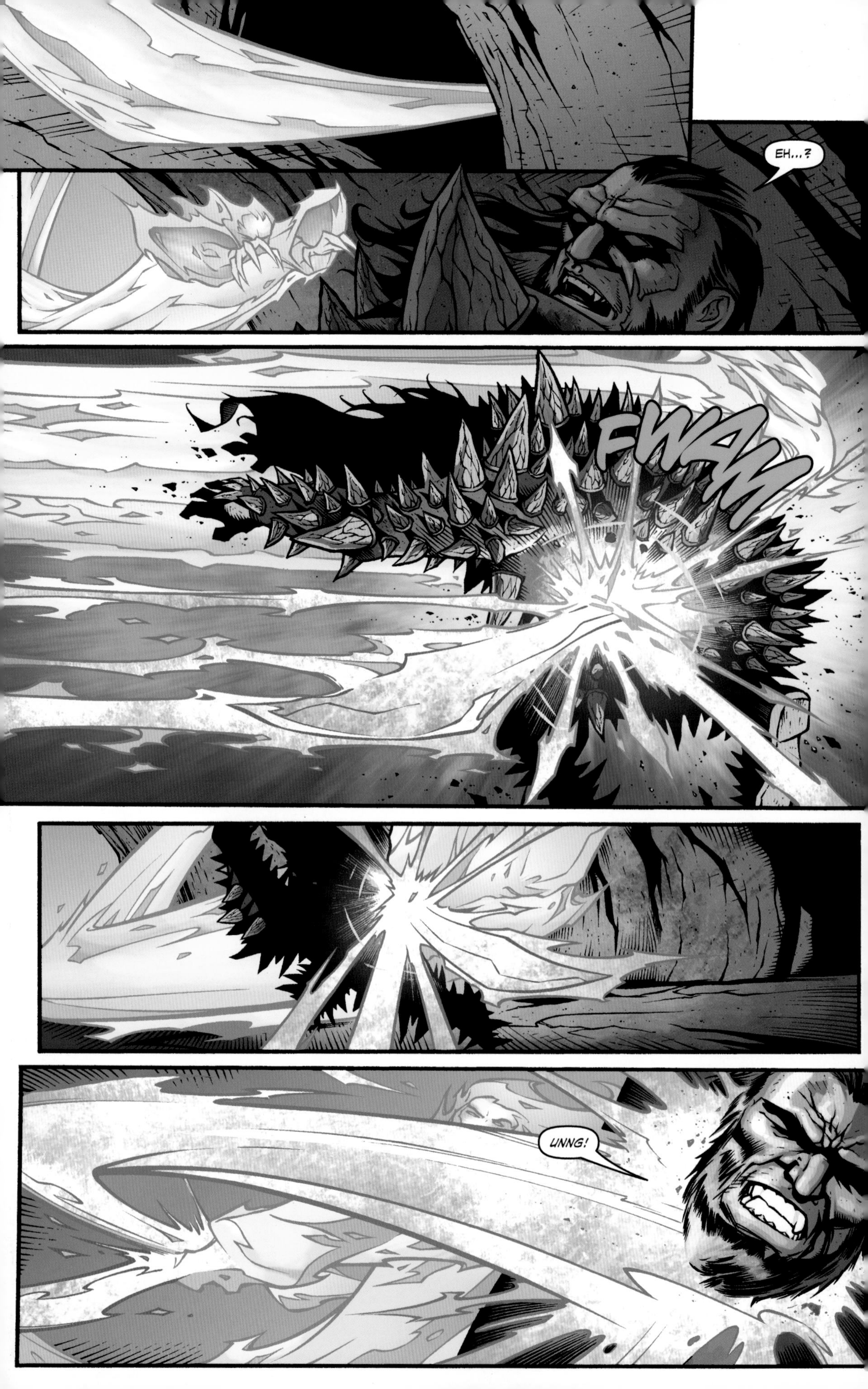
EH...?
FWAM
UNNG!

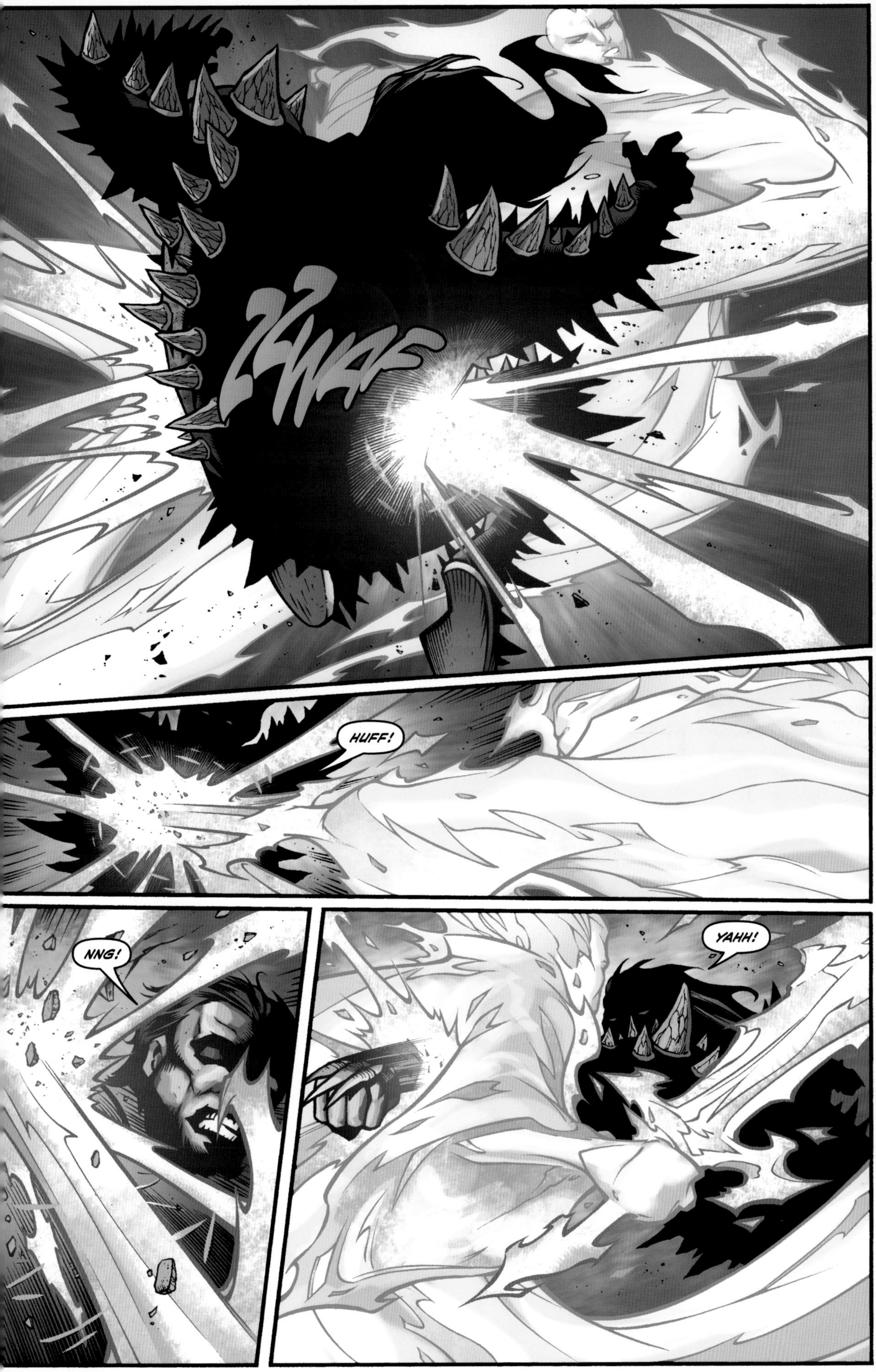
ZWAF
HUFF!
NNG!
YAHH!

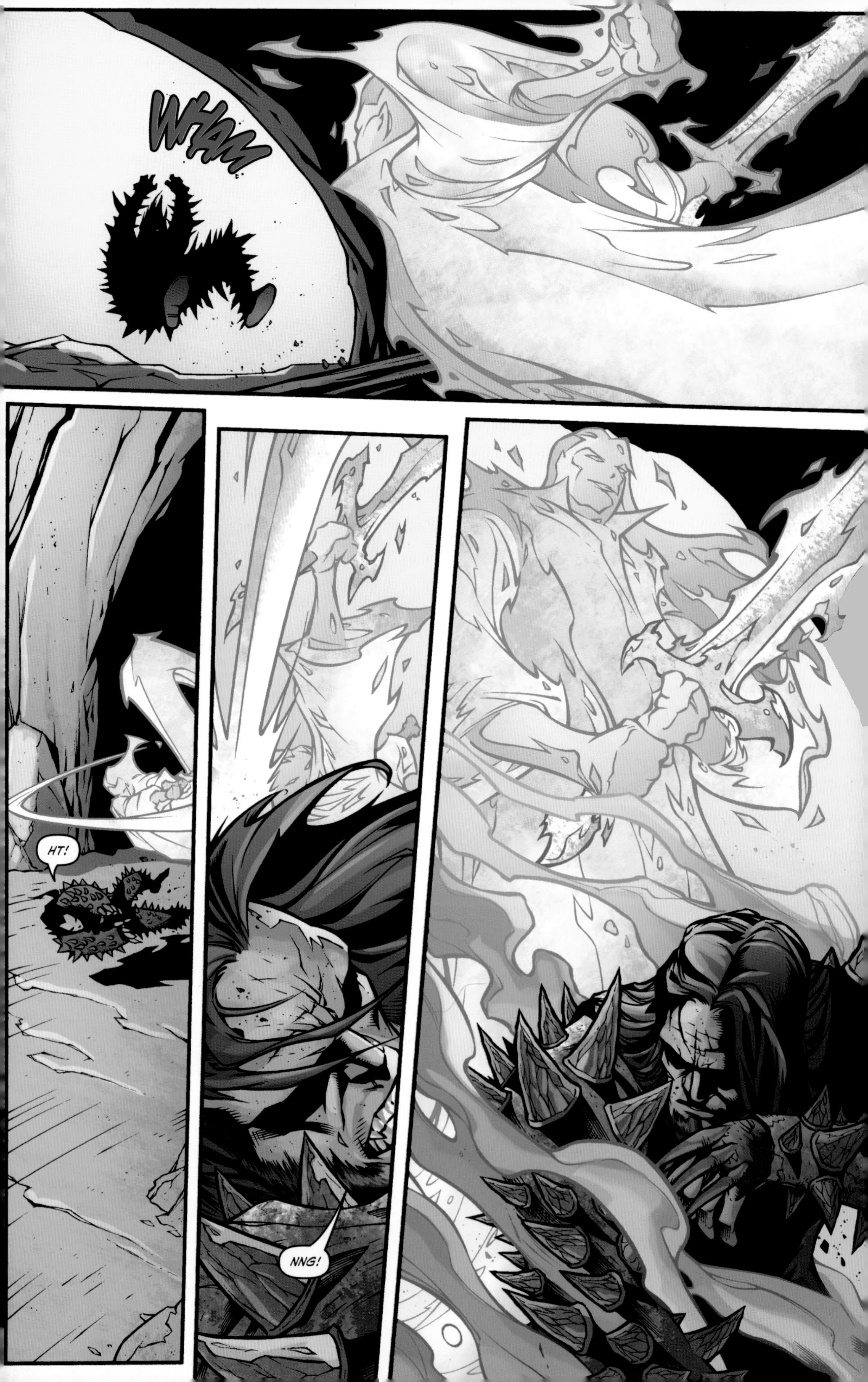
WHAM
HT!
NNG!

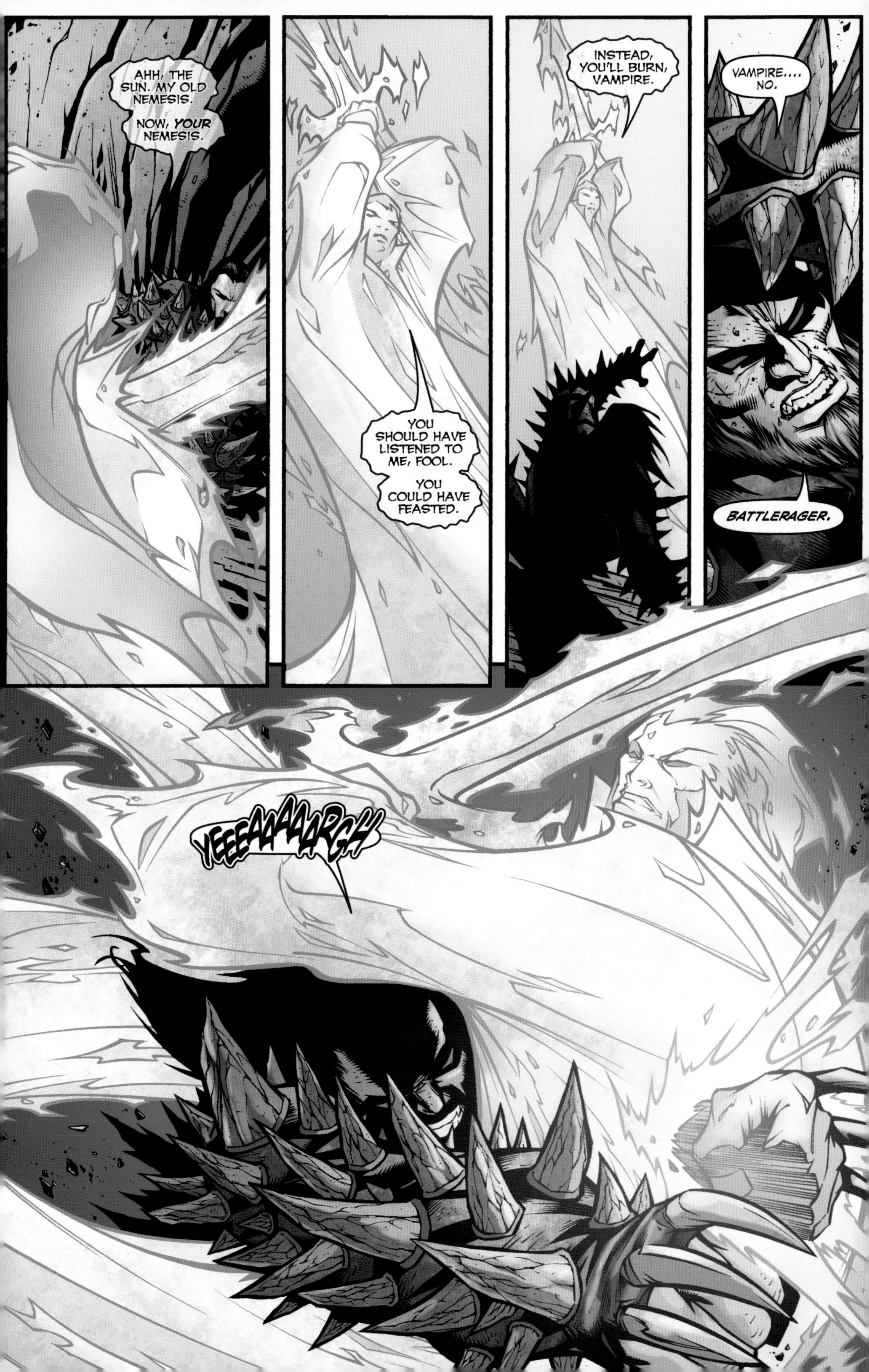
AHH, THE SUN. MY OLD NEMESIS.
NOW, YOUR NEMESIS.
YOU SHOULD HAVE LISTENED TO ME, FOOL.
YOU COULD HAVE FEASTED.
INSTEAD, YOU'LL BURN, VAMPIRE.
VAMPIRE.... NO.
BATTLERAGER.
YEEEAAAAARGH

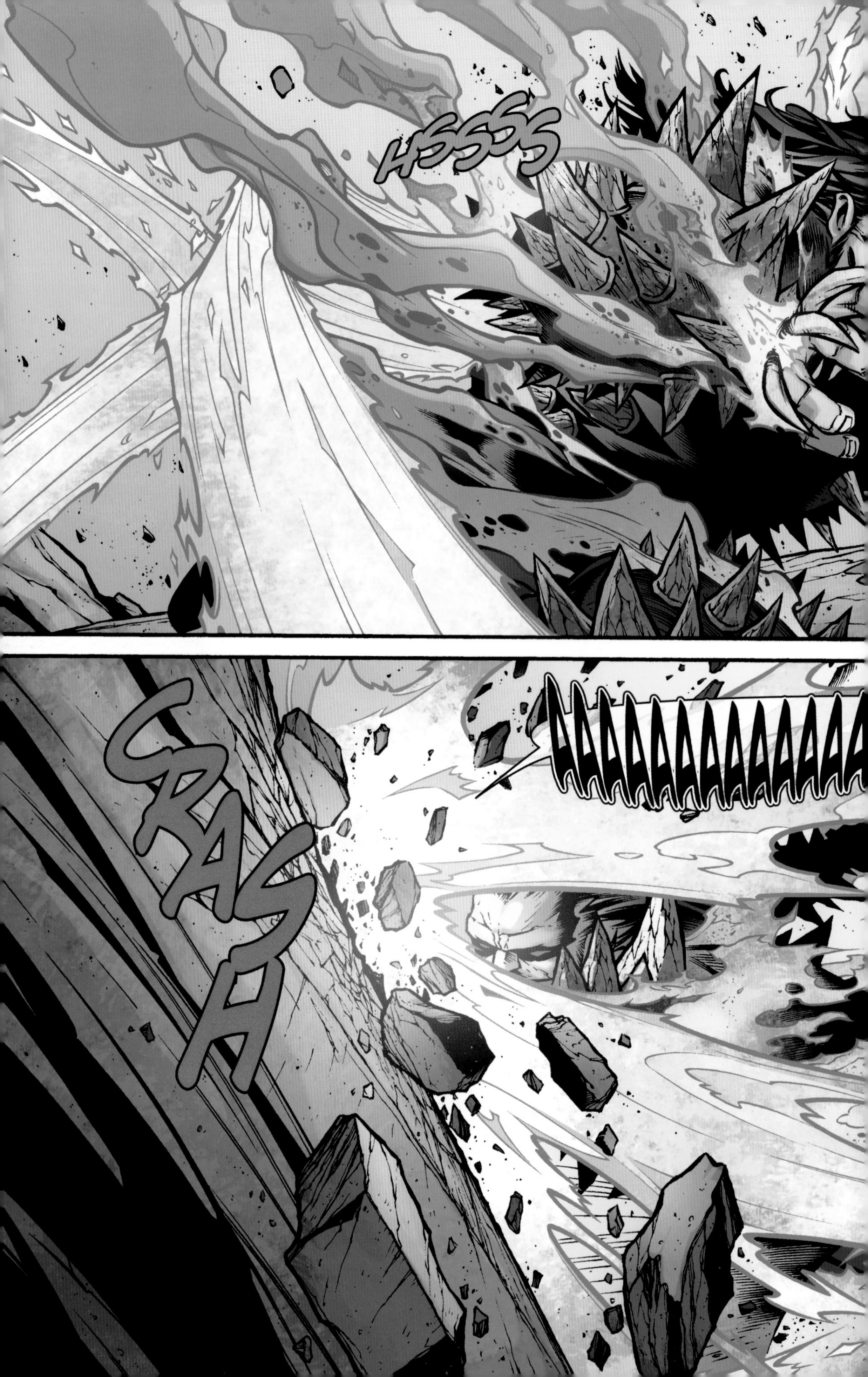
HSSSS
CRASH
AAAAAAAAAAAAA

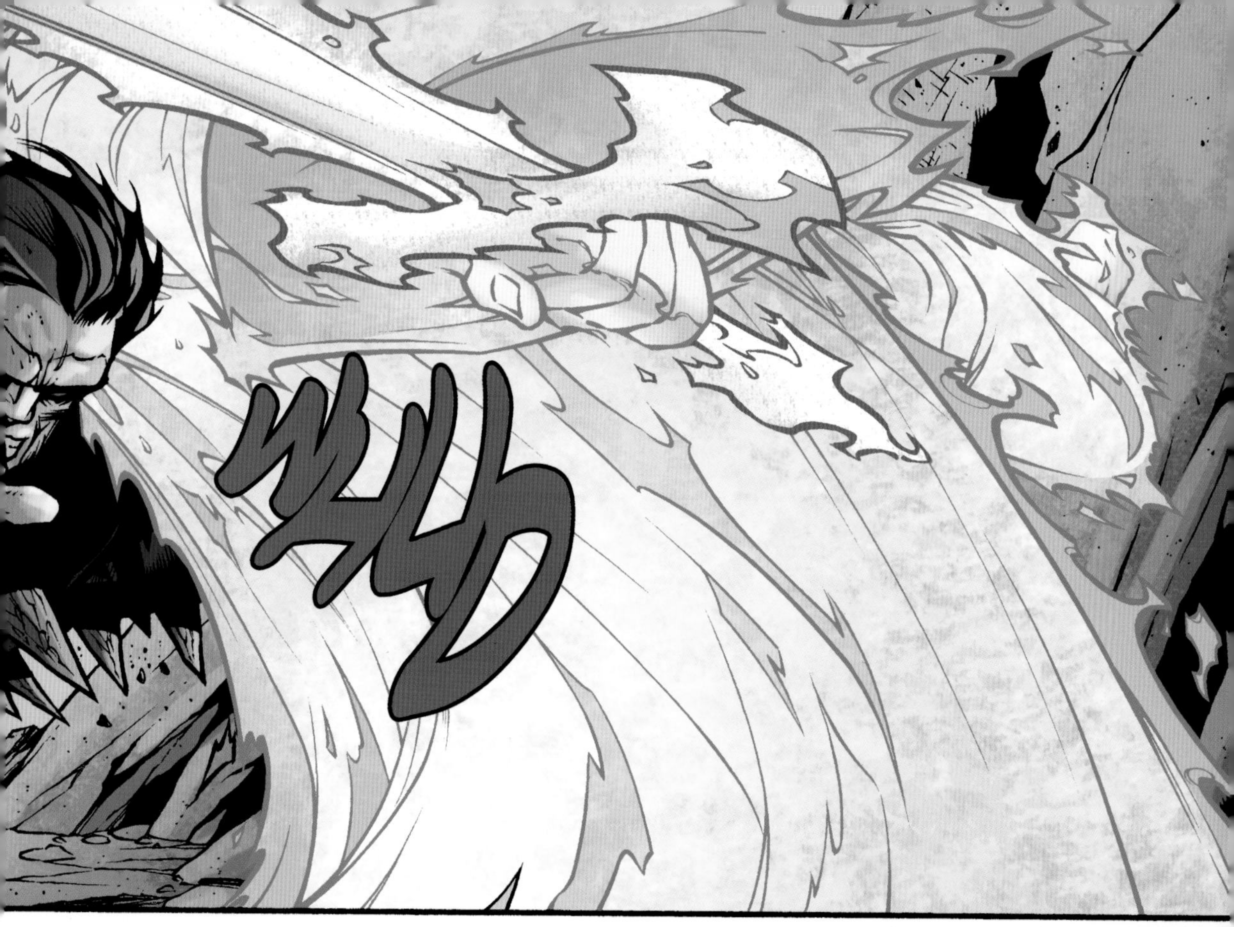
WHUD

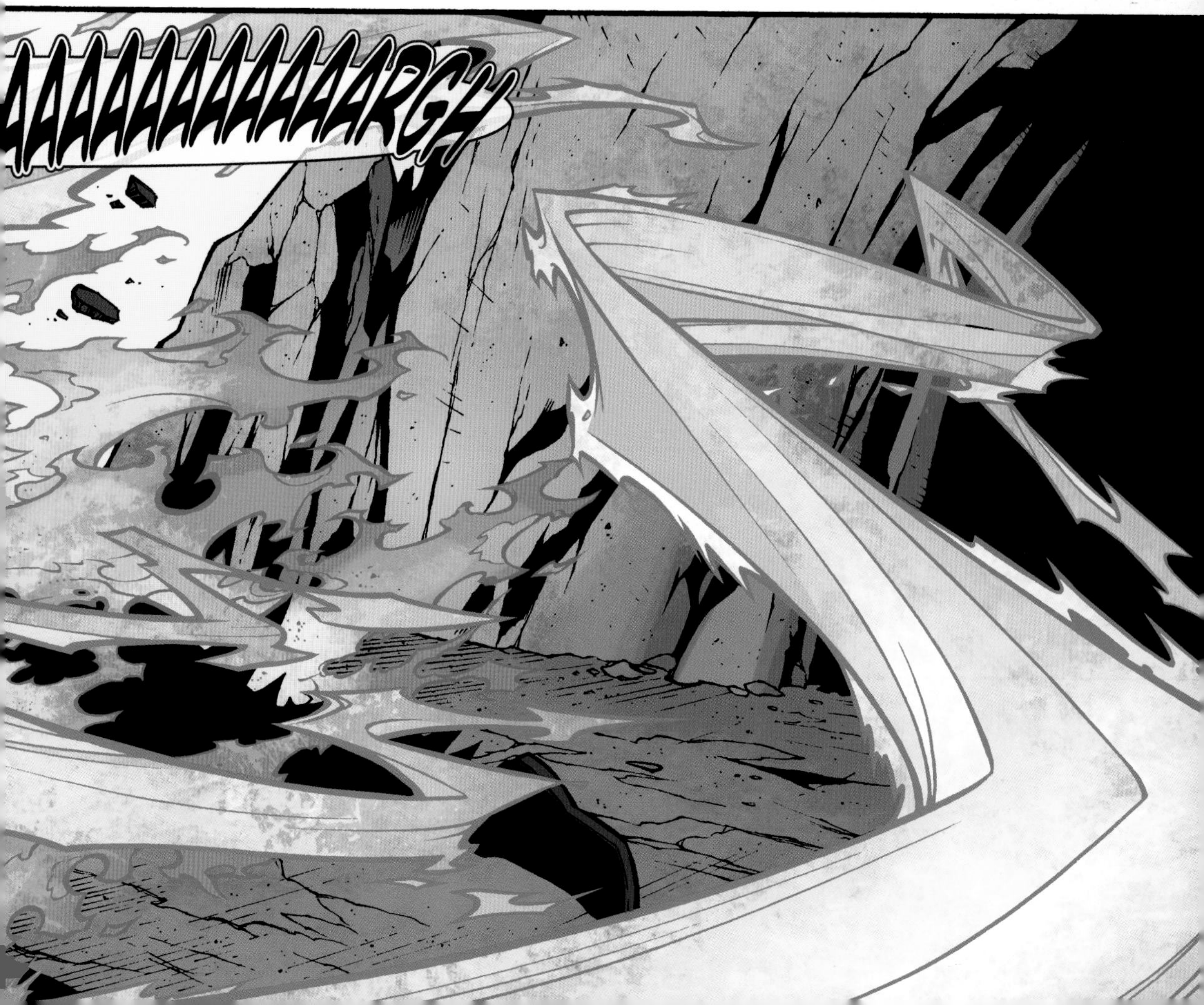
AAAAAAAAAAAAARGH

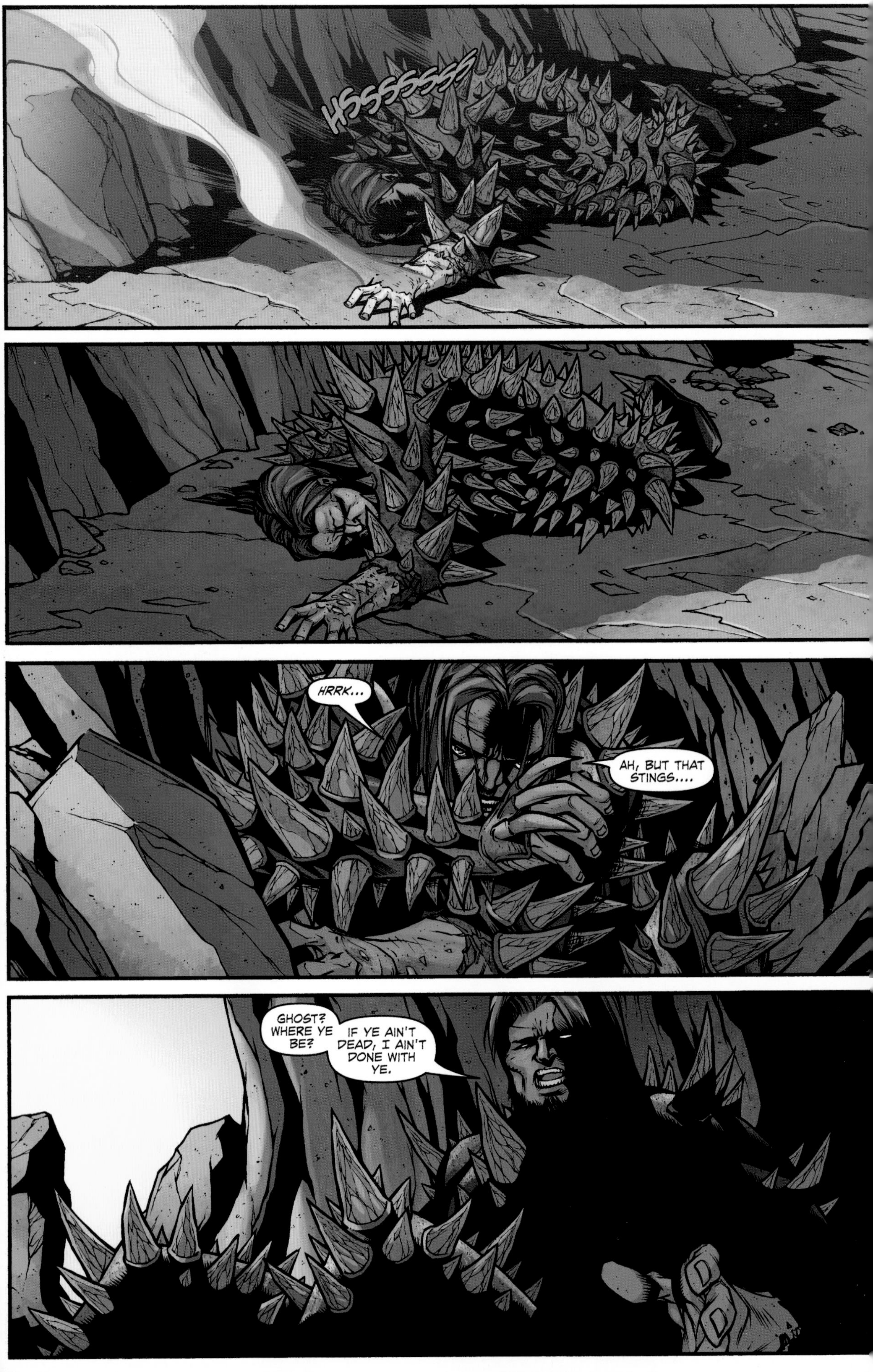
HSSSSSSSS
HRRK...
AH, BUT THAT STINGS....
GHOST? WHERE YE BE?
IF YE AIN'T DEAD, I AIN'T DONE WITH YE.

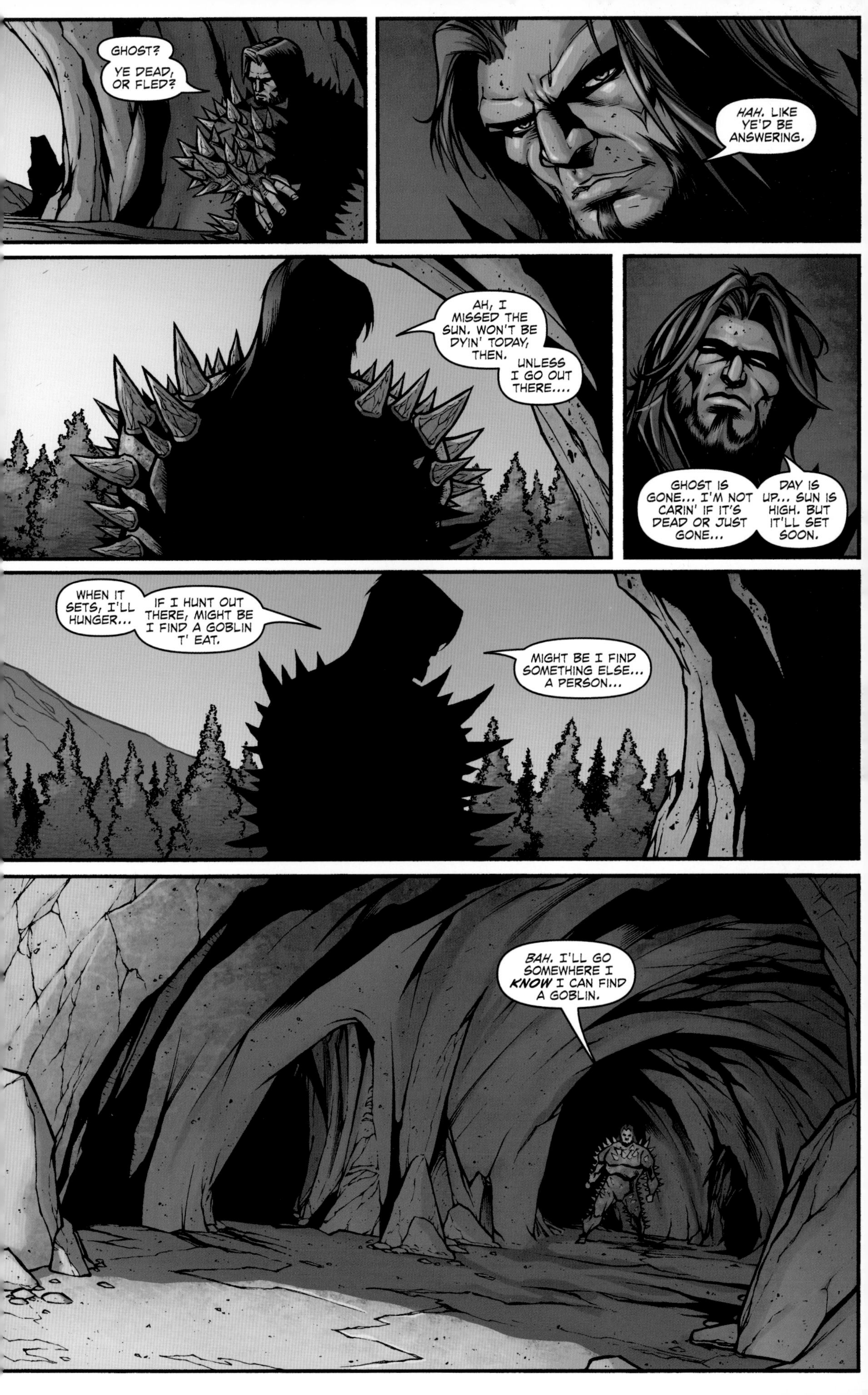
GHOST?
YE DEAD, OR FLED?
HAH. LIKE YE'D BE ANSWERING.
AH, I MISSED THE SUN. WON'T BE DYIN' TODAY, THEN.
UNLESS I GO OUT THERE....
GHOST IS GONE... I'M NOT CARIN' IF IT'S DEAD OR JUST GONE...
DAY IS UP... SUN IS HIGH. BUT IT'LL SET SOON.
WHEN IT SETS, I'LL HUNGER...
IF I HUNT OUT THERE, MIGHT BE I FIND A GOBLIN T' EAT.
MIGHT BE I FIND SOMETHING ELSE... A PERSON...
BAH. I'LL GO SOMEWHERE I KNOW I CAN FIND A GOBLIN.

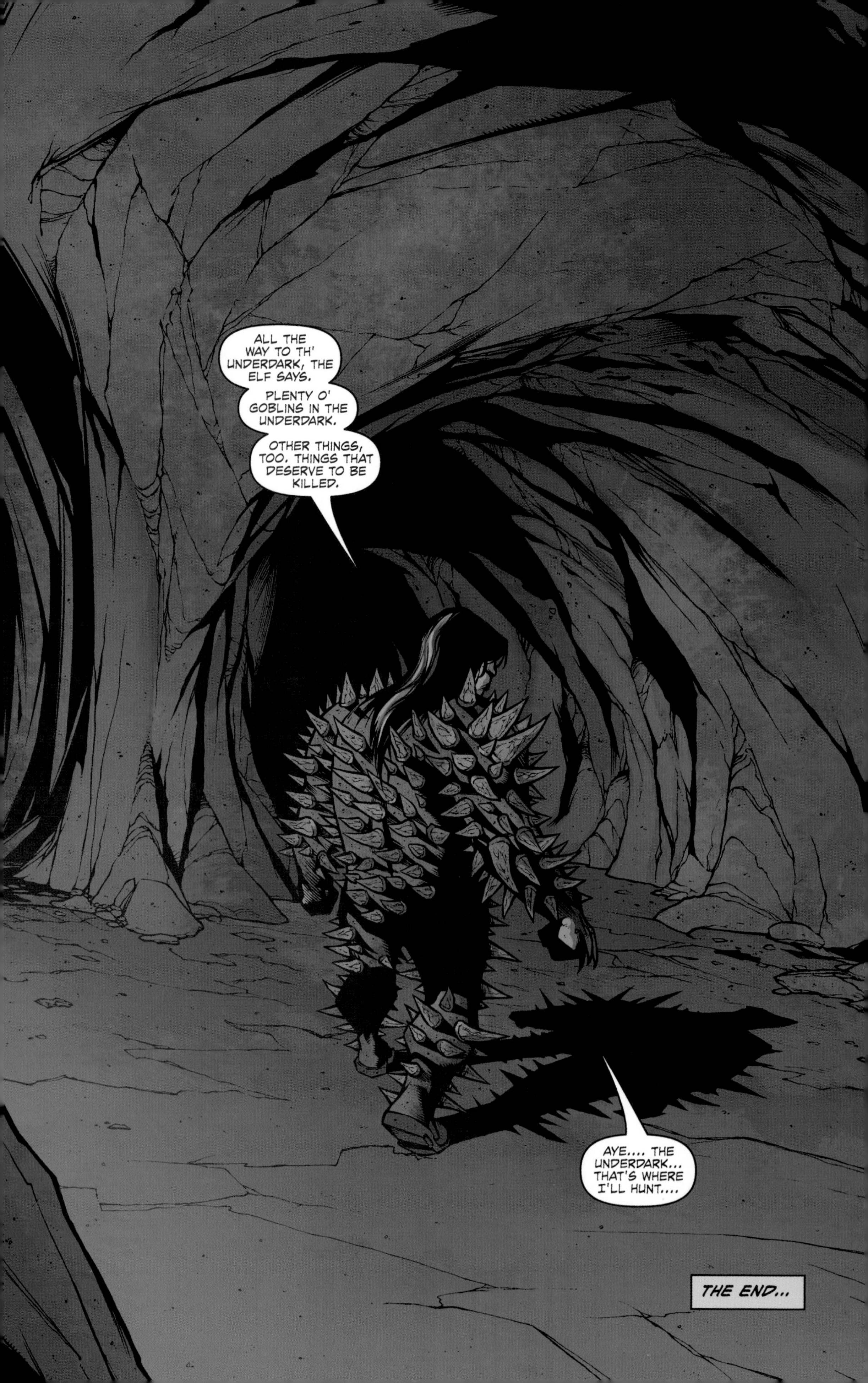
ALL THE WAY TO TH' UNDERDARK, THE ELF SAYS.
PLENTY O' GOBLINS IN THE UNDERDARK.
OTHER THINGS, TOO. THINGS THAT DESERVE TO BE KILLED.
AYE.... THE UNDERDARK... THAT'S WHERE I'LL HUNT....
THE END...

D1 An Adventure for 4 to 6 Characters, Level 1 and up

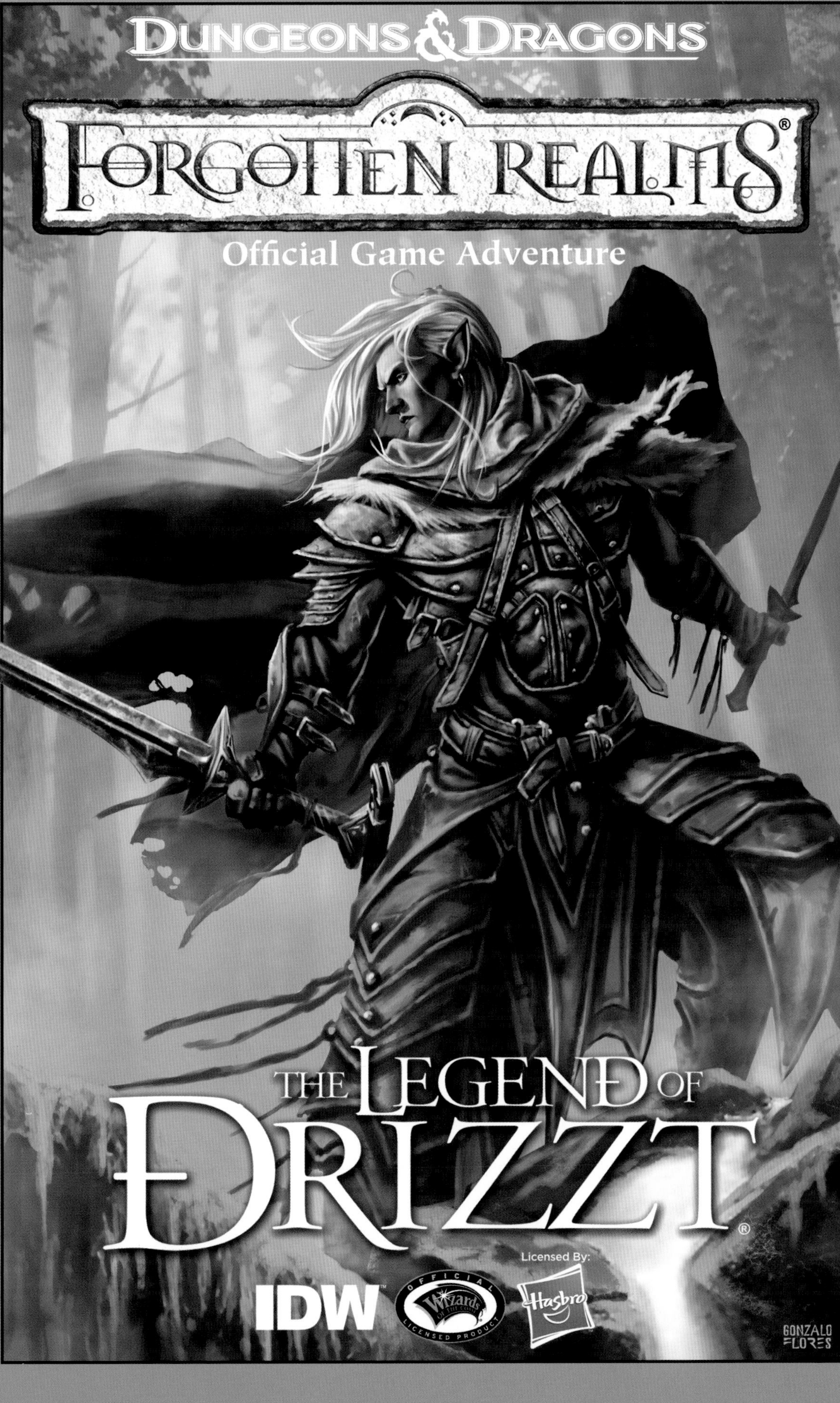

DUNGEONS & DRAGONS
FORGOTTEN REALMS®
Official Game Adventure
THE LEGEND OF DRIZZT®
Licensed By:
IDW
OFFICIAL Wizards OF THE COAST LICENSED PRODUCT
Hasbro
GONZALO FLORES

Dungeons & Dragons

Comic and Game Adventure

NEVERWINTER TALES

By Logan Bonner
Cartography by Jonathan Roberts

Introduction

In DUNGEONS & DRAGONS: THE LEGEND OF DRIZZT: NEVERWINTER TALES #1, you've witnessed the unfortunate fate of Thibbledorf Pwent. It's truly a terrifying prospect to find yourself turned into a vampire, so what better torture to inflict on your players? We've adapted the basic storyline of this issue to fit a DUNGEONS & DRAGONS® group. The characters will see flashes of themselves in a possible future—a dark one they'll want to prevent! This works equally well as an early encounter in an ongoing campaign or a single session with temporary characters. If you're going to use it in an ongoing game, you can repeat the "time flashes" in future sessions and invent a greater phenomenon that causes them.

These encounters are best for 1st- or 2nd-level adventurers. For a higher-level group, you can substitute different monsters or increase their levels.

Adventure Background

The action takes place near the long-lost dwarf city of Gauntlgrym, not far from the city of Neverwinter. The city was destroyed by a great primordial dwelling deep within Gauntlgrym, and is slowly being rebuilt. Jobs for adventurers are plentiful—tasks to tame the wilds nearby and stop the monsters that roam freely.

The dwarves of Delzoun blood still search for the lost capital of their ancient society. Old Toldor searched for every hint to its location. When he heard rumors about the exploits of Bruenor Battlehammer and Thibbledorf Pwent (plus that drow with his kitten, and those other folks), he knew he had a lead. He spent his entire savings to travel to Neverwinter and secure a peculiar item: the Monocle of Ages. The monocle, it is said, can look into the past. In fact, it's more powerful than the rumors, as the adventurers will soon find out. If used incorrectly, it fractures time. When this happens, the adventurers will become conscious of their counterparts in a horrifying possible future. Only if they use the resources and knowledge of both sides can they put things right.

Toldor set out into the wilderness on his own. His granddaughter Tollora, greatly worried, searched for brave adventurers to help her locate him. Out in the wilds, they saw a band of traveling goblins with an old dwarf in tow.

The first encounter begins when the adventurers and Tollora sneak up on the goblins' camp where her grandfather is held prisoner. You can either start right at the cusp of the encounter, or you can run a roleplaying scene with the adventurers meeting Tollora. Choose whichever you think your players will prefer. If you start with the encounter, summarize the previous paragraph to set it up.

Getting Started

Dungeon Masters need a copy of the DUNGEONS & DRAGONS game rules, which you can find in either the DUNGEONS & DRAGONS *Fantasy Roleplaying Game Starter Set* or the *Dungeon Master's Kit™*. Players need a copy of *Heroes of the Fallen Lands™* or *Heroes of the Forgotten Kingdoms™* and a character sheet to make characters to use in the adventure.

Once you're ready to begin, flip to Encounter 1 and give your players a glimpse of what terrible things the future might bring!

Encounter 1:
A Present for the Goblins

Encounter Level 1 (500 XP)

4 goblin snipers (S)
2 goblin cutthroats (C)
(2 more goblin snipers and a goblin hex hurler are inside the tents. See "Tactics.")

To start the encounter, read or paraphrase:
The sun hangs low on the horizon, and a band of goblins has just finished setting up camp for the night. They cluster around a small campfire, roasting lizards and rats for their dinner. Two sentries with bows stand at the far corners of camp.

The young dwarf Tollora squints her eyes as she looks out through the trees. She whispers, "Grandfather is in that small tent across from the fire. I see him moving. Get him out, please! Surely these goblins can't be that tough."

Have the adventurers place their miniatures in the bottom right corner of the map, behind the cluster of trees. Also place a miniature for Tollora and have one handy to use for Old Toldor. The goblins haven't seen them yet.

When the adventurers attack or the goblins become aware of them, roll for initiative! Even though the hex hurler isn't on the map, roll its initiative check now.

The Two Dwarves

Old Toldor and his granddaughter Tollora are very close, even as the girl reaches adulthood. Toldor came to Neverwinter just this year, spending the last of his savings on the trip. Tollora followed without her parents' permission, planning to keep an eye on her granddad since he was acting so strangely.

Old Toldor can be a bit scattered, and has grown more so since he became obsessed with finding Gauntlgrym. Stories of King Bruenor and faithful Pwent brought this area to his attention. He wants to walk in these heroes' footsteps, and nothing will stop him from finding the ancient city.

Tollora inherited her grandfather's stubbornness, and traveled all this way to find him. As long as she can remember, Old Toldor protected her, and now it's her turn to watch his back. Though she's said she plans to take him back home, she secretly desires to help him find Gauntlgrym.

Tactics

The goblins respond to intruders the same way they respond to most things: stabbing! Snipers cower behind trees and tents for cover as they fire their bows. Cutthroats flank their enemies, even using snipers who get stuck in melee as unwitting co-flankers. If the goblins are reduced to only minions remaining, they run for their lives.

A goblin hex hurler and two more snipers rest inside tents. When their initiative counts come up, they come outside to join the battle. The hex hurler uses *stinging hex* to punish melee characters. It keeps close to its allies so it can protect itself using *lead from the rear*.

Tollora runs toward the tents to rescue her grandfather.

Development

When someone releases Old Toldor and unties his bonds, he makes a mad dash for his magic lens.

When Toldor is rescued, read:
Old Toldor runs out of the tent and starts rummaging through a goblin's knapsack. He quickly finds a five-inch-wide lens with an ornate gold rim. Holding it in front of his face, he chants.

First, he is overjoyed. "That cave! Gauntlgrym be there!"

Then, the lens flies from his hand, and his face fills with dread. He yells, "No! Somethin's gone wrong!

An invisible wave pulses out from the lens, and it feels like the world has been ripped in two. Toldor seems to flicker in and out of existence. He runs into the cave, taking the lens.

Nothing else changes overtly, but it all feels somehow less real.

When the adventurers complete the encounter,

either give them time to enter the cave, or immediately go to Encounter 2.

Features of the Area

Illumination: Bright light.

Tents: These are filled with beverages, foodstuffs, and other mundane items. Squares containing crates or barrels are difficult terrain.

Campfire: The goblins have already started up their campfire. Any creature that enters or ends its turn in the campfire takes 5 fire damage.

Stones: Moving onto a stone costs 1 extra square of movement.

Trees: Squares with trees in them are difficult terrain. A creature standing in a tree's square gains partial cover.

6 Goblin Snipers (S) Level 1 Minion Artillery

Small natural humanoid   XP 25 each
HP 1; a missed attack never damages a minion.
Initiative +3
AC 13, **Fortitude** 12, **Reflex** 14, **Will** 12
Perception +1 **Speed** 6   Low-light vision

TRAITS
Sniper
   If the goblin misses with a ranged attack while hidden, it remains hidden.

STANDARD ACTIONS
⊕ **Short Sword** (weapon) ✦ At-Will
   Attack: Melee 1 (one creature); +8 vs. AC
   Hit: 4 damage.
⊗ **Shortbow** (weapon) ✦ At-Will
   Attack: Ranged 20 (one creature); +8 vs. AC
   Hit: 4 damage.

TRIGGERED ACTIONS
Goblin Tactics ✦ At-Will
   Trigger: The goblin is missed by a melee attack.
   Effect (Immediate Reaction): The goblin shifts 1 square.

Skills Stealth +8, Thievery +8
Str 13 (+1)   **Dex** 17 (+3)   **Wis** 12 (+1)
Con 13 (+1)   **Int** 8 (–1)   **Cha** 8 (–1)
Alignment evil   **Languages** Common, Goblin
Equipment leather armor, short sword, shortbow, 20 arrows

2 Goblin Cutthroat (C)   Level 1 Skirmisher

Small natural humanoid   XP 100 each
HP 30; **Bloodied** 15   **Initiative** +5
AC 15, **Fortitude** 13, **Reflex** 14, **Will** 13
Perception +2
Speed 6   Low-light vision

STANDARD ACTIONS
⊕ **Short Sword** (weapon) ✦ At-Will
   Attack: Melee 1 (one creature); +6 vs. AC
   Hit: 1d6 + 5 damage, or 2d6 + 5 if the goblin has combat advantage against the target. In addition, the goblin can shift 1 square.
⊗ **Dagger** (weapon) ✦ At-Will

Attack: Ranged 10 (one creature); +6 vs. AC

MOVE ACTIONS

Deft Scurry ✦ At-Will
Effect: The goblin shifts up to 3 squares.

TRIGGERED ACTIONS

Goblin Tactics ✦ At-Will
Trigger: The goblin is missed by a melee attack.
Effect (Immediate Reaction): The goblin shifts 1 square.

Skills Stealth +8, Thievery +8

Str 13 (+1)	**Dex** 17 (+3)	**Wis** 14 (+2)
Con 14 (+2)	**Int** 8 (–1)	**Cha** 8 (–1)

Alignment evil **Languages** Common, Goblin
Equipment leather armor, light shield, short sword, 2 daggers

Goblin Hex Hurler Level 3 Controller (Leader)

Small natural humanoid   XP 150
HP 46; **Bloodied** 23
AC 17, **Fortitude** 14, **Reflex** 15, **Will** 16
Perception +2
Speed 6   Low-light vision

STANDARD ACTIONS

⊕ Staff (weapon) ✦ At-Will
Attack: Melee 1 (one creature); +8 vs. AC
Hit: 1d6 + 7 damage, and the goblin can slide the target 1 square.

⇗ Blinding Hex ✦ At-Will
Attack: Ranged 10 (one creature); +6 vs. Fortitude
Hit: 2d6 + 1 damage, and the target is blinded until the end of the goblin's next turn.

⇗ Stinging Hex ✦ Recharge ⚄ ⚅
Attack: Ranged 10 (one creature); +6 vs. Will
Hit: The target takes 3d6 + 1 damage if it moves during its turn (save ends).

❋ Vexing Cloud (zone) ✦ Encounter
Effect: Area burst 3 within 10. The burst creates a zone that lasts until the end of the goblin's next turn. Enemies take a –2 penalty to attack rolls while in the zone.
Sustain Minor: The zone persists until the end of the goblin's next turn, and the goblin can move it up to 5 squares.

TRIGGERED ACTIONS

Goblin Tactics ✦ At-Will
Trigger: The goblin is missed by a melee attack.
Effect (Immediate Reaction): The goblin shifts 1 square.

Lead from the Rear ✦ At-Will
Trigger: An enemy hits the goblin with a ranged attack.
Effect (Immediate Interrupt): The goblin can change the attack's target to an adjacent ally of the goblin's level or lower.

Skills Stealth +10, Thievery +10

Str 10 (+1)	**Dex** 15 (+3)	**Wis** 13 (+2)
Con 14 (+3)	**Int** 9 (+0)	**Cha** 18 (+5)

Alignment evil **Languages** Common, Goblin
Equipment leather armor, staff

Encounter 2: Troubles of Time

Encounter Level 2 (727 XP)

2 dwarf clan guards (G)
1 duergar scout (S)
(8 duergar thugs appear on round 2. See "Tactics.")

This encounter takes place in the same location as the previous encounter, but with alternate future selves of the adventurers. The Monocle of Ages has split their minds, and they sense that they're in different forms. And these versions of themselves are vampires! Note that dwarves remain unchanged.

Read or paraphrase:
You blink, and the grove goes dark. The sky is dark, but the first rays of sunlight rise over the horizon. Corpses litter the ground, and a blazing pyre piled high with bodies sends smoke and embers into the air. The flames seem to take on a white tinge. The trees in the grove have been chopped down to make the pyre.
You feel like you've been split in two. One half of you is here, another half in the grove as it was. You suddenly realize that your dark half is running.
Two dwarves and a duergar stand near the cave entrance—two groups that would never fight together.

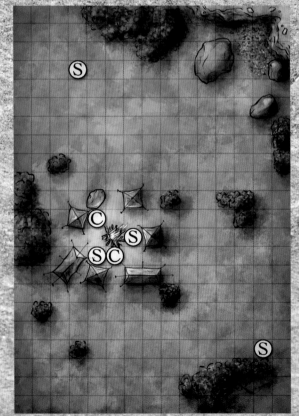

They heft their weapons and shout, "The foul vampires have returned! Keep them out of Gauntlgrym!"

Only now do you notice the coldness of your limbs, the sharp fangs in your mouth, and an overwhelming hunger for blood.

Explain the character modifications listed under "Vampire Additions," then place the miniatures on the map and roll for initiative.

Vampire Additions

Players gain the following traits when they become vampires.

Vampire's Form: You have darkvision, resist 5 necrotic, and vulnerable 5 radiant.

Sunlight Vulnerability: When you end your turn in direct sunlight and lack a protective covering such as a cloak or other heavy clothing, you take 5 radiant damage (plus additional damage from your radiant vulnerability) from the sunlight, and you are weakened (save ends). If you drop below 1 hit point from this damage, you are instantly destroyed.

Blood Feast: You gain the *blood feast* power.

Blood Feast   Utility
You sink your fangs into a fallen foe, sapping their blood to reinvigorate your unnatural life.
Encounter ✦ Shadow
Minor Action   Melee touch
Target: One unconscious or dead creature.
Effect: You regain 5 hit points.

Tactics

The enemies try to stop the adventurers from entering the cave. The clan guards use *warhammer* attacks to push back the adventurers.

At the start of the second round, the duergar thugs appear on the bottom edge of the map. They rush in to flank the adventurers.

When the new troops arrive, read:
More duergar run into the clearing. A pitched, running battle rages behind them. Dozens of vampires battle dwarves and duergar. In the middle is a lone drow. He whirls, fighting with two swords, cutting down vampire after vampire. A vicious panther fights alongside him.

The vampires fall quickly. If the battle reaches the grove, the fight will be swift, and your side will fall.

Development

Once the new troops show up, the adventurers have two rounds to get into the cave before Drizzt and the other combatants reach them. If they don't make it there by the end of the third round, it's game over. There's no escape.

Features of the Area

Illumination: Bright light from the pyre.

Corpses: Human, elf, and halfling corpses lie strewn over the ground. Some were killed violently, but others look like they died of old age or sickness. It looks like they were dragged here to be put on the pyre.

Sanctified Pyre: Moving onto the pyre takes 1 extra square of movement. This is a holy fire, sanctified to prevent the bodies from rising as undead. A creature that enters the pyre or a square adjacent to it, or that ends its turn there, takes 5 fire and radiant damage.

Stones: Moving onto a stone costs 1 extra square of movement.

Trees: Squares with trees in them are difficult terrain. A creature standing in a tree's square gains partial cover.

Duergar Scout (D)	**Level 4 Lurker**
Medium natural humanoid	XP 175
HP 48; **Bloodied** 24	**Initiative** +8

AC 18, **Fortitude** 18, **Reflex** 16, **Will** 16
Perception +9
Speed 5   Darkvision
Resist 5 fire, 5 poison
TRAITS
Shadow Attack
    The duergar scout's attacks deal 4d6 extra damage when the scout hits a target that cannot see it.
STANDARD ACTIONS
⊕ **Warhammer** (weapon) ✦ **At-Will**
    Attack: Melee 1 (one creature); +9 vs. AC
    Hit: 1d10 + 4 damage.
⊗ **Crossbow** (weapon) ✦ **At-Will**
    Attack: Ranged 20 (one creature); +9 vs. AC
    Hit: 1d8 + 5 damage.
Underdark Sneak ✦ At-Will
    Effect: The scout becomes invisible until the end of its next turn or until it hits or misses with an attack.
MINOR ACTIONS
⊗ **Infernal Quills** (poison) ✦ **Encounter**
    Attack: Ranged 3 (one creature); +9 vs. AC
    Hit: 1d8 + 4 damage, and the target takes a –2 penalty to attack rolls and ongoing 5 poison damage (save ends both).
Skills Dungeoneering +9, Stealth +9

Str 13 (+3)	**Dex** 15 (+4)	**Wis** 14 (+4)
Con 18 (+6)	**Int** 10 (+2)	**Cha** 8 (+1)

Alignment evil   **Languages** Common, Deep Speech, Dwarven
Equipment chainmail, warhammer, crossbow

2 Dwarf Clan Guards (G)	**Level 1 Soldier**
Medium natural humanoid	XP 100 each
HP 33; **Bloodied** 16	**Initiative** +3

AC 17, **Fortitude** 15, **Reflex** 13, **Will** 15
Perception +8
Speed 5   Low-light vision

TRAITS

Stand the Ground

The dwarf can move 1 square fewer than the effect specifies when subjected to a pull, a push, or a slide.

Steady-Footed

The dwarf can make a saving throw to avoid falling prone when an attack would knock it prone.

STANDARD ACTIONS

⊕ **Warhammer** (weapon) ✦ At-Will

Attack: Melee 1 (one creature); +6 vs. AC

Hit: 1d10 + 3 damage, and the dwarf can push the target 1 square. The dwarf can then shift 1 square to a square the target vacated.

Effect: The dwarf marks the target until the end of the dwarf's next turn.

↗ **Throwing Hammer** (weapon) ✦ At-Will

Attack: Ranged 10 (one creature); +6 vs. AC

Hit: 1d6 + 4 damage, and the dwarf marks the target until the end of the dwarf's next turn.

↓↗ **Double Hammer Strike** ✦ Recharge ⚅ ⚅ ⚅

Effect: The dwarf uses *warhammer* and then uses *throwing hammer*. The dwarf does not provoke opportunity attacks for this use of *throwing hammer*.

Str 16 (+3)	**Dex** 12 (+1)	**Wis** 17 (+3)
Con 17 (+3)	**Int** 10 (+0)	**Cha** 10 (+0)

Alignment unaligned

Languages Common, Dwarven

Equipment plate armor, heavy shield, warhammer, 4 throwing hammers

---

8 Duergar Thugs (T)   Level 4 Minion Brute

Medium natural humanoid   XP 44 each

HP 1; a missed attack never damages a minion

Initiative +4

AC 16, **Fortitude** 17, **Reflex** 15, **Will** 14

Perception +4

Speed 5   Darkvision

Resist 5 fire, 5 poison

STANDARD ACTIONS

⊕ **Warhammer** (weapon) ✦ At-Will

Attack: Melee 1 (one creature); +9 vs. AC

Hit: 8 damage.

MINOR ACTIONS

⊙ **Infernal Quills** (poison) ✦ Encounter

Attack: Ranged 3 (one creature); +9 vs. AC

Hit: 6 damage, and ongoing 2 poison damage (save ends).

Str 14 (+4)	**Dex** 15 (+4)	**Wis** 15 (+4)
Con 18 (+6)	**Int** 10 (+2)	**Cha** 8 (+1)

Alignment evil

Languages Common, Deep Speech, Dwarven

Equipment chainmail, warhammer

Encounter 3: The Once and Future King

Encounter Level 3 (750 XP)

2 flesh-crazed zombies (F)

(Up to 5 grasping zombies appear over the course of the encounter. See "Tactics.")

The adventurers find refuge in the cave, and rush deeper into the halls of Gauntlgrym. They manage to temporarily lose their pursuers, and they can take a short rest.

When they reach the throne room, they find Old Toldor sitting on the throne and reigning over this dark future.

Read:

During the frantic race through Gauntlgrym, memories of this future began flooding back. An undead blight spread out from within Gauntlgrym. It quickly infected most of Neverwinter's populace.

Races that live underground seem immune. Dwarves, duergar, and drow formed a reluctant alliance, but Gauntlgrym became their last refuge.

The mob will soon flood back into Gauntlgrym. Only the throne room is safe, left alone out of respect for the dead dwarven kings.

Jump back to the "present." Since the two versions of the characters can sense one another, the present characters have traveled to roughly the same place as those in the future.

If the "present" adventurers enter the throne room, read:
At the far end of this room, a throne stands on a dais. Old Toldor sits there, still blinking in and out. The lens floats in the air in front of him. It spins and glows a faint blue. Tollora rushes to her grandfather, but when she tries to touch him, her hands pass through.

Toldor lifts his weary head and begs, "Please. The lens be evil. It smells o' death. Shatter th' foul thing!"

Jump back to the future and read:
Toldor sits on the throne, smiling. The lens floats in the air in front of him. Tollora rushes to her grandfather, sobbing. She asks, "What's happened? What caused all this?"

Toldor speaks. "Don' worry, sweet. Ye be a dwarf, so ye'll live. Let those lot die. Gauntlgrym be restored. Dwarves roam these halls. All be well!

"Can't be havin' outsiders. Rise up, fallen ones! Strike down th' intruders in th' name o' Toldor, new King of Gauntlgrym!"

At his bidding, two cairns topple (on the future map) and unleash the zombies of fallen warriors. Place miniatures and roll initiative!

Fighting in Two Eras
On an adventurer's initiative, the player can take complete turns for both the present and the future form of that character (in either order).

The two halves share one hit point total, and any powers one expends, the other does as well. Keep only location and conditions separate. For example, if a character in the future is bitten by a flesh-crazed zombie, the damage affects both halves, but only the half in the future is dazed.

Destroying the Monocle of Ages
To set things right, the adventurers have to destroy the monocle in the "present" timeline. A DC 8 Arcana or Religion check reveals how: Both versions of one adventurer stand next to the lens and spend a minor action to grab it. When the second version does so, the lens becomes real, appearing in the "present" version's hand and disappearing entirely from the future. The adventure needs only drop the lens (a free action) to shatter it, fixing time.

The future time frame disappears. Toldor returns to his "present" self, and any zombies in the present remain.

Tactics
Zombies shamble toward the adventurers and try to kill them. They're just zombies, after all.

When the grasping zombies' initiative count comes up, two of them appear. On a grasping zombie's first turn, it uses its standard action to smash out of one of the small cairns, and its move action to stand up.

You can have both zombies appear in the same time frame or one in each. If one in rises in the past, that cairn is also destroyed in the future (and no zombie can rise from it). If one rises in the future, a zombie can't rise from that cairn in the present (because, well, it wouldn't still be intact in the future if it had risen in the past). However, an adventurer in the present can knock over that cairn to make the zombie in the future disappear. (If you're not sure which it was, destroy the one closest to death). That does bring a zombie into the present fight at full health, though!

Conclusion
In the comic, Drizzt faces potent adversaries working behind the scenes. Your adventurers might have one of their own. Time has been set right, but somebody must have made that lens and sold it to Old Toldor. Can the adventurers find the culprit? If the villain is too much for them to handle, maybe they can seek the help of that drow ranger. In any case, a dark force is at work around Gauntlgrym.

Features of the Area
Illumination: Dim light.

Cairns: A cairn can be knocked over as a standard action. Doing so releases a grasping zombie. The larger cairns' inhabitants don't rise as undead. A cairn knocked over becomes a square of rubble.

Rubble (Future Half): Parts of the ceiling have fallen down. This rubble is difficult terrain.

Old Toldor: The dwarf can talk, but can't be interacted with until time is set right.

2 Flesh-Crazed Zombies (F) Level 4
  Skirmisher

Medium natural animate (undead)	XP 175
HP 55; Bloodied 27	Initiative +6
AC 18, Fortitude 17, Reflex 16, Will 14	
Perception +3	
Speed 6 (8 when charging)	Darkvision
Immune disease, poison	

TRAITS
Flesh-Crazed Charge
  While the zombie is charging, its movement does not provoke opportunity attacks.
Zombie Weakness
  A critical hit automatically reduces the zombie to 0 hit points.
STANDARD ACTIONS

⊕ **Club** (weapon) ✦ **At-Will**

  Attack: Melee 1 (one creature); +9 vs. AC

  Hit: 1d8 + 6 damage, or 2d8 + 6 if the zombie
  charged the target.

⸸ **Bite** ✦ **At-Will**

  Attack: Melee 1 (one creature); +9 vs. AC

  Hit: 2d6 + 5 damage, and the target is dazed until
  the end of the zombie's next turn.

TRIGGERED ACTIONS

Deathless Hunger ✦ **Encounter**

  Trigger: The zombie is reduced to 0 hit points, but
  not by a critical hit.

  Effect (No Action): Roll a d20. On a 15 or higher,
  the zombie is instead reduced to 1 hit point.

Str 18 (+6)	**Dex** 15 (+4)	**Wis** 13 (+3)
Con 15 (+4)	**Int** 1 (−3)	**Cha** 3 (−2)

Alignment unaligned   **Languages** —

Equipment club

---

4 Grasping Zombies   **Level 1 Brute**

Medium natural animate (undead)   XP 100

HP 33; **Bloodied** 16   **Initiative** −1

AC 13, **Fortitude** 14, **Reflex** 11, **Will** 11

Perception −1

Speed 4   Darkvision

Immune disease, poison

TRAITS

Zombie Weakness

  A critical hit automatically reduces the zombie to
  0 hit points.

STANDARD ACTIONS

⊕ **Slam** ✦ **At-Will**

  Attack: Melee 1 (one creature); +6 vs. AC

  Hit: 1d12 + 3 damage, or 1d12 + 8 against a
  grabbed target.

⸸ **Zombie Grasp** ✦ **At-Will**, **Recharge** ⚅,
  Recharge condition, **Encounter**

  Attack: Melee 1 (one creature); +4 vs. Reflex

  Hit: 1d6 + 3 damage, and the zombie grabs the
  target (escape DC 12) if it does not have a
  creature grabbed.

TRIGGERED ACTIONS

Deathless Hunger ✦ **Encounter**

  Trigger: The zombie is reduced to 0 hit points, but
  not by a critical hit.

  Effect (No Action): Roll a d20. On a 15 or higher,
  the zombie is instead reduced to 1 hit point.

Str 16 (+3)	**Dex** 8 (−1)	**Wis** 8 (−1)
Con 13 (+1)	**Int** 1 (−5)	**Cha** 3 (−4)

Alignment unaligned **Languages** —

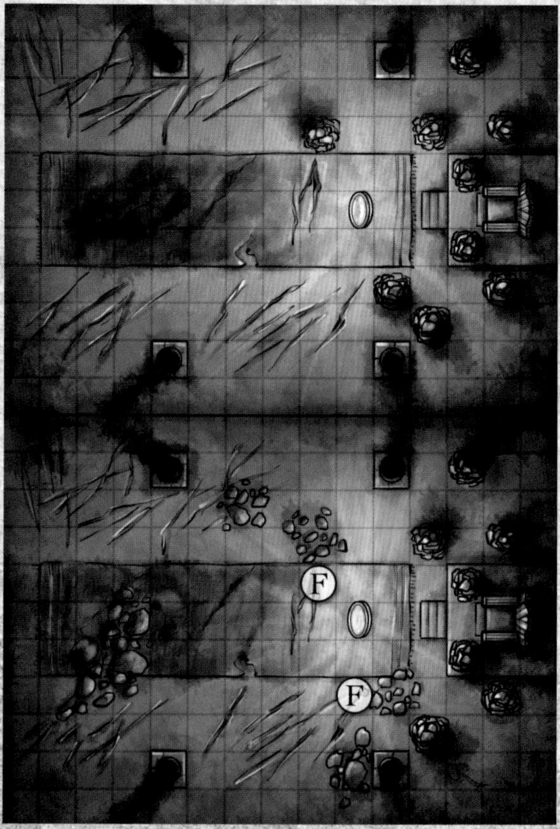

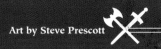

Art by Steve Prescott

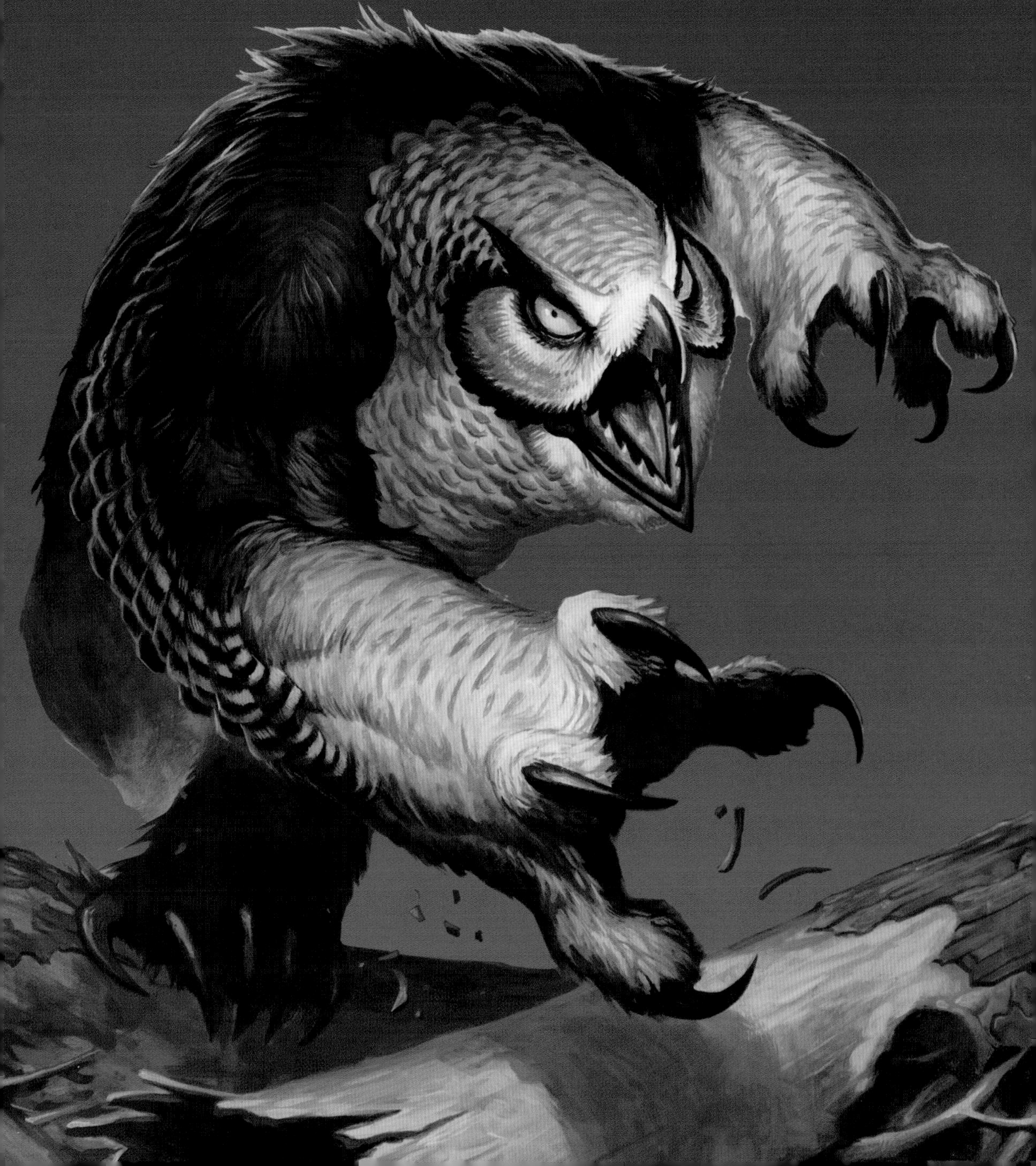

Art by Todd Lockwood

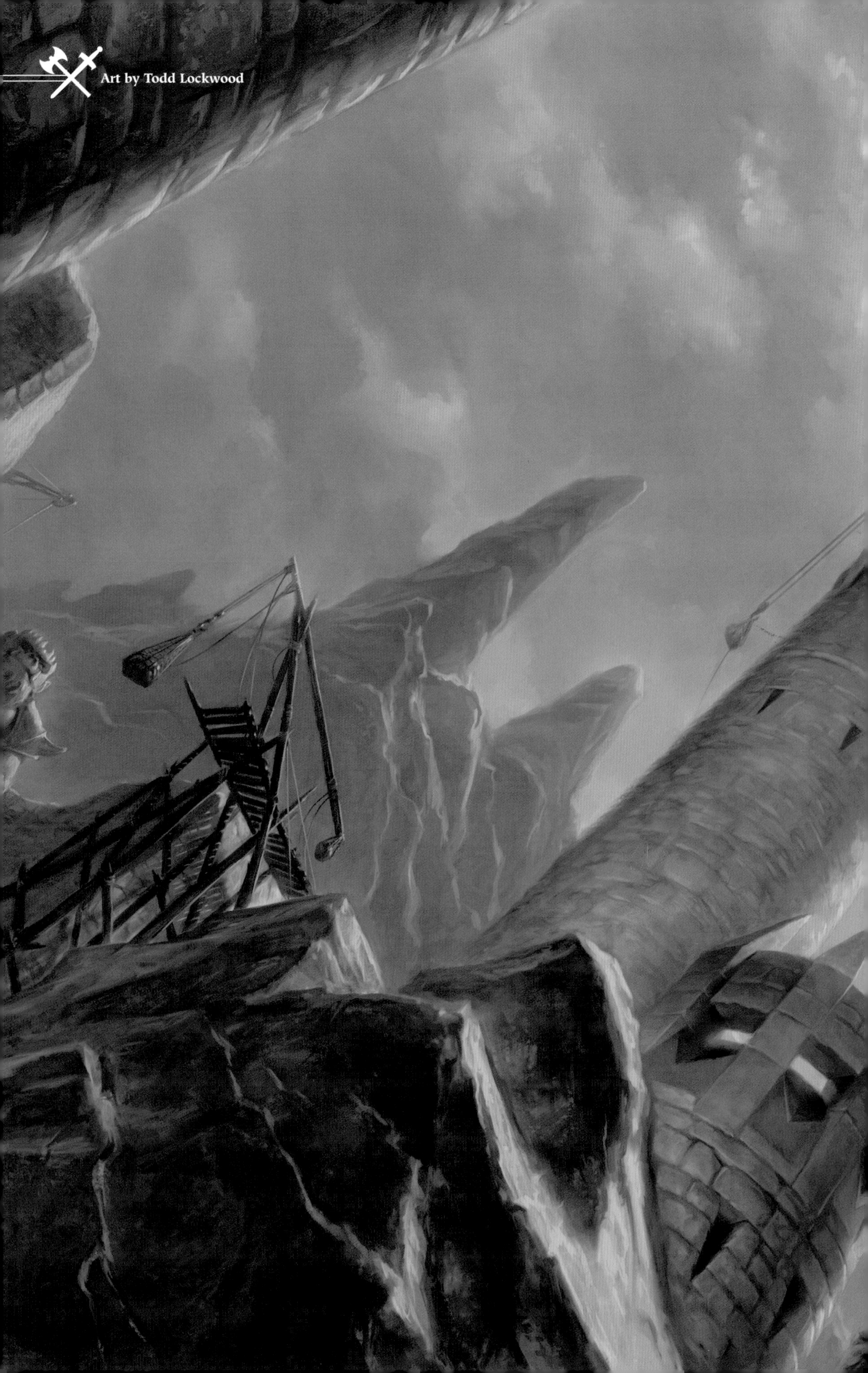

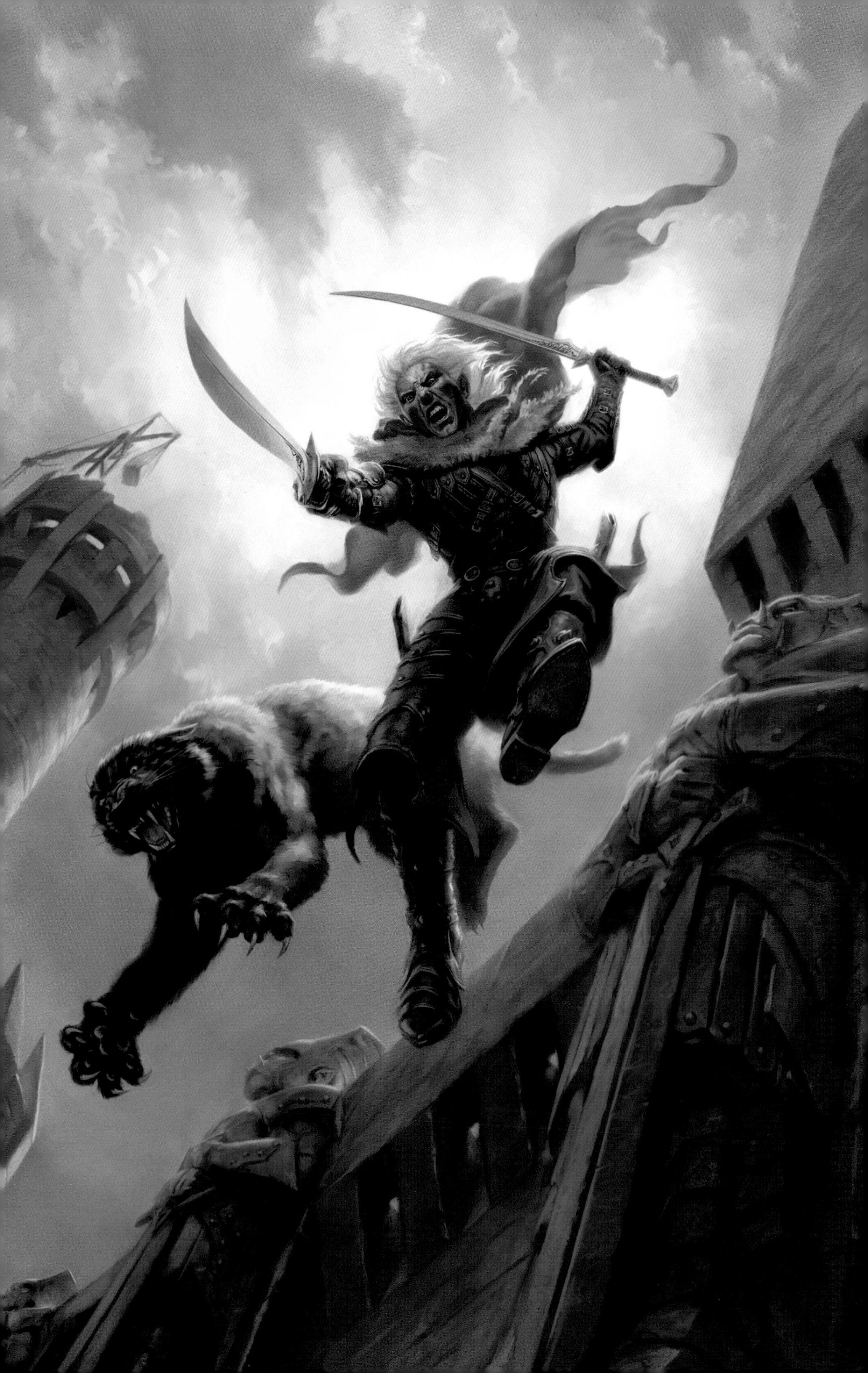

Art by Eric Deschamps

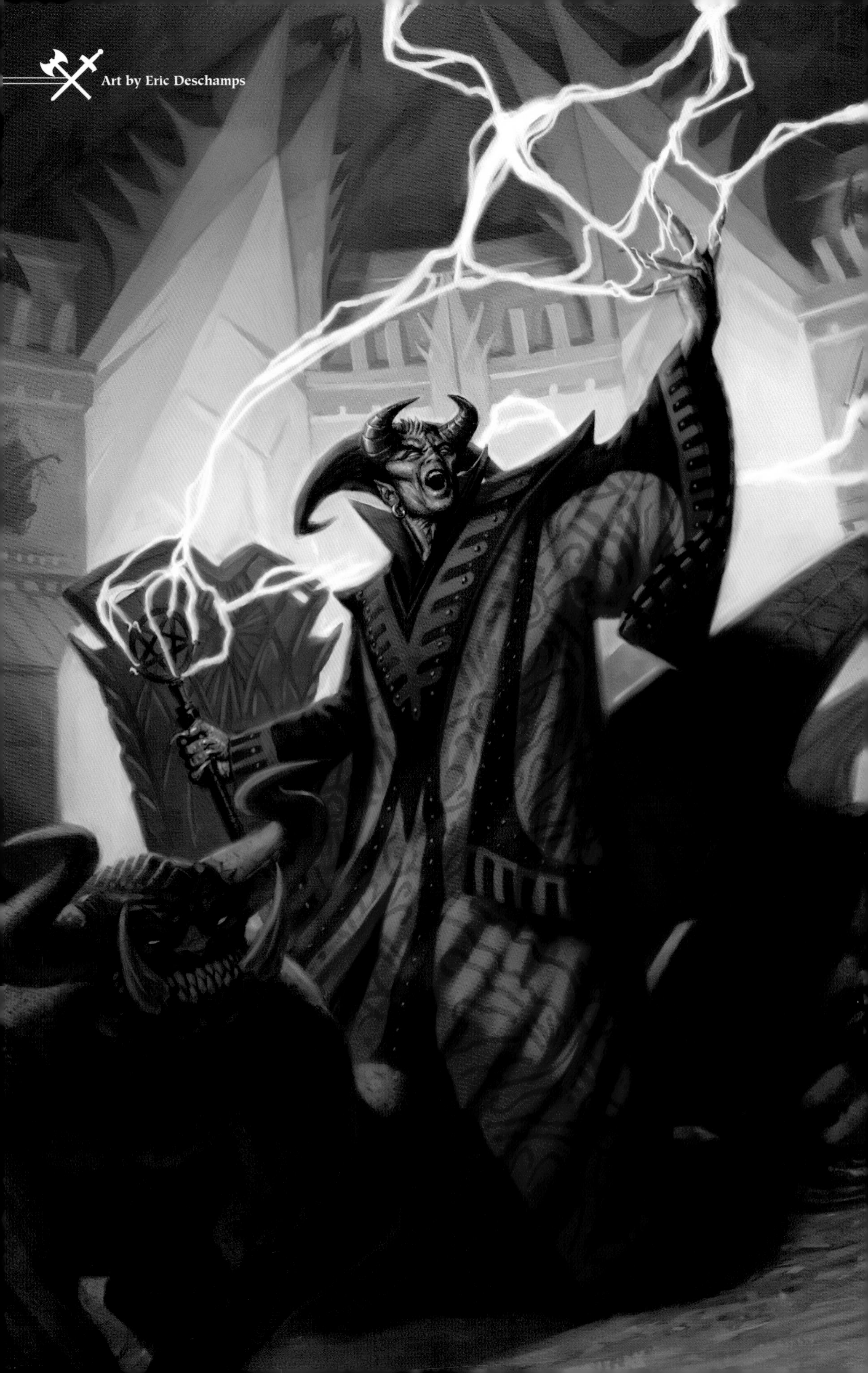

Glossary

Battlerager: Members of this elite dwarven order, usually covered in scars, runes and tattoos, will scream out battle cries and religious oaths as they charge recklessly forward into battle. Few aspects of life give them the charge that being in the heat of battle does, and they build up a fury when enemies manage to hurt them. Battleragers live on the fringes of Dwarven society.

Gutbuster: The Gutbuster Brigade is a famous battlerager squad lead by Thibbledorf Pwent. They are loyal to to Mithral Hall and its former king, Bruenor Battlehammer. They have their own brand of gung-ho tactics and often disregard the order and discipline for which the Mithral Hall army is known, in favor of a more direct approach.

Mithral Hall: The fabled ancestral home of Bruenor Battlehammer, Mithral Hall is a prosperous dwarven mine with tunnels often lined with natural veins of mithral, a precious metal strong as steel, but at half the weight.

Neverwinter: Also known as the Jewel of the North, Neverwinter is a metropolis sitting on the northwestern Sword Coast and is regarded as the most cosmopolitan and civilized city on the continent of Faerûn.

Owlbear: Likely the result of a wizard's experiment, the owlbear is infamous for its bad temper and attacking anything it thinks it can kill. Also, because it's a cross between a bear and an owl. See below for this creature's stat block.

Owlbear	Level 8 Elite Brute
Large fey beast	XP 700

Initiative +6   **Senses** Perception +12; low-light vision
HP 212; **Bloodied** 106; see also *stunning screech*
AC 22; **Fortitude** 22, **Reflex** 19, **Will** 20
Saving Throws +2
Speed 7
Action Points 1

⊕ **Claw** (standard; at-will)
    Reach 2; +12 vs. AC; 2d6 + 5 damage.

✦ **Double Attack** (standard; at-will)
    The owlbear makes two claw attacks. If both claws hit the same target, the target is grabbed (until escape).

✦ **Bite** (standard; at-will)
    Grabbed target only; automatic hit; 4d8 + 5 damage.

⤝ **Stunning Screech** (free, when first bloodied; encounter)
    Close burst 1; +10 vs. Fortitude; the target is stunned (save ends).

Alignment Unaligned   **Languages** –
Str 20 (+9)   **Dex** 14 (+6)   **Wis** 16 (+7)
Con 16 (+7)   **Int** 2 (+0)   **Cha** 10 (+4)

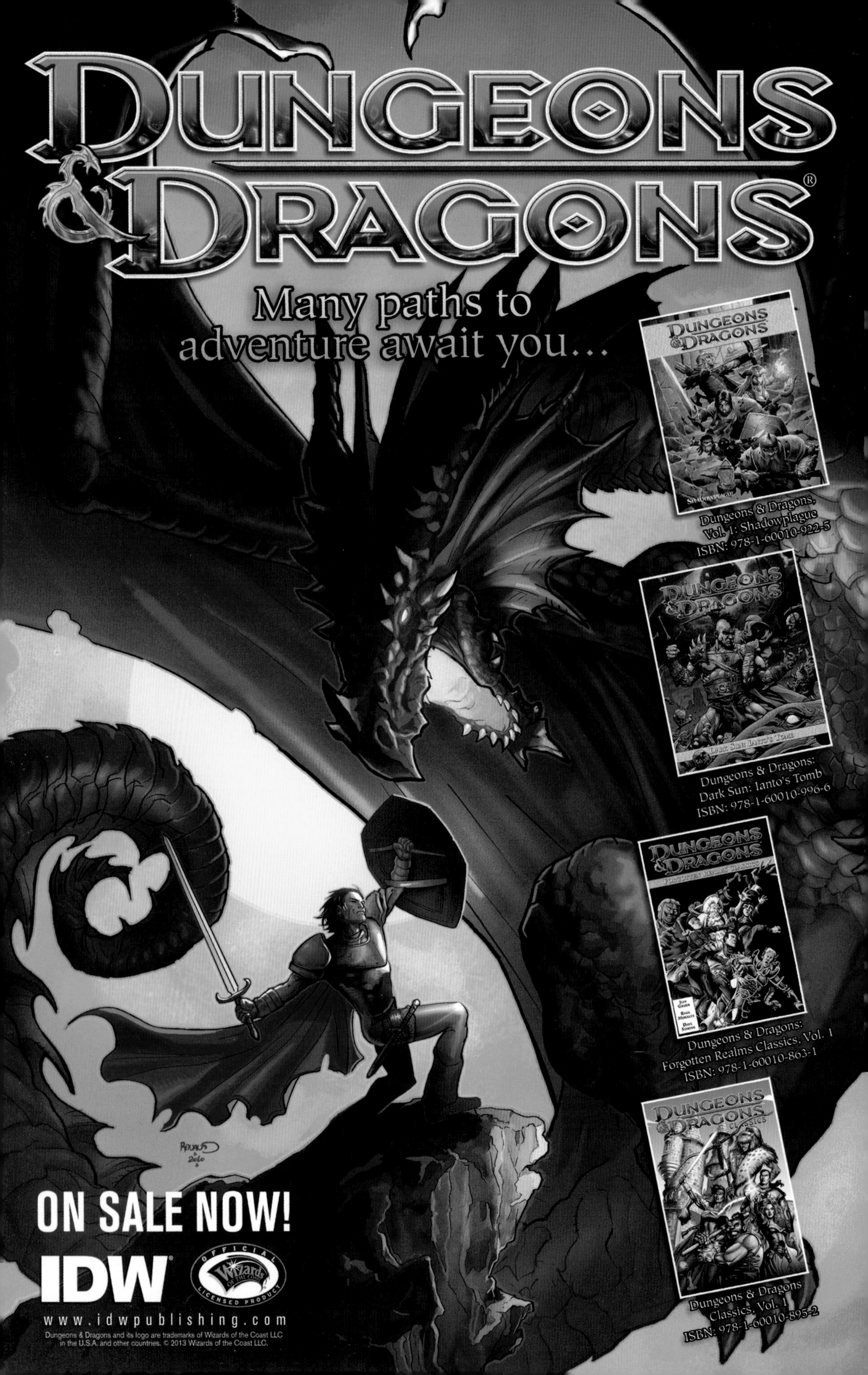

DUNGEONS & DRAGONS®
Many paths to adventure await you…
Dungeons & Dragons, Vol. 1: Shadowplague
ISBN: 978-1-60010-922-5
Dungeons & Dragons: Dark Sun: Ianto's Tomb
ISBN: 978-1-60010-996-6
Dungeons & Dragons: Forgotten Realms Classics, Vol. 1
ISBN: 978-1-60010-863-1
Dungeons & Dragons Classics, Vol. 1
ISBN: 978-1-60010-895-2
ON SALE NOW!
IDW
OFFICIAL Wizards of the Coast LICENSED PRODUCT
www.idwpublishing.com
Dungeons & Dragons and its logo are trademarks of Wizards of the Coast LLC in the U.S.A. and other countries. © 2013 Wizards of the Coast LLC.